# skip case.

by

r. e. derouin

Other books by R. E. Derouin:

*Time Trial*
*San Juan Solution*
*Mountain Ice*
*Dead on the Fourth of July*

**Skip Case**

Published by Hats Off Books™
610 East Delano Street, Suite 104, Tucson, Arizona 85705 U.S.A.
www.hatsoffbooks.com

International Standard Book Number: 1-58736-305-4
Library of Congress Control Number: 2004101255

*To*
*Elizabeth Blair, sister, friend and more*


A special thank you to Summer Mullins and Penny Chilton
for work above and beyond—
with apologies for the dangling preposition!

# PROLOGUE

The man took a deep breath of the hot and salty night air and firmly closed the door marked Room 22. After turning the knob once to confirm it was locked, he paused, somewhat unsteadily, and glanced across the motel parking lot. He looked at his wrist, but then remembered the watch was on the dresser in the motel room. In his right hand he clutched the motel key. A large bath towel was draped across his shoulder. He wore bathing trunks, a Phillies baseball cap and a t-shirt with the imprint "Eastern PA Century Bicycle Tour" and a date four years earlier. The man was about 40. His hair was a tad past barbering time and he wore polished black shoes and black socks, inconsistent with the rest of his attire.

The motel was an independent, adequate at best, barely holding its own against the national chains. It served an occasional thrifty traveler but mostly catered to salesmen, many on a repeat basis. They were given reasonable service and whispered offers to, "Stay three nights, the next one's free, and we'll give you a receipt for four."

The motel consisted of 40 units on two floors, ten to either side of a main entrance that led to the office and restaurant. A red neon sign blinked "Ocean Shore Motel," painting the parking lot and the bathing-suited man in a pulsating crimson glow. A scattering of cars dotted the parking lot but due to the late hour the avenue beyond was nearly devoid of traffic.

As the man turned from his room, a young man emerged from the main entrance several yards away and stepped outside. He was

1

dressed casually in jeans and a t-shirt and moved with the swagger of youth, someone without a care in the world. The man in the bathing suit recognized him as Leo, his waiter from an earlier dinner, and waved.

Leo shook his head and smiled. "Going for a midnight swim, mister?" he called.

The man paused, leaning against a post, and confirmed in a somewhat slurred voice that indeed he was about to take a dip. He added it was too damned hot for this early in May.

"Aw, this is cool weather for Norfolk," Leo replied. "Come back in July if you want to really sweat."

The man muttered a "No, thanks," released his support and continued on his way to the beach across the road.

"You be careful now," Leo called after him, "it's pitch black over there on the beach." The man just waved over his shoulder. Leo thought to himself that with one more drink he'd try to swim across the Chesapeake. He considered warning the Indian night clerk that they had a real winner wandering out on the sand in the middle of the night but discarded the idea. There were better things to do with his time. Francie was waiting and there was cold beer in the fridge. He hurried to his rusty Ford and by the time he pulled out on Ocean View Avenue, the man was out of sight and out of mind.

On the far side of the roadway, the man walked the short distance to the pathway that led to the beach. Once past the scrub brush and small trees, the near-total darkness surprised him, causing him to pause until his eyes became accustomed to this darkened world. When he could finally focus through the black of the night, he plodded forward, feet wallowing in the soft sand like a boat in a heavy sea.

The man stopped, thinking he'd heard some movement behind him, but after listening a few minutes could discern no human sound and was satisfied he was alone. Aside from the infrequent sound of a passing car on the avenue, only the murmur of unseen waves lapping at the sand broke the stillness. He moved forward until the sound of the sea and the firmness of the sand suggested he was close to the water's edge. He retraced his steps a few paces to assure he was on the soft dry sand above the high-tide line, carefully placed his towel down, sat on it and removed his shoes and socks. He slipped the motel key in the left shoe and then rolled each sock, pushing it into its corresponding shoe.

By the time the man had finished, his night vision was better and he could make out the tiny necklace of lights in the distance, the Chesapeake Bridge-Tunnel that ran 17 miles to the Eastern shore. A breeze picked up at the shoreline, wrinkling the water as the waves slowly rolled toward him in silver lines. He considered once more the folly of his undertaking, but pushed away his second thoughts. He stood, removed first his hat, then his t-shirt. The t-shirt was carefully placed front-side up on the towel. He secured it with a shoe on either side. He slapped the hat back on his head, took a deep breath and began to slowly walk toward the water.

# CHAPTER I

Detective David Dean sat in the Parkside Pennsylvania Police Headquarters with his feet in his lower desk drawer. He was slowly picking pieces of Styrofoam flotsam from his early morning cup of black coffee. Years from now, when he was comfortably ensconced in his Ouray, Colorado bed and breakfast, he'd often look back on this day as the turning point in his life, but for now it was only the start of yet another five work days.

He had awakened a few moments before the usual time, ordinarily a good sign, but after rubbing open his eyes, he discovered it was a white day, hazy and sultry, without a speck of blue in the sky. White days weren't supposed to show up until at least July, certainly not in early May. Dean felt cheated, doubly so because yesterday, a comp day off, it had rained as if St. Swithin was ticked off at the world, denying him the pleasure of biking the Pennsylvania countryside. So, when the alarm shrilled its two cents' worth, Dean had cussed the sadist who invented it and figured it wasn't going to be a pleasant Wednesday.

Fellow detectives Tom DeLeo and Andy Sackler, seated across the room, were arguing as usual while the only other occupant, newcomer Detective Lenny Harrigan, was either catching a quick nap or meditating. Harrigan was usually Dean's partner but Dean was content to work alone often, while Harrigan was happy to pick up odd chores the other more senior detectives would toss his way.

Rita Angeltoni, the token skirt, as she referred to herself, was usually there banging on her keyboard or answering the phone while keeping the quartet in line. Today she was absent, home nursing child number five, down with a spring fever, or just plain Spring Fever.

"It's a skip case," DeLeo said with a know-it-all air that defied anyone to doubt him. "A skip case, pure and simple. The guy got sick of looking at the old lady and took a hike."

Sackler shook his head. "DeLeo, you have an opinion about everything, whether you know a damn thing about it or not. And you sure don't know a damn thing about this case." Sackler, easily baited by DeLeo, was quick to show his temper.

"I know you don't go for a midnight swim on a dark beach by yourself, especially in the Chesapeake Bay." Then he added for emphasis, "That's where Philadelphia flushes its toilets."

"Your geography isn't even right," Sackler answered. "Besides, the Norfolk cops said the guy had a snoot-full of booze."

DeLeo tilted his head back, finishing the last of his coffee. "I'll believe it when they fish his body out of the drink, which they won't, 'cause it ain't there."

Sackler and DeLeo, partners for nearly 12 years, had more in common than their constant arguing would suggest. Both were in their late 30's, losing their hair, gaining a mid-section and happily married. Each was a father to three kids, aged between tot and teenager. Dean, who'd been on the force for their entire tenure, was used to their early morning bickering and paid no attention.

David Dean was 38 years old and the only unmarried detective. He didn't share the encroaching baldness or the spreading waistline of the others. He was in fairly good shape, thanks mostly to weekend biking more than any innate athletic ability. While Sackler and DeLeo owned homes in the same subdivision, Dean rented a small house in the older part of town with Fred O'Connor, his elderly stepfather.

The first word on the case Sackler and DeLeo were arguing about had come by way of a call from the Norfolk, Virginia Police Department the prior afternoon, Dean's day off. The uniformed guys downstairs had drawn lots to see who got stuck informing the next of kin, and since that time, speculation on the disappearance of Jeffrey Byrne had been the chief topic of conversation at the Parkside Police Department.

Any new happening outside the mundane assortment of drug cases, burglaries, domestic disturbances or a semi-annual Saturday night passion killing came as a welcome change. Parkside was a small city of 40,000 located 50 miles northwest of Philadelphia. While it was close enough to catch broadcasts of Phillies baseball and Eagles football, it was far enough away to be isolated from most of the brutality associated with the city of Brotherly Love. Each passing year brought the mayhem further northward, causing the old timers and the local newspaper to fret for the good old days when violence was no worse than a dog fight. Still, a case that spawned a novel basis for argument was always a welcomed diversion from their increasing caseload.

DeLeo, already bored with the exchange, got up and moved toward the door. "A skip case, pure and simple. The guy's sitting on some tropical beach with a babe in his lap."

Sackler was unwilling to let it go. "McCarthy got to talk to the widow. He says nobody in their right mind would skip out on her. I'll bet you a cup of coffee it was a stupid accident."

"You're on!" answered DeLeo, never willing to pass up a bet. He looked to the others for approval. "Anybody else?"

Harrigan, the youngster of the group at 28, continued to nod away. The red-haired detective was never without a smile, even when snoozing. Since his marriage two weeks ago, his catnaps were becoming even more frequent than in his pre-nuptial days. Dean simply shook his head, committed to being grumpy for the entire day.

"What's a matter, Dean?" DeLeo asked. "Are you buying the accident theory too?"

Dean continued to shake his head. "I don't know anything about the case, but I know it would take a room full of CPA's to figure out how many cups of coffee you guys owe each other."

Sackler crossed the room to the trashcan, retrieved the prior day's edition of the *Parkside Sentinel* and read aloud.

"Jeffrey Byrne, age 38, of 156 Maid Marian Lane, Parkside, apparently drowned in the early morning hours of Tuesday, May fourth while on a business trip in Norfolk, Virginia. According to sources at the Ocean Shore Motel, Byrne was last seen on his way to the beach shortly after midnight by Leo Sutter, a waiter at the motel. When Byrne failed to answer a wake-up call the following morning, a clerk finally opened his room. According to Detective Norman Hunter of the Norfolk Police Department, Byrne's bed had not been slept in. Motel personnel conducted a search and a motel employee later found the Parkside man's clothing and room key on the public beach across the road. Police are continuing to investigate while a search for the body is underway. Detective Hunter advised the *Sentinel* by phone that tidal conditions on the Chesapeake might make retrieving a body difficult.

"Byrne, a nine-year resident of Parkside, was born in Bucks County, Pennsylvania. He was the husband of Cynthia Cosgrove Byrne and the father of Randy Byrne, a Parkside High School senior. Jeffrey Byrne was employed in a regional marketing position by The World Wide Insurance Company of Philadelphia."

"Hell of a baseball player," Dean said glumly, finishing the dregs of his coffee.

"Who?" asked Sackler.

"The son, Randy Byrne," Dean answered. "I saw him play last spring when I went out to the high school to bust the Cummings kid for breaking and entering. They were on the same team, only Cummings rode the bench and Byrne was the star—he played shortstop. He's good. The whole team was pretty sharp, but he was far and away the standout. The kid could have a future, at least get a college education out of the game."

"So?" Sackler asked, his eyes brightening. "All the more reason for hubby to stick around. Why would he skip, answer me that? If my kid were a future all-star, I'd want to see it. Like I told you, it was just a stupid accident."

"What do you think, Dean?" DeLeo asked.

"I reserve judgment," Dean answered, just as Lieutenant Anderson entered the room. Harrigan woke up, as if on cue, smiling broadly at everyone.

"At least one of you guys is still objective about this case," the white-haired Anderson said. He tossed a file to Dean. "It's all yours. Norfolk wants us to dig around up here before they go busting their backsides trying to drag the Chesapeake Bay for a body."

"That makes sense, Lieutenant," DeLeo said. "If you ask me, those Norfolk guys would be better off checking the airports than the bottom of the bay."

The lieutenant motioned for Dean to follow into his office at the end of the hall where Anderson reiterated the meager details of the Byrne case. Dean made up his mind not to make up his mind until he knew more about the case.

Lieutenant Anderson was leaning toward natural causes. "He got loaded and went for a dip, pure and simple. Sure, it looks like a phony and we've got to check it out, but my money says it's a drowning. Talk to the wife and go down to Philly where he works and maybe check out some of the neighbors. Norfolk wants to clean this up and they're looking for direction on which way to lean."

"Just what I need," Dean grumbled. "First I get to third-degree a woman who just lost her husband and then I get to fight Philadelphia traffic."

Anderson looked up, irritated at Dean's mood. "Boy, have you been bitchy lately."

Dean had to agree, but going to Philadelphia was like a visit to the dentist: once in a while you had to do it but nobody liked it. Not even the commuters who lied to themselves and everyone else by saying the hour and a half at each end of the day was a pleasurable time to relax and read the paper. Dean muttered an apology to his superior and left the lieutenant's office.

When he returned to the main room, Harrigan had left to talk to a class of grade-school children, a job at which he excelled, much to the pleasure of the others who shunned playing Officer Friendly. Sackler and DeLeo were packing up, off to follow a lead on the whereabouts of a forger of Social Security checks who had been working overtime in recent months.

Dean spent a few minutes at his desk finishing up some routine paperwork before telephoning the alleged widow Byrne at 9:15, the earliest time he deemed respectable. The phone was answered by a woman who identified herself as Mrs. Riley, a neighbor. After offering his condolences, Dean asked if it might be convenient for him to come by and speak with Mrs. Byrne. He held the phone for a few moments while Mrs. Riley checked. She returned, saying that 10:30 would be fine. Dean had hoped to make it as soon as possible so he could beat the worst of the late afternoon traffic when he returned from his chores in Philadelphia. It didn't look good. White days were always like that.

When Dean telephoned the office of World Wide Insurance Company, his luck was no better. No one was available to speak with him until 2:00. A Mr. Edwin Mayer hoped to be able to sneak him in at that time, or so squeaked his nasal-voiced secretary. Dean, unable to concentrate further on his files, pushed closed his desk drawer, packed a tape recorder in his briefcase, and left the office.

The Byrne address was on the east side of town, but as Dean had time to kill, he decided to drive west to what the locals called the beltway, a loop road around the city. The route more than doubled the distance, but Dean needed little incentive for a drive in the country. Maybe the rural air would dispel his blahs. He only wished he were on his bicycle instead of the stuffy Chevrolet pool car he was assigned to drive.

Dean left the parking lot on Elm Street, turned left on Church, and after dutifully pausing for a calico cat to stalk a pigeon, he continued out Yoder Avenue, watching the city slowly dissolve in his rearview mirror.

Police Headquarters was located in the center of town between the City Hall and the library, across from a well-kept park that contained the obligatory statue of a civil war hero. Parkside had held up well, faring much better than some of its sister cities in eastern Pennsylvania. Many of the older homes dating back to the last century were still owned by families with sufficient money to maintain them in at least some semblance of their prior grandeur. A few had been converted to apartments, but a recent wave of historical consciousness had temporarily halted the decay. Parkside's economy was less than spectacular, but at least it didn't require dependency on the fickle business of mines, steel or manufacturing for its fiscal survival.

While Parkside was officially beyond the limits of sensible commuting, enough hardy souls made the long daily trek into Philadelphia to label the town an outlying bedroom community. Most of these commuters lived on the eastern perimeter, as if the extra mile or two made their daily trek somehow more acceptable. Clusters of sixties and seventies-style subdivisions had blossomed during the post-war era of rush to the 'burbs. These look-alikes that originally carried names like Camelot or South Pacific were at first scorned by Parkside's gentry but had slowly gained a level of respectability. Untold hours of do-it-yourself-manship and emergency repair had finally overcome poor septic design and generally shoddy workmanship to create communities of adequate comfort and living.

Sherwood Forest, where Dean headed, was one of these communities, and the best of the bunch in his opinion. Dean remembered reading about Adolph Messner, a craftsman of the old school who was a stickler for perfection, if not business acumen. His company went belly up only days after he dropped dead spackling the front hall of his 87th house, a bi-level on Friar Tuck Drive. But old Adolph could rest in peace beneath the crabgrass in Pine Grove Cemetery, content in the knowledge that his handiwork had held up well while more than quadrupling in value.

The neighborhood had slowly changed over the years. Babysitters now outnumbered their potential customers, as families with young children could seldom afford the little three-bedroom "Norman," much less "The Saxon" or the bi-level "King Richard." Nowadays, not even the models looked alike, altered by porches and additions and a variety of landscaping tastes.

One hundred fifty-six Maid Marian Lane was a neatly kept ranch to which a one-car garage had been added. Rows of red tulips stood like sentinels along the walkway, struggling to survive against the encroachment of summer. Dean pulled into the empty driveway. The detective's knock was answered by a woman who introduced herself as Janice Riley, the neighbor he had spoken to on the phone. She was in her early thirties, overweight, dimpled, and dressed in a flowered shirt and slacks. Dean entered a living room, furnished tastefully but on a limited budget. A bookcase containing a dozen baseball trophies highlighted the far wall of the small room.

"Cindy's in the john," Mrs. Riley said nervously. "She's so upset—all this waiting, and still no word." She looked at Dean as if to ask.

Dean shook his head no just as the phone rang from the front hall. Mrs. Riley jumped at the sound and bit her lip. "My heart's in my mouth ever time it rings," she said and added an apology as she moved to answer it, just as Cynthia Byrne entered the room.

Years later Dean would think back to this first time he saw Cynthia Byrne. Her size surprised him. She was no more than five foot one, he guessed, but she moved with the grace of a much taller woman. She wore neither makeup nor jewelry, but her blouse and skirt demonstrated that she had made a half-hearted attempt to dress for company. Her hair was short and dark and worn in an easy style that seemed to require little care. Cynthia Byrne, in spite of reddened eyes and trembling nervousness, was a very attractive woman. And, if first impressions meant anything, as Dean believed they did, this woman was sincerely distraught over her husband's disappearance. He felt it in the quiver of her handshake and saw it in the empty look in her eyes.

"I'm sorry. It's pretty hectic around here," she said, motioning toward the phone. "I don't know what I'd have done without the neighbors—they've been unbelievably kind."

Dean offered his condolences just as the doorbell rang. Mrs. Riley set down the phone and moved to the door to answer it. Mrs. Byrne, looking embarrassed at the confusion, suggested that she and Dean might be better off talking on the back deck. She led the detective through a kitchen cluttered with coffee cups, soiled plates and two half-eaten cakes.

"People came by all last evening and everyone brought food," she said by way of apology. "I think it's a way to force you to eat by guilt, when you're not at all hungry." She opened the back door to a pleasant redwood deck overlooking a small, well-kept back yard.

"Jeff finished the deck last fall," she said, "just before the snow. You should have seen us out here cooking steaks in our mittens."

The deck was furnished with wicker furniture, two chairs facing each other and a sofa with a coffee table in front of it. A milk glass vase with a spray of daffodils rested atop the table. Mrs. Byrne sat on the sofa and Dean took the chair to her left. The air was hot and heavy but the small backyard setting remained pleasant. Birds sang in the mature trees that ringed the deck and there was a country smell of spring.

Cynthia Byrne explained, in nervous little spurts, how she had heard the news of her husband's disappearance. Dean let her talk on, not interrupting her with questions for fear the tears would start. She had received notice from Parkside's police officer McCarthy the prior day, Tuesday, late in the afternoon. She was alone at the time but McCarthy would not leave until there was someone with her. At his insistence she summoned Janice Riley.

Another neighbor's husband drove to the high school for her son Randy, who was at baseball practice.

"Randy was so good—so brave about it. He tried for the longest time not to cry. When he finally did, he was all apologies. 'I don't do the death bit very well,' he said." Then she too began to cry, making Dean feel like a bastard for imposing on her grief.

He rose from the chair. "Look, I really can do this later. The timing is lousy for me to be bugging you with questions."

"No, please stay. I know you're just doing your job." She made an effort to compose herself, taking deep breaths. "It's better if I have something to take my mind off—other matters."

"Do you have people who can stay with you?" Dean asked. "Relatives?"

"I called my mother. She lives in Indiana but it's so difficult to make any plans until...they find Jeff. Mother's head librarian in a small town and it isn't easy for her to get away. Jeff's father is dead and his mother is in a nursing home. We're both only children so there aren't any brothers or sisters. Janice's husband called a doctor last night and he gave me something. And the priest from the church where Jeff and I sometimes go came by." She looked up at him. "I'm sorry, I keep talking as if Jeff is still alive."

"No problem. It's natural."

"I know he's gone, but I can't say it yet. Is that okay? I guess I'm not making much sense, period."

"Are you sure you don't want me to come back later?"

She shook her head. "The doctor said I should talk about it. Really, I'm all right. It's just such...such a shock. One day everything is...like every other day and then...nothing will ever be the same...forever." She rose and crossed to the railing of the deck. "Do you think I should go down there? To Norfolk? I just don't know. I don't know what to do."

"I think you should stay here. At least in Parkside you're around friends." Then he added hesitantly, "The paper said the current on the bay is strong. It might be a number of days before they find him." He stopped when he saw her begin to shudder.

"Mostly, I'm scared. I'm scared to death they'll find him and I'm scared to death they won't." She took a deep breath and plopped down of the sofa. "Please, I know you have questions and here I am babbling away taking up your time."

"I'm sorry if some of the questions may sound...distasteful. They're just things we have to ask." She nodded and insisted he continue.

Dean started slowly and she answered in a straightforward manner, her voice becoming stronger as she proceeded. Jeffrey Byrne had telephoned home in early evening, his usual practice when he was traveling on business trips. The call came between 7:00 and 7:30 and there had been nothing unusual about it. Jeffrey Byrne asked about Randy's ball game and inquired about the mail. His drive to Virginia had been uneventful and he promised to bring back some fresh crabmeat when he returned. He would leave the next day, after taking care of some business.

When the police appeared at the door the next day, she was sure something had happened to her son, not her husband. Later she received a telephone call from the Norfolk Police Department, but it only confirmed what Officer McCarthy had already told her. She was too upset to remember much of what was said and she'd not spoken directly with Norfolk since that first call. Phil Riley, Janice's husband, telephoned Virginia several times but there was no additional news. They were simply "doing their best."

She closed her eyes, remembering. "Little things keep popping into mind—like Jeff won't be here for Randy's graduation, or he'll miss a neighbor's surprise party, or we'll never get to the Top of the Mark." Dean's eyes questioned and Mrs. Byrne clarified, "The Mark Hopkins Hotel, in San Francisco—it was our little joke. Neither of us had ever traveled further west than Ohio but when we were old and retired, we were going there and drink manhattans at sunset. As if we could afford to. When things were going badly, we'd say, 'Think of manhattans at the Mark.'"

"Did your husband drink manhattans?"

She laughed. "Lord, no. I don't think he's ever tasted one! They just sounded incredibly romantic—our fantasy." The smile disappeared. "Phil Riley said the Norfolk police suggested Jeff was drunk. They didn't come out and say it—but that was Phil's inference. He wasn't drunk—I'm sure. Jeff was a careful drinker. We'd have a little wine when we had something to celebrate and once in a while a beer in the summer."

"Out of town gets boring and lonely," Dean suggested, but she just shook her head. Dean changed the subject. "Was your husband a swimmer?" he asked cautiously.

There was no pause before she answered. "Jeff liked the water and especially loved the ocean. He was a reasonably good swimmer. He always took a bathing suit along on his trips but more times than not he was too busy to use them."

"Were you surprised to hear he'd gone swimming—out to the beach alone at midnight?"

She took her time considering this question. "Jeff does silly things sometimes—it wouldn't be totally out of character for him to do something on a whim. But this? I just don't know. He's usually very predictable but he surprises everyone once in a while with something totally off the wall." She looked up at Dean. "But little things, not important things—not dangerous things." Dean sensed part of her was upset by her husband's irresponsible actions.

Before he could respond, Mrs. Riley entered carrying a tray with coffee, two mugs and a plate of homemade doughnuts. She apologized for disturbing them, and set the tray on the wicker table, explaining they were fresh and had just been delivered by a neighbor.

"They're delicious," she added self-consciously as she turned and left.

Dean poured the coffee while Cynthia Byrne rubbed her hands on her skirt as if to smooth out the nervous quiver she couldn't seem to shake. Both drank their coffee black and although both took a doughnut, Mrs. Byrne simply picked at hers, lifting the tiniest of crumbs with dampened fingertips.

Dean tried to phrase the next question as delicately as possible, repeating it in his mind before releasing the words. "Is there any reason you can think of for your husband...to just leave?"

"No." She answered without pause and then spent long seconds looking down at her coffee, as if searching for words to clarify her statement. "Emphatically no. Definitely no. Positively no. It simply wouldn't be Jeff."

"Why?" Dean asked cautiously.

She paused before answering. "You'd have to know him. Jeff is too simple. I don't mean stupid-simple, I mean...uncomplicated. We both are. We don't owe millions, or have lovers, or rare diseases, or tons of life insurance, or work for the CIA, or do drugs or any of that. The three of us live in a five-room ranch with a fat mortgage and less than a thousand dollars in the bank. We've been married 20 years and..." She turned, wiping away a tear with her sleeve, "we love each other."

Dean said nothing and she finally broke the silence. "Jeff is very moral. He has a black and white sense of right and wrong. It's difficult to put in words, but if he were to leave, he'd do it up front—he'd never just sneak away." She looked up at him. "I'm sorry. There's no reason I should expect you to understand. I know you had to ask but I'll save you the next question," she added. "There wasn't another woman...ever."

Dean didn't press the point. He was curious why she was so emphatic and he didn't even consider mentioning the wife was the last to know.

She seemed to read his mind and smiled. "We just didn't have secrets—at least not the sneaky kind."

"What kind did you have?" he asked with a smile.

She paused. "None about important things. Sometimes Jeff had this notion about protecting me from anything unpleasant. It infuriates me, but he keeps doing it—some macho thing, I guess. When there is a problem at work, he keeps it to himself or mini- mize it. Jeff does kind things for people, sometimes to a fault, but he seldom talks about it."

"What sort of things?"

"Picking up a hitch-hiker, giving a homeless person a dollar— things like that. He says he doesn't want me to worry. But impor- tant things, like his health or our budget or Randy—those we share."

Dean continued with the rest of his questions and she dutiful- ly responded. Sometimes she answered as if she were alone, talk- ing out loud, reminiscing, remembering the tiniest of details of a life now forever changed.

Most of their friends were local to Maid Marian Lane where they had lived for nine years. Slowly a portrait of the missing man emerged. Jeff Byrne had worked for World Wide for 15 years and seemed at least content with the work he was doing. His health was excellent and he had never expressed more than mild dis- pleasure with his lot in life. Between job, commuting and home life there was little extra time. Nor did he personally have access to much money. Cynthia Byrne handled the finances.

"Jeff was terrible with money. I handled the checkbook from the very first. I don't remember us ever not being on a tight budget. Jeff doesn't make much, but we make do, and he's tickled pink to let me do the paper work." She named a salary figure close to the small amount Dean drew from the Parkside Police Department. He could imagine the difficulty in supporting a family of three on the figure.

The Byrne family had finally scraped aside enough for Cynthia to go back to school. She was close to completing training to become a physical therapist and would graduate at the end of the summer. The second income would be a must if Randy were to attend college. Otherwise, it had looked as if further education was out of the question.

"But now Randy may have a chance for a baseball scholarship," she said proudly. "A number of schools are interested. That would be a Godsend." She added, "Especially now."

"He's a great player. I saw him last spring. Your son has real talent."

"He's at school now," she said hesitantly. "I practically made him go. He didn't want to go but I felt it was important for him to be around friends his own age. He has a game this afternoon, too." She added somewhat sheepishly, "He's had perfect attendance for all of high school. His father kids with him about it. Jeff is never sick and is a real stickler for that sort of thing. He and Randy have a bet going about it. Do you think I was wrong in sending him?"

Dean recalled his own father's death when he was 12 years old and how well his mother had brought him through the ordeal. It was not until years later after his mother too was gone that he realized the grief and confusion she must have felt. "I don't think there is a right or wrong in a situation like this," Dean replied. "Follow a mother's instincts and it'll come out just fine."

"You're a very kind man." She said it matter-of-factly. Her statement had a surprising effect on Dean. In spite of his discomfort with having to conduct the interview, he found he was now reluctant to leave. He felt an urge to stay and offer some modicum of comfort to this woman he hardly knew. He felt strangely sorry for her, suddenly left alone by death, or perhaps duplicity. And he felt guilty as hell for his own foul mood and the insignificant reasons behind it.

Dean finished the interview by obtaining the names of Jeffrey Byrne's doctor and insurance agent although, according to his wife, Byrne seldom visited a doctor and the only life insurance he carried was whatever his employer provided. Dean had already overstayed his visit, so with promises to return if he had any more questions and to keep in telephone contact, he took his leave, shaking Cynthia Byrne's hand and waving to Janice Riley, who was again on the phone.

Dean was no stranger to interviews with people recently exposed to the violent side of life. Neither the years nor the number of interviews made his dislike for the task any less, but experience did help in knowing who to believe and who was telling stories. While that intuition was far from foolproof, it was pretty damn good. And as Dean left Sherwood Forest behind, he had a strong feeling Cynthia Byrne wasn't telling stories.

# CHAPTER II

Dean usually devoted the solitary time behind the wheel to sorting out details of a case, putting little facts in their slots like letters in a country post office. But after two hours with Cynthia Byrne, he had to fight the inclination to take all of her comments at face value, thereby kissing off any degree of objectivity. There was far more to learn about Jeffrey Byrne before he could report an informed opinion on the happenings in Norfolk two nights earlier.

Dean made surprisingly good time driving to Philadelphia in spite of having taken longer than he had planned interviewing the wife of the missing man. He knew the return trip would be far different, crawling his way back in the snarl of rush hour. His route to Philly looked like a drunkard's path, zigzagging a series of country roads that were at times crowded with local traffic. The hills and farmlands gradually turned to inner suburbia and then to the harshness of urban streets, choked tightly with the crush, smells and sounds of the city. He grabbed an order of French fries and a burger at the drive-in of a national chain, eating on the road, licking the salt from his fingers as he searched among the glass and steel structures for the address he had jotted down earlier.

World Wide Insurance Company was in the heart of Philadelphia, occupying a towering structure that glared down on city hall and a thousand tired buildings, many dating back to the horse-drawn carriage days. Parking wasn't a problem if you didn't mind paying the price of a good country dinner, but Dean didn't have time to hunt down a bargain so he reluctantly pulled into the closest lot. He'd fight the expense account battle at the end of the month.

After a brief wait, Dean was led to the sixteenth-floor cubbyhole of Mr. Edwin Mayer, an incredibly gaunt giant who slumped as if to tell the world he was just as short as the rest of them. He wore an ill-fitting suit and his neck seemed to be untouched by an oversized collar. His high-water trousers exposed black silk socks with little ladders up the sides, held in place with garters, something Dean hadn't seen in decades. But in spite of his uninspiring appearance, Edwin Mayer was fully in command. A half dozen workers whose desks were in sight of their superior all pretended unsuccessfully to act busy while sneaking peeks at the stranger.

"Don't mind those guys," Mayer said after introductions. "They're just interested in Jeff. We all are. Damn shame, isn't it? I didn't get the word until last night—I was out of town. Anything new? He hasn't floated in, has he?"

Dean confirmed there were no developments nor had the body been located. He asked if he might record the interview in addition to taking notes. Mayer readily agreed and Dean produced a hand-held recorder from his briefcase. Dean had used a less intrusive pad and pencil with Cynthia Byrne.

"This whole business is a damn shame," Mayer repeated. "I can't get over it. You just don't know what to say." He paused. "It was kind of a dumb thing for ol' Jeff to do, wasn't it?"

"It seems that way, at least in retrospect. Does swimming alone late at night strike you as in character for Byrne?"

Mayer took no time in responding. "I suppose any of us might act stupid, given the circumstances. You're out of town, you have a few snorts at dinner, it's a hot night, there's a beach. Why not?"

"I suppose you're right. We've all done things we regret later." Dean changed the subject. "What was it exactly Byrne did for World Wide?"

"We called his position Regional Marketing Manager, but in reality he was a glorified errand boy—a paper pusher. He didn't make any decisions; he just went out and visited the local offices and some of our independent agents, you know, pumping up our product line, troubleshooting, that sort of thing."

"Was he good at it?"

"Sure. Well, good enough." Mayer pushed up his sleeve and scratched a bony elbow before continuing. "Let me put it this way, there are fast-track guys and day-to-day guys—the guys who just get the job done. Byrne was a day-to-day guy. He wasn't going anywhere in the organization, but he didn't really want to, either."

"You're saying he was content at his job?"

"Hell, yes. Like a frog in a mill pond. He never liked being on the hot seat and he'd found his niche with this job. Yeah, ol' Jeff was content. We liked his work and he liked what he was doing. You can't beat that, can you? You know, I never once heard him bitch in all the years he worked for me."

"Tell me about this last trip—the one to Norfolk, Virginia."

"What's to tell? It was the usual swing down to Norfolk."

"Nothing out of the ordinary?" Dean asked.

"Naw. Jeff would hit all of the districts a few times a year, spend two, sometimes three days depending on the need."

"Did he make up his schedule, or did you?" Dean asked.

"A little of each, I guess. I gave him a general overview and he picked the times, unless something hot was cooking."

"Was something hot cooking in Norfolk?"

Mayer shook his head. "Just routine." He rocked back in his chair and added, "There was a little shindig for the marketing guy—Fletch Brunell. It was his last day—finally. Good riddance."

"Why do you say that?"

"Fletcher Brunell? He was a pain in the ass. Hated the hot and stickies of Norfolk weather and was always after me to transfer him back to Scranton—fat chance of that—or to some bread-basket state out west. Then he went over my head—put in a request to senior management. You don't pull that shit with me."

"Did he get his transfer?"

"Hell, no! I saw to that. He knew his days were numbered and gave his notice—said he had a job out west. I'm surprised the office even bothered with a send off party. I'm still waiting for his last expense account. He never turned it in."

"He was a problem?"

"Naw, not really. He replaced me in Scranton when I got this promotion here to the head office. He screwed up. Lousy production. Scranton was my baby—I wanted to see it hum but Brunell wasn't the hummer for the job. I transferred him to Norfolk but he didn't fit in there either and now he's gone. Big send off and all." He added, "I guess that's why Jeff had too much booze."

"Was Jeff much of a drinker?"

"No. Maybe one or two. I never heard he got loaded. Someone would have mentioned it. I keep pretty good tabs on my boys."

"What you're saying goes along with the wife's statement—she said he was a careful drinker."

"Who really knows? Maybe this was the one time he let it all hang out—or maybe you don't have to be drunk to be stupid."

Dean looked at his notes. "He was to return after some early morning business, the next day, Tuesday—same day, I guess—he died after midnight, Tuesday."

"The office said he wrapped it up Monday—was supposed to take off first thing Tuesday morning. The trip was really just for Brunell's send off."

"How often was Byrne out of the office?"

"Oh, two, maybe three times a month. Want to see his expense account?" Before Dean could answer, Mayer hollered over his partition. "Hey, Chernak. Get Jeff's expense reports, will you?" The most curious looker, who sat at the first desk, scurried to an empty desk three stations away and began rummaging through the drawers.

"Is that Byrne's desk?" Dean asked.

"Yeah, you want to look at it?"

"Sure," Dean answered and the two men rose, leaving the cubicle for the open office area.

Chernak handed a thick folder to Dean, smiling at Mayer as if he were waiting to be introduced. "Thanks, Joe," Mayer said, excusing Chernak, who looked disappointed as he reluctantly left. Mayer's telephone rang and he excused himself to answer it, leaving Dean at Jeffrey Byrne's grey steel desk.

A stack of file folders was neatly arranged on one side, while a half-dozen pens, all facing in the same direction, were perfectly centered on the desk blotter. The only non-business items were a digital clock and two framed pictures. The first picture was of a young man dressed in a suit, looking as if he'd rather be anywhere else. Dean assumed it was Jeff Byrne's son, Randy. Next to it was a full-face picture of Cynthia Byrne. Her hair was shorter and the smile on her face made her all the more attractive.

A large drawer on the left side of the desk contained files on various branch offices of the company while the drawers on the right, three in all, contained blank paper, company circulars and a few maps. Apart from the pictures, there was nothing personal in or on the desk. The top drawer contained the usual assortment of pens, pencils and paperclips. There was no computer.

Dean felt a movement behind him and looked up to see a young man in his early twenties looking down at him. He wore an Alfred E. Newman smile and was dressed in a short-sleeved shirt without a tie.

"Hi," he said, "That there's Mrs. Byrne, Jeff's wife."

"Yes, I know. I've met her." Dean rose and introduced himself

"Me too. My sister lives up in Parkside and sometimes I hook a ride up with Jeff so's I can visit." He extended his hand. "I'm Jackie Rudman. We're all sorry as hell Jeff's gone. He was okay. Do you guys think he skipped?" Dean shrugged his shoulders and perused the reports, hoping the young man would take a hint and leave. "Neat writer, ain't he? He was great with detail—always by hand. Never saw him type. I suppose you get lots of skips, don't you?"

Before Dean could answer, Mayer returned and Rudman beat a hasty retreat to his cubby hole. Dean was left standing there, Cynthia Byrne's picture in hand, a report in another.

"She's quite a looker, isn't she?" Mayer said, "And quite a lady."

"Yes," replied Dean. "I guess you've met her."

"A few Christmas parties, that sort of thing." Mayer answered. Dean replaced the picture. "Did they get along?"

Mayer thought a minute. "Are you married?" he asked.

"No, why?" answered Dean.

"Then maybe you wouldn't understand but they were what marriage is supposed to be. I know. And I know what marriage ought not to be! I'm working on wife number three and I think she's working on somebody else. Jeff and Cindy? They were like Barbie and Ken, for cripe's sake."

"Did Byrne fool around?" Someone behind them laughed out loud and Dean turned to see a young man cover his mouth and apologize.

"What's so funny, Clancy?" asked Mayer.

"Just the thought of Jeff having a chick on the side struck me funny, that's all," he answered. "Sorry, Mr. Mayer."

"Yeah." Mayer turned to Dean as he and the detective moved back to Mayer's office. "That is pretty funny. You'd just have to know Jeff Byrne to appreciate it. A 100 percent home body."

Further questioning revealed that Byrne had signed out a pool company car for the seven-hour trip to Virginia. The vehicle was in police custody in Norfolk but the authorities there said it would be released to the World Wide local office shortly.

The life insurance World Wide provided its employees was equal to one year's pay, hardly enough to leave a rich widow. Mayer did not think Byrne had carried any additional coverage because, according to Mayer, Byrne hardly had enough money to blow his nose. "But who needs life insurance?" It was a line of business World Wide didn't sell. Besides, Jeff Byrne's health was good. He was in better shape than half the office, by Mayer's assessment.

"Jeff used to jog and all but he got a bum knee. Nothing serious, but it bothered him if he ran. He swims, or at least he did. But not very good, I guess."

Dean continued to question Mayer but learned nothing more of substance. A picture of Byrne continued to emerge: Mr. Ordinary, homebody, well liked, in a blah job like a million other guys, on a train to nowhere but happy enough to keep chugging along with the ride. It was beginning to look more as if Jeffrey Byrne pulled a stupid stunt after a few too many drinks in a lonely motel, leaving a widow and a teenaged son to fend for themselves.

Dean began packing up to leave but Mayer drew him aside.

"Look, could I ask you something? This is really bugging me. Byrne's on the payroll, right? Say they don't even find his body? Like never. I don't want to terminate him but he's not dead, official-like, so they can't just pay off his life insurance. But we can't just pretend he's gonna come strolling back in the door either. He's not disabled, so we can't pay disability. I don't mean to be harsh, but we'll have to replace him pretty damn soon and we've only got so much budget. It's a real bitch. Imagine me giving Cindy Byrne a call and telling her she's cut off, at least until ol' Jeff floats in? How would that look? I'll tell you—it'd make me look like a real bastard, that's how it'd look." Dean simply shrugged his shoulders.

It was after 4:00 when Dean signed a receipt for the bulky expense folder. He also asked for and received Byrne's department personnel file. Mayer promised to send the full file with Byrne's picture from the now near-closing personnel office, located in another building. Dean passed out his business card to Mayer and a few of the other workers in case anything important came to mind. He stowed his recorder and descended to street level in an elevator packed tightly with exiting employees. From a pay phone in the lobby of the large building, he placed a call to the Parkside Police Department. He spoke to Harrigan, who was filling out a report on a daylight burglary. Lieutenant Anderson had already left, but wanted Dean to call him at home with an update. It had been a good day for DeLeo and Sackler. They had collared a suspect in their search for the pension check thief. Their case was weak, but they had a strong feeling they had the right man and with a little work could put it together.

Dean retrieved his car and fought his way out of town on roads thick with retreating commuters. It was an hour later when he pulled into an upscale tap house and while waiting for ribs and coffee, called Anderson. Anderson's wife Marian answered on the first ring.

"David? Quick, tell me. I've a bet with Leland—a night of unforgettable pleasure for him against a new golf outfit for me. Was it a skip, or wasn't it?"

Dean smiled. "Which did you pick, Marian?"

"The skip, naturally. Don't tell me you believe the jerk just drowned!" Dean could picture Marian Anderson standing there in a silk robe, cigarette holder in hand, looking every bit the wealthy socialite she was.

"Marian, it's too early for a definitive answer, but don't give away your old golf outfit just yet."

"Oh, you poop. You're just stalling. You know I'm right. But hurry up with an answer. I have to leave town. Do you know where Ouray, Colorado is?"

"No. Why?"

"I inherited property there from some uncle I never even met. I have to go check it out." Marian Anderson, with more money than a small city bank, was always inheriting something. "Oops, here's Leland," she added.

Dean filled in Lieutenant Leland Anderson on the happenings of the day, detailing his conversations with Cynthia Byrne and her husband's employer. When he had summed up his findings, Anderson agreed that the evidence gathered to date pointed to a simple accident.

"Norfolk called three times today. They're pretty anxious to put this thing to bed," Anderson stated. "They want to know if you could fly down and back for a day." Dean had mixed feelings. The trip would make for a 15-hour tour but it would certainly break up the usual routine. "Take tomorrow and check out the details, like the life insurance and that stuff and catch up on your paper work," Anderson continued. "Fly down on Friday and we can put this whole thing in a file cabinet by the weekend. This case is looking like a no-brainer." Dean agreed, and ended the conversation as dinner arrived. He hadn't even had time to do the teaser puzzles on the place mat.

By the time Dean had finished his meal, the traffic had thinned out, making the balance of the trip northward much more pleasant. The late spring sun had finally fought its way out of the white haze and was slipping down in the west, painting the countryside in yellow brush strokes. An unusual number of people were enjoying the unseasonable weather, spending the last few hours out of doors; fathers playing catch with sons, youngsters riding trikes or skipping rope, and others content to just drink in the springtime evening. While Dean's mood had slowly improved, he still envied their contentment. Punching the buttons on his car radio, he finally found music that didn't assault his senses and pushed ahead toward Parkside, ready to call it a day.

It was dark by the time Dean reached the town and maneuvered his way through the familiar streets to 422 Collingswood Avenue. The downstairs lights were on, giving the house a welcoming glow. The two-story home had been built in the depression years and although there was little land around it, it was comfortable, well constructed and had answered Dean's limited needs—at least "temporarily"—for the past 15 years.

Dean's mother had raised her only son alone after her husband's death, relying on life insurance proceeds and a series of part-time jobs. During those years no man had shared her life, but just before Dean was released from the Army, he received surprising word of his mother's second marriage. Two days after landing in the United States, Dean received a phone call from Fred O'Connor, the stepfather he'd yet to meet, informing him his mother was gravely ill. Dean rushed to the Philadelphia hospital where three days later a third heart attack claimed the woman's life.

During this trying time, the funeral and the days that followed, Dean stayed with Fred O'Connor in the Collingswood Avenue house Fred and Dean's mother had rented after their marriage. A few weeks later Dean was discharged from the service and he gravitated back to Parkside and, temporarily he thought, to Collingswood Avenue. Fifteen years later he was still there.

Fred O'Connor, at 74, had long since finished his working career, a calico collection of jobs which changed with the telling, none of which gave him a pension. His small social security check was barely enough to provide spending money and keep him supplied with paperback mysteries, his passion. But it was more than Dean's charity that kept the two together, although at times Dean questioned the relationship as well as his sanity for putting up with the old man.

"How's it going?" the detective asked as he draped his suit jacket on the railing and pulled off his tie before slumping down in the rocker across the room from the old man.

"Wait a minute," O'Connor said, without looking up. Dean dutifully paused a few moments until Fred took off his glasses, slammed down the book on a table and said with a broad smile, "I knew it! The cousin had to be the illegitimate daughter of the old man. That was the only way it would work!"

"The cousin is always the illegitimate daughter of the old man," Dean answered. "Any mail?"

"Only your bicycling magazine, a few circulars and a couple of bills. I pitched out the junk mail and paid the bills." He paused, "You just have to sign the checks."

"You don't have to do that," Dean said, meaning every word of it.

"Glad to help. Don't the place look great? Me and Mrs. Porter cleaned it up today." Mrs. Porter, the housekeeper, came in weekly and Dean could guess the percentage of work performed by each. "You got a phone call too," Fred added, "The guy said it was important."

"Who was he?" Dean asked.

"Don't know. He wouldn't leave his name. He sounded kinda wacky. He's going to call back tomorrow night, at exactly 9:00."

"Tomorrow's Thursday."

Fred snapped his fingers. "I forgot," he said sarcastically. "Thursday's your night for sex." Dean simply ignored him.

Fred O'Connor had a sharp mind and a sharp tongue to match it. He was remarkably spry, healthy for his age, and had broken the hearts of half the widows in Parkside. Fred possessed a full head of snow-white hair, carried himself ramrod straight and was a familiar sight and well-liked figure about town.

Dean went to the kitchen and poured beers for himself and Fred. When he returned, he opened the compact disc player, a recent indulgence they both enjoyed, and checked the selections before turning it on. He and Fred did not enjoy the same music so when both were home the five-disc machine usually contained two jazz selections for Dean, two country and western for Fred, and a pop group neither liked but both could tolerate. The machine was set for "random selection" so no one was cheated. The right mix was in so Dean turned on the machine. He'd lucked out. It was Gerry Mulligan with a nineteen-fifties piece that filled the room with familiar strains. He returned to his rocker, sipped his beer and began to patiently answer the barrage of Fred's questions about his day's activities. Fred's level of interest was sky-high when he learned Dean had been assigned the Byrne disappearance.

"I was hoping we'd get that caper soon as I read it in the paper," Fred said as he reached for a pad and pencil to take notes. Dean ignored the pronoun we. "Give me all the details. Finally you've got something interesting—a case we can really sink our teeth into."

"Sorry to disappoint you, Sherlock, but it looks like a simple drowning. I'm going down to Norfolk Friday to talk to the local police, but so far, there isn't a thing to point to the guy skipping." He ticked off the items he had learned about Jeffrey Byrne during the course of the day, as much for his own review as to answer

Fred's rapid-fire questions. Fred finally leaned back with the knowing look of a kid with a pocket full of gumdrops.

"Churchy la fam," he said smugly.

Dean smiled. "You mean, 'Cherchez la femme,' don't you?"

"That's what I said. It means, 'look for the gal.'" Fred's answer came just as the music switched to a shrill voice pleading for her lover to come back to the hills.

"Rough translation and close enough. But you're all wet on this one. Jeff Byrne is the last of the straight arrows. He's about to be nominated for sainthood."

"You're just starting to investigate. Don't go jumping to conclusions."

"I haven't finished but I'll tell you, I haven't met anyone who thought there was a ghost of a chance he was fooling around."

Fred ignored Dean's response and began to scratch his head in thought. "I remember a case like this. I think it was an Agatha Christie or maybe Nero Wolfe. The guy skipped out with his secretary after he faked his drowning and embezzled a million dollars."

"Fred, this is the real world. Given Byrne's job at World Wide, I don't think he was in a position to embezzle anything but the coffee money."

"I keep telling you, this stuff happens in the real world. If you read some of these here mystery books, you'd pick up lots of pointers for that job of yours. Just because it's fiction doesn't mean you can't learn from it. This type of skip comes up all the time. By the way, I'm free to ride down to Norfolk on Friday if you want a little company."

"I'm flying to Norfolk. This is business. Anderson would have a fit if you tagged along even if I were driving and you know it."

"Two eyes are better than one," grumbled Fred, disappointed.

"I have two eyes," Dean answered, as he crossed to the kitchen for two more beers.

"That's not what I meant." Fred growled, as he added more notes to his pad. "I'm making a list so's you don't forget stuff."

"Put on your glasses, you'll go blind doing that," Dean said, handing Fred his beer and reclaiming his rocker from Mrs. Lincoln, the large black cat that had adopted the pair the prior February.

("He" had been named Abe for the occasion before they discovered their mistake.)

"I got 20-20 eyes. Those glasses are only for reading," Fred replied, without looking up.

"And seeing. What's on your list?"

"Just things," Fred muttered, putting on his glasses. "This here case may be a lot more complicated than you think. Don't go jumping to conclusions. There's elements to consider."

Dean smiled as he picked up the evening newspaper. There was nothing new on the Byrne case—just a comment to that effect. After a quick look at the sports section he tossed the paper aside and glanced at the bicycling magazine. That too held little interest, so he began to peruse the papers he had accumulated at World Wide.

Dean found it difficult concentrating on the expense reports with Fred's foot keeping time against the coffee table to an early cut of Hank Williams, but gradually his mind began to focus on the forms. The reports went back nearly three years and listed dates, locations and dollars expended, with each entry carefully and manually recording names, locations, reasons for visits and persons present. The names and offices visited recurred regularly as Mayer had described. While there was no precise pattern to the trips, no locations seemed to be more frequently visited than others. Dean found himself able to predict for instance, it was time to visit Baltimore again, and a week or two later, Byrne would travel there.

Most trips commenced early in the week if the destination was closer, and Byrne was home by late Wednesday or Thursday. Even though some of the destinations might have been more efficiently visited by plane, Byrne always took a company car, often resulting in very long workdays. The mileage was scrupulously recorded, as was everything else. Receipts were attached to all reports, mostly for inexpensive meals and an occasional beer or two. There were ten cities serviced by Byrne, all on the eastern seaboard, and his itineraries were detailed on practically an hour-by-hour basis. There was absolutely nothing that Dean could see to indicate any unusual pattern or unaccounted time. Jeffrey Byrne was a boringly precise man. The files were better than a sleeping pill.

Dean rose with a yawn just as Errol Garner was replaced by Hank Snow. He began his ritual of locking up and putting out a bowl of canned cat food for Mrs. Lincoln, who came on the run at the sound of the refrigerator door.

"Aren't you going to bed?" Dean asked as he returned to the living room. Fred had spotted the World Wide files and had begun to read them, as Dean suspected he would.

"Nope," Fred answered. "I want to work on some stuff."

Dean didn't ask, "What stuff?" but instead climbed the stairs to the smaller of the two bedrooms, and in less than ten minutes was asleep. White days and Philadelphia had that effect.

Much later, sometime in the deep hours of the night, he awoke to the sound of thunder and the rush of wind. The lights downstairs were off, so Fred too had retired. Dean began to float back to sleep, half content in the thought that the storm might wash out the steamy, unseasonable humidity. Thunder had never bothered him, even as a child. He and his mother would sit out on their porch in the most frenzied storm, watching the wild and wonderful display. But he realized not everyone felt the same way. His mind pictured Cynthia Byrne, perhaps awake and alone with her grief, listening to Mother Nature's fury.

# CHAPTER III

Fred was still sleeping when Dean left the house the next morning. The expense reports and the personnel file from World Wide were neatly stacked on the table, but not in the same position Dean had left them the night before and his tape recorder hadn't been re-wound. He felt little concern, however; let the old man read about a real mystery instead of his fictional sleuth stories. Besides, it would give them meat for conversation. They were wearing out politics, baseball and the current status of the widows of Collingswood Avenue.

The late night storm had blown Wednesday's hazy whiteness east to New Jersey and the Atlantic beyond, leaving in its place a high pressure system, a sky painted deep blue and patched with just enough puffy clouds for contrast. It greatly improved Dean's frame of mind and he was in fine spirits when he reached his desk. DeLeo and Sackler were off to Philadelphia chasing down evidence on their check thieves. Rita had returned and Harrigan was knee-deep in paper work, smiling as usual, but looking as if his heart wasn't in it.

Rita Angeltoni was the sloppiest woman Dean had ever known. She rarely combed her hair, owned no more than three or four shapeless dresses, which appeared in all seasons, most of which were stained and wrinkled. Her shoes were crunched down in the back and no one had ever seen her in stockings. Angie, her eighteen-wheeler husband, kept her in a constant state of pregnancy. None of this was meant to say Rita was absent redeeming qualities. Just the opposite. Not only was Rita the fastest typist in

Parkside, she was the neatest. The detectives kidded that the last time she had made an error, she wore stockings and her dress was new. Rita never forgot anything important—or anything, period. She was their diary, their calendar and their conscience, and they loved her like a sister.

Plane tickets for the next day's flight to Virginia were on Dean's desk with a list of the time he was to leave his house, where he should park at the airport and a description of Detective Norman Hunter whom he was to meet in Norfolk. There was also a large note reminding him of a 10:00 court appearance today and two telephone messages. An assistant District Attorney had called about prosecuting a felony drug possession, but the second note was upsetting.

"Hey, Rita, how come I'm supposed to call back Ida Wassermann? I wasn't even in the office yesterday."

Harrigan looked up. "We drew lots. You lost."

"Oh, sure. I'll bet. Why didn't the person who answered her call talk to her?"

"I don't know. I was out too. But DeLeo said you won it fair and square. And you'd better call her right back. Mrs. Wassermann wants to hear from someone first thing."

Harrigan got up, still smiling, and went to the can, effectively cutting off further conversation. Rita laughed, but neither looked up nor broke the rhythm of her flying fingers. Dean gritted his teeth to retain his good mood.

"What's so funny?" he muttered to Rita.

"Not a thing, honey. Not a thing." She continued to bang away on her keyboard, the smile etched on her face.

Dean looked at the message again, sighed deeply and dialed the number.

Ida Wassermann was the mother of the Wassermann twins, a pair of 30-year-old misfits whose I.Q.'s didn't equal their waist sizes. Billie and Willie were journeymen criminals, and both had spent time in jail for a number of offenses, mostly physical in nature. They hurt people for fun and money, ran errands for more talented malefactors, and generally kept themselves in constant trouble. While the pair was a definite annoyance to the Parkside police, the two were seldom a serious problem, principally because they were too stupid to get away with much, and their size—six-feet-five and at least 500 pounds between them—made escaping detection difficult. But they did have one thing going for them. No one, save possibly their mother, could tell them apart.

This little gambit drove not only the police, but everyone else who encountered the pair, downright batty. The boys had been playing switch and swap every time it suited their fancy since they had shared a crib. Teachers, cops, girls, judges and fellow gangsters had all shared the frustration of not knowing Billie from Willie. Once a fed-up loan shark who'd had enough hog-tied the one he caught—he didn't care which—and branded a "B" on the left cheek of his backside. "I don't care who you were before, you're Billie now," rumor had it he'd said. But that didn't stop the twins. The un-branded brother let his twin burn a "B" on him as well. Then, just to make the whole business come out even, each branded "W" on the other cheek.

But for the past six weeks or so, neither Billie nor Willie could be found anywhere. They were missing and the only person who gave a damn was Mrs. Wassermann, the mother of the bouncing boys.

Once Dean introduced himself, he sat with the phone several inches from his ear, unable to inject a word as she built up her tirade. He began to doodle, listing the names she was calling not only him, but the entire, inept, Parkside police force. The woman certainly had a vocabulary, and an imagination. She accused them of jailing her sons without trial, hiding them away or simply not telling her of their whereabouts. One minute they were dead for sure, the next kidnapped or in some FBI safe house. Dean waited until she stopped for a breath and then rapidly explained they were doing all they could, would be in touch, thanked her and hung up. Rita began to clap in appreciation of his performance.

With that odious chore behind him, Dean began to formalize his notes on yesterday's interviews. Because of his 10:00 court date, he asked Harrigan to contact Byrne's doctor and try to run down any additional life insurance the missing man might have purchased. Rita would type up the taped transcript of the conversation with Mayer. Norfolk called to confirm Dean's flight, adding there was nothing much new on the case from their end. A fisherman had thought he'd sighted a body in the bay, but it was too far away to confirm and, with night approaching, the shape was lost in the darkening swells. Dean saw no reason to trouble Mrs. Byrne with this nebulous sighting. By the time he left the office for the ten-minute walk across the square to the courthouse, he felt comfortable with the progress of the case.

The old courthouse was a massive structure dominating the town square. The interior was marble and polished wood, dating back to a time when first generation craftsmen took pride in their workmanship. As Dean climbed the steep steps, Bobby Witherspoon from the District Attorney's office caught up with him. Bobby was assigned to the pending burglary case and Dean had made the arrest. The young attorney was always well prepared, and the police appreciated how tenaciously he pursued his cases. Unfortunately, his efforts were all too often thwarted by a sympathetic judge or a system that could not find jail space for the numbers of criminals brought before it.

Bobby and Dean had reviewed the testimony the prior week. Witherspoon felt optimistic about their case against Shakey Jake Morrison, the "alleged" felon.

The courtroom was half filled, mostly with pensioners who looked to the system for their daily entertainment. Dean could not understand someone voluntarily subjecting themselves to the tedium of the molasses-process of justice. Many of the women knitted and a number of the men caught catnaps when the action was dull—which was most of the time. The entire procedure operated with a casualness to it that seemed to make fun of the serious nature of what was happening, while the rules seemed more important than what they were designed to accomplish.

Shakey Jake, named for a nervous tic, looked less nervous than he should have for someone facing heavy time. The reason soon became apparent. Jake was led forward by his attorney, a newcomer, a dapper little man resplendent in vest, patent leather shoes and a gold watch chain, all topped off by a condescending smile that seemed to say, "Look out, rubes, I'm going to spring this poor victim before you finish administrating the oath." His appearance was in marked contrast to the public defender who usually inherited the Shakey Jakes of the world.

"What happened? Did Jake hit the lottery?" Dean asked.

"No," answered Witherspoon. "I hear Jake's got a new employer in Philly. He's graduated to the family and papa takes care of his boys. He either sends in out-of-towners like this guy or gets big-dollar local counsel." He named two or three prominent lawyers Dean knew.

Judge Adamson arrived and there followed more conversation at the bench and in the judge's chambers than in the courtroom. All of this was off the record so no one had any idea what was transpiring. Dean wished he could follow the lead of the pensioners and catch a nap. As it turned out, he could have. It was nearly noon when the session ended. A deal was struck, without Dean's testimony. At first he was disappointed, but the look on the faces of Shakey Jake and his dapper counsel indicated the deal was not to their liking. The only one smiling was Bobby Witherspoon.

"Adamson tossed the book at the little twerp! He ate the bastard for lunch!" Witherspoon was ecstatic as they left the courthouse. "This is what makes it all worthwhile! Adamson was terrific!"

"What happened?" Dean asked.

"I'll spare you the details, but our judge doesn't like hired guns from out of town and he doesn't like being instructed in the law. Before this started, I'd have settled for half of what Shakey Jake caught, all because his lawyer didn't know when to shut up!"

The two men celebrated with a deli pastrami sandwich pasted with horseradish that made your eyes burn. It wasn't the war, but it was a battle won, and one more slug was off the street. One more red conviction star could go on Lieutenant Anderson's chart.

Harrigan was out interviewing Byrne's doctor and Rita's printed version of Mayer's interview was on Dean's desk when he returned. His only phone message sounded like the same person who had telephoned the house the night before—again leaving neither name nor number. Dean spent the remainder of the workday sorting reports and more closely reviewing the Byrne papers.

The job evaluations of Jeffrey Byrne in the personnel file surprised Dean, as they were considerably more glowing than the picture Mayer had painted of the missing man. There was no derogatory information at all. Byrne was an outstanding employee who was thorough, conscientious, a self-starter and had missed but one day in the 15 years with the company. Dean made a note to check into the evaluation with Mayer, but Byrne's Philadelphia boss called Dean first to see if anything new had developed. After Dean had informed him of the lack of progress, he questioned Mayer about the glowing appraisal.

"Oh, that crap," Mayer answered. "That's just a walk-on-water letter. We put one in everyone's file. Hey, you've got to take care of your own, don't you? No way I'd get any of these poor slobs a raise if I were really honest. Besides, how would I look if all my people were average?" There were some things about the business world Dean would never understand.

Dean also asked Mayer about the one day Byrne had been absent—a Thursday the fourth of March—about two months earlier. The file had listed the reason as "personal."

"Byrne just telephoned and said he wouldn't be coming in. Something had come up. I'd have asked anyone else for more reason, but nobody could remember Jeff taking a day off—ever." Mayer added that Byrne was back to work the following day, but made no reference to his absence. Dean made a note to ask Cynthia Byrne about the incident and, after promising Mayer he'd keep in touch, hung up.

Rita wished him a nice flight the next day, pulled on a sweater with a hole through which her elbow protruded, reminded him it was after 5:00, and left the office. Dean was closing up his desk when Harrigan called. The doctor had taken his sweet time seeing him, but had finally confirmed that Byrne was in excellent health. The knee injury Mayer mentioned had occurred a year before and while it might have kept Byrne from jogging, it was no more than a temporary ailment. The doctor suggested as much exercise could be gained by walking without the added risk of injury.

Fred had taken the geezer bus to Atlantic City—ten free silver dollars plus a free meal—so Dean was on his own for the early evening. The lunchtime pastrami more than eliminated the need for an early dinner, so he drove home, changed into shorts and set out at a leisurely pace on his 18-speed touring bike.

Dean had a later appointment so he limited his ride to the area around Parkside. Given more time, he'd have preferred to put the bike on the car's rack and chew up some countryside miles, touring the hills and farm lands that surrounded Parkside. In the rural areas, there was less concern with traffic, although an occasional farm dog forced him to practice his sprints.

The late afternoon was delightful as he wound his way through the city streets north of town. He had no particular destination, but his meandering brought him to a hillside overlooking the new high school complex. In spite of the relative lateness of the hour, a baseball game was still in progress. He altered his course and coasted down to the edge of the field.

In Dean's playing days the high school was still in town, but otherwise, nothing had changed. Old Coach Grayson was still at the helm and probably always would be. The title "Coach" was so branded to the old man that few ever considered he had a first name. The "old" was a natural—he'd never see 70 again. The man had an additional distinction. Coach Grayson was the only resident of Parkside who had ever played major league baseball. This distinction granted him the position—nay, the obligation—of coaching Parkside High Baseball, and so he did, for as far back as anyone could remember. Consensus held he had taken an abominable collection of losers and quickly honed them into perennial also-rans. The exception was this year when Parkside had a legitimate shot at success.

Dean once looked up Coach Grayson's professional record in the Baseball Encyclopedia at the Parkside Library. Unfortunately, someone had torn out the page. Curiosity got the better of him and later, on a trip to Philadelphia, he checked the city's library. Coach Grayson, first name Henry, had gone oh-for-four, lifetime, in just two games for the Boston Braves in the late forties. He apparently was given a whiff of the bigs in a losing September when a few fortunate minor leaguers get a peek of how the other side lives. A moment in the sun for a lucky few prior to a life of obscurity in the Parksides of the world. Dean never mentioned this bit of detective work to anyone, but he could guess who had torn the page from the Parkside Library edition.

Coach Grayson wouldn't have remembered David Dean even if he hadn't been busy with piloting his crew and glanced Dean's way. There was absolutely nothing memorable in Dean's baseball career to give reason for lasting impressions.

The scene brought back a flood of memories to Dean. Just making the Parkside High baseball team had been a miraculous ascension from being the-you-take-him-we-don't-want-him-boy when the kids chose sides in sandlot games. Never mind he spent three years constantly riding the bench, hoping against hope for a miracle, as he practiced, cheered and hustled with unbridled enthusiasm. He meticulously kept his stats, listing his infrequent ups with the care of an accountant. He could still remember them. Seven hits in 41 plate appearances for a lifetime bating average of .171. All seven hits were singles and all were in routs, usually by the other side. He had scored once, in his junior year, producing one-third of his team's production in a 13-to-3 lapper for Easton High. But all his disappointments, if not forgotten, at least were put on hold when he qualified for a Varsity letter and the right to wear the maroon sweater of the Parkside Bulldogs. He began humming the school song as he watched the play.

Parkside was leading seven-zip with one inning remaining. Randy Byrne was in his usual place at shortstop, but the young man was much more subdued than the last time Dean had seen him play. There was none of his animated chatter, and Dean guessed he was anxious for the game to finish. But his play was as sharp as usual as he handled a hard ground ball to his left, cleanly gunning the runner out by three steps. The game finished but Dean ignored an impulse to introduce himself and chat with the boy. Instead he mounted his bike and began the long climb up the hill, killing time before his Thursday night date.

Detective David Dean had been seeing Attorney Ethel Rosewater three or four times a month for more than two years. Their little get-togethers took place on Thursday nights unless one or the other had a pressing engagement. Monday had been their original preference but pro football on T.V. had preempted their trysts. Fred O'Connor's description of the Thursday encounters were right on the button.

Dean's involvement with Ethel Rosewater, like most of the elements in his present life, developed through little overt action on his part. He met Ethel at a cocktail party both were attending by obligation and neither were enjoying. Small talk progressed to let's-go-someplace-else and before Dean knew it, he was between Ethel Rosewater's white silk sheets. They had rated each other highly in the entanglement, and by mutual consent began repeating the performance regularly. Both recognized from the very start that aside from sex, they had absolutely nothing in common. Ethel took one glance at Dean's occupation and knew she had hit neither a financial bonanza nor a stepping-stone to anything but fiscal mediocrity. For Dean's part, that was no problem. He recognized Ethel held the door in the relationship, be it the entrance or exit.

Early on they had attempted to find some modicum of common ground in the relationship aside from raw, physical sex. Dean once suggested a bike ride in the country. Ethel looked at him as if he'd proposed a trip to the moon, stating emphatically the only activity worthy of sweat would take place in her king size bed. Thereafter each accepted the emotional limits of their arrangement—it would never evolve to something like love or even affection and surely not a long-term relationship. But the convenience of a nice weekly roll in the hay without the threat of future complications and long-term commitments appealed to both and kept the fires of the strange partnership smoldering.

If Dean had been entirely honest with himself, he would have admitted he considered Ethel Rosewater a social-climbing, ambulance-chasing bitch. Ethel would have listed him as a lazy, unambitious civil servant with a lifestyle as exciting as limp toast. All in all, it was a most satisfactory relationship.

Their secret opinion of one another didn't preclude them from being mutually polite. Each tolerated the other's non-conjugal company. They talked. They alternated discussing what was happening in their lives while the other nodded, injecting a polite one word answer occasionally, just to properly pretend interest. Each took turns at this unconscious game and probably thought he or she communicated with the other. In reality, neither ever gave a flip about the other's life or career. Once in a while they did things together socially, usually to fulfill mandated coupling at necessary functions and seldom for the entertainment of either. When Ethel did the inviting, the function was nearly always out of town. She would make Dean promise not to divulge his occupation, giving some weak excuse neither believed. While mildly annoyed, he went along. "Wind me up and take me anywhere," he'd say, much to her irritation.

Ethel was not attractive in spite of spending more money in the beauty salon and boutique than Dean's entire salary. Her hawk-shaped nose, most pronounced in profile, must have led to numerous grade school nicknames. Once, in a rare instance of candor, she'd admitted to Dean she considered a nose job but rejected the idea on the basis that either people would think her vain, or it would so alter her appearance as to make her unrecognizable. But in spite of her lack of beauty, Ethel Rosewater was hell on wheels in bed.

Dean did not know Ethel's age and she wouldn't have told him if he had been interested enough to ask. He assumed she was somewhat older than he, but her body parts were firm and functional and he cared little about the model year of the equipment.

Ethel was an attorney who specialized in making money, so she never crossed paths with Dean's area of the law. She was particularly adept at suing anyone in the same county as an injured victim, but only after carefully deciding they either had a bankroll or sufficient insurance limits to justify her attention.

Rosewater and Atherton, Attorneys-at-Law, was a partnership of Ethel Rosewater and Arthur Atherton, a pompous bastard that Dean had busted for soliciting a plainclothesman outside a gay bar. Atherton had managed to beat the rap, avoiding embarrassing notoriety, but he had despised David Dean from that day forward.

"Bobby Witherspoon mentioned Arthur's name today," Dean commented during a pause in their activities. "Hear-tell he's one of the local lawyers defending some of the Philadelphia family's bad boys. Has he been expanding his clientele?"

"Arthur's always a little short of cash. He grabs 'em where he can find 'em," she answered as she began to coo and squirm.

"Those are rough customers. He'd better watch his P's and Q's."

"I'm sure they're just dropping him crumbs. He can take care of himself." Dean didn't agree but held his tongue.

"Arthur asked me to marry him," Ethel pronounced as Dean struggled with an obstinate bra snap.

"I thought he liked boys—not women," Dean answered.

"Of course he does. He likes any type of male. He's as queer as a three-dollar bill."

"It's not 'queer' nowadays, Ethel. The proper term is 'gay'."

"There's absolutely nothing 'gay' about Arthur," she answered. "He's a worse glum-bum than you when you're in one of your moods. But he was so cute today. He got down on his knees, right there in my office. He said he had been thinking of asking me for weeks."

"Have you slept with him?"

She pushed away. "God, no! What on earth would we do?"

"The same thing you'd do if you were married, I suppose."

"I can tell you what *I'd* do if I were married to Arthur—the same thing we're doing right now, with my same little playmate." She laughed as she tickled him.

"I'm afraid I'd have to take a hike once there was a wedding," he said, as he rolled over.

"Why David darling, you're jealous!"

"Nothing of the sort, but there's a difference between consenting adults and adultery. I just don't fool around with married women, especially a woman wed to a Mafia lawyer."

"That's nonsense! And Arthur's not smart enough to be a Mafia lawyer. Besides, he'd be in total agreement with the arrangement. It would eliminate his watching me pant around the house, looking for it, and him mooning away because he couldn't deliver."

"And that wouldn't bother dear old Arthur?"

"David, sometimes you're so naive, it's incredible. He just wants a wife so people won't question his sexuality."

"Maybe they'd question it less if he'd stop trying to pick up pretty men at gay bars."

"That was a one-time mistake. Arthur's much more discreet now."

"That may be so, but I'd still pass on the offer," he answered. "I could never be sure the old boy wouldn't have a change of heart some night and blow me away just to prove his masculinity, or send some of his Philadelphia clients around to work me over." Then he added, "Are you going to marry him?"

"Oh, hell. I don't know. Let's get down to business," she said, pulling him to her.

Ethel lived in the pride of Parkside, a new six-story luxury apartment building southeast of town. She occupied the largest suite in the structure, seven spacious rooms on the top floor. The living room and kitchen, which faced to the south, provided an exquisite view of the surrounding countryside. Presumably, the other rooms too offered calendar-quality scenes, but Dean never viewed them. Ethel always performed her lovemaking in a darkened room. Any suggestion of an open window shade or even a night-light was summarily dismissed. He once dreamed her naked torso was horribly disfigured by a giant birthmark but the truth was more likely childlike modesty kept in check by a general arrogance that forbade her to admit anything deemed to be a weakness.

While the rest of Ethel's wardrobe was nothing short of spectacular, her underwear was a throwback to another era. Instead of designer thongs or flimsy lace things, Ethel wore the plainest of cotton panties, the type described by past generations as 'practical.' Dean remembered them from the dime stores of his youth, tightly rolled little balls of cotton in every color of the rainbow, all stuffed in long plastic tubes. Some came with the days of the week emblazoned on them. As Dean lay in the dark, he absentmindedly wondered if Ethel always wore "Thursday" when he came to call. He leisurely began to trace a finger along the elastic waistband in search of a telltale imperfection he could locate on a later date, giving identifying confirmation to his theory. But his mind was soon engaged in earthier matters.

When their lovemaking finished, Dean remained in bed, his arms folded behind his head, awaiting Ethel's return from her obligatory post coital trip to the bathroom. His mind kept thinking, not of Ethel, but of Cynthia Byrne. He wondered about the last time she and her husband had made love, never knowing it would be the very last, ever. How different if must be, he thought, making love with someone for whom you really cared.

The toilet flushed and Ethel returned, proceeded in the darkness by the tiny pinpoint light of her cigarette. He felt her sit on the bed next to him. He disliked her smoking and the stale smell that always surrounded her like a bar room musk. While she'd never admit to concern for his wishes, Ethel seemed to limit her smoking around Dean, but never abstinence from the mandatory one "after."

"What happens to someone's estate when they go missing?" he asked.

She turned abruptly, surprised at the question. "Legally?"

"Yeah. Do their heirs have to wait seven years or something like that?"

"It depends on the state law and on the circumstances," she replied.

"Just like a lawyer." He chuckled as she stretched out beside him.

She adjusted the pillow and reached across him to extinguish her cigarette. "That's what I am, honey bunch. Are you talking about the Byrne case?"

"I'm impressed," he replied. "No wonder you sharp lawyers charge so much."

"I read about it in the paper. And Arthur was talking about it. He used to do some work for World Wide Insurance—where Byrne worked."

"Did he know Byrne?"

"Heavens, no. Arthur never deals with the peons. But to answer your question, I'm serious—it depends on where it happened. Different laws apply in different jurisdictions. The circumstances have a lot to do with it too. If an airplane crashes in the middle of the ocean and someone is listed as a passenger on it, it's pretty simple, even if there's never a body. The presumption of death is high so obtaining a death certificate would probably be easy. Often it's a judgment thing—the court weighs all the facts and makes a determination. If there's a serious doubt, the heirs may have to wait a good long time, even seven years."

"Then someone's up the creek."

"Paddle-less. Right. Does it look like Byrne skipped?"

"No. Just the opposite, but it's too early to be positive. I'm going down to Norfolk tomorrow."

"So you think he got tanked and took a midnight dip?"

"Looks that way. But his wife claims he wasn't much of a drinker."

"Yeah, and I'll bet she swears he wasn't screwing around either. If you ask me," she said, "I'll bet he skipped off with his secretary or girlfriend."

"Cherchez la femme," he muttered.

"That's right. 'Look for the woman.'"

"Fred already used that line. He agrees with you."

"Don't spoil the evening by bringing up that old bastard!"

Although Ethel and Fred had never met, that didn't stop them from developing a strong mutual dislike, fueled via telephone messages and third-party comments.

When he didn't comment, she asked, "Who owns the beach?"

"You mean where Byrne drowned?"

"Of course—where he *allegedly* drowned." There was annoyance in her voice.

"I haven't the foggiest idea."

"Did they have a lifeguard?"

"At midnight?"

"The city probably owns the beach and sovereign immunity makes that angle a waste of time. How about the motel? The newspaper says someone talked with Byrne—an employee. If Byrne was tanked, they should have stopped him. Sounds like a right of action to me."

"Why would they be responsible because Byrne acted like a jerk and decided to go for a midnight swim—drunk or sober?"

"Hey darling, you just muddy the waters by suing everyone in sight. Sooner or later you hit the guys with the bucks and somebody tosses you money so you'll go away. That's how the system works. Just thinking about it gets me all hot and tingly," she said, snuggling closer.

He responded, with just a hint of reluctance, thinking of the 5:00 alarm call, very few hours away.

# CHAPTER IV

**FRIDAY, MAY 7, 1999 5:00 A.M.**

The early morning fog blanketing eastern Pennsylvania was thicker than the frosting on grandma's cake, but no thicker than the early morning fog shrouding David Dean's sleep-deprived brain. He felt like a packaged pound of dog meat after slightly less than three hours sandwiched in his warm and comfortable bed between Ethel Rosewater's last frenzied spasm of pleasure and the screaming alarm clock. For the first hour of his trip to the airport, Dean's vision was restricted to two red eyes of the taillights in front of him, glaring out of a haze as thick as chowder. The traffic crawled to a near standstill as Dean's blood pressure mounted, sure the 8:00 direct flight to Norfolk would leave without him.

He need not have been concerned. The airport was coping with the fog no better than the harried commuters. The place was a morgue of mannequins, all clutching briefcases, their faces in newspapers as the planes stood silently by.

It was 10:00 by the time the fog lifted enough for a bumpy take off and Dean gratefully accepted a much-needed cup of coffee from the pleasant attendant. He declined her offer of a magazine. They were all designed for Fortune 500 executives, not poorly paid detectives sworn to keep the streets safe for orphans and widows. He tried to snooze but only managed a wink or two before the plane began its descent into Norfolk.

Detective Norman Hunter, who met the arriving aircraft, was unperturbed by the overdue flight. The 32-year-old detective with bright red crew cut and opened-collar sports shirt looked as if nothing short of a catastrophe would cause him a lick of concern.

Dean took an immediate liking to his southern counterpart as soon as the two shook hands and left the terminal.

"No problem," Hunter responded to Dean's apology. "I'm used to planes being late more often than on time. Your return flight back isn't until 4:00 so we've got hours to grab a bite and check out that motel. By the way, welcome to God's country."

Although Dean didn't say it, he figured God must be partial to roasting temperature and off the scale humidity that quickly drenched his clothes like an afternoon shower. By the time they reached Hunter's double-parked car, Dean felt like limp lettuce at a summer picnic. He loosened his collar and tie out of absolute necessity.

"The wife wants you to give her a call," Hunter said, as he started up the automobile and turned on that miraculous invention, the air conditioner.

"Mrs. Byrne?" asked Dean, somewhat surprised.

"Sure enough. I gave her a ring last night, just to tell her nothing's new and I mentioned you were coming down. She asked that I have you buzz her. She sure seems like a nice enough gal. Think he skipped out on her?"

"I suppose that's the 64-dollar question. At first everyone was positive he'd taken a hike, but personally, I haven't seen a thing yet to tell me he didn't just do something stupid and pay the price for it. We're about ready to close our end of the case unless you've found something that looks fishy."

"I haven't got any smoking gun down here," answered Hunter. He added, "but I haven't seen any body float up either. The ol' boys at the station are about split down the middle but we're not privy to Byrne's lifestyle and I suppose that's the key. Some of the guys figure a dumb trick like a midnight swim ain't so surprising for a Yankee with a snoot full. No offense intended."

"None taken," Dean answered, with a smile. "But the wife claims he wasn't much of a drinker. I'd like to see a body wash up and put an end to the argument. What are the chances it'll turn up?"

"Pretty good, I'd say. The tide was coming in the time of night he was supposed to have drowned so the body would drift up the bay. If it sank up there, it'd most likely float up to the surface after a few days or a week and then drift back down this way with the tide. If the tide had been going out, he'd be in the Atlantic by now."

Detective Hunter pointed out the sights as they left the airport and drove toward the center city police headquarters. Although Hunter had been born in North Carolina—on 16 acres of red mud, as he described it—he'd moved to Norfolk in high school and never left. To hear him tell, Norfolk was God's chosen paradise. There was no place like it, anywhere. Dean smiled at Hunter's adoration for a location where the weather alone would turn him around, scurrying back north. But the detective's enthusiasm was contagious and Dean was content to not interrupt the friendly officer's nonstop chatter.

The level of activity at Norfolk Police Headquarters made Parkside's much smaller operation look like the front porch of an old folk home. Hunter chuckled as they threaded their way around cluttered desks and scores of busy bodies. "You ought to see it on Saturday night," he said.

Hunter' desk was on the second floor, tightly squeezed between two others where uniformed offices sat with telephones pressed to their ears. It reminded Dean to check in with Lieutenant Anderson and call Cynthia Byrne. Hunter connected him to an outside line before leaving to get them both coffee.

"Hello, beautiful," Dean said to Rita who answered the phone. "The eagle has landed."

"More like the turkey," she answered. "Leland wants to talk to you."

After a series of clicks, the lieutenant barked into the phone. "Do you know Ida Wassermann has a sister-in-law on the *Sentinel*?"

"I didn't think any of the Wassermanns could read, much less work for a newspaper."

"Well, she does, and the woman's a pain in the ass. She wrote a cover story about how the police force is sitting around on their thumbs while the poor widow's little twin darlings remain missing. I pulled Sackler off that check fraud case and gave him the Wasserman business full time. Harrigan too."

"I thought Harrigan was supposed to help me finish up this Byrne case," Dean protested.

"Naw. You have to go that alone. What's to finish? It's pretty well wrapped up anyway, isn't it?"

"I don't know. I just got here. Philly was fogged in," he answered.

"Well, hurry up and wrap it. I need all the help I can get back here. That damned reporter is supposed to interview me at 3:00."

"Just tell her the Parkside Betterment Society voted for Billie and Willie to improve the city by getting lost." But Leland Anderson wasn't in a mood for smart talk. He grumbled something unintelligible and hung up. "No sense of humor," Dean smiled to himself as he dialed Cynthia Byrne's number and congratulated his luck at being in Norfolk and missing the Wasserman business.

Cynthia Byrne answered in a tentative voice on the first ring. She let out a sigh of relief when Dean identified himself.

"Don't mind me. I'm still scared to death to pick up the phone," she said, and added, "Please, call me Cynthia," when he addressed her more formally.

Dean explained he'd just arrived in Norfolk and there was nothing new in the search for her husband's body.

"It's been four days now," she said.

"Is there anyone there with you?" he asked.

"No. But I'm all right." He didn't believe her. "Janice Riley will be by this afternoon. She had some errands to run. I have to start getting used to the fact life goes on. Everyone's been wonderful, really. Even Detective Hunter down there. Tell him I appreciate his taking time to call me."

"I will," answered Dean. "You'd like him. He's a nice guy."

"I have a favor to ask," she said, a hint of hesitation in her voice. "Detective Hunter asked me what I wanted to do about Jeff's things. World Wide will take care of the company car, but Jeff's luggage—his clothes and stuff—could you possibly bring them back? It's only one suitcase...."

Dean agreed and promised to call when he returned and arrange to deliver the articles to her. Hunter returned with the coffee while he was still talking and pulled over a chair with his toe.

Cynthia Byrne thanked Dean. She paused before adding softly, "Will you be going there? To the motel?"

"Yes," he answered, as he sipped the hot coffee, burning his lip. She didn't respond. "One other thing," he added. "Just a detail. Do you remember if your husband was sick on March fourth?" He had to repeat the question.

"No," she answered quickly. "I mean, I don't know anything about March fourth but I know Jeff hasn't been sick for years and years. Why?"

"I remembered your mentioning the perfect attendance—how your son and husband had a little bet going but his personnel record shows he took a day off, on the fourth of March. I was just wondering...."

"No. That's a mistake. I'm sure of it."

"Couldn't he have gone to the doctor or the dentist or someplace? Maybe had the car inspected?"

"I usually run all the errands. We use local doctors and dentists and Jeff tries to schedule evening appointments because it's difficult with his working in Philadelphia. His office must have mixed his file up with someone else."

"You're probably right," Dean said. "But just to make sure, would you check the date to see if anything out of the ordinary happened that day?"

"Yes," she said hesitantly. "If you think it's important."

"No," he answered, lightly. "It's not really important. I'm just trying to be thorough."

She thanked him again and wished him a safe return trip before hanging up.

"Problems?" asked Hunter.

"No," Dean answered. "Just the first little inconsistency."

"Okay," said Hunter as he rose. "Let's get out of this here kennel and let the hound dogs scrap for themselves."

Hunter and Dean exchanged information during the short drive to the Ocean Shore Motel. Dean detailed what he'd learned from speaking with Cynthia Byrne and meeting with Byrne's boss in Philadelphia and gave the detective a written copy of his interviews. When Dean described Jeffrey Byrne's quiet life style, Hunter nodded in agreement.

"That's pretty much the picture the local office gave me. Byrne would come into town, do his business, but that's all. He was friendly enough, but no threat to anyone and no corporate climber. When some of the Philadelphia big-wigs flew down, everyone would sweat and jump. When Byrne came, no one got out of his chair."

Hunter had interviewed the fisherman who thought he saw a body floating in the bay. However, an empty pint of Jack Daniel's on the galley table made the observation somewhat less credible. Further investigation revealed nothing. There was no taxi report of a pick-up in the area. Bus station and airport personnel had been questioned, but no one remembered anything of note. Byrne's description was far too common to stand out but no one recalled a man hurriedly leaving the city in the middle of the night, Tuesday-Wednesday.

Hunter had personally interviewed the employees at the Ocean Shore Motel, but with little success. They had vaguely remembered Jeffrey Byrne from his repeat trips, but Byrne hadn't made much of an impression on anyone. He was a loner and no one could recall him having contact with anyone else during his short stay. The party for the departing employee, if you could call it that, had been a quick affair—a pat on the back, a few appropriate words and a token going away present. According to Byrne's expense file, his prior trip to Norfolk had been in late January and, earlier, in October of last year. The motel records confirmed these trips.

"I'll give you a whack at 'em," Hunter said as he pulled his tan Ford into the parking lot. "I didn't get diddly-damn from a one of 'em. This guy Byrne was so ordinary, talking about him put me to sleep."

"Ordinary guy in an ordinary motel," Dean replied as he stepped from the car and looked around. The motel was past its prime certainly, but had not yet descended to seedy. If you were looking for a place to stay and save a buck, you'd have found it. The two detectives entered the office, and the clerk, a bored and balding retiree, looked up from a crossword puzzle and, recognizing Hunter, frowned.

"I just hope you fellows are here to clear out number 22. We're not running 'Police Investigation 101,' so you can use it as a classroom to play detective. This here's a going business."

"Glad to see y'all are still in a happy mood," Hunter said, an exaggerated smile on his face. "This here's Detective Dean from up in Yankee land. If you're real nice to him, maybe we'll clear out your room. That way you'll have 20 vacant rooms 'stead of just 19."

"Very funny," the clerk said as he shook Dean's hand and handed him a key. "I surely don't know what you guys figure you'll find
as many times as you've looked around. The guy drowned. Period.
Give him a week and he'll float in somewhere down south of here
if the fish don't eat him first."

They left the man to his puzzle and attitude and walked
around the corner to room 22. Hunter opened the drape, painting
Jeffrey Byrne's sparse belongings in early afternoon sunlight. The
room had a musty closed-up smell and looked like a thousand other
motel rooms in a thousand other cities. Dean took a quick tour.
Bucolic pictures were screwed to the walls as if someone might
want to steal them and shampoo came not in little bottles but in
hard-to-open plastic envelopes. You could see light through the
towels when you held them up. A suit jacket and pants were laid
out across the bed, and underwear was dropped on the floor next to
it, apparently discarded by Byrne when he changed to his bathing
suit. A suitcase was open on a rack by the door and an imitation
leather briefcase stood next to it. Pocket change, watch and wallet
were on the nightstand by the bed. The bedspread was pulled back
enough to prop up the pillow by the phone, but the bed had not
been uncovered for sleeping. Polished shoes, with the socks still in
them and a shirt, recovered from the beach, rested on a chair.

"Move anything you like," Hunter said. "We took all the pho-
tographs we need and we've inventoried everything. I even read
the list to Mrs. Byrne over the phone. Everything's here...but the
bathing suit and ball cap. When you've finished we'll stuff it all in
the suitcase and you can haul it back up north to her."

Dean methodically searched the room, examining each of the
missing man's items slowly, not knowing exactly what he was looking for. Hunter stood off to one side, nodding as if to say he too had
done the same thing. The suitcase contained three sets of underwear and socks, all neatly folded and strapped in place with an
elastic cord. The closet contained a second suit and three shirts,
each on its own hanger with a necktie looped over it. A toilet kit
containing nothing out of the ordinary was on the bathroom counter. The only item that appeared out of place was a matchbook on
the bureau. Dean picked it up and examined it.

"That was under the bed, in the back corner. I'd guess it's
been there a spell—there was a fair amount of dust on it." Two of

the matches were missing. The cover advertised art lessons for anyone drawing cartoon pictures and seeking "A rewarding career." Dean tossed it back on the table as Hunter said, "If this were the movies, that matchbook would be to a Hootchy-Cootchy night club where some sexy broad would come on to us both and then get her throat slit by a gangster boyfriend."

Dean laughed. "This place sure isn't the movies." He began to look through the wallet. It contained 78 dollars, a half-dozen credit cards, a few business cards and two pictures, one a duplicate of the desktop photo of Cynthia Byrne and the other a grade school picture Dean assumed to be of Byrne's son, Randy. There was also a small sheet of white paper listing 11.2 gallons of gas purchased in Aberdeen, Maryland, a mileage figure and the amount of the purchase. It was dated Monday, the day before Byrne's disappearance.

"We checked out the tank and the mileage. It's about right for him to have filled it up there. I called the station in Maryland but it was a cash sale so they don't have a record. But the price per gallon's right so it don't look like he faked it."

"So why did he pay cash if he had a pocket full of credit cards?"

"It was a Texaco station. He didn't have a Texaco charge card and they don't take Visa or MasterCard," Hunter replied, and then added, "but I've driven that route. There are lots of stations along there. He could have stopped where he could charge it."

"So, what do you think?"

Hunter smiled. "One of life's little mysteries—emphasis on the *little*."

Dean began to fill the suitcase and Hunter helped him by folding the suits. Neither man said anything for a few moments. Finally, Hunter said, "The only thing peculiar about this whole thing is that there ain't nothing peculiar about it. That's the problem. Does that make any sense?"

"It's too damn easy, isn't it? I'm used to everything being all screwed up. We don't even have any unanswered questions to play with."

"There are only four possibilities—accident, suicide, murder or skip." Dean counted them off on his fingers. "Murder seems a real stretch, given lack of motive—nothing missing, no evidence or anything else usual to a homicide. Suicide lacks reason if you listen to what everyone is saying."

"Plus we don't have the usual nice little note saying, 'See you in the next life, honey. This one sucks.'"

"Not much motive for a skip, either."

Hunter nodded in agreement. "Let's play devil's advocate just the same." He thought a moment. "I want to skip. I don't take anything from the room—that's a dead giveaway. I set the game up, pretend to tie one on."

"What about the local guy they gave a send off—Fletcher something. Did you talk to him?"

"Fletcher Brunell. Vanished," Hunter said, his voice dripping with mock melodrama. Then he smiled. "He's already left town. His last day was Friday but he stuck around because Byrne was coming down from the head office with his last paycheck. The office confirmed he and Byrne went out to have a drink or three, just the two of them. It seems Brunell burned a lot of bridges in the office and no one else wanted to buy him a send off snort."

"The head office didn't think much of him either. Only 'St. Jeffrey,'" Dean commented. "Too bad Brunell's gone. He was the last person to spend any time with Byrne. I'd like to hear how much Byrne had to drink."

"We tried to run him down but he was hush-hush with everyone at World Wide on his new job and where he was going. We're checking with the Post Office for a change of address. As to the booze, Byrne only had two beers here with dinner."

"So," Dean mused as he continued their speculation, "if you want to let the world know you're loaded and your drinking partner's gone, you..."

"...make sure someone else sees you leave your room, like Leo, the waiter," Hunter finished.

"But you're in a bathing suit, a poor choice of traveling duds."

"I'd have stashed some clothes on the beach earlier."

Dean paused. "So how do you split? It's after midnight and you can't drive two cars. The cabs didn't record anything and it's too far to walk. Do you sleep on the beach and leave in the morning?"

"He could have. It was a nice night. But I checked out the morning cab calls too. No dice. Maybe somebody else is involved—a honey. That would answer a lot of questions."

"It doesn't fit with Byrne's lifestyle. In fact, the whole idea of the skip doesn't fit any better than murder or suicide."

Hunter smiled. "Can't say we didn't give it the old college try. Unless his body floats in with a bullet hole in the head or he gets pinched for speeding in Vegas, it's going down as an accident in my report."

After leaving the room, Hunter stopped by a green Ford with Pennsylvania license plates. "That's his car. The insurance boys at the local office are picking it up tonight." Hunter took out a set of keys and unlocked the doors and trunk. "Check it out."

"Looks brand new."

"Damn near is—only 3,000 miles. It's a pool car—random assignment. I guess he lucked out and got a new one for this trip."

The glove compartment contained a registration in the name of World Wide Insurance Company and maps of the east coast states. There was a log listing mileage and dates in a variety of different handwritings. The latest entry dated Monday showed a mileage figure and the starting point of Parkside, Pennsylvania.

"There was nothing else in the car, except this." Hunter held out a small scrap of paper. Dean looked at the bottom half of a small register receipt showing the amount of $59.95. The top half, which might have identified the date and the store was missing as if the slip had been torn in two. "Not here long, as new as the car is. It might have even blown in the open window from a passing car."

"Or maybe that half blew back in the window when someone tore it in two and tossed it."

"That's why I'm hanging on to it," Hunter answered.

Dean looked at the odometer and then at the mileage log. The figures differed.

"The mileage checks pretty good. The log stays with the car. Looks like he recorded it when he got here, then put another 23 miles on it, running to the office and around town."

"The trunk's clean too," Hunter remarked as Dean moved around to look. He lifted up the mat as Hunter added, "The spare never touched the ground—usually doesn't nowadays. Not like the old times. If I had a buck for every flat I fixed, I could retire...no pun intended."

Dean chuckled as he reached beneath the mat to a back corner for something that caught his eye. It was a small metal container no larger than a matchbox. The top slid open to reveal a tire patch kit containing two small patches and a tube of sealing adhesive.

"Then why would anyone need this?" Dean asked.

"Looks like Norfolk's finest missed something," Hunter mused as he examined the box. "Suppose it belonged to our friend?"

"Even odd, I'd guess. Not too many have used the car as new as it is. But it doesn't make sense either; nobody patches tires anymore. Add it to your inventory." Dean slipped the container into his pocket as he walked around the car.

"Clean as a whistle," Hunter said. "I wish mine had as few scratches."

The two detectives spoke with Leo the waiter, the night clerk and the maid. None could add anything to their earlier stories and none was particularly happy being called in for questioning when they should have been enjoying their time off. According to the time-stamped dinner receipt, Byrne had dined on fish, and had two beers as Hunter had remarked. Any celebratory drinks with departing Fletcher Brunell had occurred earlier and elsewhere.

"We checked a couple of bars local to the World Wide office but they were crazy-busy after-work places and no one remembers diddly." Then Hunter added, "No credit card receipt either but there's a raft of places between the office and the motel and they could have stopped anywhere."

"He was back in the motel at 7:00 or so," Dean said. "He called his wife."

"If you're sure you can believe her." Dean turned quickly and Hunter grinned. "Life ain't always what it seems to be, is it?"

Before leaving, Hunter showed Dean the beach across the road where it was presumed Jeffrey Byrne took his last steps on land. The area was nearly empty except for crying gulls, a man running with his dog, and an elderly lady propped up in a half chair reading. Hunter pointed out where Byrne's things were found but Dean learned nothing from the excursion. They left the seashore and, after a quick bite to eat, Hunter drove Dean back to the airport for his return plane trip to Parkside.

It was after 9:00 by the time Dean finally returned to Collingswood Avenue. He was dog tired and his stomach grumbled its dissatisfaction at being limited to the airline's toy dinner. He half-hoped Fred would either be out socializing or asleep but lost on both counts. The old man opened the door with a barrage of questions, allowing Dean no chance to escape the interrogation. Even Mrs. Lincoln seemed eager to see him, giving his leg a welcoming rub. Resigned to the inquisition, he settled down in his chair with two cans of beer and a piece of apple pie, devouring the pie with a combination of guilt and gusto. Between bites he answered Fred's questions, filling in the details of the trip south.

As soon as Dean mentioned the luggage and briefcase locked in the trunk of the car, Fred insisted on protecting this valuable evidence by bringing them in—just for safekeeping. Dean didn't doubt for a minute the booty would be examined in detail as soon as he was asleep.

Fred made careful notes of everything Dean said, shuffling papers in his lined notebook. He was interested but perplexed about the March date when Byrne was excused from work—without his wife's knowledge. He was also curious about the tire repair kit and examined it closely, as if looking for a secret compartment. He carefully detailed the information on the torn sales receipt but made no comment. By the time Fred had finished his questioning it was nearly midnight. Dean could hardly keep his eyes open as he rose to go to bed.

"Just wait until a week from next Tuesday," said Fred with a smugness that caught Dean's attention.

"What happens then?"

Fred reached for the newspaper, tapping a small article with his fingers as he handed it to Dean. "Read it. They're going to hold a memorial service for Byrne at the Catholic Church."

"So?"

"So, that's when we stake it out and spot Byrne!"

"You've got to be kidding!"

"Everybody wants to go to their own funeral! I've read about it lots of times. Just imagine being a little mouse in the corner, seeing who shows up, what they have to say about you. He's gonna make an appearance, just you watch!"

Dean slumped down in his chair, his mind picturing a veiled fugitive, costumed as an old lady, slinking into a back pew. "Fred," he said, "I think you've finally popped your cork!"

Fred prattled on about a mystery where something similar had occurred but Dean paid him no attention as he glanced through the newspaper. The story of the inefficiencies of the Parkside Police caught his attention. The Wassermann twins, sainted boys according to the stilted account, had been all but ignored, according to the writer, Linda Segal, a name Dean didn't recognize. Lieutenant Anderson's response sounded more like an apology for being unable to locate two pillars of the community than a proper description of the two as a couple of leg-breaking punks. Dean tossed the paper aside and rose.

"Don't wake me early," he said as he walked toward the stairs.

Fred called after him, "your mysterious buddy called again, twice. This time he left a message." He looked through his notes. "Here it is. 'Yellow 42.' That's what he said to tell you, whatever it means. He said you'd know."

Dean looked annoyed. "Yeah, I know what it means. It means Vinnie Baratto is in a jam again."

"Who's Vinnie Baratto?"

"We played high school football—at least Vinnie played—I mostly sat. 'Yellow 42' was a running play."

"I didn't know you played football."

"Neither did anyone else," Dean replied. "I spent two years on the bench and never played a down until the last game of my junior year. Nick Volpe had his bell rung and they sent me in for one play, 'Yellow 42.' Vinnie Baratto was the star running back for three years. He was one of those guys who drank beer all night, smoked Camels and never practiced while I broke my butt and sat on the bench. Just as Vinnie was tackled he flipped me the ball and I scored. We tied Doylestown—my one athletic claim to fame. The only one—I didn't even make the team the next year. We finished the season with eight losses and that one tie."

"So what's he want and why is he so secretive?"

"Beats me. He's probably looking for help to keep from going back to jail. I hear he's been messing with the bad guys again. Ol' Vinnie was a hell of a jock but not 'the most likely' at anything but getting in trouble."

"Well, he said he'd call back later," Fred answered. Dean was already on the stairs, just about asleep on his feet.

# CHAPTER V

Much later, in the darkest part of the night, Dean's mind was creating picture stories to amuse itself while his body lay in frozen and unmoving slumber like a fallen mannequin. Ghostly, veiled ladies of exceptional height passed in somber silence past an empty bier while a shadowy figure looking like a cross between Hercule Poirot and Fred O'Connor lurked behind a pillar, watching. The unearthly shrill of the telephone shattered the scene, once, twice, three times before Dean clawed at the instrument and grumbled something.

"Yellow 42," said an anxious voice on the other line.

Dean rubbed his eyes to consciousness. "For God's sake, Vinnie. Do you know what time it is?"

"Don't use my name! The phone may be bugged!"

"Stop playing games, Vinnie. It's the middle of the night."

Rapid fire. "Be at the corner of Locust and Ninth in 20 minutes or I'm a dead man!" Then Dean was listening to a dial tone.

"Vinnie, you son-of-a-bitch, you'll be a dead man if I catch up to you!" Dean yelled to the empty phone, slamming down the receiver and mashing his pillow into a ball.

Try as he might, the mourning ladies of dreamland wouldn't return to the empty coffin. They'd floated away from the church of his slumber and refused to make a second appearance. In exasperation he turned and squinted at the illuminated hands of his clock radio. Ten minutes after four. The son-of-a-bitch. He turned over. He turned again. Locust and Ninth. His mind tried to picture what was located on that corner but couldn't. It was a crappy

59

neighborhood, he remembered that much. A liquor store, a pawn shop? He told himself he didn't give a damn about Locust and Ninth but his mind wouldn't let go. Finally, as wide awake as a kid on Christmas morning, he gave up the ghosts and dressed, intent on making the trip for the sole satisfaction of punching out Vinnie Baratto.

The crosstown trip through deserted streets took less than ten minutes. The entire city was deep in slumber with the exception of a crazy ex-running back and an exhausted cop intent on killing him.

There was nothing at Ninth and Locust but a boarded-up storefront and a stillness like the day after the end of the world. Nothing but a standalone phone booth. Dean closed his eyes and said to himself, "Vinnie, you wouldn't...." Then, as if on cue, the phone began to ring. Dean slowly unwound himself from behind the steering wheel and crossed to answer it.

"Yellow 42!" came the same anxious voice.

"Vinnie..."

"Don't hang up, Davey. I got no more quarters!"

"Vinnie, tell me where you are so I can come and kill you!" yelled Dean.

"I had to make sure you weren't followed! Fourth and Oak! Fourth and Oak! I swear to God I'll be there!" Dial tone again.

Dean sighed and went back to the car. He couldn't believe he was stupid enough to play Vinnie's silly game. It was like a high school scavenger hunt, absent the babes and fun. But back then he hadn't been dragged from a soft bed and the dream-movies of his mind to chase around the slums of his city.

Fourth and Oak were just as desolate as Ninth and Locust, but as soon as Dean stopped the car, a disheveled figure jumped from the darkness and clawed at the passenger door until Dean reached over and opened it. Vinnie Baratto scrambled into the car, locked the door and buried himself on the floor of the vehicle.

"Get going! Get going!"

Dean slowly pulled away, looking down at his passenger, and shook his head slowly. "Vinnie, this better be damn good."

"Ol' buddy, my old buddy—I knew you'd come through!"

"I'm not your old buddy or your new buddy. I've seen you once in 13 years and you were in a lineup. Just tell me what in hell this is all about."

"They're after me! They really are, Davey, no kidding! They got a contract out on me! Look at me! I'm shaking like a leaf! My fingernails are bitten off. I been puking all day!"

Dean glanced down in the light of a passing street lamp. "You do look like hell."

"I ain't slept like in three days...I ain't even eaten! They're watching my place...and I didn't do nothing...I got no money, no place to go.... I spent my last coins calling you!" He looked up and Dean could see his wild eyes in the glow. "It's all a big mistake! I ain't done nothing! You gotta help me! You gotta get me like a new identity...a new life!"

"Vinnie, I'm a cop. I'm not J. Edgar Hoover's replacement."

"It's all a mistake."

"Vinnie, those guys don't make mistakes. The only mistake was you screwing around with the big boys in the first place."

"It's not me! It's Billie and Willie!"

Dean slammed on his brakes, causing Vinnie to whack his head on the underside of the dash. "What do you know about those two piles of dump?"

"The family's got 'em!" he cried as he rubbed his head, "I swear! They were like, kinda lying low...because of this mistake. They heard some guys were looking for 'em, so they hid out in this here...place. For weeks. And then they got sick of sitting around, and maybe ran out of dough I guess and figured the heat was off, so they came out. Zingo! They're gone and the street says they're history and now there's a contract out on me! The twins must have fingered me! For the mistake."

"What 'mistake'?"

Vinnie was as sullen as a three-year-old. "I can't tell you. But you've got to get me a place, a new life—like on TV.... I ain't eaten. I ain't even had a bath in more than a week!"

"*That* I guessed."

"I saw the papers. They're giving you guys the business for not finding the twins. Get me a place to stay and I can help you! There's stuff I know—stuff I can tell you!"

"Vinnie, it isn't even 5:00 in the morning. I'm not doing any-thing until you tell me something that makes sense."

Vinnie began to rummage through the ashtray, finally picking out a butt left over from Ethel Rosewater. He jammed in the cig-arette lighter from his sitting position on the floor. "I ain't had a whole cigarette in days. Have a heart, Davey. Get me something to eat, for God's sake! If I don't get some food, I'll faint or die or something. Go to a truck stop—out of town where they don't know me."

"Vinnie, the only place anyone knows you is in jail."

"You're not taking me serious!"

"No, Vinnie. I'm not taking you seriously. I want to kick the crap out of you for dragging me out of bed!"

"Cops don't do that!"

"I'm off duty. I want to do it as a sleep-deprived Saturday morning citizen. Now, tell me what's going on or so help me God I'll dump your ass right here in the middle of the square!"

"For old times...."

"Vinnie, there aren't any 'old times.' Get this through your thick head—you're the bad guy. I'm the good guy. I'd have my white hat on but it was still dark when I dressed. Now, start mak-ing sense!"

Vinnie sounded close to tears as he coughed on another of Ethel's cigarette butts. "You gotta help me! I got nobody! There's stuff I know...I don't want to be a squealer, but they got a contract on me, for God's sake! I can point you right to 'em—just get me a new life!"

"Vinnie, I'm a minor league cop. I play for Parkside, strictly double 'A' at best. I don't want to screw around and play against the big leagues in Philadelphia; all your friends with the crazy middle names like, 'The Shiv' and 'The Hunchback' and 'Three Fingers'—really neat nicknames like that."

"You're a cop! You took an oath!"

"I didn't take an oath to do something stupid!"

"You owe a responsibility to Mrs. Wassermann! I read the paper! And I can spill my guts, honest to God, I can! But you've got to protect me!"

Whatever Vinnie was babbling about sounded like the last thing in the world Dean wanted to get involved with, but he had no choice but to at least hear out the terrified man. They reached a compromise and Baratto began to half-tell his story until Dean found an all-night truck stop, miles north of Parkside.

The twins had been involved in some escapade for the Philadelphia crime family that Vinnie refused to describe. The Wassermans dragged him along for the ride without the knowledge of their employer. Something had gone awry, or so the twins found out a day or two later, although Vinnie swore everything went according to plan and they hadn't done anything wrong. The word spread on the street that the family was hot after Billie and Willie Wassermann. Vinnie hadn't been marked because no one knew he'd accompanied the boys, until the twins came out from under their rock the prior weekend and were quickly nabbed and "questioned." Vinnie claimed to be able to show the police where Billie and Willie had been hiding and continued to brag that he had enough information to make headlines and sink half the Philadelphia mobsters.

Vinnie Baratto stuffed his face with a double breakfast order and gained confidence with every bite. "The bastards are going to find out they can't screw with me. A contract, for God's sake! You set this up with the Feds, Davey, and I'll maybe get you a promotion or something. This is big, really big."

Dean had two choices, neither of which was appealing. He could call Lieutenant Anderson and explain the situation to him, but it was still far too early to wake up his boss. He could babysit Baratto until a reasonable hour and then either call Anderson and turn him over to Andy Sackler, who was now in charge of the Wassermann case. He considered taking Vinnie to jail for safekeeping, but the petrified man wouldn't hear of it.

"They have spies everywhere. I'd be dead before you turned the key! When you're on their list, you're history! But I'm not going to make it easy for 'em. I'm not stupid, you know. You remember me in school." Dean remembered him in school. He was stupid.

Exasperated, Dean drove toward Easton, Pennsylvania until he found a motel that satisfied Baratto. It was not unlike the Ocean Shore in Norfolk, only smaller and completely deserted. Dean was down to 11 dollars and change, so he used his Visa card, holding his breath that it wasn't maxed-out while the clerk ran it through the

recording machine. At the earliest reasonable time he called
Lieutenant Anderson, who grumbled his reluctant agreement to
let Vinnie stay at the motel until they could question him further
and find out if he actually possessed any useful information. Dean
located Sackler, who was less than pleased at getting a Saturday
assignment of questionable worth. Sackler made Dean wait until
his son finished Little League practice before he would leave for
the motel. It was after 11:00 by the time Sackler arrived.

The two detectives agreed to keep Baratto at the motel until
Monday as neither wanted to waste their weekend checking out
his dubious story. No one expressed any sympathy for Billie and
Willie, not even Baratto. If the twins had been in the hands of the
family for three days, two more wouldn't matter. Sackler questioned Vinnie briefly but got no further than Dean. Vinnie reluctantly agreed to stay put until Monday as long as he had enough
money for cigarettes and meals at the diner across the street and
the TV continued to work. They summarily dismissed his request
for a mustache and disguise and refused to give him a gun for pro-
tection. Sackler handed him his son's Little League bat.

Dean and Sackler had 26 dollars between them. Baratto started to grumble but took one look at their faces and decided to leave
well enough alone. Saturday was more than half over before Dean
was able to leave.

Vinnie had given Dean his address: 879 Parsons—two rooms
over a laundromat. Dean planned to send a patrol car by later to
pick up some clothes but his trip home passed within a block of
Parsons Street and on an impulse, he drove by the building. It was
not a neighborhood one would be proud to call home.

As Dean looked for a place to park, he noticed a late model
Chevrolet with a rental sticker on the rear bumper parked across
the street. Dean could see two men in the front seat as he drove
by. He circled the block, approached from the other direction, and
parked up the block.

Dean walked up to the open driver's side window, startling the
man behind the wheel, mid-bite in his hamburger. The other
occupant was slouching down in the passenger's seat with his hat
pulled over his eyes, apparently napping.

Dean put on his silliest grin. "Hi, fellows...."

"Get lost, asshole," the man answered, not bothering to pause in his eating.

"Oh, no," Dean said. "You fellows have got it all wrong. I'm not a mugger. I'm one of the good guys. See?" He showed his badge, inches from the man's face. The driver, tall, dark-haired and unshaven with a pencil-thin mustache, set down his hamburger. The passenger, skinny and much younger, had a facial tic that was very noticeable after he pushed back his hat and looked slowly at Dean who, in turn, continued to smile his silly smile.

"So?" the mustache finally said. "You got yourself a little tin badge. Isn't that nice?"

"Whatcha doing here? Anything I can help you with?" Dean did a quick look-see in the car. Discarded wrappers and soft drink cans littered the floor, a magazine and a folded newspaper lay between the men on the seat. It looked as if they had been waiting a long time.

"We're waiting for a friend. Is that against the law in this burg?"

"Oh, gee whiz, no. I just thought I might be able to help you out. Your friend wouldn't be Vinnie Baratto, would he?" He asked the question almost gleefully.

Both of the men took notice. "Vinnie, who?" asked the mustache.

"Vinnie Baratto. He lives right up there, over the Laundromat. Is he a friend of yours?"

"Yeah. You know where Vinnie is?"

"Tell you what. If you fellows show me some identification, then I'll know who to tell Vinnie was looking for him...if I happen to see him."

They both thought about it before extracting driver's licenses from their wallets. Mustache was Alfred Nota, from Boston, and tic-face was Homer Flanders, from Philadelphia. Dean meticulously copied the names and addresses in a notebook.

"You don't meet many folks named 'Homer,' do you, Homer? Most old ladies wouldn't name their kids 'Homer.' They'd figure the poor kid would get all kinds of razing in school and all." Homer did not look happy. "Have you fellows known ol' Vinnie very long?"

"We go way back. Now, can we cut out all this shit and...."

"I go way back with ol' Vinnie, too. Ol' Vinnie and I went to school together."

Homer laughed. "I didn't know Vinnie ever went to school."

Dean reached in the car, pointing, scarcely an inch from a bulge beneath Alfred's shoulder, causing him to pull away. "I guess you carry that gun 'cause it's such a piss-poor neighborhood where our old buddy Vinnie lives. Huh?"

Alfred turned, a smile on his face but a sneer in his voice. "I don't have no gun, Mr. Policeman," and he added, "you don't have no 'probable cause' now, do you?"

Dean retained his smile. "Well, I guess you got me there. But I'm just interested in our old pal Vinnie. It looks like ol' Vinnie is missing, doesn't it? I can't understand it. Seems there's an epidemic of 'missing' going around. All my buddies seem to be missing. You haven't seen anything of Billie and Willie Wassermann, have you? Word is they're missing too."

The name startled them. "We don't know no guys named Wassermann," answered Alfred.

"Naw, we don't know no twins at all," piped up Flanders, who Dean pegged as the really smart one of the pair.

Alfred interrupted him. "We better get going. I got to catch a plane back up to Boston—tickets for the Symphony and stuff like that."

"I'll certainly let ol' Vinnie know you're looking for him. I'm sure he'll be tickled pink." Dean stepped back from the car.

"Yeah," said Homer. "And tell 'em Papa down in Philly is anxious about him too. Papa wants to take him fishing." Both of them laughed as Alfred started the car. Dean stepped back further, the smile fading from his face as the two men drove away at a very sedate pace.

It was mid afternoon when Dean returned home.

"Where the heck did you go?" Fred asked, looking up from his notebook—a now familiar accessory. "I thought you were out on your bicycle."

"Not at 4:00 in the morning. I was babysitting 'yellow 42'." He capsulized his session with Vinnie as he turned on the ball game.

"I told Mrs. Byrne you were bicycling. I said she could come by about 6:00 and pick up her husband's stuff. I already wrote up an inventory. She was going to headquarters for the belongings but I told her Saturday is your day off and the things were still here."

Dean heaved a deep sigh and plodded out to the kitchen for coffee.

"I've been working since 4:00," he called over his shoulder, "I really wish she'd wait until Monday. There's always a scene when relatives view what the victim left behind. Besides," he added, looking around, "the place is a mess."

Dean was sure Fred simply wanted to meet Jeffrey Byrne's wife and had suggested Cynthia Byrne come by the house for her husband's belongings. While Dean wanted the opportunity to speak with her in person after his Norfolk trip, he didn't feel in the best mood to do it after spending half the night and day coping with Vinnie Baratto and his sleazy friends.

Fred knew he'd overstepped his bounds and commenced to make amends. "You go up and take a little nap. You've got to keep your strength up. I'll just pick up around here, spruce it up like the preacher's coming to call. Mrs. Byrne will probably just come to the door anyway."

There were four phone messages in Dean's absence. Ethel Rosewater called to confirm Thursday night. Leland Anderson wanted Dean to spend Sunday with Vinnie at the motel. Andy Sackler was checking on clothes for Vinnie. A lady from Visa had called, probably to tell him he was overextended. He called all but Visa. Reluctantly, he agreed to waste his Sunday with Vinnie and learned from Sackler that a uniformed officer had delivered Vinnie's clothes earlier. Dean passed along the information on the two hoods staking out Vinnie's apartment. Sackler sounded ready to look them up and hand them Vinnie with a red bow around his neck. Ol' Vinnie was being, as usual, a pain in the butt. Finally Dean stumbled up the stairs for a short nap.

The last sound to reach his ears as he dropped off to sleep was the hum of the vacuum cleaner competing with the twang of Merle Haggard on the disc player. If any dreams disturbed his much-needed slumber, he had no recollection of them when Fred tapped on his door telling him to rise and shine. Dean staggered to the shower, letting the ice-cold water start his day anew. It was ten past six, according to his bedside clock. He assumed Cynthia Byrne was a few minutes late, but when he descended the stairs, there she sat, opposite Fred O'Connor, who was decked out in an elegant blue pinstripe suit complete with pocket handkerchief and bow tie. Both Fred and Cynthia were smiling, lemonade in hand, like lifelong friends. Dean, his hair still soaking wet, wearing an open-neck polo shirt while carrying his shoes, felt like the village idiot.

Mrs. Byrne was dressed in a black jersey dress with a single strand of pearls around her neck. In spite of little or no makeup, she looked knockout gorgeous. Dean stopped dead in his tracks.

"I'm sorry," he managed to blurt out. "I didn't know you were here." He ran his hand through his hair self-consciously.

"That's all right. I'm in good company. Mr. O'Connor has been the perfect host. We've had a lovely chat." She smiled at Fred, who bowed. Errol Garner was playing in the background. The conniving old son-of-a-bitch had probably told her the soft jazz was his choice and the barnyard music Dean's.

But you had to give him credit. It was inspirational to see Fred O'Connor at work with a lady. He had changed before Dean's eyes to a perfect balance of charm and elegance, guaranteed to have any female eating out of his hand. It was uncanny—must be something in the hormones. The very presence of the opposite sex turned him to a totally different person, a regular lady-killer.

"Mrs. Byrne's son drove her over but the lad had an engagement so I suggested she join us for dinner and allow us to drive her home. I know you want to discuss your trip to Norfolk and I hated to see the poor young man delayed. I made the reservations at Café Richard."

Dean couldn't believe his ears. The old bastard had set the whole thing up! He wasn't dressed like opening night at the opera by accident! It was a damn wonder he hadn't ordered roses! And Café Richard! Common folk never ate there. It would cost the price of a car payment for the early evening special, if the posh place had such a thing!

Dean mustered his best smile. "I'm delighted. That's very generous of Mr. O'Connor. Atlantic City must have paid well this week. He takes the bus down every Wednesday—with the rest of the old folks." Fred made a professional recovery with the help of a gulp of lemonade as Dean continued to address Mrs. Byrne. "Have you been here long?"

"Just since 5:30. I had to stop at the church to make arrangements. We're...going to have a service next week. Mr. Mayer at World Wide suggested it."

Dean held his tongue. Mayer was something else—have a service, bury the guy in absentia and get him the hell off the books.

"You'd better put on a shirt and tie," Fred said. "Café Richard is a pretty swank place," Fred said, rising and refilling Mrs. Byrne's glass from a crystal pitcher Dean hadn't seen since his mother died.

Dean ignored his stepfather and instead pointed out Jeffrey Byrne's belongings and suggested Mrs. Byrne might want to check them over before signing a receipt.

"Can't I just sign for them without having to go through everything? I'd rather sort them out at home...alone." Then she asked, "Was there a wallet..."

"Yes. It's in the suitcase."

"Good," she answered with a slight smile. "There should be about seventy-five dollars."

"Seventy-eight," answered Dean.

"This is embarrassing, but I really need the money for groceries. World Wide can't issue any more paychecks. Something to do with their legal department. Mr. Mayer did say he was going to talk to them about some sort of advance to hold me over. Mr. Mayer has been very kind. He's called three or four times."

*Kind, my ass!* thought Dean. The lecherous bastard didn't waste any time getting Byrne off the payroll and now he's trying to hustle his wife before the body even floats in.

Fred reached for a paper from his notes. "This is sort of an inventory of the stuff. Perhaps if you just sign it...."

Dean grumbled some sort of agreement, trying to keep the edge from his voice, as he turned and climbed the stairs to change.

Café Richard was new, sleek, pretentious and looked like its half-page newspaper ads, Dean's only previous exposure to the establishment. While not strictly a meat-and-potatoes guy, he felt more comfortable with a meal he could recognize, like the weekday special at Uncle Sally's Galley, not something tiny and exotic, wrapped in dainty strands of imported grass.

The most enjoyable part of the meal was Cynthia Byrne.
Though the weight of sadness from the past few days was still in
evidence, she was obviously brightened by Fred O'Connor, the perfect host. The old man perused the wine menu with a studious
eye, mispronouncing the items with enough of a smile so you
never knew if he was kidding or ignorant.

After the tuxedoed maitre d' had seated them, Fred had made
a pronouncement in his best French accent, "There are no problems, no worries at Café Richard. You, madam, for the evening
shall be Cynthia, head mistress of a poor, but academically superi-
or school for restless girls. You are taking a much deserved vacation
in Europe." He pointed at David. "Our friend here, is Prince David
of Dean, vacationing incognito. We're all trapped by a raging bliz-
zard in an obscure little hotel on the French Riviera."

"Snow on the French Riviera?" Cynthia laughed.

"A most unusual occurrence for the season, Madam," Fred
replied.

"And who are you?" Dean asked.

"Chief Inspector Hercule O'Connor, at your service," he
answered, with a bow. "Taking a short holiday after freeing this
august establishment from the scourge of an international jewel
thief."

There was total absence of mention of the disappearance of
Jeffrey Byrne, Dean's trip to Norfolk, or any real-life matters for
the entire evening. All pedestrian concerns were put aside and col-
lectively forgotten while the group concentrated on the created
adventures of the mythical three. The characters became more
absurd with each passing round of tales. They whispered conspir-
atorially about the "true" identity of the other guests—the bearded gentleman on the left, by the palm tree? A defrocked priest
conspiring to blow up the local abbey. The gorgeous blonde on the
far side of the room? A famous movie star on a secret rendezvous
away from her alcoholic husband, a graft-taking senator from the
mid-west. In spite of himself, Dean enjoyed the evening, more
than he had in weeks. They laughed their way through two bottles
of good Bordeaux and a dessert, brought in flaming splendor to
their darkened table. They were still giddy when Fred paid the
check, by peeling a large number of ten-dollar bills from a roll that
started twice as large as it finished.

"Just thank the quarter slot machine at Mr. Trump's place," Fred said, as they rose to leave. Dean brushed aside a pang of guilt for sticking the old man, but it served him right.

It was still early when the group left Café Richard, but to Dean's surprise Fred suggested Dean drop him off before taking Cynthia Byrne back to Sherwood Forest.

"Us old timers need to hit the sack early," Fred lied.

Cynthia kissed him on the cheek, telling him he didn't look a day over 50.

"I'm so old I won't even buy green bananas no more," he smiled as Dean rolled his eyes.

The moon was out, the evening was mild and had circumstances been different, Dean would have put in a plug for continuing the evening's pleasure. Instead, he spent a half-hour in her driveway, discussing the Norfolk trip and the search for her missing husband. She accepted his report, not without obvious sadness but with business-like decorum and no sign of tears. She, in turn, brought him up to date. Her mother was to arrive the next day and stay through the memorial service on the following Wednesday. The neighbors continued to help, but they had their own lives to live and she was encouraging them to get back to their normal activities. She was coping, forcing herself to acknowledge that it might be weeks, or possibly never, before her husband's body was recovered. Yes, money was a problem and she hadn't any idea how to tackle the matter.

"I have a friend who's an attorney," Dean said, on the spur of the moment. "I don't know if she can help very much but she may be able to steer you in the right direction." He scribbled Ethel Rosewater's name and address on a scrap of paper. She thanked him and placed it in her purse.

"Randy and I tried to remember the day you said Jeff was absent from work," she said. "Neither of us could recall anything unusual. It was a Tuesday so I was at class and Randy at baseball practice—otherwise we remembered nothing. I'm sure it's a mix up on the part of World Wide."

Dean agreed she was probably right and didn't press the subject. He then told her the Parkside Police Department would close the investigation from this end unless something new came to light.

Cynthia Byrne held out her hand and said, with what Dean hoped was at least a hint of reluctance, "I guess I won't be seeing you again. I really appreciate everything you've done. And tonight was perfect—it was just what I needed. Mr. O'Connor is a doll."

"Mr. O'Connor is a scoundrel," Dean replied. "I wouldn't leave you alone with him for a minute."

She laughed. "I'm sure he's broken a thousand hearts!"

He walked her to the door, carrying her husband's suitcase. "If there is anything missing, let me know."

"I will," she smiled, but the sadness was returning. He went back to his car and started the engine, glancing back, but she had already closed the door.

# CHAPTER VI

Just as Dean backed from the driveway, another car turned the corner and waited for him to clear the entrance. Evidently it was Randy Byrne. As soon as Dean was clear, the other car pulled in, stopping in front of the garage. On an impulse, Dean drove back in behind it and strolled over to meet the young man who stepped from the vehicle.

Dean introduced himself to the tall, good-looking boy who shook his hand firmly. Randy Byrne was dressed in jeans and sweater and seemed at ease around adults, more so than most his age.

After offering condolences for Randy's father, Dean added, "It's a little early for a Saturday night, isn't it?"

"It was a party. They started hauling out the booze and I don't want to do anything to screw up a scholarship—especially now."

"Good thinking and good luck with the scholarship. You should be a shoe-in. I watched your game on Thursday. They ought to be begging you."

"Thanks," the boy answered. "But I've been a little out of sorts lately."

"I can understand why."

The boy shuffled his feet, looking down at the ground. "I appreciate all the help you've given mom. She says you've been really good about all this."

"Tough times."

"Yeah. Especially the waiting around. And not knowing. It gets to you."

73

Dean patted him on the shoulder and started to leave but Randy stopped him. "You know that date you asked my ma about, March fourth?"

"Yes."

"Is it really important?"

"No. It was just one of those unanswered details I picked up on and figured I'd ask. Your ma told me you had baseball practice and nothing unusual happened."

"Yeah, well...that's the truth, sort of. But there's something else. I don't know if it means anything, but I guessed I'd better say something." He moved around to the far side of the car, as if to get out of earshot of the house. Dean followed him. "There's this guy in my trig class, Bobby Ridner. He said he saw our car at Whitney's Motel. That's out 309, maybe 20 miles from town."

Dean had bicycled the area and recognized the location. "I know where it is."

"Ridner and this girl skipped school and tried to find somewhere, you know, to get together. He thought it was a big joke, making all these plans and there in the back of the motel is our car."

"How could he be sure?"

"We have this funny license plate. The first three letters are SXX. Like, 'SEX,' you know? And besides, it's got a caved in front left. Ridner's been in it lots of times."

"And it was March fourth?"

"I'm not sure. I know it was back when baseball practice started. Around that time."

"Did Ridner see your father?"

"No. Their room was on the other side."

"You never asked your father about it?"

"Naw. I guess I should have. It really bugged me. I lied to Bobby—told him dad lent the car to a friend while he took the train into Philly, like he usually does. I thought about it a lot. Now I'll never know. Unless I hear it from the other person."

"Don't condemn him before you hear the evidence."

"Do you know any other reason to go to a motel in the middle of the day?" he asked, harshly.

Dean didn't. "Tell you what. I'll check it out. I'll fill you in on what I find. We'll keep it between us. Okay? I'm sure there's a logical explanation."

"Yeah, okay." Randy Byrne managed a smile but a fool could tell he wasn't buying.

As Dean drove away from Maid Marian Lane, he made up his mind to find out if the world had put a crown on Saint Jeffrey a little prematurely. It wasn't yet midnight and his afternoon nap had worked so well he was far from ready for bed. He knew Fred would be waiting up for him, but decided to let the old man cool his heels, punishment enough for setting up the evening's activity on the sly. Dean turned the car away from town, opened the window to let in the fresh May night, and headed south toward route 309 and Whitney's Motel. Why wait to find out about Jeffrey Byrne's little escapade?

This was Dean's week for second-rate motels, and they weren't getting better. Whitney's was the bottom rung.

A little bell jingled in the empty office as Dean entered and an unshaven man in his sixties took his time sauntering out from behind a curtain, hoisting up his suspenders as he moved behind the desk. "Twenty-eight dollars, plus tax." He said, hardly looking up. He had a personality that would tick off Mother Theresa.

Dean didn't answer, but held out his wallet to show his ID. It took a few moments before the man focused, looked down at it and sighed. "So, you don't want a room."

"No, just some information."

"Look, I don't ask their age. I don't guarantee nothing...."

"I just want to see your registration cards for March fourth. That's all."

The man stared at him with the same glum look. Finally, he turned and reached beneath the counter and handed Dean a box containing hundreds of cards. "If you're looking for John Doe, I think you're in luck. The cards probably ain't in order, but help yourself. You all come back, you hear."

The man started to return to the back room when a car pulled up. As Dean began to search the cards, a teenaged boy entered with a girl no more than 16 or 17 hanging on his arm. The boy asked for a room and paid for it in cash, getting the last two dollars from the girl.

"I suppose you folks are on your way for a vacation in Florida and just stopped off for the night," the man said with mock innocence.

"Yeah," the boy said with a smile. "We're just a couple of tourists." The girl giggled, clinging tighter to his arm.

"Are you sure you don't need some help with all your luggage?" They all had a good laugh over that too, all but Dean. It wasn't that they didn't do the same stuff when Dean was young, but at least back then the girl stayed in the car.

After the young couple took their key and fairly skipped away, the old man retreated to the back room, leaving Dean alone with the stack of registration forms. After ten minutes he had found 14 cards for March fourth. One of the three 'Smiths' of the group listed his auto registration with the telltale 'SXX.' The last three digits were similar, but different. The number in the party was listed as *one*.

Dean could not tell from the writing if it compared to the signature Jeffrey Byrne left on the many expense forms Dean had reviewed—it was only a scrawl. He checked the room number and searched the cards until he found the occupants of the two adjoining rooms. There were three in all—Room 15, to the left, had been rented twice. There was a Smith and a Jones, each with local addresses that sounded fake, and Zeke Ambrowski of Raleigh, North Carolina. All three rentals listed two occupants. Dean copied the information from the forms, including the license numbers, and then rang the bell summoning the manager.

"I'm interested in this guy," he said, showing the car that listed the license number beginning 'SXX.'

"Oh sure, Mr. Smith," the night manager grinned. "We get lots of his relatives too—the whole Smith family."

"There are 14 cards for the fourth of March. This place only has 12 units."

"So, we do a good business. We advertise."

"In all the high school yearbooks?" Dean asked.

"Funny. Look, some folks check out early. What's the heat if I double rent once in awhile? A guy has to make a buck."

"It's against the law."

"So's spitting on the sidewalk. It's a bullshit law," he said defensively. "I change the sheets. The place is clean."

"So, tell me about this 'Smith.'"

"Give me a break. That's two months ago. I couldn't tell you who was here this afternoon. In this business it don't pay to have a good memory, even if I did have one."

Dean tried to take the card but the manager protested, saying it was part of his records. He began to talk court order so Dean backed off, thanked him and left. Two more cars containing teenagers pulled in the as he drove away.

"Where the heck have you been?" Fred challenged as Dean entered the door. "You should have been here two hours ago. She's hardly a widow."

Dean answered in a voice as nonchalant as he could muster. "I've been up to the Whitney Motel."

"The hell you say!"

Dean took his sweet time before explaining it was police business. "Without Mrs. Byrne. And the next time you pull a fast one like tonight, I'm going to personally stick you in an old folks home! You haven't had 50 bucks to your name in a year! Now you blow four times that on one meal!"

"There are occasions in life when financial caution gets tossed out the window," he added, "*son*. That's all water under the bridge. Now, let's get down to this case."

"The 'case' is a police matter if it's a case at all. Come Monday morning, Anderson is going to make it a closed case." But before he could continue, Fred had launched into his opening statement.

"That's one fine woman back there and quite a looker. I'm hard pressed to figure why any man in his right mind would dump her. It's makes me falter a bit on the 'Churchy la Fam' theory."

"Well, don't quit on it entirely. The angel Jeffrey's halo may be rusty." Dean described his conversation with Randy Byrne and detailed his reason for visiting the Whitney Motel.

"Kinda puts matters in a different light, doesn't it?" Fred said as he sat in his rocker. Mrs. Lincoln hopped up, stretching her languid body and yawning, as if wondering why these two idiots were keeping such late hours. She jumped off in her graceful way, a ballerina in a black fur coat. Fred began to pick cat hairs from his blue suit.

"Even if he did fool around a bit, it doesn't mean he skipped," Dean said.

"It makes everything you've heard a tad suspect, doesn't it?"

"Just that maybe Sherwood Forest wasn't heaven for Mr. Byrne after all."

"Heaven's where cats don't shed and the Red Sox win in October—not a dead-end job and money problems," Fred offered.

"It bothers me he only listed one person at the motel," Dean said, almost to himself.

"Why?" Fred answered. "He wouldn't have been anxious for someone to find out he was with some floozy."

"No, but he signed an anonymous name in the first place and probably changed the last three digits of his car license plate. Then why bother to lie about the number of people in the room? One person in that place looks more suspicious than two."

"He could have checked in early and had the gal meet him."

"I suppose so. It's just another nagging question."

"Any idea how long he stayed at the motel?" Fred asked.

"No." Then he added, "Maybe I'll look up this Ridner kid and ask him if the car was still there when he finished, but I'm just checking it out because I promised Randy Byrne I would. It's chasing ghosts. Just because Byrne might have gotten a quickie two months ago doesn't mean he faked his drowning and skipped."

"Maybe. But I been making these lists. There's a lot more angles to this here caper—options we ain't touched on yet."

"Such as?" Dean asked, hardly listening.

"Such as someone else could've killed him."

"Why?" Dean asked with a yawn as the night caught up with him.

"That opens up a whole new list of sub-topics, like was it just a random mugger or someone he knew? If it was someone he knew, then that opens up another list—his wife, a business enemy, an old grudge, or he could have been scooped."

"'Scooped?' What in hell does 'scooped' mean?"

Fred looked at Dean as if the detective was clueless. "It means kidnapped."

"Not in the real world, it doesn't."

But Fred was undaunted. "You got to consider the bizarre. That's what reading does for me. My mind's not tied down like yours. You have to be inventive, try to get into the criminal mind, think of all the angles...."

"How about considering the obvious? Like maybe Jeffrey Byrne was just stupid enough to drown himself—half-drunk or sober." Dean rose and stretched. "Whoever gets up first, don't wake the other." He climbed the stairs and never even remembered hitting the bed.

# CHAPTER VII

Sunday was eight hours of listening to Vinnie's uninformative babble, followed by a TV ball game, a couple or three beers and a steak. But if Sunday was peaceful, at least by recent standards, Monday was anything but. The day started with Fred meeting Dean at the breakfast table, a most unusual occurrence. As Dean smeared his whole-wheat toast with a coating of peanut butter, Fred poured the coffee, a sure sign he was looking for a favor.

"I've been thinking," he began. "You may be right about Byrne not showing up at his funeral next week."

"Memorial service," Dean corrected him.

"Yeah, but all the same, if it was you who skipped, wouldn't you be a bit anxious about what was happening? Wouldn't you wonder if everyone was really buying the drowning bit? Now, you can't just call up your best buddy and ask, can you?"

"Not hardly," said Dean, reaching for his coffee.

"So what do you do? I'll tell you what you do. You read the newspaper—not the *New York Times*—you read the *Parkside Sentinel*."

"Okay, so what are you getting at?"

"They don't stock the *Parkside Sentinel* in all the libraries around the country like they do the big city papers."

"So?"

"So, a smart detective would go downtown and ask his old friend Monica Cutler at the *Sentinel* for a list of out of town people who've ordered the paper to be mailed to 'em. The ones who've

80

signed up over the past few weeks. Smart, huh? Then I'll just check 'em out from here by phone."

Dean reluctantly agreed it was a clever idea even though he thought it was a waste of time. While he should have turned the project over to Rita at headquarters, it had, after all, been Fred's idea, so he didn't complain about giving it a shot. "I still think it's whistling in the wind, but it'll keep you out of trouble. Just don't overload the phone bill if I come up with some names."

Dean knew the *Parkside Sentinel* would be going full steam later in the day, so he stopped by the red brick building on his way to work. It was located around the corner from headquarters and he was early anyway. Monica Cutler was seated in her usual corner amid a clutter of used coffee cups and thousands of old newspapers.

"You here to kill Linda Segal, The Ice Lady, or is this a social call?" Monica asked. Ms. Segal was the reporter who was giving Leland Anderson and the department such a hard time over the missing Wassermann twins. Monica grumbled that Segal was more interested in selling papers than the truth so if he wanted to kill her that was fine with her. Dean laughed and told her his visit was neither social nor to perform mayhem—it was police business, sort of.

Monica Cutler had performed every duty but setting type at the *Parkside Sentinel* for the past 20 years. Four years ago, she and Dean were a weekly item, as they say. But no comparison to Ethel Rosewater need be made. Monica was a sweetheart who never said an unkind word about a soul. Dean often wondered to himself why their romantic attraction to one another never grew to something permanent. Perhaps the time was wrong. In any event, they remained as they always had been, the very best of friends.

Monica ended their romance immediately after meeting Harry Turnball, a young and energetic truck driver who delivered the *Parkside Sentinel*. They married within weeks and Monica was set for a lifetime of martial happiness until, six months into her marriage, she was diagnosed with cancer, which began to ravage her body. It pained Dean to see her 30 pounds thinner, wearing an ill fitting wig in place of her waist-length ebony hair, but her indomitable spirit continued to leave him in awe.

He gave the frail woman a hug and described the reason for his visit.

"What detective story did the old gent pull that one out of?" she said with a smile.

"He claims he thought it up himself," Dean answered.

"It makes a certain amount of sense. Do you think Byrne skipped?"

"No. Just the opposite. I'm really just humoring Fred—rewarding him for his first idea in years that isn't totally hare-brained."

"How far back do you want me to check?"

"He disappeared on Tuesday. The last day or so, I guess," Dean answered.

"If I were planning on dumping Harry and leaving town, I'd work at it longer than that! That stuff takes planning. Let's go back three months," she said with a twinkle in her eye. "We'll give old Fred something to do—besides chasing widows around Parkside."

A check of the records listed 22 individuals who had ordered the paper from out of town over the last three months. Four of these customers had since canceled their subscription and four more were personally known to Monica. Dean started to copy the names but Monica stopped him. She took a plain sheet of white paper from her desk and proceeded with flying fingers to type the 14 names and addresses using an old manual typewriter.

"It keeps me in shape," she said over her shoulder. "And reminds me of the old days. Newspaper offices should have type-writers, not those damn computers. They make life too easy. You get soft."

There was a pause after she stood up and handed him the paper. "How are you really doing, Monica?" Dean asked.

She looked him in the eye, the smile momentarily gone. "There are a few days I don't feel like a bucket of dog puke, but I'll tell you this—I thank God every morning I wake up and see Harry snoring beside me. I'd have blown my brains all over the wall months ago if I didn't have him to give me a hard time. You know what? I'd rather have a year of agony with Harry than a lifetime of never having met him. Silly, huh? Sounds like a dime novel, does-n't it?" She gave him a hug. "Get yourself a good woman, David.

You'll find out. There's nothing in the world like love. Everything else pales by comparison."

He didn't say a word as she turned away. "Look at me," she said. "If I had any pride, I'd stay in bed and hide this body under the covers. What a mess!"

"You're beautiful, Monica. You always have been and you always will be."

Dean tucked the list in his pocket and walked the short distance around the corner to Police Headquarters.

The door to Leland Anderson's office was closed when Dean arrived, and Lenny Harrigan was the only detective at his desk. Tom DeLeo had the day off and Andy Sackler was back at the motel holding hands with Vinnie Baratto. Rita Angeltoni banged away on her keyboard, complaining of a terminal case of morning sickness.

"What's going on in there?" said Dean, motioning toward the closed door.

"Anderson's got the FBI on the line. Looks like they're interested in your high school sweetheart," Rita answered without looking up.

"I didn't know you were a football hero," said Harrigan through his permanent smile. "Your buddy was telling me all about it."

"He's not my buddy," answered Dean. He turned to Rita, "The *real* FBI?"

"Yup. They're sending some honcho up from Philly later this morning. The two goons you let walk from outside of Baratto's apartment? They got all hot and bothered over them too."

Dean winced. "With my luck, they'll be mass murderers wanted in 20 states and I'll get my butt kicked for not checking them out. Anything new on our favorite twins, the brothers Wassermann?"

"Nothing to contradict what Baratto said," answered Harrigan. "Me and DeLeo interviewed half their sleazy friends and got nowhere. Looks like they dropped off the face of the earth. No one's sorry to see them gone, I can tell you that much."

"Only Mrs. Wassermann," piped in Rita.

"I was talking to Leland before he barred the gate," said Harrigan. "He wants to close up that Byrne case unless you've found a real good reason to keep it open. He says this Baratto thing is too hot to waste time. I guess that means DeLeo won a cup of coffee, huh? I get to clean up the crumbs on the Byrne business and you get to play chauffeur for the federal guy—take him up to meet your old football buddy."

Dean was primed to respond when Lieutenant Anderson stepped out of his office. "I checked out Nota and Flanders. Flanders is wanted in Philly for skipping child support and he hasn't seen his parole officer in weeks, but no one's gotten around to putting out a call for him, so officially they weren't looking for him. Everybody would like to see Alfred Nota locked up but nobody has been able to make anything stick. The word on the street is he works for a crime family in Boston and hires out for special projects. He's one mean dude."

"Good riddance. Let our Federal friends from Philly have the bunch of them. They'll get no argument from me. But I have to question their smarts if they're interested in Vinnie."

"No argument here but no dice on our dumping the whole business in their laps. They want Parkside to be involved. You get to go out there with them."

"I've got a couple of last minute things to check out on Byrne...."

"Don't waste any more time on it—just get the report finished. This new stuff is too important. Byrne disappeared in Norfolk's jurisdiction and if they're satisfied, let's drop it. Case closed." He turned on his heels and returned to his office. The Ice Lady must have really gotten Leland's goat, Dean thought.

Dean asked Harrigan to work up his end of the report on the Byrne matter and make a few last minute return phone calls to neighbors, just to dot the I's. He filled out the paperwork on his visit to Norfolk and answered some of his phone messages. Visa, he was happy to learn, didn't call to say he was overdrawn but to offer to increase his credit limit. The prime must be up again.

While the case might be officially closed, Dean felt an obligation to Randy Byrne, as well as his own curiosity, to follow up the March fourth Whitney Motel incident. He unobtrusively managed to locate all of the three renters of the adjoining rooms through their license plate numbers and was able to speak to two of them. The couple from North Carolina, the only guests using their own names, hadn't checked in until evening and remembered nothing.

"Mr. Jones," was Jack Webster, a local realtor, who was apparently having an affair with the wife of a city council member. He whispered to Dean he was, "in and out quickly, as the expression goes," and heard nothing in the adjoining room.

The third guest was an 18-year-old from a nearby township, although the name on the registered vehicle was different than the motel listing. He assumed the young man occupied the room for the same purposes as Randy's friend, Bobby Ridner. Dean felt guilty about pursuing the case but made a note to try and speak with the youth.

Mid-morning, Fred O'Connor came by, ostensibly out for a stroll, casually asking for the list of newspaper subscribers. Dean gave him the list but informed him the case was closed. Fred was unperturbed. He would continue until he was satisfied. It was shortly before 11:00 when the federal visitor from Philadelphia arrived, heralding Dean's return to legitimate police work.

Leland Anderson buzzed Dean from his office. A very tall, perfectly proportioned black man, looking like the front page of a fashion magazine, smiled and held out his hand. Everything about him was perfect, from the glass polish of his black shoes to the knife-like crease in his thousand-dollar suit. He stood ramrod straight—a movie star, not a government employee. The guy exuded confidence to the point where Dean felt as if he had just dropped a plateful of mashed potatoes in his lap while this tall, dark stranger was toasting the queen. *Major League, good guys team, Philadelphia franchise*, Dean thought to himself, as he held out his hand.

"Jonathan Winston, meet David Dean," Leland announced. After handshakes and a brief chat, the pair left in Dean's pool car for the motel where Vinnie Baratto awaited.

The two men chatted amiably on the trip from Parkside. Winston was most personable and seemed genuinely interested in the small town and surrounding countryside. He had spent his career in the city, the last seven months investigating the crime family as a part of a special task force.

"Other than a nice drive in the country," Dean said, "I suspect today's going to be a waste of time for you."

"I'm not so sure," Winston said. "I'm interested in these Wassermann guys. Tell me about them."

"They're a pair of fat, stupid, nasty punks who got in over their heads."

Winston paused before answering. "They've been running errands for the family for quite a few months now. The word is, they've been on the fringes of some deals. The fact that they're stupid makes sense. The family likes the stupid ones; they're too dumb to pull a double cross and if they overhear something, chances are they won't know what's being discussed."

"So why snatch them?" Dean found himself wanting to say "scoop."

"That's the intriguing part and what I hope Vinnie Baratto will tell us. Something's happened over the last few weeks. I don't know what it is, but it stirred up the soup. It's not business as usual. The whole distribution system broke down. Baratto could be helpful. If he is, I want him out of that motel. If the boys sent Alfred Nota looking for him, they want this guy very badly."

Just then, Dean noticed a sign for Delbart Regional High School, which serviced the township where young "Mr. Jones," the third guest at Whitney's Motel, was attending school. He briefly explained the situation to Winston, who had no problem detouring for the short time it would take to question the youth. The principal located the boy, who willingly answered Dean's questions once he learned his own activities were of no interest to the police.

"Damn, you guys are good! Here I used an assumed name and all and you ran me down." He brushed back what seemed like a foot of wavy blond hair.

"All in a day's work," Dean answered, winking at Winston as he said it. "How long were you at the Whitney Motel?"

"All day. It was fantastic! We got there about eight in the morning and didn't leave until about nine that night!"

"You and...a friend?"

"Yeah. I wouldn't be no gentleman if I told you her name but she wasn't just some pig. We were going steady and all."

"We're interested in the occupant of the next room," Dean asked.

The boy stopped to think. "On the side by the bed, the right side, some guy came in about 1:00—right after lunch. He and his lady friend were drunk, at least it sounded like it, laughing and all. You could hear everything. She was hell on wheels, moaning and carrying on something wicked! Me and Carrie kept making fun of 'em, quiet like. It was a real turn-on, not that we needed it. They left around three. Some other couple came in just before we left, hauling bags and all."

"What about the other room, the one on your left?"

"That was some guy alone."

"Tell me about him," Dean asked.

"Not much to tell. He was by himself. He came in a little after us, early. We heard him drive up and open the door. There was some moving around so we knew he was there but he didn't even turn on the TV. He left sometime before lunch. I heard the car."

"Are you sure he was alone?"

"He drove up alone and no other car came back there—all day. His room was on the far side—away from the bed, so we couldn't hear as well as the other. If he wasn't alone, she was real quiet." He smiled. "There wasn't any bumping and grinding and those beds are noisy."

Dean looked at him quizzically. "How come you can remember everything? It was two months ago."

The young man smiled. "Hey, it was one memorable day!"

Dean thanked him, a hint of envy in his voice, and he and Winston continued their trip to the motel.

"You're pretty good at interviewing," Winston noted, as they joined the sparse midday traffic northward. "You let the other fellow do all the talking. I like that. Just prompt them once in awhile."

"Just the way you've been doing with me about the Wassermanns and Vinnie Baratto," Dean answered.

Winston smiled. "You're also very perceptive."

The federal agent was interested to learn Vinnie and Dean had played sports together, but Dean put to early rest any misconception about his prowess on the playing field. Winston, the son of a Connecticut congressman, admitted modestly after some prodding he was educated at Yale on a sports scholarship and had played both baseball and football for four years. "They won't let you do that anymore. Everyone has to be a specialist nowadays," he added, a hint of regret in his voice. "But it sure made you burn the night oil to keep up the grades."

*Sure,* Dean thought to himself, more in awe than sarcasm, *Only a three-point-eight instead of four-oh.*

Andy Sackler met them at the door of the motel with a mouth full of doughnut and a coffee cup in his hand. Baratto was in the john, but as soon as he emerged, he took one look at Winston and turned away.

"I ain't talking to no nigger cop," he said defiantly.

"Vinnie, you're scum..." Dean said, but the federal agent held out a hand and stopped him.

Jonathan Winston never flinched and his smile remained in place as he moved very close to Vinnie, nearly touching him. "Frankly, I'm not all that partial about talking to a honky low-life piece of shit like you either, but I guess the winds of fate tossed us together." He pushed Baratto down on the bed. "Let's get it out on the table. I'd give you about ten minutes to live if you walked out this door, and maybe a day or two if you stay in the motel. Your sole prayer is to play ball with me. And you know what? I'm not even sure you've got the stuff to get in the ball game—and if that's the case, you're already a dead man."

The look on Baratto's face showed he bought every word Jonathan Winston was saying.

Winston motioned to Sackler and Dean. "Why don't you guys run down the road and get another cup of coffee? My newfound friend and I want to get better acquainted." Vinnie was beginning to lose his color.

"Want me to get the rubber hose from the car?" Sackler asked, smiling at Vinnie as he and Dean started for the door.

"No. We're just going to have a friendly chit-chat," Winston answered. Vinnie started to rise but Winston bounced him back down on the bed.

Dean and Sackler drove about a mile down old Route 22 to a chrome and Formica railroad-car diner straight out of the fifties. The coffee was good and so was the blueberry pie. Sackler brought Dean up to date on his recent stay with Baratto but nothing of importance was learned. Sackler was sick of the man's company. Like everyone else, he'd hoped Parkside was out of the case and was disappointed to learn the FBI was expecting Parkside's continued assistance in the investigation. The two men gave Winston a half-hour alone with Baratto before returning to the motel.

As they alighted from the car, Winston came out to meet them. "Your buddy is being a little coy but he's hung around the wrong people long enough to pick up some information. If we can open him up, I think he'll be useful. We've got a place up in the Poconos we want to store him. Too many people know he's here at the motel. I want to move him before the bad boys track him down and try to whack him."

Only Sackler and Dean of the Parkside crew would know the new location where the Feds would store Baratto until they figured out what to do with him more permanently. As Sackler had worked the night, he was excused for the balance of the day. Dean and Winston would transport Baratto northward that afternoon. Winston stressed the secrecy of the location. "I don't care if they blow Vinnie's head off, but I don't want my guys getting hurt."

Vinnie Baratto came out of the motel, suitcase in hand, a smile from ear to ear. "These Feds got class, Davey, not like you hicks. Me and Johnny here, my colored buddy, are going to do us some business."

"Only if your memory starts working and you start spouting some useful information. We're not looking for stuff we can read in the phone book or the newspaper." There was no smile on Winston's face.

As it turned out, the safe house location was safe with Dean as he had no idea where they were after the first half dozen turns. He thought he was still in Pennsylvania—he hadn't seen a sign welcoming him to another state. Dean hadn't been around this many trees since he was a Boy Scout.

Winston glanced over his shoulder frequently, checking to see if they were being followed. Dean hoped it was simply from force of habit, not because he possessed information he wasn't sharing.

The final leg of the journey was a long dirt road that climbed first through a grove of fir followed by an unbroken forest of hardwood just beginning to bud. The trail dead-ended at a faded white house at the edge of a clearing that commanded a view of the valley below. It was a small house, no more than four or five rooms. While no other vehicle was visible, two men, dressed more casually than Winston, emerged from the house. They shook hands, but no names were exchanged. Most of Baratto's bravado had disappeared. He was uneasy—the kid being dropped off at the hospital for a tonsil operation, hearing about the ice cream but now realizing something dire might be in store before dessert.

The two ushered Baratto into the house before he could change his mind, while Winston held out his hand to Dean.

"I'm sure you want to get back to Parkside. I'll give you a call tomorrow," he said as he turned and followed the others, adding, "Keep an eye out over your shoulder."

Winston assumed Dean would know his way back, and Dean was too embarrassed to ask for directions. After an hour of circles he spotted a numbered highway he recognized, although he was much further from Parkside than he'd suspected. It was well after 4:00 by the time he found the correct route leading toward home. In view of the lateness of the hour, Dean pulled into a pay phone and called the office to check his messages.

"Three phone messages," Rita said, with no emotion. He could picture her sitting there, in her wraparound paisley with the torn-out hem. "Fred has a date with Mrs. Abernathy and won't be home for supper but wants you to wait up for him. Mrs. Byrne asked that you call her and the lady lawyer you ball on Thursday nights telephoned." She added, "Leland Anderson's wife Marian says you're a schmuck for not solving the Byrne thing and causing her to lose her bet."

He called Ethel Rosewater first, catching her at the office. "I talked to your Mrs. Byrne this afternoon. Do you have the hots for her or something? She thinks you're the greatest thing since God died."

"Strictly business," Dean answered, automatically.

"I'll bet," Ethel said sarcastically. "But maybe you can talk some sense to her. It looks like she's too goody-goody to sue anybody, but I haven't given up yet. I did tell her what's needed to begin the process of getting the jerk declared dead." Before Dean could ask her to explain, she added, "I gotta run. Arthur's buzzing me. He needs help with fat-cat client—one of his Philadelphia gangsters. My pocketbook calls. See you Thursday night, stud." He was left listening to a dial tone and beginning to seriously question their bizarre relationship.

Dean telephoned Cynthia Byrne next, but Randy answered. "No baseball practice today?" Dean asked.

"No. The coach gave us a breather. Exams are starting."

"Can we talk?" Dean asked quietly.

"Yes," came the cautious reply.

"Your dad, or whoever was in his car, was alone at that motel. No one else was there."

"He was really alone?"

"I wouldn't lie to you. I don't know why the car was there. Maybe we'll never know, but I'll bet it was harmless. I'll explain how we found out when I see you, but there was only one person in the room the whole time. No woman. No hot date."

"Thanks. Thanks a lot. I really appreciate this."

"There's a lesson there," Dean added, although he wasn't exactly sure just what the lesson was. Somehow it sounded appropriate.

"Yeah, I guess you're right," Randy answered. "I'll get Ma. And thanks again."

Cynthia Byrne apologized for not answering the phone. "Things are a little hectic around here planning for the memorial service next week. Will you be able to come?"

"I'm on a new case now, and things are a little confusing."

"Oh," she said, sounding disappointed.

"...but I'll try to sneak away, if I can."

"Thank you," she said. "I'd like for you to be there."

"How have you been—generally speaking?"

She was slow answering. "Pretty good. This was a tough day. I received a post card from Jeff—from Norfolk. He often does that when he's out of town even though he's always home before they get here."

Dean wanted to ask what the card said but was far too civilized to ask. Instead he said nothing.

Cynthia paused, and added, "I saw your attorney friend this afternoon...Ms. Rosewater."

"Yes," he said. "She called and said she'd spoken with you."

"She seems like a very nice woman." Dean wondered if they were speaking about the same Ethel Rosewater. "I think she was disappointed I didn't want to sue someone." It was the same Ethel Rosewater. "She was very helpful. I was afraid the insurance company might try to claim Jeff committed suicide and deny coverage, but Ms. Rosewater said that wasn't a policy exclusion anyway."

"That's good," Dean said. Then he asked, "Have you checked the items I brought back from Norfolk? I held the inventory to make sure."

"Yes," she answered. "Everything was there." Then added, "Except the bathing suit—and his cap." Dean had forgotten the waiter saying Byrne also wore a baseball cap when he left the room. Cynthia Byrne continued. "Jeff loved his Phillies cap. He's had it for years."

"I've got a few old things like that myself."

She hesitated. "There's one more thing. I have a really big favor to ask of you."

"What is it?"

"Ms. Rosewater says the more thorough the investigation into Jeff's drowning, the better the chance to have a judge issue a death certificate. If the court thinks there's any possibility Jeff's alive, I'd have to wait years and years. I really don't know what I'd do."

"We've closed the police investigation," Dean interjected. "There wasn't any evidence to suggest other than an unfortunate accident."

"I know," Cynthia Byrne said quickly. "But Ms. Rosewater said the more detail, the better—bury them in paper, she called it. I asked about a private detective—God knows how I would pay— but she said a hired person wouldn't be seen as objective." Dean was silent. "I know I'm asking a lot, but...."

"I've just started writing up my final report. I'll go into as much detail as I can," Dean answered.

She sighed with relief. "Thank you very much."

"If I don't see you next week at the service, it won't be because I didn't try to get there," he added.

By 5:00 Dean was ravenous and, as he was on his own for dinner, stopped at the dining room of a national chain motel for a full meal. What the hell, Visa liked him again. A waitress wearing a lace cap denoting her Pennsylvania Dutch heritage seated him at a small corner table by the window. As it was early in the evening, there were few customers in the room. Three men, at three separate tables, evidently on the road for business, were all dining alone. They reminded Dean of Jeffrey Byrne, doing the same thing a week earlier.

The only exception to the lonely customers was a young family of four, husband, wife, girl about nine and boy about six. They were seated two tables away from Dean and appeared to be celebrating something unusual in an otherwise Spartan life. They were dressed in their best and both children and adults seems perfectly at ease with each other's company, even if they all seemed somewhat in awe of their surroundings. The children, in particular, caught Dean's attention.

The little girl was a beauty: her blond curls were pinned with a bright red ribbon and her white dress had a red sash about the waist. Her smile lit the table and she and her little brother, who was being the perfect gentlemen in his spring suit, were obviously the pride and joy of Ma and Pa.

All four perused the menu judiciously, with father and mother occasionally offering comments and explanations. At one point, the girl dropped her napkin and the boy reached beneath the table, picked it up, and replaced it daintily on her lap. She scowled at him at first, but then understanding the generosity of his evidently out-of-character act, bowed politely in acknowledgment.

The boy discovered something on the menu to his liking and enthusiastically pointed it out to his father. The girl too, smiled and nodded. The father frowned, ever so slightly, and surreptitiously opened his wallet and counted his money. He whispered something to his wife. She too frowned, and then reached for her purse and withdrew an envelope, extracted a bill and slipped the money to her husband.

"A good woman," Monica Cutler had said, "makes all the difference in the world." Suddenly Dean felt incredibly lonely. Just as quickly, a picture of Cynthia Byrne began crowding his mind. He'd be at the service next week and not to see if a missing man would turn up in veiled drag, but simply because Cynthia Byrne told him she'd be pleased with his presence.

"Don't get involved," he said to himself, "you're getting involved in your head." He dismissed the intrusive thought. The case was over. Forget Jeffrey Byrne and forget his grieving wife. Let her mourn her drowned husband. No, he hadn't skipped. He lacked opportunity, money or reason to take off. So why this nagging feeling to the contrary, like he was missing something?"

He rose abruptly, his coffee only half finished, and paid his bill. It was before 6:30 so the early bird special was in effect, making the meal a tad cheaper than he'd figured. On an impulse, he turned and looked at the family seated near his table still enjoying their meal. He handed his Visa card back to the cashier.

"Pay for theirs too," he said. She stared at him. "The family over there. Tell them it's from a friend." The cashier shrugged but complied with his request, writing up an additional charge slip. Their unknowing company at his meal was well worth the price of the charge.

# CHAPTER VIII

Dean spent most of the evening flipping through TV channels, but as none of the inane programs held even minimal interest, he took out his voice recorder and began summarizing his notes for the detailed report on Jeffrey Byrne, adding as much minutia as he could muster, as Cynthia Byrne had requested.

The report methodically listed each person interviewed and what they said about Jeffrey Byrne. Mayer's assessment of Byrne's true abilities were kept to a minimum. Dean included the "walk-on water" evaluation from Byrne's personnel file so he didn't have to lie. There was a detailed itinerary of Byrne's movements and information on Byrne's health, finances, personnel records and lifestyle. He included a picture of Jeffrey Byrne, recently forwarded from World Wide's personnel department. It showed a good looking, much younger man, as Dean guessed it dated from when Byrne was first employed, 15 years earlier. Dean tried to be as objective as possible and let the report speak for itself. He did not mention the March fourth date Byrne was absent from work. When he replayed his dictated first draft, the report seemed dry but the evidence produced an overwhelming endorsement that there was no logical reason why Jeffrey Byrne might skip. Dean even convinced himself as he listened to his unexciting voice. He hoped he wouldn't put Rita to sleep transcribing it when he was finished. Dictating it had certainly had that effect on him. He remembered Fred O'Connor left word for Dean to wait up for him but it was already 11:00 and he figured he could wake Fred in the morning.

95

Dean was knee-deep in a dream, trying to pull his Visa card away from Jeffrey Byrne, who was sitting on a cloud playing a harp, when his bedroom was suddenly filled with light. He jerked awake to see Fred O'Connor standing at the foot of his bed, in his Sunday go-a-courting clothes, a smirk upon his face. Arrested slumber was becoming a common occurrence in David Dean's bedroom.

"Sorry to wake you up, but we've got an important hot clue!"

Dean rubbed the sleep from his eyes. "Got what? What time is it?"

"It's only 1:15; Cora Abernathy's an early date. Listen, I checked out the names of the people who ordered the *Sentinel* and caught a winner! There's someone who had it sent to Scranton!"

"So?"

"Scranton, Pennsylvania! According to Byrne's expense account he was in Scranton for two days just before he shacked up at the Whitney Motel!"

Dean rubbed his bloodshot eyes. "He didn't shack up at the Whitney Motel." He mumbled a summary of his interview with the high school lover who'd lodged in the next room.

Fred dismissed the news with a wave of his hand. "That doesn't matter now. This here clue's a lot more important. Byrne was in Scranton on the sixth and seventh of April. The newspaper subscription was called in on April eight, the first day he's back in Parkside!" Dean yawned, refusing to open his eyes as Fred continued. "There's no listing in the Scranton phone book for this guy either!"

"What's his name?" Dean figured he ought to say something.

"J. Cleary, 157 Bascomb Place, Apartment C. You gotta check it out!"

That was the sum and substance of the conversation, as far as Dean could remember the following morning. If Fred had said more, Dean had fallen back asleep and missed it. He assumed he must have agreed to do something because Fred had finally turned out the light and left him alone. There was a note on his night-stand listing Cleary's address.

Dean was out of the house before Fred arose and the morning passed uneventfully with Dean, Harrigan and Tom DeLeo addressing the usual assortment of Parkside offenses. Rita typed the second expanded Byrne report, with only a mildly raised eyebrow after Dean explained more would be added later. He made some reference to the needs of the insurance company. Winston called to leave word he would see Dean tomorrow—Wednesday— at the safe house. He reiterated his concern for the utmost confidentiality concerning the location. Confidentiality, ha! Dean hoped he could find the place again.

After a late lunch on the run, Dean spent most of the afternoon interviewing a burglary victim only three blocks from his Collingswood Avenue home. It was the second break-in in the neighborhood in the last month. Things were returning to normal and in a strange way, Dean was glad of it.

Dean stopped by the office later in the afternoon to clean up a few details as he wouldn't be back in the office for two days— tomorrow, the safe house, Thursday a day off. Larry Harrigan was packing up to leave. He had finished his portion of the Byrne report and the interviews he'd conducted with Byrne's friends and associates.

"Case finished," he said as he added his file to Rita's desk.

Dean made no mention to Harrigan of his promise of more detailed documentation to Cynthia Byrne. This was already far enough beyond his official duties to make him feel a twinge of guilt. Harrigan, smiling as usual, was anxious to get home to his new wife and turned down Dean's offer of a beer.

Just as Dean was about to follow Harrigan out the door, Rita turned from the phone to tell Dean he had a visitor downstairs. He considered sneaking out the back door but it was still early and the look on Rita's face told him he'd better behave.

A young man in a tan jacket waited at the foot of the stairs looking ill at ease. Dean recognized Jackie Rudman, the employee from World Wide Insurance in Philadelphia. He remembered the young man mentioning he had a sister in Parkside. Dean offered him a seat but he declined.

"Sis needed me to babysit," he said, as if to apologize for his weekday presence in Parkside. "I just thought I'd stop by."

"Nice to see you," Dean said, waiting to hear the real reason for Rudman's visit.

"I worked with Jeff, see? All the guys told you what a straight arrow he was." He moved from one foot to the other. "But that ain't so."

"Go on."

"I saw Jeff having lunch with this girl just a few weeks ago. I got thinking about it and figured maybe you ought to know."

"Why didn't you say something when I was in the office?"

"Look, I'm just trying to help," he answered defensively.

"There are a lot of business reasons to have lunch with a girl, or anyone else," Dean offered.

"Not with this girl. It was Cece Baldwin. Take my word for it, there was no business reason for Jeff to be having lunch with Cece Baldwin—just monkey business. I ought to know. And she quit two weeks ago." Dean started to say something but Rudman shoved a piece of paper at him. "Here. This is her address. I don't want to start nothing—don't tell her it was me who told you." He turned and left without another word.

Dean waited until he was home before looking at the address Rudman had given him. He had stopped off for a bowl of spaghetti so it was 7:00 before he dialed the girl's Bala Cynwyd, Pennsylvania number. The ringing went unanswered, but at least the phone hadn't been disconnected.

Fred came in just as Dean was hanging up. Dean explained about his visit from Byrne's fellow employee and the young man's story about the possible girl friend. Fred didn't seem surprised. "Churchy la fem," he said, on his way up the stairs to bed. Dean expected a spirited argument at the very least, but tomorrow was Wednesday, Atlantic City day, and Fred needed a good night's sleep.


Wednesday morning dawned with air so crisp Dean was awake before the alarm, awake to a knock down gorgeous day, "one of the ten best" prattled a cheery voice on the kitchen table radio. Even the drive to the Poconos went well, with Dean only making two wrong turns. Baratto and Winston were alone in the safe house when Dean entered.

"Where are the rest of the federal troops?" Dean asked as he took the cup of coffee Winston offered.

"They're checking some of the info our good pal Vinnie gave us. But, if I were guessing, I'd say he's still holding out on us."

"I told you. The whole damn thing is a mistake. I just can't get nobody to believe me." Vinnie paced up and down, grumbling like a bear on the first day of spring.

"Let's hear it again," said Winston with a sigh.

"I already told you about 50 times," Baratto protested.

"Dean hasn't heard it," Winston said.

Vinnie plopped down at the kitchen table. "It was all because of the chicks," he began. "Me and Billie and Willie had these three broads lined up but the twins had this job to do first. They were supposed to do it alone but I rode along with them so's we could get a head start on meeting up with the girls afterwards, you know? We had these two big-ass suitcases in the trunk of the Caddy and we was to go down this highway 'til someone phoned us and told us what to do. Right on cue we gets this call to pull into a closed down rest area. We have to drive around the barricades and all. When we get there, we open up the trunk and drop these two suitcases back by the building, just like they told us. It's dark out, as black as Winston here, and we drop 'em and scoot. That was it. We weren't there a minute, I swear. Then we get this call and tell 'em it's done and they say turn off at the next exit and get the hell out of there. So that's what we do—we go back to the broads." He looked at them as if to be congratulated. "Only a couple of days later we hear all hell's broken loose 'cause something ain't where it's supposed to be."

Winston explained to Dean. "When there's a major drug buy, nobody trusts anyone else—especially face to face. This way, as soon as one car makes its drop, the other car is signaled to drop the product at another location and it comes out even. There's no advance notice except the general area. It works perfectly."

"'Cept this time it didn't," Baratto cut in.

Winston continued. "No one can follow the car and beat the pick up to the spot— it happens too quickly. They know the time, distance and location of the car and say 'turn in' at the last minute. It's usually foolproof."

"So what happened?" asked Dean.

Winston paced up and down. "I assume the Colombians think the family tried to rip them off and the family figures it the other way around. Or, they both think our friend here and his buddies the Wassermann twins are all a few bucks richer! In any event, there's a lot of money missing and both sides are at war over it. It's practically halted distribution. It gives you a hint why the whole crowd wants to carve up Mr. Baratto a piece at a time."

"It must have been one hell of a drop," Dean said.

"Angie the Mule heard it was 2.8 million bucks," said Baratto glumly. "I swear on my old lady's head we never touched a nickel of it—never even opened the damn suitcases. We got off the highway where we were supposed to and drove back to Scranton to see the broads."

"Scranton's popping up a lot lately," Dean muttered, more to himself than the others.

"In connection with the Byrne case?" asked Winston, his interest piqued.

Dean dismissed the comment with a wave of his hand, sorry he'd opened his mouth. "It was one of the branches offices Byrne serviced, that's all."

"Hey! Byrne's that guy who was supposed to have drowned! I read about him! Maybe he swiped the dough and skipped!" Baratto looked from one to the other.

"Stop grabbing at straws, Vinnie," Winston said sternly.

"Well, somebody took the dough and it weren't me or the twins."

"When did all this happen?" Dean asked, changing the subject.

"A couple of months ago. Like I told you, when the twins found out half the state was after their ass, they laid low—for a long time, couple of months. The heat wouldn't let up." He stopped to think, an arduous task. "It was a Thursday. I know, because the twins always went up to Scranton on Wednesday night 'cause that's when this country and western band they liked played. That's where they met these broads. It was way back in March."

"What highway was the drop on?" Dean asked.

"I-84. We got off at an exit for a state park. Kingdom Come or something. The closed-down rest stop was just before it. You think maybe Byrne might have swiped the dough?"

It was Winston who answered, anger in his voice. "Vinnie, this guy Byrne's life was as far away from yours as the Pope's from a whorehouse. Just keep talking to me and stop chasing dreams."

Vinnie looked like a hurt kid. "Hey, somebody ripped off the bucks and if you find who, I'm off the hook."

Winston rose and steered Dean out to the porch abruptly. Dean had the feeling he was in trouble and Winston seemed to search for the right words to say. "What's the standing of this Byrne business?" he finally growled.

"It's closed—officially."

"Good. Let's leave it that way. There's not a chance in a million your boy was 50 miles from the drop so don't give Baratto any excuse to clam up on me." Dean started to say something but Winston cut him off. "Let's drop it. Okay?"

Dean, feeling duly chastised, didn't mention the subject again, nor did Baratto. The questioning continued throughout the day but Dean's mind was not on it. It was total nonsense to even consider the million-to-one-shot coincidence that Byrne was somehow involved with the missing money but his mind wouldn't leave it alone. He kept sorting through the facts as he knew them and argued with himself on the long drive back to Parkside. Someone grabbed the dough and Dean didn't believe Baratto or the twins had either the brains or nerve to pull off a heist like that, much less stay mum about it for months. If they had, why stick around and pretend otherwise? It didn't make sense. One thing was certain, Fred O'Connor would jump on this new angle like Ellery Queen! It was right out of one of his books. Too bad it was Wednesday, Atlantic City day.

After a quick supper of pastrami and fruit at Uncle Sally's Galley, Dean pedaled 27 hard miles, working up a good sweat and a painful case of shin splints. He was still wobbly as he stood in the hot shower while the sun dipped below the horizon. He felt good, though he couldn't put his finger on the reason. The Byrne case was closed but in spite of Winston's admonishment, the matter wouldn't leave his mind. All he needed was a nice brick wall to halt the nagging speculation Byrne might have skipped—like a body or something equally definitive. Instead, there were sneaky little maybes and what-ifs. Perhaps his continued attachment to the case was simple curiosity or his promise to Cynthia Byrne to be thorough, or, he reluctantly admitted, a reason to maintain contact with the attractive woman. Or maybe it was the intriguing matter of 2.8 million dollars.

Three more telephone calls to Cece Baldwin were as unsuccessful as the first and Dean spent the rest of the evening poring over the Byrne file. He paid particular attention to the March expense accounts and itineraries. Jeffrey Byrne spent Tuesday and Wednesday in early March in Scranton. He listed *Markham Party on Thursday*, but no overnight lodging. His evening dinner tab was $23.88 and the receipt showed pizza and beer. Dean had no way of checking Byrne's mileage and if by chance he had detoured east on Interstate 84, probably 30 miles further, instead of taking the more direct south-easterly route between Scranton and Parkside. Milage logs were kept not with the drivers but with the pool cars, and World Wide must have more than 100.

Dean was still shuffling papers when Fred ambled in the door. The beautiful sounds of The Coleman Hawkins Quartet doing "The Man I Love" as it ought to be done were playing and Mrs. Lincoln never looked more content. The smile on Dean's face made Fred wonder which cat swallowed which canary.

"I won 67 dollars," Fred said. "Two winning weeks in a row!"

Dean let him explain the details of his latest roulette system until Fred asked Dean for an update on the events of the day. Dean presented the facts unemotionally but as soon as he mentioned Scranton, the old man caught the coincidence and could hardly contain himself. Dean laughed. "Give me a plausible scenario."

Fred thought a minute. "Try this on for size. You're in Scranton on business. You go out with the local World Wide guy and have pizza and beer—lots of beer, considering what he spent. Then you start home."

"Wrong direction. He'd take the turnpike extension south. Going due east out I-84 is way out of his way. Two sides of a triangle instead of one."

"We'll work on that part. Maybe World Wide has business in Milford, Pennsylvania. That's on the Delaware river—on the Jersey border."

"Keep going. We don't know, but for the sake of discussion, let's say it's the night the money turned up missing. Then what?"

Fred thought a minute. "Milford's 50 or 60 miles from Scranton. Before you get there, what do you have to do?"

"Fred, you ought to write your mystery books, not just read them."

The old man was undeterred. "Seriously, what do you have to do? I'll tell you—you have to pee! You just had a pitcher of beer or two, right?"

"Remember, Mrs. Byrne said Jeffrey wasn't much of a drinker."

Fred brushed that aside and continued. "But it's late at night and there's nothing along the Interstate. Then there's a sign for a rest area so you start to pull in but it's closed. You're ticked off; your bladder's full, so you drive in anyway."

"If you followed the car making the drop, someone would have shot you."

"Maybe you were in front of it! Maybe you're modest or scared you'll get caught so you pull way up out of sight and while you're doing your business, this other car comes in, leaves a couple of suitcases and drives away!"

Dean held up Mrs. Lincoln and looked her in the eye. "Doesn't Mr. O'Connor have a marvelous imagination, pussy cat?"

Fred was on a roll as Dean knew he'd be. "On the spur of the moment you pick up the suitcases, put them in your trunk, and drive off. Do you open them first?" He answered his own question. "No—you just want to get out of there. Then you start to get worried. You know whatever's in there, it don't belong to you."

"If you're an honest, law-abiding guy, like everyone says Jeffrey Byrne was or is, why don't you just turn it in to the closest police station? There's a State Police Barracks somewhere along that Interstate." Fred thought a minute, but Dean answered his own question. "You've had a snoot full of beer and you're driving. The last thing you want to do is walk into a police station with a couple of suitcases of what's most likely stolen money."

"That's what I was gonna say," Fred muttered. "When you see what you've got, you're in a tizzy. There's no one you can tell. You don't know what to do so you take the next day off when you're sober, find some quiet motel and try and figure out what you've got or what to do with the stuff."

"That doesn't take all day, does it?"

Fred shrugged as he paced up and down the room. "Two-point-eight million! Maybe it takes that long to count it! This guy's got the answer to every little kid's what-would-you-do-if-you-had-a-million-bucks question. Only he really has it. Unmarked and no one could tie it to him in a hundred years! What a scenario, huh?"

"So, what *does* he do?" prompted Dean.

"He looks around for a place to stash the dough and start a new identity. He rents an address, not too close to Parkside but not too far away, like maybe Scranton!"

Dean thought a minute. "Scranton is close to where he grabbed the dough. If it were me, I'd go in the opposite direction."

Fred considered. "He'd need a place where he was supposed to go frequently, so's no one would get suspicious. Maybe Scranton was the best spot to fill the bill. It's the closest city with a World Wide branch to Parkside. Bingo! Mr. J. Cleary is born!" He smiled from ear to ear. "So, do you buy it?"

"Not for a minute—but it's a great story."

"Tell me what's wrong?" Fred asked, a bit peeved.

"It's total speculation. There isn't a lick of evidence to put Byrne anywhere near that dough. If I went to Leland Anderson with this I'd be back directing traffic—if Jonathan Winston didn't nail me first for not following his orders."

"What about J. Cleary and the newspaper?"

"What about it? That's a total stretch. If you're Byrne, why order the Parkside paper way back in April? Byrne could read his own copy for at least another month. After he's gone missing, I can buy wanting to know what's going on back home but a month before he skips is too soon. I'll bet Cleary is a legitimate customer."

"One way to find out," Fred said with a smug smile. "Tomorrow you've got a comp day off. Let's you and me take a little drive to Scranton and meet Mr. Cleary."

"It would be a wasted day," Dean answered but his voice lacked conviction and he couldn't think of a good excuse.

"You've got to admit it answers a bunch of questions. I think it deserves a look-see, right?" Fred prodded. Then he added, "I'll take care of lunch."

That was a first—Fred volunteering to buy. Just a short pleasure trip on his day off, Dean lied to himself. Maybe Scranton would provide the brick wall he was looking for and end this silly speculation. His curiosity won the argument. "Okay, Fred. You earned the trip, even though it's a waste of time."

Fred's reaction startled Mrs. Lincoln from the sofa. Dean smiled, gave a wave goodnight and climbed the stairs. There was no way he would admit it, but his personal scenario matched Fred O'Connor's to a tee, even though his practical side was embarrassed to even consider the possibility. Neither slept very well that night, and Dean was awake before the alarm, up fixing the morning coffee.

# CHAPTER IX

**THURSDAY, MAY 13, 1999  8:00 A.M.**

Scranton, Pennsylvania is one of those eastern cities whose past glories were years earlier than the memory of any living citizen. The city had struggled through the drabness of poverty and joblessness in an effort to raise itself from the ashes of long-dead industries. The effort, while commendable, was not wholly successful. The city had a tired, old look about it, especially in neighborhoods like the purported residence of J. Cleary.

One fifty-seven Bascomb Place was a drab old building in a drab old section of the city with a faded "For Rent" sign permanently fixed to the front. It listed apartments, furnished or unfurnished and a telephone number, just in case someone should happen by. Fred wrote the number on his note pad. Four apartments, cleverly labeled A, B, C, and D were visible through the grimy windowpane of the front door. There were two units on either side, on both floors, divided by a central hall and staircase. Four mailboxes with corresponding letters were visible just inside the door: Apartment A listed the name, Aaron Levy, while B appeared vacant. Second floor apartment D showed the name Burgess but C, where J. Cleary was to reside, was also empty. Dean pushed each of the four buzzers, with zero response.

Fred tried the outside door and found it open. The years of habitation gave the place a thousand smells, none of them pleasant. A rap on the doors of the bottom two apartments brought no better results than the doorbell. They climbed the stairs but there was no sign of life and no answer to knocks. The door to C was bolted with a new padlock.

"It looks like our Mr. Cleary flew the coop," Fred said reluctantly. Dean agreed.

"The poor guy's probably some henpecked bank teller who rented this place trying to shack up with a honey and struck out. And here we are, acting like two heavies from the Church of Yesterday's Morals giving him a hard time."

Dean had given Fred the business the entire trip from Parkside but the old man remained undeterred. "Sex-starved bank tellers don't go subscribing to out of town newspapers," Fred grumbled in response.

It was still early and Dean figured they'd get back to Parkside in time for a few hours of biking. There was an upscale coffee shop a couple of blocks away and Fred suggested they stop for coffee. The place catered to the espresso crowd but Dean acquiesced.

"I'll order for us," Fred said. "Just give me a ten." Fred motioned to the telephone across the room. "You can call the landlord from here." Dean raised his eyebrows. "You ain't thinking of giving up so soon, are you?"

Protesting was out of the question. If Dean balked, Fred wouldn't be fit to live with. He handed the old man ten dollars and was handed a slip of paper with the phone number from the rental sign

Mrs. Glass was apparently an early riser and answered the phone on the second ring. She listened patiently to Dean's detailed explanation that he was from the police and interested in a tenant, Mr. J. Cleary of Bascomb Place. She promptly asked if he wanted a furnished or unfurnished apartment. Utilizing the best of his detective training, he deduced she was as deaf as a turnip.

With the combination of patience and increased volume, Dean managed to obtain her address and a promise she would see them, if they gave her 20 minutes to "freshen herself up." Dean returned to the table and conveyed the news as he picked up his coffee—no roll, no change.

"I have an address," Dean added. "All we have to do is find it, spend ten minutes yelling at an old lady and then get back to Parkside."

Fred nodded, sipped at his tea and made a face.

"What's a matter?" Dean asked as he sniffed a highly flavored—and apparently expensive—coffee.

"All I wanted was a cup of tea," said Fred as they killed time. "You'd think that would be a simple request. Instead they ask me if I want some Burmese Rain forest mixture or some leaves pressed by cloistered nuns in Nepal. What ever happened to Arthur Godfrey and regular ol' Lipton tea?"

"Who's Arthur Godfrey?" Dean asked with a smile as he took a sip of his sweet mixture. "What did you get me?"

"I just pointed," came the muttered reply.

Neither finished his beverage; Fred because he was anxious to get going and Dean because he could only take a small dose of the perfumed blend. A bearded counter man in bare feet pointed them off in the right direction. They were still early when ten minutes later they located Mrs. Glass's address.

Mrs. Glass ushered them into a frilly little apartment in a restored brownstone located in a neighborhood that was a marked improvement over Bascomb Place. They were seated on the type of furniture you're afraid will break, amid a thousand little figurines of dancing girls that must have presented a monumental dusting job. If the figurines were representative of Mrs. Glass's past, it was an era 50 years and 200 pounds earlier.

Fred O'Connor immediately took charge and played the woman like an old harmonica. He was not only able to control the volume of his voice without appearing to yell, but had her giggling like a schoolgirl in a matter of minutes. After the amenities were put to rest, Fred casually mentioned they were interested in Mr. Cleary, on Bascomb Place.

"Oh, yes. Bascomb Place. It's so hard to keep good people down there." She went on to explain she had 68 apartments scattered about the city with 22 vacancies. Life was tough. "Terrible, simply terrible," she complained.

"Mr. Cleary?" Dean prodded gently.

"A fine gentleman, most certainly. Never gives me a speck of concern."

Dean wished he'd brought the picture of Jeffrey Byrne that World Wide had recently sent but it remained in the case file at the office. "Could you describe Mr. Cleary?" he asked.

She took her time considering her answer. "He sounded like a handsome looking gentleman, but I really couldn't tell you." Dean looked at her, awaiting an explanation. Mrs. Glass added, "You see, I've never met Mr. Cleary."

Cleary had contacted her by telephone, saying he was looking for a furnished apartment to use when he traveled to the city. She referred him to Bascomb Place and offered to meet him there. He said he was pressed for time and declined. A day later he called again, saying he had driven by the place and was willing to take it, sight unseen. She wouldn't normally have rented on that basis but he sent her three months payment, in cash, and she left a key in an agreed location. Later she went by to meet him, but not only was he not in, he had changed the lock. Mrs. Glass considered complaining but with 22 vacancies she didn't want to antagonize a new tenant and jeopardize a three-month advance.

The original telephone call had come on April sixth. Fred stage-whispered to Dean that the sixth was one of the dates when Byrne was in Scranton. The apartment had been rented the following day—the day of the newspaper subscription. Fred now wore an "I-told-you-so," smile as broad as Mrs. Glass.

"Mr. Cleary mostly comes at night I suspect. There hasn't been any mail for quite awhile but the rent is still paid—for another two months."

Fred mentioned there was no name on the mailbox for apartment C. Mrs. Glass said there had been a name the last time she was there, a couple of weeks ago.

She looked perplexed. "I suppose I'll have to get a locksmith if he doesn't send me the key." Mrs. Glass shook her head. "I'm sorry I wasn't much help to you but I just never met Mr. Cleary...or his friend."

Both men said, in unison, "Friend?"

Mrs. Glass snickered. "Pat Corbin. I'm just guessing, mind you, but I think our Mr. Cleary rented the place so the two of them could have a little rendezvous, if you know what I mean." She patted Fred's knee playfully. "Boys will be boys, you know."

"Churchy la fem," Fred said, loud enough for Dean to hear but below Mrs. Glass's audio perception.

Dean ignored him and turned to Mrs. Glass. "How did you find out about the roommate?"

"The mailbox. I still have a key to it. I was going to give him a note about the new lock. I saw the two or three letters in there."

"What kind of letters were they?" asked Dean, a little too loudly.

"Goodness, I wouldn't know. I'm not snoopy!"

"Tell me about the downstairs tenant in the building, Aaron Levy," Fred asked.

"Mr. Levy was one of my best tenants. Always on time. He was there for seven years. He did something at the university. He played that boom, boom, boom classical music all the time. Between you and me, I think he chased out some of the earlier tenants with the volume. I could hear it before I'd get to the front door. I don't know if you noticed, but I have a little hearing problem."

"You said *was* a good tenant?" Fred prodded.

"Mr. Levy departed."

"Did he leave a forwarding address?" Dean asked.

"You best check with his Rabbi. Mr. Levy *departed*." Mrs. Glass bowed her head.

Fred joined her as Dean felt his ears redden. "And Mr. Burgees?" Fred asked after a proper moment of silence.

"Oh, he's a nice man too—he's in construction. At first he paid a few days late but I had a little talk with him and he's straightened out nicely. Been here nearly a year but his project will be over soon and he'll be gone too—but not *departed*." She smiled at Fred, as if sharing their little joke. "Dear me, that will make 23 vacancies—24 if Mr. Cleary is gone too." Dean's multiplication table of 44, the number of *rented* apartments, wasn't perfect, but that number times even a reasonable monthly rental lessened any sympathy he might have felt for the woman's financial plight.

She rose, a clear indication she'd devoted enough time to these non-paying visitors. They took their leave with her following them to the door, babbling on about unrelated subjects. Dean managed to hand her his business card but she seemed to dismiss it, with eyes only for the charming Fred O'Connor.

"Do come back when we can spend more time together. You're such a charming man...." she crooned.

Once on the street, Dean put up a halting hand. "Don't start! It's probably some traveling salesman who has a local married dame...."

"I can't believe you don't buy this! You're as stubborn as my uncle Henry and his Studebaker! It's as plain as the nose on your face! All we have to do is find out who this female is and she'll lead us right to the both of them! It's most likely the girl from his office, Cece what's-her-name. *Cece*—C. C.—like Cleary-Corbin!"

Dean kept his silence lest he have to hear *why* Uncle Henry and/or his automobile was considered the epitome of stubbornness. He didn't bother to point out that Bala Cynwyd, Cece Baldwin's address, was near Philadelphia, the opposite direction from Parkside. But their little sojourn to Scranton had not yielded once and for all what Dean had hoped for, a dead end to close off speculation on this business.

The return trip took them past Bascomb Place and as they rounded the corner, Fred yelled "Stop!" so violently Dean thought he was about to run down an unseen nun. After a frenzied honk and finger from a following motorist, Fred pointed out a man alighting from a bicycle and climbing the steps of 137. Dean pulled to the curb.

The man was about Dean's age, shorter, with dark hair and moustache and dressed in full biking attire. Fred was out of the car and had introduced himself and Dean before Dean could open his mouth.

"Nice bike," Dean said as he stuck out his hand.

"Chip Burgess," the man answered. "Yeah, this is one slick pair of wheels."

Fred O'Connor looked peeved that Dean delayed the interrogation by taking time to discuss biking. Fred could have Mrs. Glass and her ilk—Dean was now in his element. He and Burgess learned they'd both biked in the same 100-mile fund raiser two years earlier, before Dean caught a case of the lazies.

"We're interested in one of the tenants," Fred finally broke in.

"He croaked," Burgess answered as he turned to show Dean his gearing derailleur.

"The second floor tenant."

The statement caught Burgess's attention. "That's me."

"No. We mean the other guy—J. Cleary."

Burgess turned his full attention to Fred, a concerned look on his face. "Why?"

"Police business," Fred said before Dean could answer. The statement didn't reduce Burgess's concern an iota. He looked totally unnerved.

Dean stepped forward. "No big deal. We're just following up on a missing person. We thought it might be this Cleary fellow. Has he been around?"

Burgess stepped back, holding up his hand in a halting motion. "Whoa! What's this all about?"

Dean produced his identification as Burgess bit his lip.

"What's the problem?" Dean asked, trying to keep it light.

"I don't know. Like, I don't want to get someone in trouble. How did you know he's here? Has he done something?"

Dean ignored his question. "Can you describe him?"

"I don't really know the guy."

"You've seen him, haven't you?" Fred asked.

"A couple of times. He ain't around much."

"Look," Dean said. "If he's some married guy shacking up with his honey, we don't care. This is really pretty routine."

"Who's this guy you're looking for?"

"We're not at liberty to say," Fred quoted from a recent novel.

"I don't want some dangerous criminal living next door. I mean, look at this neighborhood. And I'm the only other person in the building! I don't want my stuff ripped off or something. He could kill me and no one would find my body—for months!"

Dean smiled and patted Burgess on the shoulder. "I'm sure Mrs. Glass would find you the first day rent's overdue."

Burgess smiled too. "Yeah, there's that. She's a beaut, isn't she?"

"How about it? If you'll just tell us what Cleary looks like we'll get out of your hair."

"Well, he was average height, I guess—not fat—not skinny. Blond hair or maybe light brown—not black. About my age—40."

"Did you talk with him?"

"Not really. Just 'how you doing' stuff and a nod."

"What kind of car does he drive?"

"I don't know. You park on the street where you can find a place. I never saw him with a car."

"Tell us about Pat Corbin. Did you see her?"

Burgess looked truly baffled. "Her?"

Fred spoke up. "Mrs. Glass said there was someone named Pat Corbin living in the same apartment as Cleary."

"How'd she know that?"

"Fished in the mail box," Fred offered, to Dean's dismay.

"I never saw no one—except Cleary. I guess it was Cleary—he never said his name but that's what's on the mailbox."

"Not anymore. The box is blank. Has he moved out?"

"How would I know? He's hardly ever there anyway."

Nor had Burgess heard any noise or conversation from apartment C to indicate there was anyone there—much less more than one person. Cleary had bumped into him only twice, maybe three times but he had no recollection of the dates. Mostly, he felt the apartment was empty. Yes, he'd noticed the new padlock, but didn't see it being installed. He spent little time on Bascomb Place himself.

"I'm in construction," he said. "I just rented this joint for a place to sleep—after I totaled my truck and couldn't get home easy. Strictly a temporary pad—home's in Jersey." Burgess added glumly that he used to have a wife there.

"Day off today?" Dean asked.

He seemed to pause. "The job's just clean up now that the tenant's in. Punch list stuff. They're inspecting today and we can't go forward until some bureaucrat clears us." Then he added, "If I see Cleary, should I tell him you're looking for him or what?"

"Just give me a call," Dean answered. "He's probably cleared out but let us know if you spot him." Then he added, "There's not much chance he's the guy we're looking for."

"Why did you think your missing guy was Cleary?" he asked again.

"The man's from Parkside and Cleary subscribed to a newspaper from there." Fred's statement volunteered far more then Dean would have offered and he cringed at the old man's candor.

Dean asked if he sent Burgess a picture of the man, if he could try and identify it. Burgess hesitated, and agreed, but when Dean asked for a phone number to follow up, Burgess said he didn't have one. "Send me the picture here and I'll call you," he answered.

There was nothing more to learn and Burgess excused himself and entered the building.

"He ain't the brightest bulb on the Christmas tree, is he?" Fred muttered as soon as he was gone. "But the description of Cleary is a dead ringer for Byrne. Too bad you forgot to bring the photo or we'd have this caper locked up."

"The description fits everyone but a red-headed midget or a woman. We don't know any more than when we got up this morning!"

They argued their way back to Parkside with Dean playing the devil's advocate while Fred quoted a dozen mystery stories that bore out his hypothesis, a hypothesis that grew in detail with each passing mile.

"Why get mail at a shack-up place, much less the newspaper?" Fred asked. Dean had no ready answer. Admittedly, Cleary was an enigma, but there remained no real connection to Byrne. But to Fred's mind, Cleary was Byrne, and nothing could dissuade him.

Fred wanted to drive the extra 30 miles or more and visit the rest stop drop location but Dean put his foot down, pointing out that it was two months earlier when the money disappeared. Fred grumbled, but didn't protest too strenuously. When Dean pointed out a nice restaurant where he could collect the lunch he'd earned for making the trip, Fred reached over to the back seat and produced a paper bag, containing two peanut butter and jelly sandwiches and an apple.

Dean still hoped to get some biking in during the remainder of his day off but the weather turned decidedly unpleasant as they pulled into Parkside. Real bikers weren't bothered by a little rain, he tried to tell himself, but the car radio spoke of a storm system moving up from the south, bringing with it high winds and torrential rain. The warmth of Collingswood and a soft chair won the argument. He was resigned to quietly reading a book until Mrs. Porter the housekeeper showed up a day early, accommodating a family wedding, and Dean's peace began competing with the sounds of a vacuum cleaner and Mrs. Porter's radio music, even worse junk than Fred's usual selections.

He moseyed to the kitchen to bolster his sparse lunch where he found Fred eating sauerkraut, a gift from a neighbor lady, directly from a jar.

"God, Fred. That'll give you more gas than the Hindenberg," Dean said but he couldn't be sure he was heard over the din of music and vacuum.

Finally, he donned his jacket and escaped up the street to a luncheonette where he ordered pie and ice cream. On the spur of the moment he picked up the phone and dialed Cece Baldwin, a number he now had committed to memory from the many unsuccessful times he'd made the call. Surprisingly, a woman's voice answered on the first ring. Dean introduced himself and told her he was interested in discussing Jeffrey Byrne.

There was a long pause. "I go to work at 5:30," she answered.

"May I meet you someplace? It won't take much time." She agreed to meet him at a highway coffee shop he remembered on the outskirts of Bala Cynwyd, in an hour and a half. Dean didn't stop at the house, knowing he'd have to explain his trip to Fred and take him along. This chore he wanted to do alone.

Cece Baldwin was the only person seated at the counter when Dean arrived at the designated shop, only a few minutes before the allotted time. She was a pretty girl, but not in a way that would attract much attention. She was no more than 20 or 21, he guessed. A stack of books rested in front of her and she sipped a cup of black coffee. There was a sad but determined look about the young lady.

"Hi," she said as he sat. "I guess you're the cop." She continued to sip her coffee.

Dean ordered a cup and showed her his credentials, but she hardly glanced at them. "You don't seem surprised to have me contact you," he asked, "How come?"

"Denise—one of the girls in the file room—said the police were doing a check on Jeff. I figured you'd get to me sooner or later."

"Why?"

She sighed. "Because someone was sure to have spotted us together. I know that office. Everybody thinks everybody else is sleeping with each other just because half of them are."

"Jeffrey Byrne was..." he hesitated, "...a friend of yours?"

She stared down at her cup. "Yes."

"You cared for him?"

She looked Dean straight in the eye. "Yes, I cared for him. He was the only one up there who had a lick of decency. It's a damn shame what happened to him. I cried for three days."

"Were you having an affair with him?" She immediately rose and started to leave. He reached out and stopped her. "I'm sorry. That was out of line."

"You bet your ass it was. Why can't two people talk to each other without the rest of the world thinking they're screwing their brains out? Who sicced you on me, anyway?"

Normally Dean wouldn't have considered for a minute betraying a confidence, but somehow he felt this young girl deserved to know. "Jackie Rudman. Young, blond hair, skinny. He saw you and Jeffrey Byrne having lunch."

"I know him. The little bastard. He followed me everywhere."

"Why?" Dean asked.

"Because the creep was hot for me and I wouldn't give him the time of day. He got really nasty."

"There are laws against that sort of thing, you know."

"Oh, sure," she said sarcastically. "If you don't need a job. Who was I supposed to tell? Mayer? He was almost as bad as Jackie. He couldn't keep his hands off half the office. There wasn't a soul up there who'd believe me. Except Jeff Byrne. He was the only decent person in the whole shitty place."

*Here we go again,* thought Dean. *Saint Jeffrey.*

"Rudman was the worst—he wouldn't let me alone. You know what he did? He said if I didn't go out with him, everyone up there would, 'know about me,' whatever that means. That's the kind of prick he is. You wouldn't believe what shit went on up there, just because I told a couple of those jerks what I thought about them pawing me."

"Tell me about Jeffrey Byrne." Dean asked quietly. He was beginning to like this girl who had hurt written all over her.

"He was the nicest guy I ever met. That's God's honest truth. He didn't want anything—he was nice without a reason. He found me crying in the stairwell one day and just took my arm and hauled me down to this little restaurant on Walnut. Never even asked. He just ordered for me and made me eat it. He didn't even ask why I was crying. I figured he was going to hit on me but he never did nothing. After that, sometimes we'd talk together. He got me to go back to school. He'd leave little notes on my desk sometimes, saying 'Stick with school,' or sometimes he'd send a postcard from his business trips saying the same thing."

"Did he send one from Norfolk?" Dean asked.

She shook her head no. "I was kind of hoping he did, after I heard." Dean thought she might cry but she continued. "I have this night waitress job now; it isn't so bad. I can study in between 'cause they don't do much business after supper. I'm going to get an education and a decent job." She looked away. "I only had lunch with him three or four times and those bastards tell you I'm...."

Dean put his hand on her shoulder. "No one said anything about you and Byrne except Rudman and we can discount anything out of his mouth, can't we? You're doing great, just keep it up. You don't have a thing to prove to anyone except yourself. You're doing that just fine."

"You know what Jeff said? He said about 99 percent of the people in the world just go along and let things happen to them. There's only a few who get the chance to do exactly what they want to, and they'd better grab it and run before responsibilities tie 'em up in knots and circumstances dictate their life for them. That's why I went back to school. I may not make it, but it won't be because I didn't give it a shot. I'm doing it—me, myself and I—no one else."

"They're holding a memorial service for Jeffrey Byrne next week. You should come up to Parkside. I think he'd have liked your being there." Dean spoke tenderly.

"I've got classes." She said it without hesitation and turned away. Silence followed for a moment before she added, "No, that's a lie. But I won't go anyway. I won't give those shit heads the satisfaction of seeing me cry. I'll do my praying and crying alone."

Cece Baldwin rose to leave and smiled a sad but pretty smile. She insisted on paying for her own coffee. Dean let her. She needed that. After leaving the building, when they were out on the street, she turned back to him.

"If Jeff had wanted, I'd have slept with him—in a minute. But you know, I'm kinda glad he didn't ask." She turned a corner and was gone.

His conversation with Cece Baldwin bothered him all the way back to Parkside. It reminded him of his talk with Monica Cutler on Monday. Everyone else's life seemed to have some force in it, a force that was driving it forward, something much stronger than his life that was plodding along like a Sunday walk to nowhere.

Dean was within ten miles of Parkside before he noticed a blue Ford that had stayed behind him for an unusual length of time. He watched it for a few minutes and then turned quickly to the right. The Ford followed. Dean slowed. So did the Ford. Dean sped up to 80 miles an hour and turned across three lanes to an exit while the Ford tried vainly, but unsuccessfully, to follow. As soon as he had lost the tail, he was sorry, sorry he'd played games and ditched it instead of trying to find out who was following him. Jonathan Winston was sure to ask.

When Dean returned to Collingswood Avenue, Fred was knee-deep in either his notes or another mystery novel, Dean didn't notice which. He filled Fred in on his conversation with Cece Baldwin and tried to dismiss the entire case as a waste of time. Once again there was no evidence to make Jeffrey Byrne's death anything but an accidental drowning. Still, Fred refused to agree.

It was Thursday evening and Dean showered and drove over to Ethel Rosewater's luxury apartment where the preliminaries seemed to move along even quicker than usual.

"I have a court case at 9:00," she said, "Let's get rolling." She finished the drink she was holding in one gulp and crossed to where he was standing. She looked him in the eye, silhouetted in the glow from beneath the door, the only light in the nearly dark room, and began to undo his belt.

Later, partway through Act I, Dean asked, "Ethel, how come you always have sex with the lights out?"

"Do you like screwing me or not?" she asked, somewhat sarcastically.

"Certainly."

"Then stop trying to get in my head and work harder at getting in my pants."

It was a one-round night and he was home before 11:00. He hadn't even remembered to check to see if she was wearing her Thursday panties.

# CHAPTER X

Friday morning had a yellow cast about it as if something ominous was about to take place. When Dean struck out at the alarm clock, he sent it flying across the room. It lay there, under the bureau, ringing away, as if out of spite for the mayhem he'd thrust upon it. It had an industrial size spring and continued its metallic scream for what seemed like five minutes as Dean buried his head beneath the pillow. No sooner had it expired when the phone took up the chorus. Dean clawed out a hand and answered it.

It was Leland Anderson. "Get your ass out of bed and down here. That guy Byrne's body floated in." He hung up, giving no further details.

Dean showered Ethel Rosewater from his body, shaved and dressed in a daze. Before leaving, he rapped on Fred's door and yelled the message, not waiting for a response. Finally, there was a nice, solid brick wall ending speculation on this matter. The photograph of Jeffrey Byrne he'd mailed to Chip Burgess in Scranton yesterday had been unnecessary. Mr. J. Cleary was safe to shack up with whomever he pleased, be it Pat Corbin or anyone else! Jeffrey Byrne had finally put it all to rest by making his appearance on the incoming tide.

It was only 7:20 when Dean entered the squad room but Rita Angeltoni was already glued to her keyboard as if she'd spent the night. Two airline tickets were on Dean's desk. Without looking up or pausing in her typing she issued directions.

119

"Norfolk called but there aren't any details. Some guy out on a yacht with his family spotted the body floating in the middle of the bay and hauled it in like Hemingway's fish. Leland wants you to go down there with Mrs. Byrne so she can identify her husband. There's two tickets. The weather's shitty so you'd better stop by your place and pick up some clothes in case you get stuck and can't fly back tonight. Your buddy Detective Norman Hunter is off fishing somewhere so you're supposed to go directly to the morgue on your own. It was too late to get a non-stop flight so I have you going out of Allentown and changing planes in Baltimore. At least you skip the Philly traffic. Someone already called Mrs. Byrne. She's waiting for you at her house. The flight's at 10:00 and they say it's on time, in spite of the weather."

"How come Parkside is springing for this trip? This is 'way above and beyond."

"It's all part of our huggy-feely PR campaign so Leland won't have to take any more crap from the Ice Lady at the *Sentinel*," Rita answered, still without a break in the rapid fire typing.

While spending the day with Cynthia Byrne was of itself a pleasant contemplation, accompanying relatives to identify corpses, especially those that had been under water for a week, was, in Dean's estimation, right up there with root canals and swift kicks in the you-know-whats. Why had he tortured himself by deciding to be a cop? He could answer that one without any effort—he hadn't decided. He had simply evolved into the profession from his duties in the Army. It was like everything else in his life—don't make a decision, just float along and see what happens.

Before leaving, Dean wrote a message to Lieutenant Anderson about the car that seemed to have followed him. If someone were trying to get a line on the whereabouts of Vinnie Baratto, they would all have to exercise more caution driving to the Pocono hideout. Rita would convey the message to Jonathan Winston as well allowing Dean to temporarily duck having to explain to the FBI why he played cowboy and lost the tail instead of getting the plate number.

Dean was halfway out to 156 Maid Marian Lane before it dawned on him he'd neglected to pick up his just-in-case change of clothes. By the time he stuffed a duffle bag with slacks, sweater, socks and underwear, he knew he was cutting the time close. It began to mist, just enough for his windshield wipers to skip and hop like a tap dancer as he reached his destination.

Cynthia Byrne was standing at the edge of her driveway when Dean pulled up. She held an umbrella and was dressed in a grey suit. There was a small overnight bag next to her. She looked absolutely terrible. He got out of the car, put his arms around her shoulders and gave her a hug. Dean could feel the tremble of her body through his raincoat.

"Hang in there," he said. "It's almost over."

"I'm scared to death," was all she answered.

Most of the ride to the Allentown airport was made in silence, save the swish-swish of the windshield wipers. Neither knew the proper thing to say. The weather remained ominous with dark clouds rolling in, pushed by an ever-increasing wind that churned the sky in threatening waves. Although the heavy rain was holding off, there was a feeling it was only a matter of time before the full fury hit.

"Do you think they'll fly in this?" she asked, breaking the silence.

"According to Rita Angeltoni, the seat of all wisdom, this part of the flight's on time. But after the first leg, we're on our own."

She sighed. "I've never flown before...either." Then quickly, "I can't tell you how much I appreciate your coming with me. I never could have done this alone."

"There are things nobody should do alone," he answered.

Dean felt it might be better if she talked instead of letting the silence and the upcoming events prey on her mind. He used the age-old method of asking questions that needed answers until she swung into something akin to conversation. She had continued her classes and was somehow maintaining acceptable grades. Randy was holding up well and it looked as if he would nail down at least a partial scholarship shortly, perhaps to Lehigh or Bucknell, as both were interested. His grades were good, which helped. Cynthia's mother was due on Sunday and would stay through the memorial service on Tuesday. Or the funeral, she added. Randy had been told before school about the telephone call from Norfolk and she had dismissed his offer to fly down with her. The Rileys would look in on him and she was to call as soon as she identified his father's body.

As they neared the airport, she became pensive. "I hope you didn't spend too much time working on the report of the accident," she said. "It looks as if it won't be needed now."

"I had to write up most of it anyway," he said. Now at least he could include a reference to Cece Baldwin's name without a guilty conscience. There was no further conversation after they parked and hurried to the terminal. They approached the ticket counter with 15 minutes to spare.

"Good luck getting back tonight," said the ticket clerk. "According to National Weather, this is a doozy of a storm."

The smaller airport was a welcome relief from the Philadelphia crowds and the large jet was loaded quickly. As soon as the plane left the runways they were enveloped in clouds, and neither ground nor sky visible during the entire one-hour flight to Baltimore. Cynthia Byrne clutched the armrest firmly during take off and landing, reacting to each noise anew. When they finally touched down, she smiled and took a deep breath.

"That wasn't so bad. I just wish I could see where I was going!"

The rain was steadier and the day was darker as they moved from their arrival gate to find the connecting flight to Norfolk. The plane was scheduled to leave in 45 minutes but one look at the departure board was indicative of things to come. "Delayed" was posted next to all flights headed south. Dean learned at the information counter it would be at least two hours before anything would depart in that direction.

The delay ended up being four hours. The two travelers killed the time picking over a bland lunch and alternating long walks with longer periods of sitting on hard seats, re-reading a discarded newspaper. Cynthia Byrne looked worse with each passing hour and just before their flight was called, excused herself and went to the ladies' room. Dean became concerned when 20 minutes passed. When she returned, looking ashen, he was sure she had been ill. He didn't embarrass her by asking and was thankful when at long last their flight was ready for boarding.

The trip between Baltimore and Norfolk was in a much smaller aircraft than the first leg of the journey. The little plane danced and swayed in the turbulence, constantly buffeted by the increasing wind. It was the roughest flight Dean had ever taken. Many of the passengers were ill and others whimpered and whined as the plane dropped, rose and rolled in the churning gusts, riding the heavy winds like a cork in a whirlpool. Cynthia Byrne never opened her eyes and clung to Dean's right arm with such a tenacious grip he thought he'd be permanently scarred.

The first sign of the ground Dean spotted was a rain puddle reflecting the glow from the lights of the plane as the wheels touched the runway—one, two, three times before the tired aircraft glided to the taxiway. All of the passengers sighed deeply and many clapped.

The weather in Norfolk was frightful. Waves of wind-driven rain pummeled the terminal with a fury. The pair was further delayed securing a rental car, and it was after 5:00 by the time the two tired travelers pulled away from the airport grounds. There would be no chance of leaving Norfolk that evening.

While Dean wasn't familiar with the city, the rental-car agent marked directions to the hospital morgue and he had no trouble locating it. He parked in a no-parking zone, figuring even the police wouldn't be out on a night like this.

As Dean shut off the engine he turned to his companion. "Do you want to sit here a few minutes and calm down?"

"No," she answered, trying to control the tremble in her voice. "I just want to get it over with."

Cynthia Byrne was shaking so badly had he not supported her with an arm about her waist he doubted she could have made it into the building on her own. He nearly broke both their necks when he slipped on the wet tile floor as he made his way to the receptionist who directed them to a flight of metal stairs that led downward to an empty hall. The chemical smell suggested they were going in the right direction. When Cynthia saw the word "Morgue" in gold letters on the frosted window, Dean thought he was going to lose her completely.

Inside, a white-jacketed attendant, who looked like a high-schooler, casually checked Dean's credentials while Cynthia waited, not quite out of ear shot.

"The doctor isn't here. A tree blew down on his house and he got called home. The police figured you weren't coming, with the storm and all. There's just me and an intern upstairs. I'm just filling in. You want the John Doe they fished out of the bay, huh?"

"Yes," answered Dean, annoyed at the young man's lack of concern for Cynthia Byrne. "Let's just do it."

The attendant ushered them into a sterile room of white tile and stainless steel. He checked a piece of paper he was carrying and mumbled, "Over here. Number six." He grasped the handle of tray number six but, before opening it, glanced down at Cynthia Byrne.

"You all right?" he asked.

"No, I'm not all right," she answered nervously. "But *please* do it!"

The attendant pulled out the tray with a jerk, nearly dislodging the body. The corpse was covered with a white sheet, but before pulling the cloth back, the attendant again looked at Cynthia, who nodded. She was clutching Dean's arm with both hands so tightly he was numb to his fingertips. His arm was about her waist, supporting her whole body. The attendant slowly withdrew the cover, exposing a grotesque, bloated face. Cynthia let out a gasp and wilted like a flower in a furnace; a dead faint.

The body looked like a flipped fish—a huge white under belly. But it wasn't Jeffrey Byrne. Dean knew immediately because he was staring at the bloated face of Billie or Willie Wassermann.

The attendant took one look at Cynthia and yelled, "Holy shit! I'll get Mr. Cole!" and ran from the room, leaving Dean holding the unconscious woman, bent at the waist, feet off the floor, like a five-foot Raggedy-Ann doll. He started to say something to the fleeing attendant but instead lifted the limp body up in his arms to a more reasonable position and carefully carried her out to the anteroom. He was sitting there a few moments later with Cynthia Byrne still unconscious when the attendant reappeared with Mr. Cole, a young intern, in tow.

The intern took charge, directing them to a small room that contained a cot. He revived Cynthia and wrapped her tightly in a bright red blanket, stark contrast to her blanched pallor. She woke with a startled look on her face until she realized where she was. She then closed her eyes and began to cry. The intern patted Dean on the shoulder and winked.

"It's a shock seeing someone's loved one like that," the doctor said in his best bedside manner. Dean wanted to explain it was far more of a shock seeing a bloated Billie or Willie Wassermann with a head looking like a bleached basketball, but simply nodded instead.

"She'll be all right now," Intern Cole added leaving as quickly as he had arrived.

When Cynthia Byrne finally stopped crying, she wiped her eyes on the corner of the red blanket. "God, that was horrible."

"Just rest a minute and we'll get the hell out of here," Dean answered. She nodded and closed her eyes. He rose and, taking the arm of the attendant, steered the young man out to the slab where Wassermann was unaware of the turmoil he'd created.

"Sorry," the man mumbled. "I never done this before. I'm just filling in. The guy's a real mess. Someone did a number on him."

"What do you mean?"

"They took a cigarette to his balls for one thing, and there's all kinds of marks on him. They really worked him over."

"What in God's name ever made anyone think this tub of blubber was Jeffrey Byrne?" Dean asked, still upset at Cynthia Byrne's unnecessary ordeal.

"He ain't her husband, huh?"

"Not even close to the same description."

"I don't know," the attendant answered defensively. "Somebody screwed up, I guess. Byrne was the only recent missing person in the file."

"Where did they find him?"

"Way up north of here, near the other side of the bay. They bring all the stiffs in here 'cause we've got the best facilities on the Lower Chesapeake."

"Roll him over," Dean directed. "I want to see his ass."

The attendant gave Dean a strange look but between the two, they managed to turn the body. Plain as day was a B tattooed on one cheek and a W on the other. The rumor was true.

"Just like it's supposed to be," said Dean with satisfaction.

"God, he's branded like a cow! What's 'BW' mean?"

"It's a long story," Dean answered.

"Can you ID this guy?"

"Sort of."

"What do you mean? Either you can or you can't?"

Dean paused. "He's a twin. He's either Billie or Willie Wassermann."

"Which? I can't put both names on a death certificate."

"Take your pick," answered Dean. "I'm not sure even his mother could ID him now. Better yet, keep an eye out in the bay for another body. Neither of those two ever did anything alone." He left the attendant standing there, a quizzical look on his face.

Dean let Cynthia Byrne rest a while longer while he telephoned the news to Parkside. At least somebody else would get the distasteful task of telling a wailing Mrs. Wassermann one of her bouncing baby boys was stretched out on a marble slab in Norfolk, Virginia. The news was not well received by Lieutenant Anderson, who was still on duty. Only the Lord knew what Linda Segal, The Ice Lady of the *Parkside Sentinel*, would do with this turn of events. It would have been much more convenient if the customer under the sheet had been Jeffrey Byrne. But it looked like Parkside could wash its hands of Wasserman's death—there was no way he'd floated out of their land-locked jurisdiction to the Chesapeake Bay. His murder was someone else's headache.

Now that Jeffrey Byrne was still among the missing, Leland Anderson promised to send someone to the Byrne residence to let Randy know the body in Norfolk was not his father. But Anderson was quick to point out that the Byrne case was still closed as far as Parkside was concerned.

Dean returned to the room where Cynthia Byrne was slowly returning to the world of the living. She sat on the edge of the bed and had been ill again, but was awake and alert. He told her of his conversation with Parkside and she was appreciative that word was being conveyed to Randy. However, she still wanted to speak to her son personally as soon as she felt able.

"God, that was terrible," she said. "I can't do this again when they find Jeff. Someone else will have to identify him." Dean didn't answer. She stood up, brushing down her skirt and looked at him. "Are they always...that bloated?" she asked.

"Wassermann had a pretty good head start," he answered. "I think he actually lost weight."

"You knew him?"

"Sort of." Dean was getting tired of telling the story of the ever-popular Wassermann twins, but related it one more time.

"What was he doing here? We're hundreds of miles from Parkside."

Dean hadn't given that much thought but he remembered what Vinnie Baratto had said about the Maryland eastern shore and explained it was across the Chesapeake Bay. "He probably floated out on the tide."

Dean left word with the attendant that he would phone the coroner and the Norfolk police in the morning. No, he didn't know where they would be staying. Somewhere near the airport, he guessed.

The weather had not improved. The wind made short work of Cynthia Byrne's dainty umbrella, wrenching it to a mass of twisted wire and ripped fabric as they scrambled into the car. Dean had been wrong about the efficiency of the Norfolk police. A soggy parking ticket was spread over his windshield by the first sweep of the wipers.

"Shit," said Dean, quickly apologizing. Cynthia laughed, the first sign of life since the ordeal had begun. It was a good sign.

Dean smiled and looked over at her. "We have to get you a good stiff drink and a stomach full of food."

"That sounds just fine," she answered. Ignoring the seatbelt, she moved closer to him. It felt good.

They drove along in silence for a few moments. "You're a nice man and I'm taking terrible advantage of you," she said.

"I'll let you buy me the first drink," he answered, "and then every other one. But first of all, we'd better find a place to stay. Given the weather, that might not be easy, especially near the airport."

She took a deep breath. "I want to stay at The Ocean Shore Motel." She said it with a firmness that left little room for arguing.

"Do you think that's a good idea?"

She didn't answer. She didn't have to. It wasn't a good idea and they both knew it. They also knew she wasn't going to change her mind.

Dean glumly tried to get his bearings. If he guessed correctly, the Chesapeake Bay was on his right, so he turned in that direction. Sure enough, after ten minutes of silent driving on nearly empty streets, he recognized Ocean View Avenue, and a few minutes later, The Ocean Shore Motel. It was even less appealing in the dark of the storm. They parked close to the building and, leaving the engine running, Dean made a dash for the office. Cynthia followed.

"Which room was Jeffrey's?" asked Cynthia softly as they stepped inside the door.

"Twenty-two," Dean responded reluctantly.

Fortunately, room 22 was taken and they settled for adjoining rooms on the second floor near the end of the building. As soon as they entered their respective quarters, Cynthia knocked on the connecting door. When Dean opened his side, Cynthia took his hand and smiled. "I know I keep saying it but you're a saint for putting up with me. Staying here was something I had to do. Otherwise I'd always wonder what it looked like, what kind of place it was and I'd never know. I'm all right, really. But I could use that drink."

She asked for a few minutes to call Randy first and Dean took the time to telephone Fred, filling him in on the latest happenings. Fred's response was surprising, a few grunts and a brief comment that it figured. He didn't offer a single I-told-you-so.

A few minutes later Cynthia knocked on the door again. "Let's get those drinks," she said with a cheery voice and, taking his hand, descended the stairs to the dining room. In spite of her words, she still looked terrible but Dean was thankful for even forced improvement.

The dining room was nearly empty and they chose a seat in a quiet corner. As soon as they were seated, Cynthia perused the menu, bit her lip and ordered manhattans for both of them. She looked over at Dean and feigned a smile. "Do you mind? It's not the Top of the Mark, but I may not get another chance."

He wasn't sure how to answer. The drinks arrived in glasses better designed for raising fish than serving alcohol—a sure hit with the traveling salesmen. He raised his glass. "I'm sorry I have to be the substitute but I feel honored," he said. "To Jeffrey."

She raised her glass and bit her lip but didn't cry, then cast her eyes downward. "You're far more than just a stand-in," she said.

Her words pleased him as he cautioned her. "Careful with those things. They're hell on an empty stomach."

"I plan to remedy the empty stomach very soon," she said, studying the menu. She smiled but it seemed more designed to give comfort to Dean than a true indication of her feelings. He sipped his manhattan. He had a feeling he might need it.

Cynthia's cheeks were quick to color as she sipped the liquid, making a face with each gulp. They each ordered a salad and steak and attacked them with surprising gusto.

"I won't be sad," she said. "Jeffrey would want that."

As the meal progressed, their conversation remained open and relaxed. To anyone watching, they were two people perfectly at ease with one another enjoying an evening meal. The ghost of Jeffrey Byrne, who had spent his final hours in the same dining room, was nowhere in evidence.

They chatted amiably about a variety of things. Both told childhood tales, stories of happy memories, each prompting the memory of yet another incident to their mutual delight. It was Dean's second meal with Cynthia Byrne and in spite of the gut-wrenching happenings earlier in the day, no less enjoyable than the first.

"Are you going to marry Ethel Rosewater?" Cynthia asked out of the blue, somewhere between manhattan number one and number two. Dean nearly choked on a string bean. She laughed aloud at his reaction, a little too loudly, quickly covering her mouth as other diners glanced her way.

"I'm sorry," she said, still giggling. "But you should have seen yourself!"

"Ethel and I are...good friends," he said, trying to look serious. "I guess I can say marriage isn't in either of our plans."

"That's good," she stated matter-of-factly.

"Why?"

"She nice enough, but I don't think she could make you happy."

Dean smiled to himself at the difference between happiness and a Thursday night romp. Just then the third round of drinks arrived, apparently as a result of a nod to the waiter by Cynthia Byrne. Dean had a good buzz going and could only imagine the effect of the booze on the five-foot frame of his dinner partner—a frame without food most of the day.

"You're not going to remember a thing in the morning," Dean warned, happy to change the subject.

"I'm not sure that's all bad," her words formed with care through the slur in her voice.

"One shouldn't drink to forget."

"One doesn't do it very often," came the reply. "You can't begrudge me that, can you?" She finished the remaining half of her drink in one gulp.

"I think it's about time we get you in bed before that stuff makes its rounds of your bloodstream," Dean said with a mock stern look. He knew she was on borrowed time given the alcohol's delayed reaction.

She laughed. "In the movies that would be considered a very"—she annunciated each syllable—"pro-voc-a-tive line." Dean felt the temperature climbing in his face.

"God, I can't believe I'm flirting with you! I have to stop this drinking!" She patted his hand. "Now I've gone and embarrassed you. I'm sorry." She started to rise but a serious look crossed her face. "I'm not sure I can get up!"

The thought passed Dean's mind that he'd already carried her to bed once today but he held his tongue. She rose, albeit unsteadily, and he grasped her in the now familiar position of his supporting arm about her waist. After paying the check he maneuvered the wobbly woman up the stairs while she chatted merrily about the meal, the weather and the price of steak. When they reached the rooms he took her key and opened her door. She put her arms about his neck in a bear hug and gave him an exuberant big sister kiss on the mouth.

She stepped back and looked him straight in the eye. "You're a nice, nice, nice, nice, nice man!" She pivoted and entered the room, taking baby steps and leaving him to close the door behind her.

When he reached his room both of the connecting doors were still open. He sighed but tactfully closed the panel on his side.

He had undressed and was in the bathroom splashing water on his booze-numbed face when the lights suddenly failed. There followed a rip of thunder. In the momentary silence that ensued Dean heard an outside door slam. At first it didn't register but then he quickly crossed to the window and looked out. There in the blur of a passing auto and mirrored in descending waves of rain was the huddled figure of Cynthia Byrne stumbling across the parking lot toward the road and the beach beyond. Dean swore to himself and fumbled for a pair of slacks and his raincoat, whacking his shin on the bed in the process. By the time he was out the door and down the stairs, Cynthia was nowhere in sight. He knew instinctively where she was headed.

Dean half-felt his way across the parking lot in his bare feet, cursing the pebbles and splashing through ankle-deep puddles at curbside before stumbling into the absolute darkness of the beachside path. He yelled her name but the call was smothered by the cry of the wind and the crash of the surf beyond. He groped his way down the path, the wind whipping his raincoat behind him, until he felt the mush of soft sand beneath his aching feet. With the power out, the darkness was absolute. He yelled Cynthia's name as he stumbled ahead until he reached the wind-driven surf splashing at his feet. A feeling of helplessness and panic welled up in him as he strained his eyes against the darkness.

At last he heard a noise off to his right, a sigh or a moan in the blackness. He wallowed through the wet sand, stumbling and staggering toward the sound. Suddenly a flash of lightening illuminated the crouched figure of Cynthia Byrne several yards away. Once again in darkness, Dean made his way toward the form, his arms outstretched before him. She was sobbing uncontrollably and he pulled her soaked frame up to him, trying to wrap his raincoat around her shaking body.

"I had to see it. I had to see it. I had to see it." She kept repeating the words over and over.

Dean lifted her in his arms and slowly picked his way up the beach in the direction from which he'd come, half staggering through the soft sand. It was an arduous trip. He made two or three false starts before he located the elusive narrow path through the thorny brush that separated the beach from the road beyond it. Emergency lights were now on outside the motel, making the return trip easier once he reached the road. Dean could now see Cynthia Byrne was unconscious though her arms remained tightly about his neck. Her added weight, though slight, caused the parking lot gravel to cut even deeper into his aching feet. She was drenched to the skin and rivulets of water ran down her shivering body. He quickened his step and his breath came in spurts as he gingerly climbed the stairs toward their rooms.

The room key was in his raincoat pocket and he managed to pull it out with two fingers and fit it into the lock, pushing the door open with his shoulder. The power remained out so the only light in the room came from the outside emergency fixture through the open door. Gently laying Cynthia on his bed, he tried to revive her but it was obvious she would be in the land of dreams for quite some time.

Dean opened his connecting door and found to his relief she had not locked her side. Her blinds remained open and he could see the room key on the nightstand. He pulled down her bed covers, felt around the darker bathroom for all the towels and opened her small overnight bag. The bag contained a dress, a slip, underwear and a two-piece pajama set but no robe or flannel running suit or anything dry and warm.

Returning to his room, he closed his door and opened the shades just enough to see. He shrugged off the raincoat and stepped out of the wet trousers, using one of his smaller towels to partially dry off before slipping on pajama bottoms and a long-sleeved shirt. He then carried Cynthia Byrne's limp but still drenched and shivering body through the connecting door to her bed and laid her on one of the towels.

Dean began to peel away her soaked clothes, half expecting her to wake and scream bloody murder that he was raping her. Had she awoken, there was no doubt she'd be petrified by his actions in the nearly dark room. It was a no-win situation.

Cynthia was as limp as a rag doll as he pulled down her skirt, which was heavy with water. He maneuvered her arms out of her jacket and white frilly blouse. Feeling like 20 kinds of pervert for doing it, he hoped to at least be spared undressing her further. One touch of her damp, cold body told him otherwise—she was soaked to the skin.

Dean rubbed and blotted Cynthia Byrne's body briskly with the towel and wrapped her head turban-like in a smaller one. He then took a deep breath and began work on her under things. Alternating bars of light cast a pale glow through the venation blinds on her near-white body. She may have been asleep and she may have been a wet shivering mess but, by God, she was still beautiful and the whole procedure was beginning to bother Dean as he tried to be objective to his task. He peeled away her panty hose. Cynthia Byrne's breasts stood firm against the lacy fabric covering them and he draped a towel across her chest as he struggled to unhook her bra from beneath her comatose body. He then draped a second towel across the lower part of her body and removed her panties, no "Thursday" cotton things, but small and white. He couldn't have felt guiltier if he were molesting a nun.

After patting her body as dry as he dared, Dean reached over and grabbed her night bag, pulling out her pajamas. She should have had a hot shower but there was no way he was going to tackle that chore. Without difficulty he pulled her arms through the pajama top and buttoned the garment. He was about to pull on the bottoms when he wondered if she would wear panties to bed. He still hoped she would awake in the morning thinking she had undressed herself and save them both the embarrassment that would otherwise follow. What the hell, he thought. He closed his eyes and tugged on a pair of lavender briefs before pulling up the bottom to the PJ's.

Dean maneuvered the still-unconscious figure beneath the covers, tucking the blanket as tightly as he dared. He hung up the sopping towels and wet clothing in the bathroom. Before returning to his room, Dean stopped to adjust the remaining towel beneath Cynthia Byrne's damp head. He gazed down upon her now-peaceful figure. She was truly beautiful, resting there, color beginning to return to her cheeks and a look of contentment that only sleep could bring, a look that would surely be absent in the morning. He bent down and kissed her lightly on the lips. A feeling of caring he had never before experienced washed over him.

In spite of the exhausting schedule of the day, Dean had difficulty falling asleep. At first he lay awake, conscious of every sound the motel uttered, fearful that Cynthia Byrne might waken to God knows what thoughts and fears. Later, when all was quiet, a restless half-sleep was all he could achieve. Later still, the power was restored, and both rooms blazed with light. He jumped to his feet flipping light switches and stumbling through both rooms, barely seeing still-sleeping Cynthia through eyes pinched nearly closed against the intrusive brightness.

But once back in bed, the complexities and the happenings of the day raised their heads like so many ghosts crying for attention in his tired brain. Sleep eluded him. Dean knew if he were honest with himself he'd admit he was tickled pink during those few hours that it appeared Jeffrey Byrne's body had been found. Now they were back to square one. His emerging feelings for Cynthia Byrne only added complications to the equation. Courting a widow was one thing, but harboring a nagging feeling she might not be widowed was quite another matter. Before, it was just police business. Had Jeffrey Byrne skipped or drowned? Let's look at the facts, make a decision and close the case. Drowned, that was the official conclusion. He'd already finished most of the report, hadn't he? Then why was it each time he was around Cynthia Byrne the question kept coming back? Dean wanted to be positive the son of a bitch was dead so he could have his wife; admit it, it was as simple as that.

There. The bastard side of him said it, much as he had tried to fight the thought down. As long as there wasn't a body, Dean could never be sure Jeffrey Byrne wouldn't jump out of the past and yell, "April Fool!" dragging Cynthia Byrne back to home and hearth.

He must have drowned. He has to be out there, caught in the seaweed at the bottom of Chesapeake Bay, with the fish and crabs having a party, getting as bloated as the fat Wassermann twin lying on the slab at the Norfolk morgue. Why not? What evidence did they have to the contrary? Nothing, unless you count a tire patch kit and a half a receipt for $59.95, neither of which probably even belonged to Byrne. There was the Whitney Motel back in Parkside. Big deal. That was two months earlier. Byrne probably needed a day off. What about the newspaper sent to Scranton and J. Cleary? Just coincidence. But some specter in his fitful half-sleep wouldn't even give permission for him to dream about Cynthia Byrne, sleeping restfully just yards away.

# CHAPTER XI

The sound of running water in the next room told Dean that daylight had finally arrived and Cynthia Byrne was up and around. The sun flooded in through the still-open drapes, announcing that the violent storm of the night before had fled out to sea. He fought off the last of his dream demons, pulled himself to an upright position, and stumbled into the bathroom. After showering and dressing, he wrote a short note explaining he would be at police headquarters until midmorning and slipped it under her door. Cynthia Byrne needed a little time on her own before he barged back into her world.

Detective Norman Hunter had returned from his mountain fishing trip and was irate at the snafu that had occurred at the morgue in his absence. He was clearly embarrassed and apologized to Dean on behalf of everyone in the Norfolk Police Department, the City of Norfolk and the entire south. Confusing a Wassermann twin with Jeffrey Byrne was inexcusable.

"The least they could have done was issue a general description. Anyone would have known that tub of lard wasn't Byrne," Hunter fumed as he paced up and down the room. Dean let him get it out of his system. He tried to appease the Norfolk detective by saying no permanent harm had been done and even Mrs. Byrne seemed to have made it through the ordeal.

The local FBI had stepped into the picture and hustled action on the body, tentatively identified as Billie Wassermann—perhaps on an alphabetical basis only. A local autopsy was rushed through

135

in the wee hours of the night and the remains of the obese thug were airborne, in route to Pennsylvania as they spoke.

Detective Hunter finally sat. "The word is someone did in Wassermann over on the Eastern Shore and the tide carried him out in the middle of the Chesapeake. Or maybe they took him out by boat. Either way, it's out of our jurisdiction. From what you say the odds are high it's only a matter of time until his brother floats in."

Dean agreed. "They'll have to put navigation markers out in the bay if they turn up any more bodies. It's getting pretty crowded out there."

"So much for closure on the Byrne case," Hunter said. "I feel badly for the missus. It must have been a shock seeing Wasserman instead of hubby."

"You don't know the half of it," Dean answered.

"Too bad she can't put the whole business to rest. Our active investigation is closed, but the file stays open until there's a body or a judge's ruling."

"Any word from Brunel—the World Wide employee who had the drink with Byrne?"

"Naw. My guys found a forwarding address someplace out west but there's no phone hooked up yet. A clerk at World Wide thought he was taking some time off before settling in out there. They're still ticked at him for not completing his paper work before he left. My chief says for us not to break our butts wasting any more time chasing him down." Dean asked Hunter for the address, just in case. "Just in case what?" Hunter asked.

Dean explained Cynthia Byrne's request for as much detail as possible in his report to help her obtain a death certificate. Then he added, "We recognize it's Norfolk's case—we're just investigating our end as a courtesy."

Hunter nodded, but seemed skeptical. Then he asked, "Did the inventory check out okay?"

"The only things missing were the swim suit and baseball cap."

Hunter smiled. "I wonder why a fella would go swimming with his hat on."

"Maybe he never intended to get his head wet—just paddle around a bit."

"Maybe he forgot he had it on—him being a little sloshed and all."

"He took off his t-shirt. He had to take off his hat first, then put it back on."

"Do I detect you're not 100 percent sure the old boy drowned?" Hunter asked.

Dean smiled. "Just turning things over in my mind. It gets to be a habit after all these years. Let's say I'm 99 percent, but it sure would be nice to find a body."

"You're gonna break your stick beating this here doggy so hard," was Hunter's response.

The coroner's report indicated Wassermann had been dead at least two weeks, the same length of time the morgue attendant had guessed. The twin had been tortured before being shot once through the back of the head. The bullet hole hadn't been visible at first due to Wassermann's long hair, the condition of the body, and the length of time in the water.

Dean called the Parkside Police Department and caught hell from Leland for not keeping him posted on the Wasserman autopsy and current details. Anderson was getting his news via the FBI. Dean didn't go into any detail explaining why he had not gone to the Norfolk Police Station the prior evening—he just mumbled that he had a very distraught widow on his hands. He wasn't in the mood to discuss Friday night in the Ocean Shore Motel with anyone. Efficient Rita, in spite of it being Saturday, arranged for a return flight north with reservations for early afternoon.

When Dean returned to the motel, the adjoining doors were open and Cynthia Byrne sat on the edge of her bed with one hand holding a phone and the other with a wet face cloth pressed to her forehead. She was dressed in a pair of light colored slacks, a pale blue blouse and was barefoot. As soon as she saw him, she ducked her head under a sheet to hide. She came up, motioning for him to come into the room. Putting a hand over the mouthpiece, she asked, "Do you know what time we'll get back?"

Dean mentally calculated the time from the airport and told her about 5:00. She conveyed the information to son Randy, told him she loved him and, after ending the conversation, flopped back down on the bed, again covering her head, this time with a pillow.

"I haven't been this sick since I was pregnant with Randy and I'm so embarrassed I could die!"

"We all drink a little too much once in a while."

"May I wear a bag over my head on the trip home? I don't think I can ever face you again. I am totally mortified."

"You were a perfect lady. You just fell asleep a little early."

She covered her ears. "Don't say it! Don't even talk about it!"

"You didn't miss a thing," then added, "except the power failure." She looked up at him as he continued. "Not a light in the place for hours. Couldn't see a thing."

She covered her face. "God, I hate not remembering!"

"Water under the bridge," he answered. "Let's get packed up and out of here. Have you eaten?"

She moaned. "Don't mention food!"

"You have to eat something. Remember what an empty stomach can do." He turned to leave. "Five minutes. I'll knock."

She caught up to him at the door, surprising him with the quiet of her bare feet on the carpet and gave him a hug from behind, burying her head against his back and holding on for a long while. "Thank you," was all she said.

They settled for sandwiches at the airport. Dean ate a chicken salad on whole wheat with a piece of cherry pie and ice cream. Cynthia nibbled half a grilled cheese. Dean had allowed what he thought was plenty of time for the flight but the rental car area was slow and the entire airport was crowded with storm-delayed travelers. The flight was on schedule and thankfully there was little time for forced conversation. It was obvious that Cynthia was still feeling terrible. She smiled and responded with one-word answers while he did most of what little conversation occurred. Neither was disappointed when they lapsed into silence for the last leg of the trip.

Cynthia was a wee bit cheerier on the ride from Allentown but the subject of the prior evening was never broached. She apologized that she would once again need his detailed report now that the body remained missing. With each passing day the possibility that Jeffrey Byrne's corpse might not be found became more realistic. While Dean was tactful enough not to mention it, it had, however, taken two weeks for Billie Wassermann to come home to port.

"I guess we'll be having the Memorial Service on Tuesday after all," she said. Again she asked he attend, if possible. He nodded and murmured he'd try his best to be there.

"Thank you. I'd like that," she said.

When Dean pulled in the drive at Maid Marian Lane, Randy was walking a bike into the open garage. His mother alighted and gave him a hug. Dean stood aside while they talked quietly, then walked around the car and shook the young man's hand. No one spoke until the silence became awkward.

"Do you do much riding?" Dean finally asked.

"No. It's my father's bike. I thought it had a flat but I guess he fixed it. You're a bit early; I was just killing some time."

Cynthia put her arm around Randy as she spoke to Dean. "Jeff used to ride, years ago. He started up again this spring. I've been meaning to get my bike fixed too. Both of my tires are flat." She added, "I could use the exercise."

"Say the word," Dean answered. "I'll be over. You just hit on my favorite pastime." Then, thinking his statement presumptive added, "When things settle down."

She smiled. "That sounds like fun." She offered her cheek and took his hand, thanking him again. She then turned to her son as if to apologize for allowing this relative stranger to kiss her. "He's been really wonderful to me."

Randy didn't seem to mind, but Dean felt more like a kindly old uncle than someone who, the prior evening, had undressed this woman and put her to bed. The unease of the entire situation put him in a foul mood all the way home.

As Dean rounded the corner of Collingswood Avenue and pulled in his driveway, he noticed a light blue car pull away from the opposite curb. A slow-moving car on his side of the street blocked him from reading the license number or giving chase. The car was around the corner and out of sight when his field of vision cleared. There were two occupants and the driver had glanced in his direction before turning away. Dean was certain the driver was Alfred Nota, one of the men he'd hassled at Vinnie Baratto's place.

*Just what I need*, Dean grumbled to himself. He jumped out of the car and dashed up the steps to the house. If he called the station quickly enough they might be able to run down the car.

Fred O'Connor stood in the center of the room, the phone in his hand, with Dolly Parton crooning from the stereo. He gave a wave to Dean. "He just came in now, Lieutenant Anderson. Do you want to speak to him?" Dean grabbed the phone.

He covered one ear against Dolly. "Leland, there was a car—"

"Yeah, I know. Your stepfather just called it in. He got the license number too. I just put an APB out on it."

"Oh," was all Dean could reply.

"We think it's your pal Nota and his sleazebag friend—the pair you hassled at Baratto's place."

"It looked like him," Dean mumbled.

"Lucky you, getting on the bad guy's list. Watch your back." Then he added, "We're probably going to have to move Vinnie Baratto again. If they're tailing you, the location's getting too hot. I already told Winston I want you to stay clear of Baratto for a few days." While it was in part at least an indictment that Dean had allowed himself to be followed, it was still the best news he'd heard in weeks.

Dean filled in to his lieutenant the details of the Norfolk trip, leaving out what he felt wasn't police business—a surprisingly large portion. Anderson, in turn, brought Dean up to date on Parkside news, especially the local excitement caused by the discovery of the body of Billie Wassermann. Billie—it was official now, identified or guessed at by the weeping Ida Wasserman, accompanied to the mortuary by Andy Sackler, who drew the short straw. The Ice Lady, Linda Segal, was going full bore at the *Sentinel*, trying to convince her reading public that the poor lad might have been saved had the local police properly conducted the search for the missing boy in a timely fashion. There was an office pool on how long it would be before Willie would float in. Dean took Thursday for five bucks, in absentia.

Rose Tisdale first sighted the blue car circling the block and called Flora Watkins. She in turn called her sister in Toledo, then Fred O'Connor because the occupants seemed to be watching his house. Fred managed to get the license number by walking around the block and returning to the house from the rear. He was proud as punch over his crime-fighting accomplishments. Dean congratulated him but issued a warning against getting too bold with characters who would burn their mother at a stake just to light their cigars.

There wasn't much left to Saturday but the time was spent lounging around, munching on Chinese takeout and drinking Coors beer. Mrs. Lincoln seemed pleased to have a variety of music instead of straight country and western, partial as she was to good jazz—plus there were two laps to alternate when the patting on one slacked off. Fred was back at it with his notes and was anxious to bring Dean up to date on the progress he'd make in Dean's absence.

"I figure it like this. If Byrne was out to set up an identity he'd apply for credit cards, a driver's license, a library card and stuff like that. So I called all around. I even checked out some of the banks, figuring credit cards would be most important."

"So?"

"So, I haven't hit yet but I'm still trying. Some of those people can get really snotty on the phone."

"You didn't tell them you were from the police, did you?" Dean asked.

"Would I do that?" Fred answered innocently and then changed the subject. "I haven't heard from the Burgess fellow yet on the picture of Byrne's you sent him. I called Mrs. Glass again, just to see if she remembered anything else." Dean started to protest but Fred continued. "She remembers a motor home parked on Bascomb Place! What do you think of that?"

"I think you ought to stick to reading mysteries instead of inventing them. Who says the motor home belonged to Cleary?"

"Well, it stands to reason, doesn't it? It was there while this guy Cleary was renting the place. There wasn't anyone else there but him and Burgess and it didn't belong to Burgess." Fred stood up suddenly, much to Mrs. Lincoln's disgust. "You can't see the woods for the forest."

"Fred, it could belong to anyone on that street, or someone visiting." Fred rolled his eyes at Dean's perceived stubbornness. "I don't suppose Mrs. Glass got a license number?"

"No, but she said it was paper—you know, a temporary plate! See? He bought it with his haul so's he could make his getaway!"

Dean smiled. "So you called all the local dealers to find out if anyone named Cleary or Byrne or Corbin bought a new motor home?"

"Yeah," Fred answered glumly. "They didn't." Then he added, "but it's a fact there was a motor home there. Stands to reason..."

"Don't go confusing 'it's a fact' with 'stands to reason.' You're making some broad jumps just because Jeffrey Byrne visited in the Scranton area."

"You're dancing to different music. The band's playing a fox-trot while you're waltzing around the floor," Fred grumbled.

They sat is silence through one whole Count Basie take before Dean finally spoke. "I settled one item for you today."

"What's that?"

"The tire repair kit. It looks like it was Byrne's. He had just fixed a flat on his bike. His son was riding it this afternoon." He sat back smugly.

Fred looked up. "So what was the patch kit doing in the trunk of his company car?"

"It fell out of his jacket or something. He probably had his suitcase and stuff in the trunk. It makes sense. He was traveling around all day and didn't want to get his things ripped off if he left them on the back seat."

Fred was quiet for a moment, thinking. He then crossed to the table and began poring over his notes. His face lit up with a broad smile. "So how come there's nothing missing from the tire kit?"

"How do you know that?" Dean asked.

Fred pointed to his notes. "It says right here, 'One large patch, three small ones and a tube of gunk to stick 'em with. None of 'em used.' Answer me that!"

Dean didn't have an answer—to that question or a few others that nagged at him for the rest of the evening.

# CHAPTER XII

The weatherman totally blew his Sunday forecast. What was supposed to be sunshine, mild temperature and puffy white clouds turned out to be intermittent showers and a sky as gray as Dean's sweat socks. In spite of the disappointing weather Dean was determined to fit some serious biking into the salvaged half of what should have been a free weekend. With his silver pride and joy secured to the bike rack, a spare change of clothes and rain gear in his pannier and some fruit and crackers for a snack, he rolled away from town to the peace and quiet of the countryside. No blue car followed.

Dean chose an area well away from town and parked at a road-side rest stop. After doing some stretching exercises and setting his bike's trip odometer, he began, slowly at first, to swing into his rhythmic cadence of 70 revs per minute, maintaining the pace by shifting gears as the country hills rolled beneath his wheels. It was a fine feeling indeed. He drank in the sights and sounds of the bucolic world around him and for the first time in days felt relaxed.

In spite of his love of music, no pocket recorder filled Dean's head with voices, strings or horns through tiny toy earphones— he'd leave that to the bikers who pedaled unaware of the sounds of birds and springtime around them. Besides, if an eighteen-wheeler was going to make "possum pizza" out of him, he wanted to hear it coming.

Slowly munching an apple at mile 23, he noted with satisfaction that his legs felt good in spite of the lack of practice. Earlier he'd signed up to take his July vacation in Iowa, biking the 400 miles across that state on a seven-day bike tour known as "RAG-BRAI," named for the sponsoring Des Moines Register newspaper. He would need all the training he could get in between now and mid-summer, even for that relatively easy tour.

Biking was usually Dean's thinking time, but his brain felt overused lately and had opted for a day off, restricting his thoughts to nothing more pressing than the next hill. He had already stopped for lunch and was rolling toward mile 47 when a sudden thought from nowhere hit him between the eyes. If Alfred Nota in his blue Ford was really interested in following Dean, why had the con taken off like a scared rabbit as soon as Dean showed up? The answer had frightening implications with Fred O'Connor at home alone.

Dean calculated he was 12 to 14 miles from his car, with nothing but corn and cows around him. He quickened his pace. It was three miles before he came to a closed gas station, but there was a phone booth outside. He dug change out of his bike bag and dialed his number but he might as well have saved his time. There was no answer at Collingswood Avenue—not a good sign. It took Dean another 40 minutes to reach his car, pull off his rain gear, and secure his bicycle. It was nearly 4:00 when he pulled into his drive.

As soon as he entered the house, he knew something was wrong. Art Farmer was blowing trumpet with the Horace Silver quintet in a piece called "Moon Rays" that Fred wouldn't have listened to on his own unless someone cut off his ears. And there was a smell of cigarette smoke, a definite no-no, one of the few points on which he and the old man agreed.

"Fred!" Dean yelled at the top of his lungs to an empty room. A glance told him things were in enough disorder to know there was trouble. Dashing from room to room downstairs produced nothing so he raced up the stairs, first to his room, then to Fred's. Again, nothing. Then he heard a muffled sound from behind the partially closed bathroom door. Yanking it open, he found his stepfather.

Fred O'Connor was seated on the toilet, a towel over his head with his pants and shorts pulled down to his ankles. He was bound to the porcelain fixture with a nylon cord around his ankles and one around his arms, which were tied behind him. His shirt and tie were in place as usual and Mrs. Lincoln was curled up on the bath mat at his feet, fast asleep.

Dean jerked the towel from his head and pulled a cloth gag from his mouth.

"The sons-of-bitches jumped me!" Fred sputtered.

"Who?"

"How the devil do I know who?" He was furious. "They wrapped that towel over my head!"

"Are you all right?" Dean asked, his heart racing nonstop.

"Hell no I'm not all right! How'd you like to sit on the damn toilet for hours? I probably got a terminal case of hemorrhoids."

"Damn!" Dean exclaimed, breaking a fingernail on a knot.

"Hurry up! I'm gonna have a ring around my be-hind for a week from sitting on this thing!"

Dean finally freed the last of the knots and Fred rose, pulling up his pants, staggered a step or two and sat back down. "Kinda woozy, I guess," he said. Dean lifted the old man in one swing and carried him to his bed. "Put me down! I'm not an invalid! I'd have beat the dickens out of 'em if they hadn't jumped me!" Dean turned to leave. "Where are you going?"

"To call the police...and a doctor."

"I don't need no doctor and *you're* the police."

Dean paid him no attention and called headquarters to report the break-in, asking them to send a doctor as well. He clicked off Art Tatum and "Willow Weep For Me" and after pulling out a bottle of scotch and two glasses, returned to Fred's room.

"How'd they get in?" the old man asked.

"I haven't looked yet. I've been too busy rescuing you."

"You took your sweet time getting to it," he grumbled. "I must have been there three hours. What time is it?"

"After four. Now tell me what happened."

Fred took a long drink from the scotch. "I was in my room and thought I heard a sound down below. I figured you'd come home early so I called out to you. When I got to the top of the stairs, they must have been hiding back of the door 'cause the next thing I knew they had a towel over my head and were dragging me into the bathroom."

"How did you know there were two of them?"

"'Cause they talked to each other."

"What did they say?"

Fred took another swig from the scotch. "Can't hear much with a towel over your head. Besides, I was concentrating on how to escape and teach them guys a thing or two."

Dean smiled and patted Fred on the shoulder. "How long were they here?"

"Not as long as they wanted. They turned your music up loud and started tearing the place apart but then someone rang the bell and they hightailed it out the back. It must have been Cora Abernathy. She watches the place like a hawk and as soon as you're gone she's at the door—comes socializing." He paused. "You don't have to tell the cops about them pulling down my pants, do you? That's kinda embarrassing. Why do you suppose they did that?"

Dean shrugged but shuddered when he remembered how information was extracted from Billie Wassermann.

Fred insisted over Dean's objections that they try and find if anything was missing. Dean was sure it was Nota and Homer Flanders, looking for information on where Vinnie Baratto was hidden, but there was nothing in the house to tell them. He was still searching and putting things back together when Officer Jack McCarty and his female partner Jenny Nachman arrived, with the doctor close on their heels. Dr. Blanchard went up to Fred's room while the police followed Dean around the downstairs, filling out their report.

"Second break-in today," said Jenny, a pretty blonde and the brightest in her recent graduating class. "I'm going to be an expert if this keeps up."

Although the intruders had started to search, it was apparent they hadn't gotten far. Only the living room showed signs of any activity. Nothing was seriously damaged, simply strewn about. A drape had been torn from the dining room and the cord used to tie Fred.

The pair finished their burglary report and agreed to try and keep the matter out of the papers in deference to Dean's other police activities. Nothing had been stolen and after yesterday's encounter with the blue Ford, all agreed they had a line on the prime suspects.

Before the uniformed officers left to interview the neighbors, Dean called Lieutenant Anderson to inform him of this latest development. The lieutenant's wife Marian answered the phone.

"I thought you were out in Colorado looking at some place you inherited," Dean said.

"Just got back. You wouldn't believe this little town, Ouray. It's up in the mountains, a zillion miles from any shopping."

"Sounds like my kind of place."

"I'd let you stay there if I wasn't still mad at you for not helping me win my bet," she said. "Now I have to give Leland a night of unforgettable pleasure just because you couldn't prove that jerk Byrne skipped out on his wife."

"Now Marian, be nice. Is a wild night with Leland such a terrible ordeal?"

"You don't know Leland the way I do!"

"If he isn't up to it, give me a call!"

"Sounds like fun!" Marian answered.

Just then, Lieutenant Anderson picked up the phone. "Dean, are you trying to put a move on my wife?"

"Certainly, wouldn't you?"

"Damn right! What's cooking?"

When Dean explained the recent happenings, both men turned serious. The blue Ford from the previous day had been located in Lansdale, Pennsylvania that morning. It had been stolen, so the police had no way of putting out a call for Nota and his friend unless someone in the neighborhood had sharp eyes. Dean was betting on Cora Abernathy.

"What gets me," said Dean, "is how they knew who I was and where I lived. I don't think I was followed until Thursday and I lost them then before I got to the house. I didn't show those punks anything but my badge when I hassled them at Baratto's place last Sunday."

"No one at the station is dumb enough to give out any information on personnel. I don't think those two goons could have gotten it there. But they found you, so keep watching your back. Their kind mean business." Dean didn't have to be told. He had seen firsthand what the folks from Philly did to Billie Wassermann.

Fred made it be known he had no intention of going to the hospital, though it wasn't suggested. The doctor told Dean his stepfather was too ornery to suffer any lasting effects from his ordeal. It was apparent the old man was feeling much more chipper, reveling in his notoriety. Dean didn't even insist he remain in bed. Later, after everyone had gone, Dean sent out for pizza and both men knocked off a large pie with the works and enough scotch to get silly.

Just after seven Cora Abernathy called, in tears. She had stopped by that afternoon but when she heard the music and the doorbell went unanswered, she assumed Fred was entertaining the competition. She had gone home to sulk causing, in her mind, Fred to suffer hours of grief and agony from her selfish inaction. Fred consoled her in his best fashion in spite of having a snoot-full at the time—the mark of a real pro. Cora had spotted a car, a black Buick this time, but had not written down the license plate number.

No sooner had Fred hung up than the phone rang again. It was patrolman Jack McCarty.

"Remember Jenny Nachman said your house was the second break-in today?" he told Dean. "The other one was at Mrs. Byrne's place, out in Sherwood Forest. Jenny didn't recognize the address. She hasn't worked on the other case...."

McCarthy spelled out the details. Cynthia and Randy discovered the break-in when they returned from church shortly after lunch. The place had been ransacked but nothing appeared missing. Two neighbors reported seeing a black car near the house. As soon as Dean hung up, he telephoned the Byrne home.

A man answered. Dean identified himself and asked for Cynthia. It was Phil Riley, the Byrnes' next-door neighbor.

"Cynthia's over at our place. I just came over to pick up a sweater for her. She tried to call you this afternoon."

"How is she?"

"Poor kid, she's pretty shook. It's been a tough couple of weeks," he answered.

"I couldn't agree more," Dean said. "I was with her in Norfolk when they popped the sheet on the wrong guy." Dean asked to have Cynthia call when she felt up to it but he didn't mention that someone had broken into his home too.

"It could have been a coincidence," Fred said after Dean hung up. "Those things happen."

"Only in your mystery stories, not in Parkside," Dean answered disgustedly.

"But why the Byrne place?"

"If they were tailing me, they must have seen me drive out there. Maybe they thought that was the place where we had Baratto stashed. They wouldn't have any idea who Cynthia was. I just feel like a bastard for dragging her and her son into something that has nothing to do with them." Dean paused. "I'm thankful she and Randy didn't come home in the middle of it."

Neither said much before calling it a day. They both had earned the rest.

# CHAPTER XIII

News of the break-in on Collingswood Avenue had traveled with the speed of an Olympic sprinter through the Parkside, Pennsylvania police department. In the first two hours at his desk, 20 people came up to Dean inquiring about poor Fred O'Connor. It must be nice to be so popular. If Dean himself had been bound and gagged, it would have been the joke of the squad room for weeks to come. To make the day no better, the telephone chirped nonstop and everyone in the station wanted a piece of him for cold cases, new cases and paper work. Dean's mood was souring by the minute. He remained annoyed at himself for involving Cynthia in the Baratto business and undecided about telling her the break-in was his fault—if she called. Which she hadn't. Maybe that was the main reason he was so pissed.

When the world wasn't expressing sympathy for the old man, they were looking for details on Billie Wassermann, his butt-brand, and all the gory details of the fat twin's execution. The only halfway pleasant phone call came from Norm Hunter in Norfolk. He said he was just asking about Dean's return trip but he was fishing for details on why the FBI was so unexpectedly interested in Billie Wassermann.

"They were all over this place like bolls on cotton. He must be part of something big."

Dean gave a capsule account of Vinnie Baratto and his connection to the murdered Wasserman. Then Hunter added, "They wanted to see the file on your pal Jeffrey Byrne as well. Now why do you suppose he'd interest them?" Dean told Hunter about his off-hand comment and how Baratto had jumped all over the Scranton connection.

"Any reason to dig that casket back up?" he asked.

"No," Dean answered. "At least not officially. But you can do me a favor on the case."

"Sure thing, old pal. Just name it."

"Have someone check out the bicycle shops in the area and see if that half receipt you found in the car came from one of them." He explained about the tire repair kit. "It's just a hunch and I'm not sure what it would mean if he did make a purchase. I'm just curious."

Hunter laughed. "You sure are curious. If you were a cat, you'd be one dead pussy." He added that he'd let Dean know if he developed any information.

When Dean replaced the phone and glanced up, the tall figure of Jonathan Winston was standing next to his desk, smiling down and, as usual, impeccably dressed. Dean wasn't sure what the FBI man had heard, if anything.

"What brings los federales out of the woods?" Dean asked, rising and shaking his hand.

"I'm just checking on David Dean, latest mob burglary victim. Sorry to hear about your house being hassled. Is your stepfather okay?"

"He's a survivor, and now he's the hero of the neighborhood. The widows will be fawning all over him—even more than usual." He paused as Winston laughed. "What's your read on why Nota busted into my place? I can't believe he thought I'd have a map to Baratto just lying around."

Winston thought a minute. "There's no telling. These guys aren't subtle and you were the only contact to Vinnie they knew about. When they want something, they act like a tank battalion and go get it."

"That's a lot of heat for a lousy two or three million. That must be coffee money for those clowns."

"Yes," Winston answered. "But it's a lot more than the money—pride's involved here. The Colombians don't want to deal now because they don't trust the family and the family doesn't trust the Colombians. The street's a mess until they get to the bottom of this business." He smiled. "We just want to keep it that way."

"That doesn't answer how Nota knew about me," Dean said.

Winston just shrugged. "Beats me. But let's hope now they're satisfied you're not the one to lead them to Baratto."

"Fine with me. I'd just as soon get back to purse snatchers and pot smokers and leave the big boys to you."

"I understand from Anderson the other case is closed...the Byrne matter? Nothing new has popped up on that, has it?"

"It's officially closed. There were a few loose ends, but no real evidence." Dean sipped the last of his cold coffee. "We thought we could lock the file drawer on this case when a body washed up, but no such luck. Norfolk has closed their investigation too."

Winston frowned. "What do you mean by *officially?*"

Dean explained he'd promised Cynthia Byrne a report, detailed beyond the usual, in an effort to help her in obtaining a death certificate. "Moonlighting a bit" was how he explained it. He didn't add that he'd mailed the report to Cynthia that morning.

Winston seemed to ponder this, then formed his words with care. "I don't want to stick my nose in your cases but it's vital to my case that heat stays high between the mob and the suppliers. Any hint that we're looking at Byrne or anyone else as having taken that money stops the war and our leverage goes out the window." Winston had more to say but held off as Rita came by, handing him a cup of coffee.

"How about me?" asked Dean.

"Only the guests rate," she replied. "The locals get their own coffee." Dean smiled as Winston thanked her.

"Tell me about these loose ends," Winston said as Rita returned to her desk.

Dean reluctantly explained Fred O'Connor's idea about the newspaper subscription and the fact that a paper had been sent to Scranton to a somewhat mysterious occupant. He brushed off the idea it could be Byrne and justified his interest as only appeasing his elderly stepfather. Winston didn't press for details—thankfully—and Dean made no mention of taking time for an off-duty trip to Scranton.

"Tell you what," Winston said, "I'll chase down the name and address with the Post Office and see if a forwarding address was filled. Then you can forget the whole business."

Dean gave Winston the information, including both names, Cleary and Corbin. Dean thanked him and changed the subject. "How are you coming with our friend Vinnie?" he asked.

"He's singing like the choir lead at a church revival." Winston glanced up. "Why don't you ask him?"

"Yellow 42!" shouted a voice and Vinnie Baratto stood by the door in the loudest sport jacket Dean had ever seen. "Yellow 42," he yelled again, charging into the room, feigning a hand-off and tossing his arms in the air. "Score!" he screamed, "Davey Dean scores! Parkside wins!" The room froze. Harrigan stopped in mid-sentence on the phone and Rita turned, fingers paralyzed above the keys. Dean closed his eyes and bowed his head on his arm. The jerk couldn't even get it right—they'd only tied the game. Even Leland Anderson turned the corner from his office to see what was causing the commotion.

"Vinnie, what are you doing here?" Dean asked disgustedly.

"What place is safer than the police station?" said Winston. "Right, Vinnie?"

"Hey, don't call me 'Vinnie.' It ain't gonna be my name from here on. My colored buddy here—see? I don't say 'nigger' no more—he and me, we're burying Vinnie Baratto for good. I'm getting a whole new identity!"

"I hope they make you a stable boy in a pig farm in Iowa and you spend the rest of your life knee-deep in what pigs do best." Dean said as the others returned to work, Rita shaking her head in disgust and Harrigan trying to talk on the phone by sticking a finger in one ear.

Winston hooked a leg around a chair and sat. "Old Vinnie here is going to be fine as long as he keeps on singing. He's even got himself a lawyer to make sure he's getting a good deal. But we're on the same track now, aren't we, Vinnie?" Vinnie nodded vigorously. "He and I are taking a little vacation trip to Maryland before he assumes his new life and disappears. Vinnie thinks he knows where some of his friends have a place around St. Michaels, on the eastern shore of the Chesapeake. We understand they give swimming lessons there."

"Swimming lessons reminds me, Vinnie. I saw your buddy Billie Wassermann Friday night," Dean said.

"Jeez, don't talk about that," Baratto said, cringing away. "Just thinking of Billie gives me the willies."

"Speaking of Willie," Harrigan piped up as he ended his phone call, "Tuesday's still an open day in the tide pool."

"Billie didn't even say hello, Vinnie," Dean continued to chide.

"Let's change the subject," Baratto protested.

"Hey, that's all right with me," said Dean. "Just make sure you play ball with the FBI and don't let your old pals find you. You'd need more than a lawyer if they catch up with you. They used Billie's privates for an ashtray. Let me tell you, it was pretty gross."

"Shit," Vinnie said, turning away. "And the whole damn thing was a big mistake."

"Watch your language, asshole," Rita snarled, not missing a beat in her typing.

"I'll bet Billie said it was all a big mistake just before they dropped him in the middle of the bay," Dean answered.

"Those guys will get smart. They'll figure out it wasn't me. I got 'em going in the right direction now." Vinnie nodded his head, a knowing look on his face.

"What are you talking about?" asked Dean, his tone suddenly cold.

"Nothing," Vinnie answered, a little too quickly.

Winston crossed over to Baratto with surprising speed and grabbed him by the collar, nearly lifting him off the ground. "Listen, you little son-of-a-bitch, I'll toss your ass right out this door to the street and then advertise on television exactly where you are and sell tickets while we watch them cut you up in little pieces. Answer the man's question."

"Okay, okay." Vinnie spoke slowly. "I just made this call...from the cabin, when your lightweight pals were out having a smoke. I told him maybe this creep Byrne—the one that's missing—maybe he copped the dough, like we were saying. He's checking it out."

"Damn!" Dean said, jumping up and charging toward Baratto, who began to backpedal. "I don't believe it! You gave your low-life friends my name and address so they could ransack my house and maybe kill someone who got in their way?"

"No, no. Just your phone number! I didn't know where you lived!" Dean took a lunging swing at Baratto that missed by a foot as Harrigan grabbed him.

Jonathan Winston pulled Baratto away, and turned to give Dean a scathing look that said *It's your fault for not keeping your mouth shut.* He pointed his finger. "What did I tell you?"

Vinnie screamed, "You can't hit me! I've got a lawyer!" and yelled over his shoulder, "Hey, Arthur, they're trying to kill me! Get your ass up here! They're going whacko!"

"Vinnie, you bastard, I'll kill you! You sicced those gangster sons-of-bitches on Cynthia Byrne too!"

"Davey, I didn't mean no harm. I didn't tell 'em to do nothing to you!"

Winston dragged him toward the doorway, pausing by Rita's desk. "Sorry 'bout the language, Ma'am."

"No problem," she answered, neither stopping her typing nor looking up.

"Oink! Oink! Oink! You bastard pig slopper!" Dean screamed after Vinnie, shrugging off Harrigan and slumping into his chair. Dean pounded his fist on the desk in disgust just as Andy Sackler entered the room.

"Your buddy Vinnie's lawyered-up with your girlfriend's partner, Arthur Atherton. The two sleaze-bags deserve each other."

"That's all I need," Dean moaned. "That son-of-a-bitch Vinnie! I never should have answered his phone call."

Leland Anderson burst out of his office. "Hold-up down on Broad Street. Sackler and Dean, get down there!"

Dean grabbed his coat, glad to be doing something that took his mind off Vinnie Baratto, Arthur Atherton and the fact he and Cynthia Byrne were items of interest to some very nasty people.

Sackler and Dean spent the afternoon listening to the exaggerated tale of a variety store owner who had been held up at gunpoint, and supposedly relieved of $1,500. The store hadn't done $500 in business the past month by the looks of things, and the two hardened robbers sounded like kids. Nevertheless, the owner was frightened enough to stain the front of his pants. He swore the water pistol found outside couldn't have been the weapon. It was nowhere near large enough and how could he have been that mistaken? But the old man, finally, with much reluctance, agreed to

re-figure the amount stolen when Dean began to ask how frequently deposits were made and *offered* to check bank records.

The investigation killed the entire afternoon and part of the
evening before they finished checking the neighborhood. By 8:00,
Dean was ready to call it a day. He'd eaten neither lunch nor dinner.

On a prompt from his answering machine, Dean called the station and checked the night desk for messages. There were two.
Cynthia Byrne called saying he needn't be concerned about the
burglary as nothing had been stolen and it was probably just kids.
He considered returning her call but dismissed the idea. He'd
already inadvertently caused her enough problems. He'd stay clear
and give her a rest.

Jonathan Winston called to report that J. Cleary was the only
listed person to receive mail at the Bascomb Street address and
there had been no form filed requesting forwarding. Dean was surprised by the FBI's prompt response to what he'd described to
Winston as an unimportant matter.

Fred was being consoled by Mrs. Abernathy or some other of
his lady friends so Dean spent the evening alone with the sound of
a little early Nat King Cole trio, vintage forties. It was a sweet
instrumental sound, recorded long before the popular velvet voice
replaced Cole's beautiful jazz. He munched on a leftover casserole
some thoughtful neighbor had donated to poor hero Fred and was
about to doze when the telephone startled Mrs. Lincoln from his
lap.

"Mr. O'Connor there?" It was an elderly woman. Dean didn't
recognize the voice.

"I'm sorry, he's out," Dean answered, feeling like a social secretary.

"Well, tell him Mrs. Glass called." She started to hang up
before Dean fairly yelled for her to wait.

"I didn't realize it was you, Mrs. Glass. I'm the other man who
was with Mr. O'Connor."

"What?" she asked. Dean repeated at a higher volume.

"Oh." She sounded disappointed. "Well, you told me to call if
Mr. Cleary came back."

"And he did?"

"Yes. I didn't see him but he telephoned...to tell me he was finished with the apartment. He said he mailed me the key to the new lock."

"Did he give you his forwarding address?" Dean found himself yelling.

"No. We were sort of cut off before I could ask for one."

"Did he say anything else?"

She paused. "Well, he surely was surprised people were asking for him."

"You told him we came by?"

"Certainly. Why not?"

"Shit!" Dean said, not caring if she heard him or not. He added, "You said yes when I asked if he came back but you didn't see him?"

"I saw his motor home when I went to lunch with Rose O'Brien. She and I always go out on Friday. That's 20 percent off day for seniors."

Dean asked her about the motor home but she could give little information except to say it was boxy looking and blue...or white...or light colored. "How do you know it belonged to Mr. Cleary?" Dean asked.

"I don't know who else," she replied, as if that made perfect sense.

Beautiful, thought Dean. Just beautiful. If Cleary didn't want to be located, any chance of Dean doing so now he knew someone was looking for him would be next to impossible.

"When did he call?" he asked, trying to salvage something from the conversation.

"This afternoon. To tell the truth, I didn't think I'd ever hear from him. I thought he might want a refund on his unused rent, not that I'd have given it to him, but he didn't even ask."

Dean thanked her and was about to hang up but she insisted he tell that nice Mr. O'Connor she had called and would hold him to his promise to stop by and see her.

Each time Dean put the Byrne disappearance to rest in his mind, another nagging item popped up to renew his attention. He silently chastised himself for even caring that some guy named Cleary had spent a few weeks in Scranton and now was traveling off in the sunset in a blue-white-or-lavender motor home. He even considered not mentioning Mrs. Glass's phone call to Fred but dismissed the idea as being too dishonest with the old man. He pledged to himself to refuse any further urge to "beat this dog," as his Norfolk detective friend had so aptly put it. But all his good intentions and promises went up in smoke minutes later with another phone call.

"This here's Chip Burgess—from Scranton." The voice sounded nervous to Dean's ear. "I got that picture you sent me. The one of the guy you're looking for?"

"Yes," Dean answered, holding his breath.

"Cleary looked a lot older."

"It's not a new picture—ten or fifteen years old."

"Yeah, well...I think it's the same guy."

"You're sure?"

"Yeah. Sort of. I mean, I didn't pay much attention those times I saw him but it looks like the guy." Then he added, "Is there a reward?"

Dean wasn't sure how to respond. "I'll have to check," he answered after a pause.

"Is the guy dangerous?"

"I understand from Mrs. Glass he was back in town but has moved out, so you don't have to worry. You didn't see him today, did you?"

"Naw. I was on the job. How about I call you in a few days to see if there's maybe a reward." He hung up before Dean could question him further.

Fred was surprised Dean was still up when he opened the front door a little after 12:00. His shirttail was out and he looked like the lady friend had put him through his paces.

"Kind of a wild night?" Dean chided with a smile.

"None of your business," Fred replied. "How come you're up this late?"

Dean eased into the latest news by first telling of Winston's unsuccessful inquiry about a Post Office forwarding address before mentioning his conversation with Mrs. Glass.

"Damn!" said the old man, sinking into his chair. "Her and her big mouth. Why did she have to go and tell Cleary we were hot on his trail asking about him?"

"It's my fault," said Dean. "I never cautioned her to keep quiet about us."

Fred shook his head and chuckled. "Cleary must be going bonkers wondering how we got on to him."

"Whoever he is," Dean muttered. Fred said nothing and Dean finally dropped the bombshell—Chip Burgess's telephone identification of Cleary-Byrne. Fred was ecstatic.

After a string of I-knew-its and I-told-you-so's he asked, "So what are you going to do?"

Dean reiterated the obvious—Burgess was less than positive and the picture he sort-of identified was years old. Additionally, his agenda was questionable—his interest was more in a reward than anything else. Admittedly, the identification elevated the entire business to a higher, more serious level of concern. However, Dean possessed no cogent thoughts on what to do with this new information. He was already topping Jonathan Winston's list by even suggesting a connection between Byrne and the money. "Let's sleep on it and see what makes sense in the morning," he said with a yawn as he rose.

"That's the problem with you young people," Fred muttered, remaining in his chair and picking up his notebook. "You give up too soon."

# CHAPTER XIV

**TUESDAY, MAY 18, 1999  10:00 A.M.**

St. Thomas the Apostle Church was a scrubbed-white structure looking like a New England calendar except for its city location. Dean arrived just as the service was beginning, having been at his desk since 7 a.m. stewing over the recent turn of events. The only decision he'd made was to do nothing until there was clear evidence tying Byrne to the money. With no firm plan of action emerging with the morning sun, Dean scooted out of the house early, not yet ready to discuss matters with Fred O'Connor. Let the old man think of something—after all, he'd been the one to make the Scranton connection, however tenuous, in the first place.

He took a few moments to sign the guest book but didn't bother looking at the names before his. He was sure Fred O'Connor would take care of that chore if he hadn't already. He knew the old man wouldn't miss the service and spotted him in the far right corner.

The crowd was respectable although it looked smaller due to the large size of the building. Dean quick-counted 138 heads from his back row seat. He recognized Edwin Mayer and a few of the other employees of World Wide, although he didn't see Jackie Rudman, the young man who had squealed on Cece Baldwin. Randy and Cynthia Byrne were in the front row seated next to a white-haired lady Dean assumed was Cynthia's mother. There were no heavily veiled figures lurking in the wings of the church.

A full funeral mass was not scheduled—only an informal memorial service. After some readings and a hymn, the priest moved to the pulpit. He seemed uncomfortable without the usual casket before him but was quite skillful in referring to Jeffrey Byrne's present status in sufficiently ambiguous terms as to not quite acknowledge Byrne was dead. He directed most of his remarks to the sadness of those left to cope with "this untimely misfortune." He spoke of Jeffrey Byrne's modest contributions to country, town, family and society in general, information probably learned only hours earlier.

Edwin Mayer rose to speak. What the man lacked in tact and diplomacy, he made up for in eloquence. He eschewed the pulpit and stood in front of the altar, looking like a caricature of Ichabod Crane, gaunt and gangling, but the words from his mouth were pure silver. The Jeffrey Byrne Mayer eulogized was a far different man than Mayer had described in his Philadelphia office. Unlike the priest, Mayer made no pretext that Byrne wasn't as dead as a Jacob Marley's knocker and, as Mayer described, was "walking the streets of gold with the angels." He directed his words directly to Cynthia Byrne with a smile of sticky sweetness that made Dean want to pop him. There was nary a dry eye in the place.

Janice Riley's husband Phil was next to speak. He stumbled as he climbed the steps to the pulpit and grasped the podium like a life preserver. He spoke of family barbecues and a week's vacation on the Jersey shore, kids growing up and Christmas eggnog shared. He was frighteningly nervous, but in Dean's mind his sincerity buried the flowery words of the Philadelphia insurance executive. Riley's comments were simple but moving and made Dean wonder if he were the eulogized party, who would speak so kindly of him—or, for that matter, even attend the memorial. The service ended in 40 minutes with the priest extending an invitation for friends to return to Mrs. Byrne's home.

As the congregation filed out the door, Dean was surprised to see attorney Arthur Atherton, Ethel Rosewater's partner and Vinnie Baratto's lawyer, rise from two rows in front of him. Arthur recognized Dean but avoided eye contact until Dean stared him down and forced a glum nod.

Dean cornered Atherton near the entrance. "Friend of the deceased?" he asked as the attorney tried to push past him.

"No," Arthur replied, adjusting his designer tie as he continued to try to step around Dean.

"I figured you'd be so busy defending the scum of the earth you wouldn't have a minute to spare. What's the matter? Are the bad boys being good this week?" Dean added, "Maybe you're just hoping someone will fall down the front steps of the church and break their neck so you can be Johnny-on-the-spot."

"If you must know, Ethel couldn't make it to the service and thought the firm should be represented." Arthur looked very uncomfortable but his voice didn't disguise his annoyance.

Dean stared coldly at the lawyer. "Arthur, I think that's bull-shit. I want to hear from your mouth your being here has nothing to do with Vinnie Baratto."

"I don't discuss privileged conversations I've had with my clients. Please get out of my way." He turned on his heels and left, making Dean sorry he'd mentioned Ethel Rosewater to Cynthia Byrne in the first place. His big mouth was continuing to place the woman in harm's way. It was as if he'd tossed out a sacrificial lamb to a flock of vultures.

Dean stepped to the sidewalk and waited for Cynthia to emerge from the church, but when she did, a crowd of friends and well wishers surrounded her, with the Mayer-the-leech encircling her shoulder with his scummy arm. Dean caught her eye from afar and waved a greeting that she acknowledged. She looked as if she wanted him to stay, or at least he told himself that, but he returned to his car. Fred could play surrogate and go back to her house, heeding the priest's invitation. One member of the Dean household was enough.

Dean wasn't sure he could greet the woman with a straight face. How could he console her for the loss of her husband while increasingly considering that the bastard's disappearance might not be as it seemed? Dean hadn't thought much about Cynthia Byrne's reaction to the ever growing possibility that her husband might be alive. While he reluctantly acknowledged his growing feelings for the lady, he couldn't help but wonder: What would she think if she learned her loving husband was a toad who'd dropped her like a rock for a measly 2.8 mil? And what would her opinion be of the guy who dug up this enlightening news and brought it to her doorstep? It was enough that he'd inadvertently set her up to be burglarized by two hoods who might have killed her had she been home. Better to stay away until the facts were known—or, hopefully, Jeffrey came in on the tide.

Dean spent the evening alone, drinking too much beer. He plugged in a Coltrane disc and then a Gerry Mulligan and laid back to commiserate with the perfect sound of it all while he closed his eyes and pretended he was happy. It was funny; he knew who blew horn with Coltrane, who played bass for Mulligan and even remembered the date Gerry's set was recorded—August 1955. When Snow stepped in on disc number three, he knew that too—the date of the jam, who was on vibes, snares and keyboard. Yet try as he may, he didn't know the names of the three little kids next door, who'd come trick-or-treating for a half dozen years, sold Girl Scout cookies and always smiled—and they knew *his* name. All he remembered was Ethel Rosewater's bra size and the price of beer at Delaney's Market. It made him feel incredibly sad, and worse, he wasn't sure why.

The next three days slid by, closer to the normal routine at both home and at the station than Dean had experienced since Jeffrey Byrne's midnight swim. Strangely, Fred made no further mention of Monday night's revealing identification of Jeffrey Byrne by Chip Burgess. There emerged a tacit agreement between the two men that Dean's position negated his direct involvement in officially pursuing the investigation. That was not to say Fred had given up on amateur detecting. His note pad was ever present and he spent a considerable amount of time on the phone. He reported his visit to the post-memorial service gathering at the Byrne's home as uneventful, adding Cynthia's mother was "a real charmer." He recounted unsuccessful calls to banks, credit bureaus and public bodies but refrained from eliciting Dean's help in these activities, nor did he seek any guidance.

Dean and Andy Sackler, his partner on the variety store hold up, methodically checked leads until they arrested two youths ages 14 and 12 who admitted to the robbery. It started out as a joke with a water pistol until the storeowner shoved 89 dollars at them and ducked under the counter screaming his head off. The two boys ran out of the store, as frightened as the old man—only they presumably held their water. By Wednesday afternoon the matter was settled and the disposition of the case was in the hands of Bobby Witherspoon, the assistant DA, and the juvenile court system.

Tom DeLeo continued doing legwork on the Wassermann case, a curious jurisdictional mess with the Federal boys in charge but legions of local flat feet in scattered municipalities doing their grunt work. The boys in suits were keeping most of the facts to themselves, much to Leland Anderson's dismay. This silence did little to get Linda Segal, the Ice Lady of the *Parkside Sentinel*, off his back. And it certainly didn't help the mood of the office. When Leland was pissed, everyone suffered.

Everyone suffered, except Dean. His blue mood following the memorial service dissipated with the passing days and he remained in fair spirits. Willie Wassermann had popped up, so to speak, on Thursday morning, so Dean was 65 dollars richer from the office pool. Willie's testicles were in the same shape as his brother's and he'd been dead about the same length of time. A family out fishing had the catch of the day, in the same general area where Billie had bobbed to light. According to Norm Hunter, the fisherwoman was so frightened she'd fainted dead away, while her 12-year-old son thought towing Willie two miles to port was super cool. Jenny Nachman pulled the short straw to carry the news to Ida Wassermann. Sex had no privilege when dirty jobs were handed out.

While Dean hadn't heard from Cynthia Byrne, it didn't mean she wasn't on his mind. As he was leaving the station for the day on Thursday, she telephoned.

"I just left Ms. Rosewater's office," she said, slightly out of breath. "I have great news! It looks as if the insurance company may be willing to advance some of the life insurance money—at least enough to tide us over for a while."

"That is good news," said Dean.

"Your report really helped. We still have to wait a little while and there are lots of details to iron out, but Ms. Rosewater says it looks positive." Dean had polished the report, adding more positive detail but not in any way referencing the Scranton connection, if there was one. He did mention his interview with Cece Baldwin, describing Byrne's relationship with the young lady as that of a compassionate mentor.

Cynthia asked him, somewhat formally, if he would come to dinner the following evening, for what she described as a surprise.

She added, as if to clarify the situation, that her son Randy would be there too. Dean agreed.

Later that evening, Ethel Rosewater confirmed Cynthia's visit as she was unzipping Dean's trousers. "It may take a while, but she shouldn't have any real difficulty having her husband declared dead—but she refuses to sue. I'd go broke if everyone was that icky-sticky moral. It's downright disgusting."

Dean ignored the remark and changed the subject. "That was a nice touch sending old Arthur to the memorial service to represent the firm." She looked at him as if he was crazy and he nodded, knowingly. "You didn't send him, did you?"

"Of course not. Why in God's name would I do that?"

"He was there. The lying bastard said you sent him."

"Well, I didn't. Arthur's getting nuttier than a Christmas fruitcake. Since I said I wouldn't marry him, he's been doing all sorts of weird things. Maybe he's going through the change or something."

"Weird things like taking on Vinnie Baratto for a client?"

"Never heard of him. He must be a referral from his Philly pals."

Dean was hesitant to discuss this or any aspects of the job with Ethel. Quite frankly, he was never sure he could trust her. But fishing was fair play. He chose his words carefully. "Whoever referred him to Vinnie, he'd better watch out. Those boys want to take Vinnie on a one-way fishing trip. What other weird things is ol' Arthur doing?"

"Oh, like snooping—looking through my files. I don't think his finances are any too strong either."

"You're partners. Shouldn't you each know what the other's doing?"

"I charge him for the office space and clerical help but we operate independently. It's my show. His name's on the sign so it looks like we're a big-ass razzle-dazzle firm just like in Philly. No one respects a one-person shop."

"So why was he at the Byrne memorial service? Bird-dogging one of your clients?"

She thought a minute. "The bastard better not be."

"How much work does Arthur really do for the bad guys? Any way of telling?" She started to protest attorney-client privilege but he shook his head. "I'm not looking for details, I'm just curious."

She laughed. "Arthur's always bragging—talking about his connections in Philly. It's mostly talk. Sometimes they toss him a crumb but they have their pros for the important stuff. Why? Is this Vinnie Baratto a big time bad guy?"

"He thinks he is. But he's gotten some wild idea about the Byrne case. Do me a favor and keep Arthur away from that file. First, it's none of his business and second, he's all wet; there is no connection. Plus, I wouldn't trust Arthur as far as I could toss him and if he screws around with this he could get someone killed."

"I wouldn't trust him either, honey bunch. I just keep him around 'cause he does have *some* clean friends in high places. Plus, I need to have a man in the firm. There are still too many shit heads out there that think a woman is only for cooking and you-know-what. If I have to boot Arthur, I'll just get another pair of long pants to take his place."

Dean folded his own long pants over the back of a chair, careful not to lose his pocket change. His mind was less on Ethel Rosewater than other matters. Ethel pulled him down on the bed. "Let's get busy," she said.

Only David Dean had some difficulty "getting busy." No, Dean had a *lot* of difficulty getting busy. In fact, he couldn't get busy at all. The majority of his body was moderately awash with passion and Ethel was as warm and soft as ever. But one vital part of his anatomy expressed no interest in the proceedings. Ethel, her usual sympathetic self, reached for her cigarettes and began to get dressed after what she deemed sufficient time to put up with the unsuccessful performance.

"They say it happens every once in a while, especially when you're getting old," she said. If this was meant as a joke, Dean didn't find it very funny.

"Thanks for your kind thoughts," he said, sarcastically. "You know, this is a man's worst nightmare. You could show a little compassion."

"Hey," she said, slapping him on the backside, "I'll give you a few more evenings to try before I turn you in for a younger model. If you want to discuss sympathy, think about poor me, pining away for a hot time and getting nada."

He was home by 9:00, shattered masculinity and all.

# CHAPTER XV

Summer moved into Parkside on Friday, if only for a preview, blanketing the city with the hot-and-stickies. Everyone lolled around the squad room, shirt collars and windows open, and neither providing much relief. Occasionally a little breeze puffed in but it was more of an annoyance than a help, scattering papers and patience in a hot breath of sweat and exhaust. The FBI had put out a statement they were handling the Wasserman case and pursuing strong leads out of state. This pulled some of the heat from the Parkside Police Department, and even the Ice Lady seemed to be backing off, improving her editorial chastisement and the mood of Lieutenant Anderson with it. Paperwork kept Dean chained to his desk until after lunch and he spent the afternoon pacing the courthouse corridor until plea-bargained to freedom shortly before five. He was due at Cynthia Byrne's by 6:00, giving short time for a shower and shave.

The drive to Maid Marian Lane was becoming more familiar with each passing trip—no more need to count the blocks. He was surprised however, when a "For Sale" sign greeted him on the front lawn. Cynthia explained it away, saying it was about time she moved to a smaller place. Randy would not be around much longer and she didn't want the sole burden and responsibility of upkeep. The realtor's estimate of the value of the property pleased her.

The past few days had done much to improve Cynthia Byrne and she beamed with pleasure when Dean presented a bottle of wine, the same brand and year they were served at Café Richard. Randy's young girlfriend, Jenny, a bright and quiet little thing, arrived just after Dean and the four chatted easily before dinner. It was heartening to see two young people who obviously cared for one another. Cynthia served a pot roast, simple but delicious, reminding Dean of Sundays in years gone by. It was his first home-cooked meal in memory, if you could discount the occasional donated casseroles from Fred O'Connor's lady friends. As soon as dinner was finished, the hostess tapped her water glass for attention.

"I have two announcements," she said with a smile.

"Two?" Randy raised his eyebrows.

"Randy and Jen know about the first, but the other is a surprise to everyone!" She paused a moment before continuing. "Announcement number one—Randy has been accepted at Bucknell! He's to start in September!" The pride in her voice lit up the room.

"Terrific!" said Dean, shaking the young man's hand.

"The baseball helped a lot," Randy said, "between it, a campus job and some loans, I should be able to swing it. It's a great school."

"And," Cynthia said, with much fanfare, "announcement number two—I have a job!"

They clapped in unison and congratulated her. "I won't finish with school until the fall but a clinic has hired me. It doesn't pay much, but it's a start. Until I'm certified, I'll do clerical jobs and help out. Hopefully, they'll use me as a full-time therapist later. The clinic understands my school hours and they are willing to work around them. I'm thrilled to death!" Dean grabbed her hand and squeezed it. "This is the start of my new life, and I wanted to share it." She looked Dean in the eye. "I didn't know how else to thank you."

Cynthia looked a bit misty-eyed as she rose and began picking up the dishes and turned to her son. "I know it's been less than a month since your father died," she said, "and it's been tough. But if I don't get on with my life I'll lose my mind. I know your dad would approve." She gave him a hug. Randy just smiled in a way that said he understood.

The four sat in the living room with everyone but Dean discussing their future. Jen, the valedictorian of her class, was to attend Ryder College in New Jersey and major in English

Literature. Randy, a science buff, was in the top third of the graduates and was also his class president. Dean, while feeling exceptionally stupid, enjoyed himself in spite of it.

Shortly after nine, Randy rose to take Jen home. The two planned an outing the next day at the Jersey shore and wanted to get an early start. Although Dean wouldn't have minded staying, he too rose to leave. Cynthia did not stop him.

"Why don't you two go biking tomorrow?" Randy suggested as he was leaving. "I fixed the flat on Mom's bike." It seemed to Dean it was the young man's way of telling his mother that he was comfortable with her allowing Dean to peek into the corners of their life.

"I'm sure Mr. Dean doesn't want to wait up for an out-of-shape old lady lagging behind him." Dean noticed she hadn't dismissed the suggestion entirely. "He'd leave me in the dust," she added, but after some joking, agreed to let Dean pick her up at ten the next morning. He sang to himself at the top of his voice all the way home to Collingswood Avenue.

When Dean pulled into his drive he was surprised to see the lights on, as he'd expected Fred to be out for the evening. He should have guessed something was up—the old man wasn't even playing his twangy music.

"You look happier than a moth on a cashmere sweater," Fred said.

"All's right with the world," Dean replied.

"Not quite *all*," Fred answered. "Your friend Detective Hunter called from Norfolk."

"On Friday night?" The smile melted from Dean's face.

"He thought it might be important, seeing as you asked the question. He was gonna just leave a message but I explained I knew all about the case. He ran down the receipt that was found in Byrne's car. It was for a pair of bike shoes." Dean started to say something but Fred continued. "Hunter showed the clerk a picture of Byrne but he couldn't identify him—it was too long ago. The guy said the face looked familiar but it's a big store, there's lots of clerks and it's an old picture."

"Another *maybe*," Dean said muttered.

"That's not all," Fred continued. "I spent 20 minutes on the phone with Mrs. Glass. She wanted to know what the devil was going on. Someone else was asking about her favorite tenant, Mr. Cleary."

"Nota!" Dean exclaimed in disbelief.

"I expect so," Fred answered. "Mrs. Glass said the guy asked for Cleary by name."

"How would Nota get Mrs. Glass's number or even know Cleary even existed?"

"I think I figured it out," Fred said. "My notes about Cleary and our investigation in Scranton were down here when those bozos broke in. Mrs. Glass's number was on the telephone pad. Later when I looked, the note pad was blank. I figured I was getting absentminded in my old age and I tossed it when I was cleaning up. They searched the living room pretty good."

"There's a chance Cleary is just a cheating husband and someone is chasing him down." Dean's scenario lacked conviction and both knew it.

"Mrs. Glass told him he wasn't the first person asking about her Bascomb Place tenant and the fellow wanted to know all about us."

"What else did she tell him?"

"Not much, by the sound of it."

Dean began to slowly pace the room. "If it was Nota, chances are he won't have any better luck chasing down Cleary than we did. Or maybe he'll find Cleary, learn he isn't Byrne, and put this whole business to rest."

"Don't wait up for the Easter Bunny for that one. And don't forget the matter of the bike shoes."

"Byrne biked. Buying the shoes could be innocent enough."

"So where are the bike shoes now?" Fred asked. "They weren't in the motel room inventory. And where'd Byrne get the money to buy them? We had his cash figured down to pocket change."

Dean thought a moment. "Who says Byrne bought them? He wasn't alone all day. He took that guy Brunel out for a drink. Maybe Brunel's a biker too and they're his shoes."

"But nobody's contacted him yet. Can't the Norfolk police chase him down?"

"It's Norfolk's case—not Parkside's or mine. They've been more than generous with help and information but the investigation is closed and I have to tip-toe on ice digging into it. There's still not a shred of proof tying Byrne to Scranton, the money, or being alive."

"If you believed that was a fact we wouldn't be sitting here talking about it. If you'd spend as much time chasing after the truth as you do trying to convince your gut instincts they're wrong maybe we'd get somewhere."

Dean let out a deep sigh. "You should have been at Byrne's house tonight and seen the warmth of that family. Cynthia's finally starting to pull her life together and now we drag up all these questions. If the sorry son-of-a-bitch isn't dead and I find him, I think I'll kill him myself!"

"So are you going to go to Lieutenant Anderson with this stuff?"

Dean looked up. "It's not enough. All we have is a few unanswered questions and circumstantial evidence. There's not a lick of factual proof and there's a chance there never will be. Winston would have my job if I blew his mob case on unfounded speculation and if I went public in any way, the news is sure to get out. It was my big mouth mentioning Byrne in front of Baratto that caused most of this problem but God knows what an open investigation would unfairly do to Cynthia Byrne. She's convinced her husband is somewhere on the bottom of Chesapeake Bay. She's just now beginning to see things clearly for the first time in weeks. How can I drag out a pile of maybes and cause her to spend the rest of her days wondering if hubby will jump out from behind some bush? It's just not fair."

"So you gonna ignore all this?"

Dean looked at him long and hard. "You know me better than that, Fred. I can't turn my back on it either. Much as I still think Byrne is dead there are too many unanswered questions."

Fred was uncommonly quiet and minutes passed before he spoke. "My read is you've got feelings for Cynthia Byrne, but not being up-front with her is like walking a tight rope on a windy day. If it comes out later you weren't truthful with her there's a good chance you can kiss any future goodbye."

Dean's silence acknowledged his agreement.

"I guess it boils down to a case of doing what's right in spite of the consequences," Fred said, sounding like the old philosopher. He poured a cup of cold coffee from the pot and picked up Mrs.

Lincoln in one arm, interrupting her licking the remains of a bowl of chocolate pudding. He sat at the kitchen table, sipping the cold coffee and patting the cat. "You can't be blamed if *I* keep doing a little snooping, independent like."

Dean took a deep breath, unsure. "Just telephone stuff—nothing public unless there's proof. Factual truth. If we hit a dead end, it's a dead issue. I'm not going to open this up—to anyone—and cause Cynthia Byrne years of doubt on suspicions, no matter how strong our feelings become."

"Fair enough," Fred answered. "Now, let's work on the premise Byrne didn't drown and start trying to find where he is instead of pretending he didn't skip!" Fred could hardly contain his excitement.

Dean smiled in spite of himself as Fred swept the kitchen table clear of cups and cat, dropping a bulky folder and spilling its paper contents. "Now, the way I see it, there's three ways to prove Byrne's alive—fingerprints, positive ID, or handwriting."

"Or," Dean said, "prove he's dead."

"Scranton's the answer," Fred said, ignoring Dean. "I'll check it out real good on Monday. Until we can prove Cleary isn't Byrne, let's assume he is. Cleary must have done something in Scranton that leaves a trail. That's probably where he bought the motor home."

"We don't even know the motor home is his."

"That's what I plan to find out when I go to Scranton."

"How will you get to Scranton? You don't have a driver's license."

"I take the dad-gum bus to Atlantic City—I sure can take one to Scranton."

A thought struck Dean and he snapped his fingers. "Call Mrs. Glass back. I've got an idea." Fred looked at him. "Go ahead. If I call her at this time of night, she'll bite my head off but she thinks you're the cat's pajamas. She should have received the key back from Cleary. Ask her where the envelope was postmarked."

Fred smiled. "Gotcha! Cleary mailed it before he knew we were looking for him! He'd have no reason to cover his tracks!" Fred began to dial. "Why do you suppose he mailed it back at all? He could have just tossed it in the drink."

"Why not? He had no reason to antagonize Mrs. Glass and have her upset with him."

Fred was so sticky-sweet on the phone with the landlady that Dean took a break and used the john just so he wouldn't have to listen to the dribble. When he returned, Fred was holding down a pad of paper with his elbow and writing with his free hand. Dean looked over his shoulder, expecting to see a local postmark but read, written in block letters, *Rollins, Kansas*. While Fred continued his conversation, Dean rummaged through the front hall closet until he located an atlas. He was thumbing through the pages when Fred leaned over to him.

"Mrs. Glass just painted apartment C. Somebody rented it. Scratch any chance of fingerprints."

"Who ever Cleary is, by design or luck, he isn't making it easy for us," Dean said as he continued to search. "Kansas is the last place I'd have guessed."

"He didn't pedal a bicycle to Kansas either, Dorothy," Fred said, peering at the map.

"Here it is, Rollins." Dean pointed to a small dot midpoint on the page. "It's out in the middle of nowhere, just off the interstate. He's headed west."

"Get your AAA book," Fred said. "See if there's a motel or something."

"I doubt he's staying in Kansas. He's probably on the road— maybe going to California." He began perusing a fat envelope of Midwest travel information secured for his July Iowa bike tour. There were no motels listed in Rollins, Kansas. "Maybe he just mailed the key from there and stayed in a larger town nearby."

"Well, it's a start," Fred answered glumly.

Dean tried to remember his earlier phone conversation with Mrs. Glass. "When Cleary spoke to his landlady on Monday, the seventeenth, he told her he'd already mailed her the key."

Fred looked at the wall calendar. "He took his time getting to Kansas. Byrne disappeared on May fourth, almost two weeks earlier."

Dean tossed aside the map and papers and flopped down on the living room sofa, startling Mrs. Lincoln. "That's too much time in between."

"He was working on his new identity. Maybe waiting for papers to come."

Dean thought a moment. "If I skipped the way you're saying he did, I'd want to get as far away as soon as possible."

"Maybe," Fred said as he plunked down beside his stepson. "Let's run it from the beginning. You're Byrne and you've found the dough—more than you'll see in a lifetime. Untraceable. You make up your mind—to keep it and skip."

"Okay—I'm just speculating," Dean closed his eyes. "You need an identity—papers in your name—charge accounts, a bank where you can feed in a little money at a time, a driver's license, all that stuff."

"You can buy an identity." Fred dismissed the problem with a wave of his hand.

"Only in your mystery stories. An insurance clerk wouldn't know where to start. Byrne was a loner and super cautious. Besides, between the time he found the money and when he disappeared, he lived a regular life. According to his expense accounts, he only went to Scranton twice that we know of—both visits only a day or two. That doesn't give him much time to apply for false papers."

"That's why it took him two weeks to make it to Kansas," Fred answered. "His first step was renting an apartment and getting an address—a mail drop. Scranton. He establishes an identity—J. Cleary."

"What about Pat Corbin?" Dean asked

"Churchez la femme," Fred said. "Just like I been saying all along."

"Her, or *him*! Pat is a pretty androgynous name. Only Burgess saw Cleary and no one saw Corbin. Say Cleary rented the place innocently—he's a coast-to-coast truck driver or something and needs a temporary place, just like Burgess. Maybe Corbin just used it too and received some mail there."

"And the *Parkside Sentinel*?" Fred reminded Dean. "Maybe Corbin is just another name—a *nom de plume*—another alias for Byrne, just in case. Like belts and suspenders."

Dean changed the subject. "Let's talk about the bicycle. How does that come into play?"

Fred thought a moment. "He buys the bike in Scranton or someplace up north and stashes it in the trunk of his company car, dropping the tire patch kit. He hides the bike on the beach, maybe with some clothes. He pretends to drown, sleeps on the beach for a few hours, and about dawn pedals off into the sunrise."

"In his new bike shoes," Dean added. "But he doesn't really need bike shoes unless he plans to bike a long distance."

"How are they different from regular shoes?" Fred asked.

"They've got a plate on the sole so your feet don't get numb and they hold on to the pedal better."

"So where does he bike to? Sure not to Kansas—bike shoes or not." Fred snapped his fingers. "To his motor home!"

Dean smiled. "Too many vehicles in one place for one person."

"Maybe we're back to Pat Corbin as an accomplice," Fred suggested.

"I like your one-guy theory better so I'll help you out here. What do you do if you have two vehicles and one driver?"

"You tow it!" Fred answered. "He bought a motor home in Scranton and towed his company car down to Norfolk!"

"I'll help you out again," Dean offered. "He could account for the correct mileage on the car if he used a tow bar that kept the wheels on the road. He could figure the gas he'd have used and written his own receipt when he filled up the motor home, stopping after filling the tank part way."

"So why haul the bike in the car and not the motor home?" Fred asked, in a reversal of rolls.

"Because he parked the motor home in some campground near Norfolk, then transferred the bike to his car, stashed the bike somewhere down the beach and used it the next morning, like you said, to get back to the motor home. He's barefoot after he leaves his shoes on the beach and needs some kind of footwear so he might as well get bike shoes; after all, he's biking."

They both looked at each other. "It plays, doesn't it?" Fred said.

Dean nodded in agreement. "Most of it *could* fit. But saying it *could* fit doesn't mean our little scenario is what actually happened. The newspaper business bothers me. Why subscribe to the paper so early? He wasn't in Scranton very often and the papers would pile up. If he subscribed to it just so he could see what was hap-

pening *after* he skipped, why not have the paper forwarded to
where he was going? It wouldn't do him any good sitting in the hall
in Scranton after he skipped. Jonathan Winston said there wasn't a
forwarding notice on file under Cleary or Corbin. The apartment
was cleared out some time ago, or at least his name was off the
mailbox. They weren't laying around when you and I were there.
So where are the newspapers?"

"Just some loose ends." Fred dismissed Dean's comments
with a wave of his hand. "It still plays. We look for a campground
near Rollins, Kansas. Not a motel. And a campground near Norfolk.
Maybe this guy isn't so smart after all."

"We haven't had much luck chasing Cleary down so far. Now
that Mrs. Glass has spilled the beans that someone's looking for
him, if he wants to remain incognito, he's going to be twice as cautious."

Fred was undeterred. "Cora Abernathy's son and his family go
camping. They've got a directory the size of the Philadelphia
phone book. I'll borrow it and start calling some places." Fred
licked the end of his pencil and began making notes.

"Who will you be asking for?" Dean asked.

"Cleary, Corbin, any single guy, a motor home with paper
Pennsylvania plates that checked in on the May dates we know—
any of those things."

"Byrne could have a pocket full of aliases for all we know,"
Dean grumbled. "Cleary and Corbin might just be the start."

"Too bad you couldn't have your FBI pal Winston check out a
few more names for us. Run down this missing fellow Brunell too,"
Fred said, a hopeful look in his eye.

"No outside involvement, remember? You're on your own on
this."

It was after one before they ran out of steam and called it a
night. Just before they turned in, Fred looked Dean in the eye and
said, "I know I'm looking ahead just a tad, but if you marry that gal,
we'll have to get a bigger house. There ain't any way this place will
fit all three of us." He had by that statement firmly established his
position for the future.

Neither slept very well.

# CHAPTER XVI

Saturday was one of those days with weather so perfect as to remember weeks after its passing. There was no humidity, an ideal temperature and enough of a breeze to perfume the air with the zillion flowers recently wakened after a tough winter or perhaps just planted to welcome the approaching summer season. No activity was more natural than spending the day like this biking the Pennsylvania countryside—with Cynthia Byrne.

The light jackets came off early as the pair pedaled along, mostly riding side by side since the rural roads carried sparse traffic. The two laughed and chattered like lifelong friends, perfectly comfortable in each other's company. Cynthia was thrilled with her new job and her school classes were finally coming together. Three prospective buyers had looked at the house and at least one seemed interested. While Dean caught brief hints of melancholy, she seemed for the most part successful in putting darker thoughts aside, content to enjoy the peace of the day.

The scent of lilacs filled the air and in the woods, white dogwood stood in stark contrast against the multi shades of green wakening to spring. Whole fields were yellow with buttercups or white with the ghosts of dandelions whose tiny parachutes floated off, seeking fertile fields in which to propagate.

Jeffrey Byrne's wife was in far better physical shape than she had let on, and the pair managed 20 miles before finally calling it quits, not because she was tired, but because, as she said, her what-sis was so sore. They picnicked on fresh bread and jam washed down with warm Gatorade and a banana for dessert, sprawled in the grass next to a country stream, in a meadow abloom with spring flowers. Their only company was an inquisitive cow that stared at these intruders in her personal domain. It was an unforgettable day and Dean never once thought of the missing Mr. Byrne until mid-afternoon while they were taking a short break and Cynthia mentioned his name.

"It was strange reading your report on Jeff—hearing what everyone thought of him. Mostly he was the man I knew but in some ways, he seemed like a stranger, especially at work."

"No one knew him as well as you," Dean answered, "It's your picture of him that's the most defined." He remembered some of the comments of Byrne's World Wide boss. "You have to take some of Mayer's remarks with a pinch of salt."

"You're right, of course." Then she added, "I was pleased by the comments of that girl Cece Baldwin—how Jeff went out of his way to help her. He'd mentioned her a number of times and I know he felt she had potential but was handicapped by her lack of self respect."

"She thought very highly of your husband," Dean said. He had spent extra time wording the young woman's remarks.

Cynthia mounted her bike. "Jeff and I used to bike a lot when Randy was just an infant," she reminisced, as she rested in the shade of a giant maple. "I had a little seat on the back for Randy and he loved it. I haven't biked for years."

While he wished she'd change the subject from her former husband, Dean handled it well. "It's great exercise," he said.

"As long as the road is flat." Cynthia laughed.

"The hills are the tough part."

"They weren't for Jeff. He loved to climb hills, the higher the better. He liked the challenge. He always wanted to bike in the mountains but we had trouble enough funding two weeks vacation on the Jersey shore with the Rileys."

At first, Cynthia seemed unaware that her reminiscences made Dean uncomfortable but when he didn't respond, she turned and looked at him. "I'm sorry. I'm being unfair. You didn't invite me out here to listen to my maudlin rambling." Dean mumbled an insipid apology. She continued. "I am getting better. I can talk about Jeff in the past tense now. That's progress, isn't it?" He returned her smile. "I still hate it when the telephone rings. I won't pick it up if I'm alone. I bought one of those answering machines and I let the phone ring until it gives my messages and I find out who's calling. I'm still frightened it will be the police in Norfolk even though I know that's silly. They told me if Jeff's body wasn't found the first couple of weeks, it had probably washed out to sea and would maybe never be located. If he were in a grave—in a cemetery somewhere—I could go there and put flowers on it. Then maybe it wouldn't be so difficult to put it out of my mind." She closed her eyes and turned her back to him. "I feel so comfortable with you—you let me forget. Even when my mother was here, we couldn't seem to say the right thing to each other. It makes me feel terribly guilty, enjoying myself with you. I should be wearing black instead of enjoying myself, even if it's only once in awhile. Randy has been so good about it—so encouraging, but even so—I feel like it's a sin to smile, or laugh."

"Comfortable. Just like an old slipper," he replied, with just a hint of melancholy in his voice.

"I like being with you, I really do. But..." she searched for the right words, "we're just friends, for now, right?" He nodded slowly. "At least for now, please? I realize I'm taking advantage of you— I'm being horribly unfair, but things are just too confusing—it's so soon after, okay?" He thought she would cry but instead she lay back on the grass, arms beneath her head, and after a time, began naming the shapes of the clouds passing across the sky.

Later, when the game had run to silence, she became serious once more. "Sometimes when I wake up I can't believe my life has changed so much in three weeks. I've gone through emotions I didn't know I possessed." She turned and looked at him. "And every time it's been really, really tough, you're the one who's been there."

"You've used up your quota of thank you's. I won't accept anymore," he said.

She raised on an elbow, a broad smile growing across her face. "You know something? You're the only man besides my husband and maybe some doctors who's ever seen me naked—at least since I was a little girl!" She laughed and clutched his arm. "God, I can't believe I told you that! I swore to myself I'd never, ever mention it!" She covered her face. "I was so embarrassed I never wanted to see you again! And look, now I've gone and embarrassed you all

over again!" He could feel his ears redden as he started to say
something but she stopped him, still laughing. "No—it's all right!
God knows you probably saved my life, at least from exposure or
pneumonia. I wasn't even conscious of what was happening."

He smiled, in spite of himself. "I was nervous as a cat that
you'd wake up but I had to do something. You were soaking wet
and shivering like a leaf."

"No, no—don't tell me about it!" She paused, then asked,
"Was there really a power failure or were you just saying that? No,
no, don't answer that either. I don't want to know!"

"Totally black. I couldn't see a thing. So how did you know?"

She laughed and bit her lip trying to stop. "You put my panties
on inside out!" Before he could reply, she jumped up, still laughing, grabbed his hand and tugged at him. "I can't stand this anymore—come on, let's put our feet in the brook!"

A perfect day doesn't make you feel less like a bastard for not
being honest, for holding back important things from someone you
care about, especially if that someone is the person making the day
perfect. That was exactly how Dean felt after he dropped off
Cynthia Byrne at her empty house. If she wanted him to come in,
she didn't suggest it and he wasn't about to rush matters. Part of
him felt like a pimply 16-year-old chasing the prom queen, while
the rest of him was a lying, cheating sneak thief. He didn't like
either feeling one bit. But being around Cynthia Byrne was worth
all the aggravation of these mixed emotions.

Dean returned home dreading what new tales of woe Fred
O'Connor might have discovered in his absence. He plunked himself down in the living room with a hit-me-with-your-best-shot
look and lifted Mrs. Lincoln to his lap for moral support.

Fred took little time with his preamble before pushing forward. "I found the campground in Virginia where he stayed. It only
took me six tries. Not many places are open weekdays that early in
the season. Our boy was 'James Rogers from Lancaster,
Pennsylvania.' He and his wife stayed one night, the third of May.
But the wife didn't come to the office so he was probably faking
it."

"What on earth made you think that camper was the one you
were looking for?"

"Paper license tag—from Pennsylvania," Fred said smugly.

Dean sighed. "How did they happen to remember one camper nearly three weeks ago?"

"Whoa! Give me a break! She remembered 'cause she hasn't had a dozen customers since. She didn't write down the license info—she skips that stuff unless the place is crowded. The rig was a Pace Arrow. It's a full-size motor home—around 32 feet, she guessed."

"Was he towing a car?" Dean asked.

"No. But he could have already parked it somewhere else, and then gone on to the camp ground." Fred sounded disappointed.

"Did you get her to send a copy of the registration card so we could check the signature?"

Fred shook his head. "This guy is cute. He had this rag wrapped around his right hand. Said he'd cut it on his tow bar. She wrote his name for him so there ain't no signature."

"Could she at least ID him if she saw a picture?" Fred fidgeted. "What's a matter?"

"I don't think so. The guy had black hair and a mustache."

"Hell, Fred! It's just some guy and his wife on vacation. We don't have any more idea it's Cleary than Napoleon!" Dean strode to the refrigerator and opened a beer.

"It's a disguise! Plain as the nose on your face! It fits, don't it?"

"*Might fit.* That's all we keep finding. Every time something starts to make sense, up pops ten other perfectly logical answers that make a lot more sense."

"I found where he stayed in Kansas too," Fred said, but with a tad less enthusiasm than before.

"And?"

"He was Harold Syms there. He stayed one night, about three miles from Rollins, Kansas. It's the only campground near the town. Again, no signature. He came in after the office was closed, put his money in an envelope and was gone in the morning."

"Was his *wife* with him?" Dean's voice had a cut of sarcasm in it.

"They don't count heads at this place," Fred answered glumly. "And before you ask, the license plate wasn't the same. It was a regular one—from Ohio."

"Ohio! What makes you think it was the same guy?"

"He was the only person who stayed there on the night of the May sixteenth and he had a Pace Arrow camper! You don't get coincidences like that!"

They were both quiet for a long time. Fred sulked while Dean felt guilty for treating the old man's efforts so cavalierly but was too pissed in general to jump up and apologize. Instead, he polished off another beer or two. After he finally got around to apologizing, the two men opened more beer and began to discuss matters more rationally.

"You're right about one thing, Fred," Dean said. "If this is Byrne we're chasing, he's cautious as a clam. He didn't have the foggiest idea anyone was looking until after he spoke with Mrs. Glass—around Rollins, Kansas, and yet he keeps changing names, not leaving his signature and not even being seen unless he can't help it. Now that he's aware someone is looking, we'll be lucky to get a sniff of where he is."

"Yeah, I thought about that. We don't even know the Ohio license plate is right. He might have just put that on the registration card when he signed in. You can bet the numbers are wrong. He was on to that trick back at the Whitney Motel, remember?" Dean didn't comment on Fred's unproved assumption. "So, what's next?" the old man asked.

Dean smiled. "You're the detective. So far, you're the only one making any progress. I'm listening."

Fred beamed. "Well, the way I see it, he's gotta figure the motor home is hot."

"Why? He doesn't know we know about it."

"He doesn't how we know about nothing, much less how we know. It must be driving him loony. So maybe he assumes we know more than we do. He'll ditch the motor home and change his plans, if he has any."

Dean thought a moment. "How do you ditch a motor home in the middle of Kansas?"

He answered his own question as he sipped on his beer. "You sell it for a song. Money is no problem."

"Where do you ditch it?"

"The next largest town," Dean answered. Fred grabbed for the map and began searching. Dean scratched his head, irritated at himself for getting so caught up in Fred's continuing scenario, a scenario totally baseless in proven fact. He went to the kitchen for two more beers.

"Figure he's going west," Fred called. "That was the direction he was headed. Hays is the only place in Kansas west of Rollins worth a snot. Sixteen thousand people. That's big enough. He buys something different under another name. 'Course we don't know which of the names he used in the first place to register the motor home when he bought it." Mrs. Lincoln sauntered into the room, blinking her eyes at the late hour, and Fred reached down and picked her up with one arm, taking a beer from Dean with the other.

"You're already chasing four different names," Dean said.

Fred began to pace the room, patting the cat as he walked back and forth. "Think of the bright side. We're only six days behind him, maybe less."

"He can go anywhere in the world in six days, especially if he has a couple of a million dollars." Dean rose to get another beer. "Just watch the phone bill. It was nearly a hundred bucks and that was just through last week!" He opened the refrigerator but there was no more beer—only a lot of empty cans scattered around the room. Dean felt more than just a little fuzzy and decided to call it a night. As he started up the stairs, the phone rang.

It was Cynthia Byrne. After apologizing for the late hour, she again thanked him for a great day. "The most fun I've had since my six-year-old Christmas," he answered. Then, in a fit of honesty, he apologized for having put away a bit too much booze after he dropped her off.

"You're not drinking those awful manhattans are you?"

"No. Only beer."

"How much have you put away?" she asked. He could hear the smile in her voice.

"Some. Quite a bit, actually." He paused. "A lot—at least too much."

"You're crocked?"

"I wouldn't say that."

"Only because you can't pronounce the words?"

"That too. It's not a frequent occurrence."

"Does this make us even?"

"Nope. I'm still dressed." He apologized immediately. "Sorry, that was tacky."

He couldn't tell from the tone of her response if she was offended. "I'm not sure you would have said that if you were fully sober."

"You're probably right. Sorry."

"I'd guess you're *sort of* drunk." She paused. "Why are you drinking?"

"I'm not sure. I think it has something to do with you."

She laughed. "You're impossible."

"That too." Then he asked, "Do you know the names of kids next door to you?"

"Sure. Mark and Joni. Why?"

"Nothing. No reason."

"Is that important?"

"Yes."

"Why?" When he didn't at first answer, she asked, cautiously, "Does it have something to do with Jeff?"

"No!"

"Than why?"

"Because I don't know the names of the kids next door to me, that's why."

"You *are* impossible and very *sort of* drunk."

"Drunk is a relative term."

"You want me out of your life." It was more of a statement than a question.

"God, no!"

"You want me *in* your life?" Silence. "I don't think I want to discuss this with a sort-of-drunk." She laughed, but ended the conversation

It was the closest they'd ever come to an honest discussion.

# CHAPTER XVII

The last three days had slid by without anything unusual transpiring, at least on the Jeffrey Byrne matter. Sunday was a sleep-in-late kind of day, followed by a Phillies game on TV and a few naps in between mental re-hashes of the prior late-night conversation with Cynthia Byrne. Dean felt a pang of guilt for not putting the day to better use but figured he deserved a little time off to reconnoiter. Fred spent most of Sunday in his room either reading or playing with his notes until Dean had enticed him out by the smell of two steaks slapped on the outside grill. It was a subdued meal with neither mentioning the prior evening's conversation. Tommy DeLeo and his wife had invited them both over for a family cookout but Dean didn't want to be around someone else's comfortable world when his was a tossed salad.

By the time Dean made it to the kitchen Monday morning, Fred had already left on the early bus to Scranton. The note on the refrigerator said he'd be back in a couple of days and would check in by phone. Dean was beginning to have serious reservations about the trip and his tacit agreement to it now that it was a reality. In the meantime, Dean had all he could do to keep up with Parkside's police day-to-day activities.

The week started with a flurry of activity. On Monday, three Colombians were brutally murdered in Philadelphia and their dismembered body parts scattered like Easter eggs around the city of Brotherly Love. The crime was selling a zillion newspapers as the bloodthirsty public read with glee details of the gruesome treasure hunt that continued throughout the week. Somebody was making

a statement and someone else wasn't taking it too well. By
Tuesday afternoon, the Colombians had retaliated. Homer
Flanders, Tic-Face to some of his friends, was found resting in a
quiet corner of the Parkside bus terminal, his throat slit like a second grin. A small Colombian flag was neatly tucked in his open
mouth. "No, Mabel, that ain't no bright red sweater on the guy in
the corner! Oh, me-God! They done opened him up like a cat-
fish!"

The Ice Lady of the *Parkside Sentinel* went bonkers. While
killings in Philadelphia were fun reading, a murder in Parkside was
a far different matter. Homer might not have been a resident, but
he was murdered in *our* bus terminal! The streets of her city were
no longer safe for women and children. Parkside was no safer than
the worst of the worst—we might as well be living in Philadelphia,
or, God forbid, *The Big Apple*! The Parkside men in blue were nothing but a bunch of incompetent misfits who should all be fired, so
continued the tirade. School crossing guards offer better protec-
tion.

There was no stopping the chaos that reigned over the entire
Parkside Police Department until Wednesday when in rode federal agent Jonathan Winston. After a brief closed-door session with a
distraught Leland Anderson, a press conference was called and
held at headquarters.

Jonathan was a prince to behold, suave beyond description,
and with silver-tongued oratory, he calmed the fears of an entire
city. Parkside was nothing more than an innocent battleground for
disreputable elements of our society, at war with one another.
Parkside would remain untainted and a favored place to live and
raise healthy, God fearing children who would become model citizens like those to whom he spoke. All this was made possible by
the untiring work of the Parkside Police Department. Without
them, lowly federal agents would still be in the dark in identifying
the combatants in this dreadful war. Yes, those city bad boys might
continue to kill one another but the innocents of this fair city had
little to fear for their own. He made the continued killings "of
those thugs" sound like good news, but emphasized it was only a
matter of time until the might of right and justice would prevail
and calm would return to Parkside.

Linda Segal, The Ice Lady, was speechless. She gawked at Jonathan like a freshman cheerleader at a senior quarterback as he gave her a smile that melted her heart. Whatever they paid this super cop, it wasn't a fraction of his worth when it came to effective PR.

Amid backslapping and handshaking, the station assumed a party atmosphere for much of the afternoon. Jonathan Winston accepted the thanks of the officers with his usual grace and dignity. Before leaving, he pulled Dean aside.

"I owe you one for delivering your buddy Baratto to us," he said. "He's working out to be quite a find."

"I'm just surprised the jerk knew anything important," Dean answered. Nevertheless, he was pleased.

"Let's say he pointed us in the right direction. He might not have opened up doors, but he showed us the keyholes where we could peek. These things have a way of falling in place. If you get close enough, sooner or later someone gets careless. We're picking up information in Maryland and we tagged where the family did in the Wassermann boys. They weren't too careful about the ownership of the property and one thing leads to another. Vinnie started a lot of action."

"No word on Nota?" Dean asked.

"He's probably back in Boston or off someplace else doing a job for hire."

Dean considered relating to Jonathan his suspicions that Nota had contacted Mrs. Glass but he was hesitant to even mention the Byrne matter to the FBI, nor did he wish to volunteer information on Fred's clandestine trip to Scranton.

Fred had called in both Monday and Tuesday evenings but had little of importance to say. He'd made a courtesy call on Mrs. Glass who had promptly donated a vacant furnished apartment for his use. Fred did say Chip Burgess was gone, his contracting job now completed. Dean knew if his stepfather had developed any worthwhile information he would have blurted it out immediately. The conversations were brief and the trip apparently uneventful, however Dean continued to have second thoughts about allowing Fred to dig into the matter on his own. He cautioned Fred to be on the lookout as they were not the only ones poking around after the past occupant of the Bascomb Place apartment.

By Wednesday afternoon police business had fallen back to routine. Andy Sackler and Dean responded to a call crosstown at Ralph's Barber Shop, where they found a crowd milling around the sidewalk and a half dozen customers seated inside. The beat cop pointed to the rear room where they found Ralph hanging from a ceiling water pipe by a thin nylon cord, slowly turning until the twist of the line tightened and reversed his direction. There was an overwhelming stench in the room. Ralph's bowels had let go. Scrawled across the wall in magic marker was his two-word epitaph, *Why not?*

When Dean returned to the outer room of the shop, everyone looked at him expectantly.

"No haircuts today, guys." He told them what they already knew. There was no telling by the blank stares on their faces if they were shocked, disappointed or just plain bored.

A short, balding man, who looked as if a haircut was more a social event than a necessity, rose to leave, and with a glance at the back room said, "Ol' Ralph always was a bit weird."

"Is someone going to tell us what happened?" asked Andy Sackler.

A younger man in a plaid shirt spoke up. "Ralph finished cutting Harry Toomey's hair and went out back. We didn't hear nothing and Phil got sick of waiting—he was next—so he went out and looked." Phil just nodded. "Harry called you guys."

Dean and Sackler took names, shooed the men out of the shop and left the back room to the medical examiner. They stepped outside for a breath of fresh air to wait. Blue skies, spring breezes, little girls playing hopscotch on the sidewalk. Not the kind of day to slowly choke to death while you leave your customers waiting. No one knew of any next of kin to notify and Dean and Sackler were back at headquarters before four.

The only phone message was from Ethel Rosewater.

"I'm just calling to check if any of your body parts are still on strike," she said cheerily when he returned her call.

"You don't beat around the bush, do you, Ethel?" Dean answered.

"Time is money, honey. If you're still having a problem I'll have to dial-a-stud. I could always call in Arthur for you, if you're changing your persuasion. I mean, if a fabulous body like mine can't get you going, maybe...."

"That's not funny, Ethel."

"Oh, don't go and get all glum-bum on me. I was just kidding."

Somehow he wasn't in the mood for Ethel's brand of jokes. He could still picture Ralph slowly turning, the flies beginning to gather. "Look, maybe we'd better slack off for a while, Ethel—what do you think?"

After a measure of dead silence came Ethel's cold voice. "It's little Miss Perfect, isn't it?" He didn't answer. "She does it better than me, huh?"

He took a deep breath. "I wouldn't know," he answered coldly. "We just talk," and then he added, "with the lights on." The phone slammed in his ear like a truck backfiring.

As soon as he'd said it he regretted it. He tried to call her back but only heard a busy signal. Sighing deeply, he told Rita he was finished for the day, jogged down the stairs to his car, and fought the late afternoon crosstown traffic to Ethel Rosewater's office.

The two women in the outer office of the Rosewater and Atherton suite looked up and started to say something as Dean waltzed by to Ethel's closed-door chamber. Ethel was standing by the window, handkerchief in hand, looking like an Indian mourner at her husband's pyre. When she saw him, a look of fury crossed her face. She grabbed the closest object, a brass paperweight, and hurled it at him, bouncing it off a picture of her shaking hands with the late governor, sending glass flying.

"Get out of here, you bastard!" she shrieked.

He crossed the room in quick strides and pinned her arms behind her back.

"I'm sorry, but I'm not about to end this business with us screaming at each other!"

"Just get out!" she sobbed, tears streaming down her face. Ethel, less than attractive in the best of times, looked horrible. Mascara ran in muddy little rivulets down her cheeks, and her eyes were as red as a three-day drunk.

"My 'lights out' crack was uncalled for, but so was what you said. Now let's acts like a couple of adults."

"I can't help it," she said, still sobbing, "I don't do rejection well." Her body began to relax as he held her tightly. Someone

knocked on the door but Ethel just yelled, "Go away." He let her
have her cry. Finally, he took out a handkerchief and wiped the
messy streaks from her cheeks and managed to get a halfhearted
smile.

"You're sweet for coming over and apologizing. Nobody does
that anymore. I don't deserve it. I'm a bitch and a middle-aged
has-been." She looked as if she might start crying again. He wished
women would stop saying nice things about him. It was becoming
annoying. David Dean, counselor of the emotionally distraught
women of the world.

"Ethel, you're just mad because you didn't dump me first.
Admit it. Let's go and have a drink and end this the right way."

"Why do we have to end it?" she said, little-girl-like.

"Because it never really started and we both know it. Now
let's get going."

"No," she sniffed, "I look terrible. I look like I'm trying out for
you-know-who in *The Wizard of Oz*. Stay a little while, please?
Here, I've got some booze." She reached down behind the desk
and brought out a bottle of gin and poured two healthy slugs into
water glasses. Dean despised gin even when properly mixed but
forced a smile as he drank it straight and warm.

He put his arm around Ethel and kissed her. "Now," he said,
"Are we still friends?"

She sniffed once. "You're too nice a guy to hate." She kicked
away a few shards of glass. "God, now I've gone and busted the
Governor. I'll have to make another contribution."

"Good," he said. "Now, I've got a question to ask."

"The answer is yes. Let's do it right here on the desk—for old
time's sake. I'll get the lights and lock the door!"

He laughed. "That's not my question. I want to know why
Arthur Atherton is interested in Jeffrey Byrne."

She gave him a pout. "You're no fun. I'd much rather fool
around than talk about that turd Arthur."

The old Ethel Rosewater was coming back and the second gin
helped. He pressed her further about Arthur and she finally
answered. "I'm not sure but I think his Philadelphia-scum friends
asked him to check around. I don't have the slightest idea why, but
I found my file on your prissy-missy girlfriend on his desk. God, to

think I only charged her half-price on her death certificate business just because she was your friend!"

"Arthur?" Dean prompted.

"You could ask Arthur yourself if he were here, but he's out on Fire Island with his latest bimboy and all their little friends. He takes long weekends every time the weather starts heating up. I want to see the sneaky bastard too. I think he's been tapping the escrow account and that's a giant no-no."

"When you see him, tell him there's nothing to check around about. It's a dead issue. I had a couple of hoods break into my house and if I find out Arthur helped them find me, I'll personally beat him into the ground."

"I'll hold him down for you," she said.

Three slugs of gin later he managed to get away, just as the desk was beginning to look appealing.


As Dean turned the corner to 422 Collingswood Avenue, another car followed and pulled into the drive behind him. He felt a momentary tightness until he recognized Randy Byrne behind the wheel.

"No practice today?" Dean asked as the two shook hands.

"No. The play-offs begin tomorrow and Coach Grayson gave us a free afternoon. We leave for State College in the morning. Ma's coming too." He seemed pleased at that. "She's not much of a baseball fan," he added.

"Best of luck. According to the *Sentinel* you guys have a good shot at taking it all."

"I hope so," Randy answered. "It would be a nice way to leave Parkside High."

The young man looked ill at ease, as if something was on his mind. Dean suggested a pizza to give him time to get it out, and the two walked a few blocks to a favorite neighborhood spot—red-checkered tablecloth and scenes of Old Sorrento on the walls. They talked mostly baseball until the mushrooms, olives, peppers, onions, sausage and extra cheese of the house special were safely put away.

Finally Randy changed the subject. "Mom let me read your report. It was...interesting, interesting to see how you guys follow up all the details."

"That's what police work is most of the time, just routine fact finding. No TV glamour." He felt like Joe Friday. "Just the facts, son."

"Cece Baldwin sounds like a nice person." Randy had a hint of hesitation in his voice.

"She is. You'd like her. She comes across like a tough gal but she's really very sweet."

Randy looked down at his empty plate. "Do you think she was...in love with my father?"

Dean paused before answering. "No. I don't think so. She needed someone who would listen and understand a little. Your father was a nice enough guy to be that person. That's all."

"You didn't mention anything about the Whitney Motel in the report."

"It didn't have anything to do with the case."

Randy thought a moment. "No, you're right. I don't suppose it did."

Finally he blurted out what was really on his mind. "You're not just seeing my mother so you can get more evidence on the case are you?" Dean started to answer but Randy continued. "'Cause if you are, that's a bum. I think she really likes you."

"No, I'm not." Dean spoke firmly and looked Randy right in the eye. He knew he was answering honestly. "I'm seeing your mother because I enjoy her company." He added, "Very much."

"Maybe I shouldn't have come to see you. It's none of my business...."

Dean reached over and took his arm. "Yes, you should have come and yes, it is your business. I'm not going to give you a now-you're-the-head-of-the-house speech but it's only been a few weeks since your father disappeared and you have a right to look out for your mother. I come along barging into your lives..."

"No, it's not that," Randy said quickly, "It's just she'd be disappointed, real disappointed if you were playing her for a sucker. It's nothing to do with dad. I'm not jealous or something; besides, it's her life, but I know she's really messed up right now and she needs someone she can count on—and trust. I just don't want her hurt any more than she has been."

They silently spooned up Italian ice cream, content in this measure of understanding that was growing between them. When the last of the dessert was scraped away, Coach Grayson, in his ever-present baseball cap and sweatshirt, entered the restaurant. The old man's face broke into a smile at the sight of Randy, and he shook the boy's hand.

"Get a good night's sleep tonight, boy. We've got some base-ball to play tomorrow; some butt to kick and we're counting on you!"

"Yes sir!" Randy answered.

Coach Grayson turned to Dean, a puzzled look on his face. He nodded and held out his hand. "Dean," he said, "not much talent but a lot of hustle. I always remember the ones with hustle." He turned and brushed past them but his remark was a bright spot in David Dean's day.

# CHAPTER XVIII

Dean dusted off a Christmas present bottle of VO with thoughts of re-igniting the glow from Ethel's gin and chasing away the gloom of the empty house but one sip and he re-capped the jug, deciding it wasn't a good idea. Better to have a clear head when Fred telephoned. He remembered Saturday night's over-indulgence in beer that made him far too loquacious with Cynthia Byrne, who incidentally had not called back. Instead he tried and discarded a who-done-it and then attempted a conversation with Mrs. Lincoln, but she seemed more interested in sleeping than listening to a bored detective. The phone rang twice, both calls from Fred's lady friends, who were anxious for his return. So was Dean, though loath to admit it. He even stooped to playing a Loretta Lynn CD, although if Fred had caught him he would have sworn it was in the wrong container. As it turned out, Fred nearly did catch him. At 11:00 Dean had given up waiting for the old man's phone call and was ready for bed when he heard a noise at the door. In dropped Fred O'Connor looking like a New York commuter during a subway strike.

"You're not due until tomorrow," Dean said as Fred dropped his cardboard suitcase and plopped into his easy chair. "How did you get here this time of night?"

It took a pot and a half of coffee and a lot of patience before Dean learned just how complicated the Scranton excursion and return trip had been. Fred spent Monday and Tuesday checking every merchant of any size in the area, to find out if J. Cleary, alias half the telephone book, had tried to establish credit and thereby a new identity. No luck—at least with any of the known names. Even visiting the banks in person produced no success.

"Those guys are as tighter with their information than Aunt Gertie's dress," the old man complained. Dean was wise enough not to ask what guise Fred used to cover his snooping—surely a technique borrowed from a mystery book hero and borderline illegal. Dean prayed it wouldn't land them both in jail.

"I stopped by World Wide Insurance's local office too," Fred continued. "They moved into a brand new building a couple of months back. Byrne came out for the moving-in party—the night the money turned up missing. A darlin' lady told me all about the shindig—said the contractor and his boys put out a big spread with lots of drinks." He didn't add "just as I said" but it didn't need saying.

"What was their opinion of Byrne?"

"Nice guy, no world beater, always friendly...."

His visit to Bascomb Place neighborhood was equally unfruitful. A new name was on the mailbox for apartment C. There were no piled up copies of the *Parkside Sentinel* lying about. No one on the block remembered the motor home, but the backyard was closed from view from the street, so unless someone was in the building it would not have been visible. But in spite of the old man's litany of failures, Dean suspected he was holding back something important. It was after midnight when Fred finally let it rip.

"I found out where Byrne bought the motor home." Dean waited until Fred continued. "I didn't have any luck with any of the dealers and then I got to thinking. Suppose he bought it private, so I started checking the old classifieds and sure enough— pay dirt—a three-year-old Pace Arrow! A plumber named Otto Gruber out in Archbald listed it. That's north of Scranton. Our guy sees the ad and calls Gruber and comes out and looks the rig over. He pays big bucks—cash on the spot, no quibbling! And get this! The date was April 7—the date Jeffrey Byrne was in Scranton!"

"Gruber told you this?"

"Not exactly. I called the number in the ad and got his wife. She was a talker—told me how she figured the guy was gonna cheat on the sales tax so he pays in cash and gets the title signed over in blank. Her husband doesn't care—he's got the dough so he closes the deal right there and the guy drives off in the Pace Arrow!

The wife said she'd never seen that many 100-dollar bills in her life."

"How much did he pay?"

"The ad didn't say and neither would Gruber's wife. But those rigs can go for a lot of dough."

"Was anyone with him when he made the purchase?" Dean asked.

"Nope."

"So how did he get there?"

Dean could feel the smugness in Fred's voice. "He rode his bicycle!"

Dean let out a long sigh. "Bingo," he said. "It's getting closer."

"Yeah," Fred answered, but with less enthusiasm than Dean expected. "That's what I said too. But I was kinda jumping the gun."

"What do you mean?"

Fred continued. "I got all this info from Gruber's wife—hubby was out on a job when I called. The wife wasn't home when the sale took place—she heard it all second hand from her husband. I asked if I can talk with him and she said sure, it's fine that I come out this evening."

"So?"

"But there ain't no bus. It's way out in the boonies." Fred paused, "So I rented this car."

"You what? You don't have a driver's license, Fred!"

"Yeah, I thought that might be a problem but it's not like I don't know how to drive. I just ain't done it for sometime—but it's like swimming—you never forget."

"I know you haven't driven in 15 years! It's a wonder you did-n't kill yourself! How did you ever get them to rent you a car with-out a license?"

"I told them the license was in my other pants. It was just a garage that rents old junkers and they ain't particular. I made it out to Gruber's place with no problem, hardly." He took a long pull on his beer.

"Keep talking," Dean said.

"This Gruber fellow tossed me out of the house like a Fuller Brush Jehovah Witness selling life insurance. Or, more rightly, never let me in."

Dean turned and crossed the room in disgust. "How come?"

"Somebody got to him—that's a fact. At first he wouldn't answer the door but I could hear his wife bawling so I kept knocking 'til he came. He was scared. I had my foot in the door and he darn near busted it, all the time saying his wife had a big mouth and didn't know what she was talking about. I managed to push the picture of Byrne in his face and he says the guy didn't look nothing like that and I should get lost. I knew he was lying, I could tell."

"Maybe he was just worried you'd turn him in for trying to beat the sales taxes..."

"No, no. It wasn't like that. I told him I was just trying to locate the guy. But Gruber was scared. I know it. Besides, whoever was there followed me when I finally gave up and left."

"You're kidding!" Dean said, with dead seriousness.

Fred took a deep breath. "Nope. He chased me like a Saturday kid's movie. He really did. It scared the you-know-what out of me. I didn't fancy getting tied to no toilet again. One time's more than enough of that business."

Fred went on to explain that a maroon late model car was waiting at the end of the driveway leading into Gruber's place. The car had quickly made a U-turn and followed Fred, not taking care to disguise its actions. After making a few turns, Fred realized he wasn't imagining the car was tailing him. He managed to get a slow-moving truck between them on a winding road and nearly lost them until the road widened near Scranton. The car was never close enough for him to see the occupant.

The old man looked up with a broad smile. "But I lost the guy! I went down a one-way street the wrong way and he didn't have the guts to follow." He paused. "I figured no need to push my good luck so I drove back here to Parkside. Besides," he added, "Mrs. Glass was getting a mite too friendly and she's not much of a cook."

"You drove all the way from Scranton?" Dean said with disbelief.

"I had my suitcase in the car anyway 'cause I was gonna get a room near the bus station." Dean continued to stare. "The car ain't due back at the garage 'til tomorrow but we gotta figure some way of returning it or they're gonna get miffed."

"Right," said Dean, still in a daze.

"'Course we don't know it was Nota for sure..."

"Fred, I want you out of this business. I'm serious. I was a fool getting you involved in the first place. I'm not about to have your dead body on my conscience."

"Scout's honor. No more Mike Hammer stuff from now on. I'm strictly a stay-at-home couch detective, behind the scenes, back-room guy, like Father Brown or Nero Wolfe. I ain't leaving the house—maybe make a few phone calls from time to time. Besides, I'm tired of leading these bozos through this case. Everywhere I go they follow me. Let 'em do their own detective work. The case is all yours." Then he added, "But you gotta admit we been making progress as a team."

Dean put his arm around the old man's shoulder. "You're doing a better job than Hercule what's-his-name."

Fred smiled, but it was quick to fade. "But now it's a dead end. The train stops in Kansas by the looks of things. Every time we're a whisker away from nailing Byrne, something crops up to slam the door in our face. If that ain't bum luck."

"I don't believe in luck, bum or otherwise," Dean said.

"What do you mean?"

"Maybe we're looking at it the wrong way."

"Like how?"

"I don't know. Like someone's playing with us, and not necessarily Byrne."

"Who'd want to convince us he's alive if he ain't?"

"Maybe someone who wants us to think Byrne swiped the millions."

Fred rubbed his chin. "We been chasing this all over the country. It'd take a legion of liars to pull that big a bluff. Someone is out there and for my money it's Byrne."

Maybe Fred was right. Maybe Dean's sleep-deprived brain was going in circles but something wasn't clicking, and it bothered him the rest of the night.

# CHAPTER XIX

The annoying little details of the Byrne case were still squirming around in the morning, and in an effort to put one of them to bed Dean stopped by the *Parkside Sentinel* on his way to work. Monica Cutler looked up from her desk, a broad smile spreading across her face, brightening up the bleakness of the cloudy day.

"Hi, cop-guy! Twice in one month!" He bent down and kissed her on the forehead as he pulled up a chair to her desk.

"I'm still chasing the same ghost," he said.

"I'm glad you caught me," she said. "Tomorrow's my last day." He started to say something but she waved her hand. "Just some more treatments. I'll be back in a few weeks." Neither believed her cheery pronouncement. She quickly changed the subject. After chatting about common friends she asked, "What can I do for you?"

Dean explained he was still interested in the J. Cleary who had ordered the *Sentinel* from a Scranton address. She checked her records and returned. The subscription remained open. The listed delivery location was still 157 Bascomb Place, Apartment C.

"If it isn't being returned, isn't being forwarded and isn't accumulating at the Scranton address, what the hell is happening to it?" He asked the question as much of himself as Monica.

"You're the detective," she replied with a smile.

As he started to leave, he turned to the frail woman who was rolling a piece of paper into her typewriter. "Monica, I took your advice. I found a good woman."

"Terrific!" she exclaimed.

"Now all I have to do is catch her," he answered as he left the busy newspaper for police headquarters.

Before Dean finished hanging up his coat, pouring a cup of over-brewed coffee and settling in his chair, Rita Angeltoni dropped a pile of telephone messages on his desk. The top one, marked urgent, was from Ethel Rosewater. Dean silently hoped the call wasn't some convoluted effort to restore their relationship, which to his mind was thankfully finished.

"That bastard Arthur skipped out on me!" Ethel yelled into the phone, loud enough for Tom DeLeo to hear at the next desk. "And he ripped off $28,000 from the escrow account! The son-of-a-bitch! First you dump me, now Arthur's gone...." She began to cry.

"Calm down, Ethel. Start at the beginning. What happened?" DeLeo was all ears now and even Harrigan wandered over in Dean's direction. Dean moved behind a post, trying to get what little privacy the squad room and the length of his phone cord allowed.

"He left a note—a damn note after 12 stinking years! He said he needs some time to straighten out his head. If I find him he'll need more than time, the son-of-a-bitch! He never even mentioned taking the money!"

"Do you want to swear out a warrant?"

"God, no! How would that look for the firm? I wouldn't have a client left. I just want you to find him..." Ethel raged on for several minutes, listing in graphic detail exactly what she'd do to her partner—now ex-partner—until Dean managed to get her to agree to sign a complaint so the police could begin a quiet search. Yes, she would come by the station with the names of all Arthur's known friends, *all the little fairies*, as she called them, and the addresses of his favorite haunts. He rocked back in his chair, catching his breath and ignoring the smiles and snickers of the others in the room.

Dean shuffled through the remaining telephone messages, recognizing most as unfinished business from pending investigations, but one caught his eye. It was from Cece Baldwin. He had nearly forgotten the young lady, the recipient of Jeffrey Byrne's kindness. Dean wondered if Jeff was not the saint she thought, not deceased, instead bopping along somewhere west of Kansas, with several million bucks in his pocket. He dialed the number but no one answered.

Before Dean could return any other messages, Leland Anderson stepped out of his office, looking like the March Hare.

"Announcement," he called. "The word's out the grand jury is inches away from returning an indictment against Big Daddy Delasandro!" A cheer went up from the squad room. Big Daddy, kingpin of the Philadelphia family, had been untouchable for as long as anyone could remember. "Dean," Anderson continued, "it looks like your buddy Baratto was a big help. Let's just hope the indictment clicks and they nail the fat bastard Delasandro to the courthouse wall."

When it quieted down, Dean explained Arthur Atherton's disappearance to the lieutenant. They agreed Lenny Harrigan should handle the matter in view of Dean's relationship with Ethel. Dean hurriedly left the office before Ethel showed.

Dean and Andy Sackler spent the rest of the day trying in vain to chase down the final movements of the late Mr. Homer Flanders before the Colombians enlarged his grin. They went through the motions of checking all the hotels and flophouses in the city, but no one had seen Homer in the days preceding his murder. One more unsolved gangland slaying. Dean tried Cece Baldwin's number several more times without success.

One more piece of unfinished business was put to rest when Dean arranged for two young friends of DeLeo to ferry Fred's rental car back to Scranton. The boys were glad to earn 50 bucks and DeLeo was polite enough not to ask why a 74-year-old man was renting a one-way automobile.

In spite of the cloudy weather and the threat of rain, Dean ended the daylight hours listening to the hum of his bike tires on the country roads west of Parkside. Crouched astride a bike was a great place to think and he surely needed training with his July week in Iowa getting closer all the time. With all other thoughts lulled from his mind by the steady cadence of the wheels, he moved step by step through every facet of the Byrne case.

Overwhelming evidence demonstrated it was totally out of character for Jeffrey Byrne to discard his world like yesterday's trash, and yet, piece by piece, the picture was emerging that he'd done just that. First, Byrne's strange day at the Whitney Motel and the date of his business in Scranton. Then there was the apartment rental with Burgess's identification of Byrne, however tenuous, followed by the newspaper subscription and the motor home purchase. Albeit none of it definitely proved to be duplicity by Byrne beyond strong circumstantial evidence, but together the coincidences were compelling. Of all, it was the newspaper that bugged Dean the most. Where was it?

Complicating the picture was Baratto's tip to the mob—probably via Arthur Atherton—that Byrne might be involved with the missing money. That unfortunate gaffe complicated matters and most likely was the impetus behind the break-in on Collingswood Avenue. But why was Fred followed from the motor home seller's house? That didn't make sense. If it was the mob, how had they gotten there first? It seemed they had but then why bother to chase down Fred? He was no threat.

How else did Arthur Atherton fit into this? He was Vinnie Baratto's attorney, so presumably Vinnie told him of his suspicions that Byrne might have taken the drug money. While Arthur might have been feeding the organization tidbits on Dean and Fred O'Connor's progress, how much could Arthur really know? Certainly his ties to Ethel helped, but Ethel herself knew little and Dean had never told her he was chasing down the possibility that Byrne was alive. Could Fred have slipped up? Might it have been one of those situations where Fred mentioned something to Cora Abernathy who told it to her second cousin, once removed, whose brother-in-law's best friend was seeing the sister of Arthur's housekeeper? Things like that happened in a town the size of Parkside. But no, Fred O'Connor was a lot of things, but loose-tongued wasn't one of his failings.

Where was Fletcher Brunel, the last person to meet with Byrne in Norfolk? Norfolk had all but ceased trying to locate the ex-World Wide employee, but Dean still considered him a missing piece in the puzzle and wanted to talk to the man. Tracking him down would be difficult without stepping on the jurisdictional toes of the Norfolk Police Department. While there was no clear reason to believe Brunel was involved in any wrongdoing, his continued absence was disturbing.

What about Cece Baldwin? Nothing led Dean to believe she was more than someone befriended by Byrne but he was anxious to learn if this new phone message would change this opinion.

The rain began, light at first, and he adjusted his helmet to deflect the droplets from blowing in his face. It felt good. The rhythm of his strokes felt good too, an order, a progression, a logical sequence, straight and definite. The investigation had been anything but that. Instead, the trail was an illogical hodgepodge of unrelated sequences that had skipped forward until evaporating someplace west of Hays, Kansas. The path led step by step from the renter of Bascomb Place, with Fred and Dean always a step behind him. Was someone else a step behind *them*, looking over their shoulder?

Logic kept sticking its nose in Dean's subconscious, prodding consideration of wider possibilities. The one that gnawed at him, blocked out but begging consideration, was the possibility that Cynthia Byrne was somehow involved. But Dean's denial of Cynthia's implication appeared well founded given her reaction to the discovery of the body in Norfolk. The emotion she displayed seemed to defy duplicity. But the policeman in him forced consideration of a possible scenario.

Suppose, he conjectured, Cynthia was involved. Jeffrey found the money, told her about it, and the two decided to fake his death and start a new life. Jeffrey fakes his death, but then fails to contact her. She's frantic he might have really drowned. That would have accounted for her reaction in Norfolk. But the whole thing didn't make sense. Where was Randy in this fairy tale? While Cynthia skipping with Jeffrey was next to impossible for Dean to buy, no one could convince him she would abandon her son. And Randy being somehow involved was ludicrous. Besides, what was the point to the whole thing? Why fake a death? Why not just move someplace else and start anew, and gradually make use of the cash? Perhaps Byrne was afraid someone would connect him to the theft, a fear that would be eliminated by his "death"—a fear that was turning out to be well founded. Someone besides Dean and Fred was dogging Byrne across the country.

Could Nota and his affiliated crime family be that sly? From all indications, they were people who went rabbit hunting with machine guns, blazing away at any obstacle in their path with total disregard for the subtleties of life, like seeking out records under assumed names and following their prey from afar. And how would Nota and associates come by this knowledge in the first place? They would've had to listen. As soon as Dean said it to himself, it began to make sense.

Suppose Alfred Nota and his pal Homer's break-in at Collingswood Avenue was just a cover-up and their true mission was to plant a listening device. That made more sense. Dean had wondered what the two hoods expected to find in his house. One didn't keep maps of the location of witnesses they were hiding. He shifted his bike into high gear as he began a long downhill, building speed, anxious to get home. His mind followed suit, racing along, constructing a plan to prove his theory and more importantly, to address it.

The house was empty when Dean returned. Fred O'Connor was out, no doubt placating his sweethearts after his four-day hiatus to Scranton. While the detective had formulated a plan to confirm the listening device, he needed help to carry it off. He wanted to check the phone but was afraid he might tip his hand if he disturbed it, so he touched nothing.

He felt fidgety. Cece Baldwin didn't answer yet another call made from a corner payphone. Patience wasn't his strong suit and Mrs. Lincoln and jazz music somehow weren't sufficient evening entertainment. It was not a night for inactivity.

Perhaps it was just Dean's unsatisfied Thursday night urge for female companionship, but he found he wanted very badly to see Cynthia Byrne. According to the *Sentinel*, Parkside had won the divisional baseball title, thanks heavily to Randy, so she should be home from State College. On the spur of the moment he telephoned her. She answered on the first ring.

"I'm bored," he said without introduction. "Want to see a movie?"

"Do you always do things so impetuously?" she laughed. "My high school girl-boy-how-to book said I should be coy and turn down all last-minute dates."

"Is that the same girl-boy book that talks about patent leather shoes?" he asked.

"The very same. Do you know it's after 9:00?"

"The cinema out in the shopping mall has a 9:40 show. We can just make it."

It was a shared-popcorn, arm-around-her-shoulder, old-fashioned-love-story-movie kind of evening, topped off by a kiss goodnight—a real one, just one, maybe not passionate but on the lips and not a brother-sister smooch at all. And yes, Monica had been right: it was much, much better than a month of Thursdays with Hot-Sheets Rosewater the Sex Machine. And there was no sign of Jeffrey Byrne, in person, in conversation or in spirit.

# CHAPTER XX

Because of his suspicion the phone was bugged, Dean did not try to call Cece Baldwin when he arrived home after midnight, home to a still empty house. Fred must have been making up for lost time with the loves of his life. Dean was tired and slept so soundly he never heard the old man come in. Early the next morning, after showering, he walked around the corner to a gas station and from an outside payphone dialed Cece Baldwin. Seven a.m. proved successful as a sleepy voice answered on the third ring.

"What time is it?"

"Early—I'm sorry. This is Detective Dean. You called me."

"Who?"

"Detective Dean, from Parkside."

"Oh, yeah. Jeez, you know, it's still practically dark out." Dean tapped his fingers, giving her time to wake up. After smothering a yawn, she asked, "Did you send me that money?"

"What money?"

"'Cause, if you did...look, I don't need any charity from anyone. I'm doing this on my own..."

"What money?"

"You didn't, huh?" He didn't answer. "I got this money in the mail. It said, 'Use it for college. A friend.' That was it. No name—nothing."

"How much?"

She paused. "A thousand bucks. Ten 100-dollar bills. Look, I don't have those kinds of friends."

"Neither do I. Where was it postmarked?" He covered one ear to mute the passing traffic.

"I ripped the envelope when I tore it open but I could read Burlington. That's in New Jersey, isn't it?"

"And other states too, I'd guess. But Burlington, New Jersey isn't far from Philadelphia. Maybe some of the people at World Wide took up a collection."

"Yeah, I'll bet," she said sarcastically.

"You didn't recognize the handwriting?"

"It was typed. That's all it said—'Use it for college. A friend'—on an index card. What should I do?"

"I suggest you take the advice. Use it for college."

She thought about it for a moment. "It's not that I can't use the dough but it bugs me, you know? Not knowing."

"What made you think I sent it?" he asked.

"I don't know. You were asking about Jeff and all. Sending the money is like something he'd do—if he had the dough." She paused before asking, "He isn't alive or something, is he?"

"No." Dean surprised himself with the firmness of his answer. After the conversation was over he felt a pang of guilt for responding so emphatically.

When Dean returned to the house he knocked on Fred's bedroom door until he heard the old man grumble to wakefulness. "Come on, get dressed. We're going out for a cup of coffee."

Fred began to protest but Dean continued to knock.

"What's a matter? The coffee pot busted?"

"Yeah, come on."

A few minutes later in Uncle Sally's Galley on Butler Street, Fred was hiding behind his menu, embarrassed to be out in public before shaving. However, as soon as Dean explained his suspicions concerning the bugging of their phone, he captured Fred's full attention.

"Son of a six-shooter!" Fred said as coffee and English muffins were served. "Here I go doing their work for 'em. I should have known."

"I know. It happens in all your books. But we're going to beat them at their own game. This afternoon, after work, I'll call you, disguising my voice. I'll tell you I have information where Jeffrey Byrne is and get you to meet me at 7:00 at Willoughby's."

"Yeah," said Fred, "Willoughby's Bar, on Diamond Street."

"If someone is listening, they'll go there too. Only I'll already be sitting there on a bar stool."

"What happens if they're from out of town—like Nota—and don't know where Willoughby's is? I got a better idea! How about I come down there just before seven so's they can follow me in case they don't know where it is. You can still be there, but this way we're sure they'll find the place."

"I thought we decided you were strictly an inside man from now on. I don't want to see you take any risk."

"There ain't no risk! Hells bells, why would they bop me on the head when all I'm doing is leading them to someone who's supposed to know where Byrne is?"

Much as Dean had misgivings and knew he was being manipulated, Fred's suggestion made sense, and he reluctantly agreed to let the old man lead the prey to him. He was beginning to feel melodramatic about the whole thing, as if he were playacting one of Fred's grade "B" thrillers. But then the seriousness of the matter began to sink in. While he knew he should report his suspicion of being bugged, he feared having to answer questions about his clandestine work in the Byrne matter. Better to be sure before going public.

"And, for God's sake, be careful Fred!" he said. "I just want to get a look at who's bugging the phone. That's all."

The two men downed a second cup of coffee as Dean brought Fred up to date, relating his phone conversation with Cece Baldwin. They both agreed—Dean still reluctantly—that the money was one more indication that Jeffrey Byrne was among the living. Unfortunately, it was another dead end. Fred said he'd check the maps and list all the Burlington locations he could find but neither was sure what that information would tell them. Then it was Fred's turn to update.

Fred had phoned a number of places in Rollins and Hays, Kansas the previous day but found no information on the disposal of the motor home. No ads were listed in the local papers. He did, however, find a sales ad for a truck camper that was sold about that time. When the ad was pulled from the paper, the seller told the clerk he had just had a cash sale for his asking price. Fred wasn't able to contact the seller. The ad was just a box at the paper and no phone number.

A conversation with the Rollins, Kansas campground gave little help. One worker talked to a man about biking in Colorado. This convinced Fred the man was Byrne but Dean gave the item little merit.

After Fred left the café for home Dean went on to work. Friday was the second day in a row to begin with a phone call from Ethel Rosewater. This time her mood was much improved.

"Guess what came this morning, special messenger?" She didn't wait for him to guess. "A certified check for 28 thou from my old pal and ex-partner, Arthur. And a note, 'Sorry about the book-keeping mix-up with the escrow account.' Can you believe it?"

"No, I can't," Dean answered honestly.

"Neither can I but I'm not going to bitch about it!" She sounded downright happy. "I suppose I better call off the hounds. There's no police reason for anyone to be bird-dogging Arthur. If he wants to leave the partnership, good riddance."

"I'll tell Harrigan to stop the investigation but Arthur's actions are pretty strange. Where would he come up with that kind of dough to repay you?"

"No place legal I can think of. I've been looking at his client files and calling some of them. He really let things go the past few months—almost no billable hours. I can make a pile of money working his accounts."

"Aren't the accounts still his?"

"Nothing in writing and he left the files. It's a puppy eat puppy world out there."

"Just keep away from the bad boys. You don't want to get your hands covered with do-do."

"No chance there. Arthur took all his funny cases with him. There were 22 files missing. I could tell—we number them in sequence."

"I hope the jerk isn't doing something stupid. He's playing in the big leagues. Did you read the Philadelphia newspaper this morning? They found two more body parts last night and they don't match up with any of the earlier ones unless some Colombian had three legs." He paused and then added, "I don't suppose there's any return address on Arthur's note?"

"Nope. I guess he misses out on a Christmas card this year."

Dean spent the balance of Friday wading through paperwork, a chore made more depressing than usual because yesterday's drizzle had given birth to a storybook spring day. Nevertheless, he muddled through the mire in a surprisingly good frame of mind. He attributed his pleasant disposition to memories of the prior evening with Cynthia Byrne, the sweetheart of Maid Marian Lane.

Dean planned to telephone Fred directly from Willoughby's to make absolutely sure no inquisitive eavesdropper could arrive at the bar before he was securely in place. Not knowing who would show presented a chance he might be recognized but as the eavesdropper wouldn't expect him to be there, it gave him an advantage. Besides, Nota was the only member of the crime family who knew Dean's face and by all accounts he'd left Parkside some time ago. Just to be on the safe side, Dean stopped at a thrift store and purchased a nondescript jacket and a slouched hat. Not bad for a buck seventy-five, mothball smell and all. As luck would have it, as he was leaving the place, he nearly knocked over Cora Abernathy, who had just left the dry cleaners next door. She smiled a knowing smile in greeting as she looked him up and down. Now all of Parkside would know where David Dean shopped for his wardrobe. Undaunted, he walked the four blocks to the bar on Diamond.

Willoughby's was old hardwood and brass under 70 years of bad breath and nicotine, catering to a tenth the crowd of bygone days. The only customers were two paint-splattered workmen arguing baseball with the bartender, an overweight bald man in a wrinkled apron. Dean slipped onto a barstool at the far end of the room where the light was a darker yellow. Before making his phone call, he ordered a Coors just to get a feel for the place and adjust his eyes to the meager light. There were three tables between the bar and the four booths that lined the far wall. A good cleaning, a coat of paint and a few working light bulbs might make the place a pleasant neighborhood tavern.

Halfway through his beer the sports argument became spirited enough that Dean took the opportunity to rise and cross to the payphone behind him. It was 6:10 by the Budweiser clock on the far wall.

Fred answered on the first ring with what Dean detected as a hint of anxiety in his voice.

"Hello?"

"Listen," said Dean, with a handkerchief in front of the mouthpiece, "I hear you're looking for Jeffrey Byrne."

"Who is this?"

"Never mind. But I know where Byrne is and he ain't dead. If you want to know, maybe we can do some business. Do you know a bar named Willoughby's on Diamond Street?"

"Yeah..."

"You meet me there at seven." He hung up before Fred had to think up a response. He returned to his stool, feeling like a complete fool. Neither of the customers nor the bartender had so much as noticed him leave his seat.

It took two more beers and 30 minutes before a couple of men looking totally out of place in spit-and-polish business suits entered the bar. Definitely a different tailor than Nota and the late Homer Flanders. *Out of towners*, thought Dean. Locals would have found Willoughby's in ten minutes—not a half-hour. The two sat on bar stools midway between Dean and the painters and ordered ginger ales. They're hiring uptown hoods these days, Dean thought to himself. Fred will be disappointed. In his books the villains always order cheap whiskey and need a shave. Neither of the men seemed to pay the slightest attention to either Dean or the painters, but one of them seemed to be keeping an eye on the door while the other spoke in low tones to his companion.

After about five minutes the man furthest from the door rose and crossed to the telephone behind Dean while the detective buried his face in his beer. His mother, God bless her, wouldn't have recognized him. Dean was waiting for the sound of the coin dropping into the pay phone when he was startled to feel a hard object jammed in his rib cage and hear a voice say, "Nice and easy, guy. Don't open your mouth. Keep drinking that beer and listen really good. We're gonna get up slowly and walk out of here like a couple of old pals."

"I ain't got no money," Dean said, trying to sound frightened, which somehow came very easily. He earned himself a sharp jab in the kidney.

"I said shut up! Now stand up slowly." The other suit at the bar had not turned around and the painters and barkeeper were in their own world of batting averages and ERA's. Dean could feel perspiration form on the top of his lip. He began to rise.

"I ain't paid for my beer," he whispered through clenched teeth.

"This one's on me, asshole," chuckled a breath that smelled of clove. Dean could feel the man begin to remove his wallet. Dean figured it was the best chance he was going to get, with one of the bastard's hands on his pocketed wallet and the other on his gun. With one motion he struck downward with his right arm and swung his left elbow with all his might on a level line at the man's jaw. Bingo! He sent the son-of-a-bitch flying against the wall with a startled yelp. Pain shot up Dean's arm, hot and sharp, but he had no time to think about it as the man's partner jumped from the bar and dashed toward him. The bartender let out a yell and one of the painters knocked his beer flying as he turned to the commotion. The man Dean had hit sat on the floor, glazed eyes open, with a look of stupor on his face.

Suit number two quickly yelled, "It's all right. We know this guy. It's just a little family argument!" A big blue gun was pointing directly at Dean's mid section, out of sight of the others by the man's position. "Ain't it, fella? Just a family argument." Dean felt strongly compelled to agree. The man reached down with one hand and pulled his partner to a standing position and nudged Dean forward all in one motion, burying his gun in the detective's side. He firmly pushed Dean toward the door as his partner stumbled behind him, still in a daze. The whole maneuver took less than a minute and Dean was out the door.

It was in the first wash of light outside that suit-two-blue-gun got a good look at Dean's face. His expression went white. "Holy shit!" he said.

The assailant shoved Dean backwards, sitting him down hard on the concrete sidewalk as his head whacked the wall. Grabbing his wobbly, stumbling partner, the man made a dash for the curb, nearly knocking down Fred O'Connor, who was only steps from the bar. Fred took one look at the situation and took off after the men. They scrambled into a late model blue car parked a few yards away and were starting their U-turn as Fred caught up. The old man grabbed a metal trashcan from the curb and in one motion swung it at the car, scoring a direct hit on the windshield. A million little diamonds of glass showered the inside of the vehicle as it swerved up the street, spinning a track of rubber. The vehicle careened down the block, narrowly missing a mail truck that honked its irritation, and sped around the corner before Dean had staggered to his feet.

Fred was still hanging on to the trashcan when the bartender, two painters and Dean, still nursing his head and his elbow, reached him. "I never even got the plate number," he grumbled.

Dean showed his badge and after determining Fred was unhurt, returned to the bar. He called the station and reported the description of the vehicle. "They can't get far with a smashed windshield," he said to Fred as he plopped down in a booth to catch his breath before the police arrived. The rest of the bar, after congratulating Fred and buying him a beer, began to settle back to their routine.

"Once the guy saw me clearly by the door, he knew my face and all hell broke loose." Dean told Fred once they were alone. "That's about the time you showed up."

"You didn't recognize either of them?"

"No," answered Dean as he wiped the perspiration from his brow and nursed his sore body. "They were from out of town."

Dean related the complete happenings to Fred but when he began to describe the scuffle, he remembered the gun. "I knocked it out of his hand!" he said and rose, looking toward the back corner. A search of the area where the first suit had fallen revealed the gun, a .38 caliber, which Dean picked up carefully so as not to disturb the prints. "This should help."

The police arrived, in the form of Jenny Nachman and a young Hispanic named Alverez and it was suggested that Dean and Fred go to the station. Jenny took one look at Dean's attire and made a "love your tailor" comment. There was no permanent damage to head or elbow but Dean was beginning to feel his years. He was reluctant to pore over mug shots as he assumed the car would be located momentarily, and hopefully his assailants. It didn't happen in the two hours the pair spent in a fruitless perusal of ugly malefactors. When they finally finished and left the station, Jenny drove the exhausted pair home. A call came just as they left. The car had been found abandoned less than a mile away. The license plate had been removed but Dean had a tracer placed on the vehicle identification number, a procedure that would take a couple of days. Between the car and the gun, he remained optimistic the two men would be identified.

Neither Dean nor Fred volunteered any information on why they were in Willoughby's or that the fracas was anything but a mugging. Thankfully, it was after-hours at the station and Lieutenant Anderson was neither there nor was he called. Jenny didn't look as if she believed their story but Dean was a detective so she simply took their statements and refrained from asking embarrassing questions. Dean began to wonder if he was laying his pension on the line by not reporting the entire case in an official manner. Instead, he felt himself sinking deeper and deeper into a pit of questionable ethics for questionable reasons. In for a penny, in for a dime, as Fred would say.

Another disappointment greeted them when they opened the door to 422 Collingswood Avenue. Someone had beaten them home. A casual observer wouldn't have noticed but the door was ajar and the phone was on the wrong side of the hall table. As soon as Dean lifted the instrument it fell apart in his hands.

"Look ma, no bugs," sighed Dean. "They didn't even take time to put the screws back in. How can we be so stupid? These guys are still two steps and a leap ahead of us." Dean went through the motions of checking the phone anyway, but found what he expected, absolutely nothing.

"Think maybe there's more bugs around here?" Fred asked as he peeked behind a picture. "They can put 'em in all kinds of things, even in olives in drinks."

Dean laughed. "No, whoever bugged us knows they're been made. Now if they heard something they wouldn't know if we were feeding them lies or not." He took two aspirins and sank down in his easy chair. He didn't even bother to report this latest break-in. His headache didn't need the paper work.

# CHAPTER XXI

What a way to start a Memorial Day weekend. Dean woke up feeling as if a truck had hit him, backed up and rolled over him a couple more times just to make sure. Every part of his body ached and he could only bend his elbow halfway. But in spite of a quantum measure of misery, it was a holiday weekend, the day was beautiful, as Dean discerned as soon as he managed to pry his eyes open and inhale the smell of Fred's coffee. By 9:00 and after four aspirins, he had stretched the worst of the pain away, filled his stomach with some fresh Danish and was beginning to feel pretty good. He declined an invitation to join Fred and two neighborhood cronies for bowling, but had no desire to stick around the house all day either. It was a day made for biking and in spite of his body problems, he gave Cynthia Byrne a call to see if she wanted to join him. He knew she'd have little trouble keeping up with him in his present condition.

Randy Byrne answered the phone and seemed surprised to hear Dean's voice.

"No, she's not here. I kind of hoped she might be with you," and then he added, a tad self-consciously, "she's been gone all night."

"What?"

Randy hesitated, as if not sure how candid he should be. "Mom was pretty upset about something—something that came in the mail yesterday."

"And she just left the house without telling you?"

215

"Sort of. I knew she was upset at suppertime but she wouldn't talk about it. She kept saying she was okay and insisted I go ahead and go out with Jen. When I got home, there was a note on the fridge. It said, 'Don't wait up. I'll be all right. Take care.'" He paused. "The neighbors haven't seen her and she isn't out with Mr. Mayer either. He called a little while ago too."

"Mayer? Your dad's old boss?"

"Yeah. He calls a lot but I don't think Ma likes it—him being married and all. Anyway, he hasn't seen her either."

Dean forced a pot full of evil thoughts about the beanpole bastard Edwin Mayer aside in deference to his concern over Cynthia's whereabouts. He dragged over a chair with his foot. "Did you see what she received in the mail—what was so upsetting?"

"Not really. She had a paper in her hand—it was just a letter."

"She didn't leave it around the house?"

"No," he said and sighed deeply. "I don't know what to do. She said not to worry, but it's hard not to."

"I'm coming over," Dean said. Randy seemed relieved to be having company.

On the drive to Maid Marian Lane, one thought plagued Dean's spinning mind. Jeffrey Byrne had contacted his wife and like a fool she was going off somewhere to meet the son-of-a-bitch. Never mind that line of logic didn't make a lick of sense. What was she going to do? Hop in a car and drive—where? Kansas? Colorado? And leave Randy to fend for himself? But Dean knew reality seldom replaces the passion of panic thinking.

The concerned look on Randy Byrne's face told Dean that Cynthia's action, while not of itself so unusual, was totally out of character for the boy's mother.

"Did she pack any clothes?" asked the detective after giving assurances that were only partially believed.

Randy hadn't checked but jogged up the stairs two at a time motioning for Dean to follow to his mother's bedroom. The only luggage missing was a small overnight bag. Dean remembered it from their trip to Norfolk two weeks earlier. Two large suitcases remained in place. If any clothing was missing, the amount was small.

Dean felt ill at ease in Cynthia Byrne's bedroom, spying on her world, seeing the small rainbow of dresses hanging in her closet, sharing space with suits and shirts looking as if they were awaiting the return of Jeffrey Byrne. He reluctantly pawed through the clutter on her bureau and the personal items in her bureau drawers, urged by Randy, who hoped the letter might have been left behind. But what made him most uncomfortable was the large four-poster bed Cynthia and Jeffrey Byrne had shared in love.

They searched the entire house, all the obvious places like the trash cans and counter tops, but found neither the letter nor the envelope.

"What did it look like? A business letter? A personal note?" Dean asked as he poked through a downstairs desk.

"It was in a business-size envelope, just one sheet of paper and handwritten. Mom kept rereading it, but she didn't want me to see it—she'd turn away when I came near. Do you think it's about my father?" Dean answered the obvious—he had no idea of the content of the missive.

The morning dragged into lunchtime and Dean remained at Randy's urging, in hopes that Cynthia would telephone. He and Randy shared the remains of nearly a dozen stale doughnuts after knocking off a quart of milk and a cheese sandwich each. They ended up in the living room, watching a baseball game in which neither had a lick of interest. The phone rang twice and Randy tripped as he dashed across the room to answer. The first call was from his girlfriend Jen. Randy cut the call short, telling the young lady his mother hadn't returned and he was awaiting her call.

The second call was Mayer. As soon as Dean heard the name, he took the phone from Randy. He identified himself, and told Mayer everything was under control and he needn't worry. Mayer responded he was leaving to play golf but would call again when he returned. Not necessary, Dean said. He'd personally call Mayer's wife and pass on her husband's deep and frequent concern for Cynthia's well being as well as any news he heard. He hung up before Mayer could protest. Dean caught Randy smiling as he turned from the phone but pretended not to notice.

By 3:00, both had run out of conversation. The ball game was a lapper and Dean began to pick over a stack of magazines in a rack by the sofa. After flipping through a *Ladies' Home Journal* and reading the jokes in a *Reader's Digest*, he dug deeper into the pile. It contained mostly women's magazines and catalogs but one periodical caught his attention. It was a bicycling magazine—one to which Dean subscribed.

"My dad brought it home from a business trip. I guess he was thinking about biking again," Randy commented.

Before Dean could reply, the telephone rang for the third time, with a shrillness that startled them both. Randy caught it before the second ring.

"Where are you?" Randy shouted as soon as he heard the voice on the other end. "I was really worried." He listened for a few moments with Dean standing by the doorway as the boy's mother talked.

"I know. I know. As long as you're okay..." More silence from Randy's end and then, "Mr. Dean's here. Yes, here in the house." After a few seconds he handed the detective the telephone.

"Are you all right?"

Her voice sounded calm but firm, a hint of coldness he'd not heard before. She evaded the direct question. "I needed some time to myself."

Dean felt like an intruder again. "I didn't mean to butt in and run over here but Randy was worried and...."

"I could hear it in his voice," she answered. "I shouldn't have left like that. It was a rash thing to do."

"Is there anything I can do to help?" he asked cautiously. The silence that followed stretched far longer than Dean would have liked.

"Yes. Maybe you can. There are some questions I have to ask you." More silence, then, "Will you have dinner with me?"

"Of course. Where are you?"

Once again, she didn't answer directly but described a well-known seafood restaurant on the New Jersey shore, at least two hours from Parkside. "I'm sure it will be mobbed for the holiday weekend but if we have to wait, I'll be in the bar. I'll make a reservation for 7:00." Then she added, "That way, it'll be early enough for you to drive back to Parkside."

Cynthia Byrne asked to talk to Randy again and Dean returned to the living room, his head in a whirl. Thank God it didn't appear she had been contacted by her husband, but something was seriously wrong and Dean was smack-dab in the middle of it.

Whatever relationship they had blooming was going south in a hell of a hurry. Dean could hear it in her voice.

He slumped down on the sofa in disgust, waiting for Randy to finish the conversation, his foot kicking open the bicycle magazine. With his brain still churning from the phone conversation, it took sometime before his eyes focused on a penciled circle on one of the articles. He reached down and read the notice. The story described an annual one-week bike tour of the Colorado Rockies and the address for information was circled and underlined. Dean recalled reading the same article in his copy. Wheels of understanding began turning but before he could collect his thoughts, Randy returned to the room.

"She's going to stay over until tomorrow," he said, looking only partially relieved. "I guess dad's dying and all finally caught up to her. She wanted to sort things out in her mind. I asked her about the envelope but she wouldn't say. She just told me not to worry." Then he added, "She sounded really pissed at you."

"It's been a tough couple of weeks for your mother. I'm going down to see her and try to straighten things out—a quick round trip." Randy just nodded and Dean felt helpless to add something more appropriate. He exited before more questions forced him to lie.

After a quick stop at home to change clothes and to leave a short note to Fred, Dean was on the road. Everyone in New Jersey was traveling to Pennsylvania while all the folks in the Keystone state were spending their weekend on the Jersey shore. Dean's initial hope that most travelers would have already reached their destinations proved foolishly optimistic as he crept his way toward the Atlantic seashore. Whatever beauty the day held was lost once he was behind the wheel, listening to a chorus of horns amid a blue haze of exhaust. His mind was awhirl with the pending confrontation, not to mention the magazine article with one more arrow pointing toward bicycling, the motor home, a trip west, the Rocky Mountains and Jeffrey Byrne, all rolled into one very plausible package.

It became obvious early on that Dean wouldn't reach his destination by 7:00 and in fact the sun was beginning to set when he finally pulled into the crowded parking lot of The Sea Mist restaurant.

The Sea Mist dated back to the 1930's. The success of the restaurant rested more on out-of-date memories than the current excellence of its bill of fare. Not that the place was without merit. The food was passable, the price reasonable and the volume excessive, but none of these things were worth the constant hassle of fighting the warm weather throngs that habitually crowded the entrance, impatiently awaiting their chance to dine in "The shore's largest dispenser of the banquet of the sea."

Dean glanced at his watch and threaded his way through the crowd to the bar, hoping Cynthia had not given up. The room, obligatorily draped in fishnet and seashells, was packed to the gunnels with as many standing as occupying the tightly clustered seats jammed into the smoky room. Cynthia was there, seated alone in a cramped corner, looking beautiful in something summery, short and yellow, unsmiling but nodding in acknowledgment of his greeting.

"I'm sorry," he said, elbowing past an overweight man with a Budweiser bottle in each hand. "The traffic was the pits."

She gave a perfunctory little smile of dismissal. "That's all right. I thought afterwards seven was too early and changed the reservation to eight."

Dean felt awkward standing above her and leaned forward in order to carry on any semblance of a conversation above the din of the crowded room. "Why did you ever pick this cattle corral?" he asked. "There must be somewhere that doesn't cater to half the eastern seaboard."

"I didn't want to meet in a romantic little intimate place with you," she said, still unsmiling. The words sent a chill down his back like an ice cold shower. He couldn't think of an appropriate comeback and found himself staring down at her drink. "Ginger Ale," she said, as if reading his mind. He wanted something a hell of a lot stronger—a double bourbon and leave the bottle but he knew the return trip to Parkside lay before him. Besides, he had the distinct impression he'd best keep his wits about him. As it turned out, there was no decision to make. No waitress ever came near them.

They remained in place for 20 minutes, occasionally exchanging a shouted comment, but mostly looking up or down at each other, self-consciously. It was well past the rescheduled reservation time when a mispronounced version of Cynthia's name was called and they were led through a babble of conversation and a clatter of silverware to a corner table, remarkably, one with a view of the now-darkened bay. They both ordered ginger ales. Cynthia wasted no more time before getting down to business. She opened her pocketbook and pulled out a white envelope and thrust it at Dean. Biting her lip, she turned away from him and stared out the window.

The letterhead was from Rosewater and Atherton and was handwritten. The message was signed by Arthur Atherton but it read as if written by a ten-year-old.

*Your husband is alive and has a lot of money. With your help we can find him. I know this must be a shock and I'm sorry but you can be a very rich woman. The police know about this. I am out of town but I will telephone you when I return on Sunday.*

"Shit!" Dean said, a little too loudly, just as the waitress arrived with the ginger ales. Cynthia tried to say something but was unable to fight back her sobs. If Arthur Atherton had been within a mile, Dean would have beaten him to death with his bare hands. He started to lean toward Cynthia but the waitress was at his elbow. "Give us a couple of minutes, will you?" he said angrily. She turned away, not even trying to hide her annoyance. Just then, Cynthia let go. In a flood of tears and half-controlled sobs she got to her feet, and handkerchief to her face, dashed across the room toward the entrance. Patrons from a dozen tables gave Dean a stare fit for the Bastard of the Year.

He chased after her, in time to catch a glimpse of yellow as she barged out the door toward the parking lot. He quickly pulled a 20-dollar bill from his wallet and shoved ahead of a cluster of customers lined up at the cashier and thrust the money at the woman. "My wife," he said, for lack of a better excuse, "She's ill." Then added, "Two ginger ales." He turned and pushed his way to the door.

At first he didn't spot her and cursed the fact that Cynthia was so short. Then he caught sight of her in the light of the opening car door. When he reached her vehicle, he could hear her anguished sobs through the closed windows. She ignored his tap on the glass until he persisted and she finally flipped open the lock and he slid in.

She cried for what seemed like an interminable time. He wanted desperately to put his arms around her but knew he'd just exacerbate the situation. "It's true, isn't it?" she said.

He sighed deeply. "Arthur Atherton is an opportunistic sleaze-ball son-of-a-bitching thief who works for gangsters and would sell his own mother for the price of a cup of coffee. This note sounds like and looks like he was blind drunk when he wrote it and he doesn't know what the hell he's talking about. I wouldn't believe the bastard if he told me Lincoln was on the penny."

"It's true, isn't it?" It was as if Dean hadn't said a damn thing. "What can I tell Randy?" she continued. "What can I do?" Then she turned toward him and with a lightening swing slapped Dean across the face with a force that shocked him cold. "You used me! How could you? How could anyone do that to another human being?" She began pummeling his chest with her fists. He grabbed her and pulled her toward him, not before catching a lick or two solidly on his aching elbow. "You lied to me! You lied to me!" She screamed. First Ethel, now Cynthia. It was the second time in two days a woman had beat the hell out of him.

He buried her against his body in a bear hug, twisting around the steering wheel. "Listen," he fairly yelled, "I never lied to you—never! And I never will." She continued to cry in muffled sobs against his chest. When her sobs began to subside, he spoke in as calm a voice as he could muster. "I haven't been lying to you and I haven't for one minute been seeing you so I could fish for information." And then he added, "I've been seeing you because I care more about you than anyone I've ever met." She shuddered against him.

"Look," he continued, "Arthur Atherton represents a petty crook the FBI is interested in. Some money turned up missing and I made a stupid off-hand comment in front of him about a connec-tion to Scranton where your husband had visited. Vinnie Baratto, the con, recognized that your husband was missing and got it into his head Jeff might have come across the money. Vinnie was des-perate to place the blame for the missing dough on anyone but himself. He most likely told his attorney. I don't know what Arthur

Atherton is up to but he has no more evidence your husband is alive than the man in the moon."

"Then why would he say that?" she sniffed.

"He's probably trying to con you out of some dough."

"I don't have any money." She added, "I don't want to talk to that man, I don't." Then she pushed away from Dean and looked straight at him with red and swollen eyes. "You can't know what it's like to even have a hint something like that is true—that someone you lived with for 20 years...."

He hoped the darkened car would mask his face. "You read my report. All the evidence points to an accident...."

She stared at him for several seconds, and then bristled, "But there's more, isn't there? You're not telling me everything." He began to protest but she waved him aside. "That's the same as lying!"

"No, it isn't. Why should I confuse you with unproven suppositions that may be totally irrelevant?"

"God," she shouted. "You're worse than Jeff—trying to protect me! I despised it when he did it and I hate it now! Am I too weak—too stupid to handle the truth? Don't you think I'd want to know if my husband—just left me—just took some stupid money and ran?"

"I'm not lying when I say there is no firm proof that your husband's death was anything more than an accidental drowning—that's what the overwhelming evidence shows. And there's no connection tying him to that money."

"Why don't I believe you?" she spat. "Tell me you think Jeffrey is dead!"

It was the question Dean didn't want to hear. Dean spoke so softly she hardly heard. "I can't say that for sure, but only because there's no direct proof—only circumstantial evidence." She turned her head to the window. He could see her reflection, but not the look in her eyes. "Some questions just don't have answers—maybe never will." He paused. "Look, let me do this my way. I promised you I'd investigate this as thoroughly as I could. It doesn't mean I'm going to screw up your world with every little suspicion and insignificant detail that crops up. If there was any factual evidence..."

"I hate it when you talk down to me like that. No one should have to go through this, no one...." She turned and looked at him, fire in her eyes. "What are you keeping from me? Are the police still..."

"The case is closed. The police aren't investigating any part of it—here or Norfolk."

The lights of a turning car caught the look in her eyes. "But you are, aren't you? There's something you're not telling me—maybe lots of things." He bent his head back on the seat and closed his eyes but he didn't answer. How could he? "Why won't you just tell me?"

He looked at her. "I can't. There's nothing to tell."

She closed her eyes. "You mean you *won't*." He didn't answer and silence dragged on. Then she said, "If you believe there's a chance Jeff's alive you'd have to consider I might be a part of it."

"No, Cynthia...."

She turned to him with fire in her eyes. "I can't see you anymore, David. I can't. I can't go through this. I don't know what's going on. I don't know who to trust—who to believe. Maybe I'm not smart enough to understand it but I deserve to know. It's just...it's just not fair!"

"Cynthia, please..."

"No—please." She breathed deeply. "I need to be alone." Once again they were both silent.

Finally, Dean was the first to speak. "I'll make sure Arthur Atherton doesn't bother you. The bar association should dump him." He reached for the door handle. She didn't try to stop him. He turned back as he stepped from the car. "Will you be all right? Are you sure you want to stay down here?"

She turned to look at him and answered, coldly. "Yes. I don't want to be home tomorrow when that man calls. I'll drive back tomorrow night; I have to be at work on Monday." She added, "I have a life to live—regardless."

The long ride back provided Dean with much needed think-time. His stomach wanted to know why he didn't stop for dinner but he ignored it. Aside from a wasted 20 minutes searching for gas in New Brunswick and a missed exit on the Garden State Parkway, the trip was uneventful. Cynthia was right; he knew she was. While he had no business clogging up her life with a potpourri of unsubstantiated garbage, it was equally unfair to have a relationship while holding back the truth from someone you cared for. More importantly, Cynthia Byrne was dead right in saying he had no business being chauvinistic in trying to protect this woman from his suspicions. Now that his opportunity for a future with her was blown, she at least deserved the truth and he would find it. David Dean had a strong idea where he might find the elusive son-of-a-bitch who was the heart of all this trouble. David Dean would be making a trip to Colorado.

# CHAPTER XXII

## SUNDAY, MAY 30, 1999  1:00 A.M.

In spite of the late hour, the lights at 422 Collingswood Avenue were still ablaze. Fred had recently discovered the library rented audio tapes of mystery stories. As Dean entered the house, Sherlock Holmes was lecturing Watson in a voice sounding very much like Basil Rathbone while a radio across the room was playing soft music.

After waving a greeting, he dropped his jacket on a chair and made a quick trip to the bathroom. When he returned, Fred commented Dean's left cheek looked kinda red. Dean tossed Arthur Atherton's note at the old man. Fred snapped off the tape, read the note and looked up at his stepson with a sober gaze.

"This must put you on a whole different ground with the lady. I guess that accounts for the cheek. Did you fess up to her?"

"Yes and no," said Dean, "I didn't lie to her, but I didn't tell her what's going on either. She didn't take it very well."

"I can understand how that might be the case," Fred said.

"I think I'm history."

"I'm truly sorry but I'm not sure how it could have played out a whole lot better. We never had anything concrete to tell her—still don't."

"You're saying my lines," Dean said.

Dean explained to his stepfather Cynthia's impromptu trip to the shore after receiving Atherton's letter. He repeated their subsequent conversation after he'd driven down and met her.

"Is she going to talk to Atherton?" Fred asked.

"I told her what I thought of Arthur Atherton and that he doesn't know what he's talking about. She won't have anything to do with him anyway. She's totally upset about the whole business. She asked point-blank if I thought her husband was alive and I wouldn't answer. She knows I'm checking something but she's so confused right now she doesn't know what to believe except that she doesn't want to see me."

"I'm sure the poor darlin' is as confused as a mouse in a maze but I'm sorry it's put you two on the outs with each other."

"There's something else," Dean said. "Turn on the radio so we can talk."

Fred switched the dial to a local talk show. "You still think we're being bugged?" he asked in a near whisper.

"No," said Dean. "I just want to make sure." He fished around until he found his copy of the bicycle magazine he'd seen at the Byrne home. He opened to the article and handed it to Fred, explaining how Jeffrey Byrne had circled the request for information. "It's beginning to make some sense."

"What is this?" Fred asked, reaching for his glasses, "some kind of a race?"

"No. It's a tour, like the one I'm signed up for in Iowa, only this one is in the Colorado mountains."

"Colorado! Dang! Remember Burlington—the postmark on the money sent to that Cece gal? There's a Burlington in Colorado, right across the border from Kansas!"

"One more tie."

Fred studied the magazine. "Tell me about this 'Ride the Rockies' bike tour," Fred said as he scribbled notes.

"Iowa is a fun tour while 'Ride the Rockies' takes some serious training. Seven days, 443 miles, and some world-class climbs. There are 2,000 cyclists who get to ride on a first-come, first-served basis. They draw a lottery from the 4,000 or so who want to ride."

"Why?" Fred asked. Dean just raised his eyebrows. "Sort of like climbing a mountain," Fred answered his own question, "'cause it's there?" Dean nodded in agreement as Mrs. Lincoln came over to join them, her long tail swishing for attention. Fred picked her up.

"It's a one-week tour, each day a separate segment, with everyone riding at their own pace—within reason. You stay in a different town each night." Dean picked up the magazine, glancing at it as he spoke. "The ride starts out fairly flat and then climbs—Wolfe Creek Pass at 10,850 feet, Poncha Pass at 9,019, Fremont at 11,318 and finally Loveland Pass at 11,992 feet. Some of the days, you only bike 40 or 50 miles but on others you do 80 or 90."

"There's a lot of damn fool crazies in the world, ain't there? I suppose we'll be joining 'em. When is it?"

"*I'll* be joining 'em—you'll be holding down the fort here in Parkside, Pennsylvania." He added, "The ride starts on June 13, two weeks from tomorrow."

"You in that kind of shape?" Fred asked, ignoring Dean's comment on going alone.

"No—not by a long shot," answered Dean, "but the way I see it, it's the best opportunity we've had to date to catch up with this guy—the closest we'll ever get to the jerk. I can't blow the chance, no matter how slim it is. Besides, you saw the guys at Willoughby's. We're not the only ones chasing Jeffrey Byrne and by the looks of things, they'd blow his head off as soon as spit on him. And for once, we've got a lead they haven't overheard."

Fred perused the article. "How are you going to get in this here bike ride? You said they draw a lottery so they must have already pulled names and filled it up."

"Flash my badge. And don't bother asking how I'm going to pick out a guy I've never seen from 2,000 bicyclists. That's only one of the details I've got to work on while I'm beating my body into shape over the next two weeks."

Dean rose to shut off the radio just as the news began. He paid no heed to the words that were droning on, until a name riveted him to attention. Arthur Atherton had been found shot in his automobile. He had been rushed to a well-known Philadelphia hospital. The last thing David Dean had wanted to do was to climb back in his tired automobile and drive to Philadelphia in the middle of the night. He telephoned the Parkside Police department but they had no news. The newscast gave no details of the shooting and a call to the hospital netted nothing but a tired sounding know-nothing switchboard operator. So, back in the car Dean climbed, with an insistent Fred O'Connor beside him, ready to kick him awake if he nodded off. It was after 4 a.m. when the pair slid into the brightly lit parking lot of the Philadelphia hospital.

The packed emergency area waiting room held a disreputable collection of weeping women, stoned teenagers and dirty derelicts, all talking at the same time over the background music of a near-constant scream of sirens hauling in more Saturday night victims. Amid the chaos, a nurse calmly filled out forms in a methodical fashion, looking as if the second coming of Christ wouldn't ruffle her. Dean showed his badge and asked about Arthur Atherton. Ms. Nightingale murmured a room number and motioned down a hall crowded with bodies like the day after Gettysburg while white-coated figures strolled among the moaning, clip boards in hand

With wide-eyed Fred following behind, Dean ran the gauntlet until he found the room, a small office packed with five men and a lot of smoke, three of them in Philadelphia Police uniforms. As he was about to introduce himself, he heard a familiar voice over his shoulder.

"Welcome to Philadelphia!" said Jonathan Winston, looking as resplendent as ever. "I'm glad to see Parkside is looking out for its citizens, regardless of the hour and whether they deserve it or not. However, I'm afraid you're too late to help Mr. Arthur Atherton, Esq. Some unfriendly lowlife put a bullet in each of his pretty blue eyes. The survival rate on wounds like that are zero."

"The newscast didn't say he was dead," Dean answered as he held out his hand.

"We thought we'd be cute and not announce it, just in case some interesting candidates showed up here to finish their handiwork. So far, no takers."

Dean introduced Fred O'Connor, who was taking it all in, and the three chatted in a quieter area at the far end of the hall, away from the worst of the mayhem. Dean explained Atherton's recent disappearance and the strange return of the escrow money. He also mentioned the files missing from Rosewater and Atherton but was silent on Arthur's note to Cynthia Byrne. Winston explained that Arthur had recently contacted the government about supplying information on his Philadelphia clients because, he claimed, he was beginning to get nervous. The government was inclined to believe the nervousness was due to Arthur's need for a lot of money in a hurry.

"We ran a quick check on him and he was up to his ass in debt. We've got his files but I don't think he had anything really important. He'd be walking a thin line facing disbarment if he related any privileged information. I'd guess the only reason they knocked him off was to set an example for anyone else who might have similar ideas."

"Are you sure it was the family that hit him?" asked Dean.

"Who else would want him dead?" asked Winston. Dean couldn't think of more than 20 names—Ethel Rosewater, Cynthia Byrne, David Dean, even Jeffrey Byrne, not to mention half of Arthur's gay friends and lovers and most of his ex-clients. But Dean just shrugged and commented that Arthur wasn't exactly popular. At least if Cynthia Byrne's phone rang Sunday, it wouldn't be Arthur Atherton calling—he was on the menu with the Wassermann twins and tic-face Home Flanders in the big barbecue down below.

"If Atherton was so broke, where did he get the dough to replace the escrow money he swiped?" Fred asked, surprising the government agent.

"Good question," Jonathan replied. "Maybe he sold something else to someone."

Dean wondered just what else Arthur had to sell. It didn't make him feel warm and fuzzy to speculate after the lawyer's letter to Cynthia Byrne. Maybe he was putting the squeeze on all over town. That would certainly lengthen the list of who might have made his blue eyes red.

Jonathan continued, "We called Atherton's partner, your friend Ethel Rosewater—ran her down at a house party in the Hamptons. She didn't seem shocked at losing her business associate. There are no close relatives so she's going to handle the arrangements."

"Ethel is a survivor, that's for sure," Dean commented, hoping Ethel wasn't cleaning her gun. "Arthur may be missed, but I don't know by whom."

Jonathan just laughed. "By the way, I'll tell your good buddy Vinnie Baratto I saw you and you gave him your love. We're draining him drier than a prune. It's really helping build up the case against Delasandro."

"Good," said Dean. "Lock up all the bad guys or at least keep them away from Parkside. Is the war still going on?"

"No letup in sight," Jonathan smiled, as they began to leave. "They may all kill each other and put us out of work."

The group shook hands and Dean and Fred took their leave. Just as they reached the outside and were nearly at the parking lot, Fred let out a yell, startling the dickens out of Dean. He pointed toward another entrance.

"That's him!" he roared.

"Who?" asked Dean, seeing no one.

"One of the guys at Willoughby's—the one with the gun!" Fred called as he took off at a geriatric jog toward the building. Dean followed on the run, passing him and reaching the door that was already closed.

"He must be here to make sure he killed Atherton!" Fred said, trying to catch his breath. When they entered the building, there was only an empty corridor. The two stood there, both panting.

"How could you be so sure? It must have been 50 yards away and it's dark." Dean walked a short distance down the hall. "You couldn't have gotten a good look."

"Good enough," said Fred in a voice that indicated he didn't like being doubted. "I know what I saw."

But they were unable to confirm or deny. Their brief search halted when a security guard swore no one had passed his way and too many corridors and stairways went in other directions, making further search difficult. Dean located Jonathan Winston and related what Fred had seen but it was clear the FBI officer doubted the identification and gave only a cursory nod and a promise to look into it. He had men posted at the various entrances and assured them no one without proper identification would pass. Fred seethed but reluctantly agreed it was best to call it a night—or rather, a morning. The next day, Dean remembered nothing of the long, early-hour drive back to Parkside.

# CHAPTER XXIII

## EARLY JUNE, 1999

The first two weeks of June were a never-ending list of chores and activities jammed full with last minute preparations, one workplace crisis following another, and an annoying series of details that demanded Dean's attention. Coupled with this tight schedule was a self-imposed training regimen so vigorous he surprised himself with its intensity. Physically, he was feeling a whole lot better than he had in years. The scales showed seven pounds less, he was eating baskets of fruit and goody-goody health food, plus he'd laid off the booze completely.

Dean was making progress. After a series of phone calls to Denver and some monstrous lies, Dean managed to finagle a slot on the bike tour, not an easy accomplishment given the short time before the popular event. A call to Leland Anderson on Memorial day secured his superior's approval to move up his vacation from July—when he'd planned to bike in Iowa and since canceled—to June. In part out of appreciation but more out of guilt, Dean voluntarily worked the holiday, sending a pleasantly shocked Lenny Harrigan home to his new wife.

On Tuesday Dean borrowed a thousand dollars from the City Employees Credit Union and booked his plane flight to Denver for the evening of Friday, June 11th. His finances were not a pretty sight. The phone bill, thanks to Fred's vigorous activities, was only a few commas less than the national debt and he was knocking on the ceiling of his newly acquired Visa limit. Not only was Ol' Yella, his car, making peculiar noises, but his landlord had just hiked up the monthly rent. This bike trip was going to stretch things tighter than his pre-training belt.

In order to minimize expenditures, Dean planned to skip the motel bit and camp out on the tour. Although it was decades since Dean's Boy Scout days and he didn't relish the thoughts of bedding his exhausted body on the ground, he felt, in addition to saving money, his chance of running into his quarry in a camp ground was better. After all, the last report, if you could call it that, involved a motor home. Dean had purchased a small tent and sleeping bag for the Iowa trip, both items light enough to be hauled on his bike. Organized tours provided sag wagons—vehicles to haul luggage from one overnight stop to another—but Dean preferred carrying his own gear rather than taking time to sift through a thousand sets of belongings nightly. But the June mountains of Colorado required more and different clothing than the July lowlands of Iowa, and he would have to pack carefully. He studiously perused the biking catalogs for the additional gear he would need for the trek and crossed his fingers he'd chosen correctly.

While Dean held out no illusions of leading the pack through the mountains, after turning out 73 miles of rolling hills on a humid Saturday, he felt more confident of his chance of least not embarrassing himself.

On June 1, Dean attended Arthur Atherton's funeral. He felt an obligation to Ethel Rosewater but by the looks of the crowd his presence was unnecessary. Arthur's social friends pawed all over one another on one side of the room, while his lawyer pals held down the other side, acting as if it were a board meeting instead of a wake. None of the Philadelphia family was in evidence but a gigantic wreath from Delasandro and Company dominated the foot of the casket. Dean thought a dead fish might have been more appropriate. A pat of sympathy on Ethel's shoulder was returned by a pat on his butt and he was out of there.

The same day the station received word from the FBI the gun Dean recovered at Willoughby's had been stolen from a security guard in Connecticut the prior March. While Dean's assailant had not worn gloves, surprisingly, to Dean at least, there were no traceable fingerprints on the weapon. The days following the incident, Dean had pored over more mug books, sure he would be able to identify at least one of the two hoods. There wasn't even a close match. He was running into more brick walls than an overworked mason.

Detective Norman Hunter called Dean from Norfolk later the same week. Weeks had passed since the two had spoken and the conversation was more social than business. The bluefish were running and Hunter tried to coax Dean down for a little R and R. Dean asked for a rain check, explaining that he was going on a biking trip out west though he made no mention of his reason behind the trip. He took the opportunity to casually pump Hunter on the Byrne disappearance.

"We've pretty much given up hope a body might float in," Hunter said. "I've had one of my men checking on Fletcher Brunel, the last guy to see Byrne. We've got an address now and understand he's back from vacation. So far, he's not returned phone calls. When I hear from him, I'll give him your phone number. Maybe Byrne said some words of wisdom you can pass on to the missus."

Dean also spoke to Cece Baldwin again, just to touch base and see if she might have heard further from her mysterious benefactor. She had not, but sounded in a much cheerier mood, giving Dean a five-minute update on her school progress. When Dean chided her about her improved mood she simply laughed and said love does that to people.

On Sunday, June 6, Randy Byrne graduated from high school. Dean sent two dress shirts with neckties and a card of congratulations but did not attend the ceremony. Randy had called a few days before with an invitation but Dean was putting in a Sunday shift and was forced to decline. The young man said he understood but sounded confused at Dean's sudden absence from their lives, though he didn't press for an explanation. It was apparent that Mom was mum on the subject and hadn't told her son that Dean was about as popular as doggy do-do on new shoes.

Dean had had no direct contact with Cynthia Byrne after their acrimonious separation at the Jersey shore restaurant's parking lot. He had telephoned Randy the following day, asking the boy to inform his mother of Arthur Atherton's death. While the lawyer's death did nothing to undo the damage his note had caused to Cynthia, it at least eliminated her need for any further dealings with the miscreant. Dean wondered if Cynthia might suspect Dean himself had blown the creep away just for spite.

While Dean was out of contact with Cynthia Byrne during the first two weeks of June, it didn't mean she was out of his thoughts. He refused to accept that he and Cynthia were other than temporarily at odds with one another. To think otherwise would have been intolerable. She was constantly on his mind. Someone would laugh and it would remind him of her laugh, turn their head to the side and it would be the way she always moved. A song would play and he'd recall hearing it when they were together. Although they'd been together but a half-dozen times, each remained with him, indelibly imprinted in his memory. It was as if this separation was by miles only, and not the great chasm created by the disappearance of Jeffrey Byrne.

On June 9, Monica Cutler, asleep in the arms of her beloved Harry Turnball, failed to wake from her snug and happy dreams. She was buried on Friday and Dean attended yet another burial service. He cried for the first time since his mother had passed away 15 years earlier.

On June 10, plans for his trip west began to come together, but not in the way Dean expected. The detective had wondered about Fred O'Connor's apparent acceptance of Dean's pronouncement he was going to Colorado alone. While Fred had chatted amiably during the course of the two weeks, he confined his discussions to methods that might be used in finding and identifying Byrne, and never complained about having to remain in Parkside. Dean learned why Fred was mum on the subject when he discovered an airline ticket in the old man's jacket.

"What do you think you're doing? Dean yelled, waving the ticket in Fred's face when he returned from an evening of bingo. "We discussed this and I told you I was going alone!"

"We didn't discuss nothing," grumbled Fred. "You said you was going alone, so I guess I'm going alone too. It's as simple as that. It seems kinda silly, if you ask me, but it's your call."

Dean tried another approach. "Look, we've gone over and over this. There are guys out there that kill people. I can't be looking for them while I'm busy looking out for your hide."

"Seems to me it might be the other way around. You weren't there when them thugs followed me in Scranton and I made out

pretty good, I'd say. You just look out for yourself and I'll do like-
wise."

"Where did you get the money? Don't tell me the slots at
Atlantic City paid off again."

"They been kinda dry lately but I've got credit too, you know."

"Where will you stay and how will you get from one town to
the next? Don't tell me you're riding a bike!"

"I'll do nothing of the kind! And I ain't staying in no skimpy
little tent neither. While you're freezing your can off, I'll be in a
nice warm bed. They're taking pretty good care of us senior volunteers." He said this with a smugness that didn't improve Dean's
mood one iota. "We patrol the course," Fred continued, "work the
rest stops—all that stuff. You gotta admit, it gives me a lot better
chance of checking out the crowds for Byrne. You'll be working
yourself ragged trying to get up them mountains, tailing behind
2,000 people. Your view won't exactly be conducive to identifying
anyone. At least I'll get to look 'em in the face."

It was Dean's turn to grumble. "So when were you going to tell
me all this?"

Fred smiled. "When it was too late for you to do something
about it—about now."

"I'm not so sure about that," snarled Dean, knowing full well
his threat was empty. "What do you propose to do about the
house? Someone has to feed Mrs. Lincoln, pick up the paper and
the mail..."

"Mrs. Porter's already signed up. She was tickled to get away
from the Mister for a week. He don't like her watching her soaps."
The old man then smiled the warmest smile Dean had seen in a
long time. "Now, let's take a peek at your ticket and see if we're
on the same flight." They were.

"Too bad you're not a senior citizen like me," chuckled Fred,
looking at the price. "My ticket cost a whole lot less dough."

# CHAPTER XXIV

"The way I figure it," Fred said, "We look for a blue '89 pick-up with a Mallard camper on the back. Them's the only details the ad in the Kansas paper gave us. But that's a start." The two men were sitting outside Dean's recently-pitched tent in Cortez, Colorado. Dean was carefully reassembling his bicycle after it had been packed for the flight from Pennsylvania.

"No guarantee it's still blue," answered Dean, just to be argumentative. "He could have painted it—if it even happens to be the same person." He continued testing the tension on his bike chain, wiping the grease on a paper napkin. "But more importantly, whatever he was driving, we don't know if he parked it down here at the start of the tour or up in Golden, Colorado where the tour ends. He can't drive the truck and ride his bike at the same time."

"Unless he has a partner," Fred said. "But a blue truck is a start, that's all I'm saying. If you're right and he's actually in this here bike ride, we've got seven days to find him."

"We have our work cut out for us. He might have a mustache, black hair or a shaved head for all we know, and two and a half million could buy a face-job making him look like Robert Redford. He could be anywhere, maybe camping in the next tent or staying anyplace in Cortez."

Fred rubbed his chin. "If I had a couple of million bucks, I'd be staying in the swellest place I could find. We'll find him if he's here. We got his picture—even if it is a few years old—and my money says he hasn't changed much."

They had considered showing Jeffrey Byrne's picture to some of the bike tour workers, especially those volunteers manning the frequent rest stops where every biker would pass sooner or later. They decided against it, cautious about frightening off Byrne if he should get wind of the search and realize someone was this close to finding him. It wasn't worth the risk, at least this early in the week. There would be time enough to panic closer to the end of the tour. Dean was well aware that when this opportunity, as tenuous as it was, was gone, locating their elusive quarry would be next to impossible.

"What kind of physical shape do you suppose Byrne is in?" asked Fred as he eyed a gorgeous blonde in scarlet bike pants.

"I don't know but he's had six weeks since he disappeared," answered Dean. "Except for buying and selling a couple of vehicles and getting here he's had nothing to do but train."

"And spend some of his millions," added Fred.

The flight out on Friday night had been a comfortable few hours spent at thirty-odd thousand feet, sandwiched between a cloud-covered countryside and a starlit sky. In spite of gaining two hours with the time change, it was still late when the cross-country travelers finally bedded down in a quiet motel in Golden, Colorado, after a shared ride from the Denver airport. Early Saturday morning, the two had boarded a charter bus with scores of bikers for the 372-mile, eight-hour trip to Cortez, Colorado, where they found a pleasant little town abuzz with the activity of 2,000 riders and hundreds of support personnel.

The last 200 miles of the bus ride traversed the first three days of the bike tour route after which the tour would turn north and enter the really tough mountain portions of the trek. Or so some of the hard-bodies on the bus said—this was the easy part! Wolfe Creek Pass at 10,850 feet was unlike anything Dean had ever seen and easy wasn't the description that came to his mind. The climb didn't quit—it keep going and going and going. It scared the dickens out of him, and Fred's constant chiding of "No way, no way," didn't help. Dean figured he was in very big trouble.

But there was a plus to Dean's first day in the west. Except for his army hitch and a few late night military flights, Dean had never been west of the Mississippi and he'd never seen scenery as spectacular as Colorado in late spring. The bus trip was glorious. Traffic was light—nonexistent by eastern standards—made up mostly of Jeeps or pickup trucks, the latter with a dog pacing the back bed in perfect balance. The backdrop was the mountains; mountains with snow tucked in their crevices and, on the higher ones, sugar dust capping their tops in white, stark contrast to the deep green of the pine forests running up their sides to the tree line and the magnificent blue of the sky above. The sky fascinated Dean. He had never in his life seen a horizon so cleanly defined, a pencil line drawn without a breath of haze. All this and air so fresh each breath was a new exhilaration.

The town of Cortez, located in the southwestern corner of Colorado, was near the only spot in the country where four states converged. This area was homeland to a civilization dating back to the time of Christ. The Anasazi, "The Ancient Ones," as the present day Navajo call them, built cities and a society for 13 centuries before abandoning this high Sonoran desert, all before Columbus ever set sail. The reason for their exodus remained open to speculation. Mesa Verde National Park, the most popular of these spectacular ruins, was but one of thousands in the area where the bikers camped. Dean was sorry he hadn't taken more time and extended his stay. Marion Anderson, his lieutenant's wife, had offered use of her recently acquired place in Ouray, Colorado, a small town just two hours to the north, but Dean had declined. Once he saw the area, he knew he'd made a mistake in not accepting her offer and staying longer.

Dean had opted to pitch his tent in City Park. He could have stayed in the gym of Cortez-Montezuma High School but the weather was pleasant and he wanted to try out his newly purchased equipment under the western skies. What's more, he enjoyed the camaraderie of the hordes of participants all with the same goal in mind.

The camping area was a riot of color, with thousands of bodies wrapped in every tone and shade of tight-fitting Lycra, each an individual fashion statement on a rock-hard frame. (If Dean's clothes made a statement, they whispered and no one was listening.) Everyone was exceptionally friendly as hundreds of bicyclists wandered about, chatting and smiling, with a hint of nervous excitement in their voices. There was a definite uniformity to the assemblage. Nearly all the riders were young, good looking and in fantastic shape. Nearly all. Some of the bikers were Dean's age or older and a few were in physical shape that made you wonder if they realized what they were undertaking.

Many of the bikers knew one another and there were groups traveling together, but there was equal representation of couples and solo bikers. "Where are you from?" and "Have you done this before?" seemed to be stock questions in addition to comments and curiosity about equipment and attire. It was a fun crowd, obviously out to have a good time while testing their personal ability to accomplish a truly grueling trial.

Without the specter of Jeffrey Byrne hanging over him, Dean could have enjoyed the festivities even more. While he loved the exhilarating feeling of biking alone or on an organized tour, the après ride time was nearly as enjoyable when you could mingle with others with like interests. One thing was for certain; this group would have one whoop-de-do of a party when the week was over.

Each community along the way was scheduled to provide inexpensive meals for the bikers. If Cortez were an example of what lay ahead, no one would go hungry. Dean and his stepfather dined on western style beans, baked potatoes, sourdough bread and the best spareribs either had ever eaten. Colorado-based Coors beer, co-sponsor of the event, was also there with its products readily available, and Dean broke his training diet to share a few Silver Bullets with Fred.

After the two men called it a night and Fred returned to his guesthouse lodging, Dean sat outside his tent lingering under more stars than he had ever viewed in his life. He finally crawled into the snug sleeping bag with mixed feelings of awe and trepidation.


Sunday morning broke with a surge of nervous excitement as 2,000 cyclists oozed out of Cortez, Colorado, bound for their first day's destination 46 miles distant. If stiff muscles didn't let them down, the group would pedal into Durango, Colorado, with one leg of the tour behind them. Only two communities separated Cortez and Durango; Mancos and Hesperus, and neither were memorable. Although the route was relatively flat by Colorado standards,

Dean learned that a body unaccustomed to elevation in the 7,000-foot range needed more oxygen to fuel its muscles. However, he was pleased to keep up a fairly respectable pace, at least a few notches above the embarrassing level.

The riders quickly spread out, but because of the numbers there were always at least several in view. To Dean's mind, it seemed everyone passed him but there were more remaining behind him as he maintained his modest pace. At least glancing at the passing riders gave him the chance to carefully look them over. The bikers wore helmets and most were in a low tuck position, making it difficult to get an identifying look at them. Dean still managed to pick out eleven riders he considered could possibly be Jeffrey Byrne. As all of the bikers were assigned numbers, Dean made a verbal note of each on a small handheld tape-recorder borrowed from his more official duties.

Dean met up with Fred O'Connor during the lunch break. The old man was dressed in jeans and a western shirt complete with a string tie, turquoise clasp and a Nero Wolfe paperback in his back pocket.

"I thought Hopalong Cassidy died," Dean said with a smile.

"When in the west, do as the westerners do," Fred answered. "Besides, the ladies love it."

The two men compared the cyclists' numbers each had listed as possible Byrne look-alikes. Surprisingly, Fred's list of twenty-four contained eight of the same riders Dean had recorded. Fred checked the numbers on a master list of the tour's advance registrations. None of the names sounded familiar, nor were the addresses in areas where Byrne was thought to have traveled. The tour seemed to have attracted most of its riders from Colorado, California, Texas or some part of the west. None of Dean's or Fred's listed candidates showed addresses in the east.

While Dean stretched his muscles and alternated between bites of peanut butter sandwich and a banana, Fred perused the rest of the master lists.

"Can't imagine this many fools want to half kill themselves on a bicycle," he muttered as he'd nearly finished. Then a name caught his attention. He let out a yell and slapped Dean on the back, nearly knocking over a Gatorade.

"Here it is! P. Corbin! Remember Pat Corbin from Scranton? I'll be danged! Number 1368. Looks like we were right all along!"

They both knew Pat Corbin was one of the names used in Scranton. It wasn't a common name and there was little chance it was a coincidence. Dean could feel his heart race as he looked over the old man's shoulder. "At least he registered. How can we be sure he showed up?"

"I'll try to sneak a peek at the latest updated list in the office," Fred said. "If he's here, his information packet would have been picked up when he signed in. I can check without having to ask anyone—and tip him off."

"He knows someone was on to him in Pennysylvania so he might have been too spooked to actually show up here. What does the name list as an address?"

"Eaton, Ohio, wherever that is," Fred answered. "I'll bet it's close to Interstate 70. He probably holed up there for a few days and set up his driver's license and the rest of his identity."

Just then a pleasant looking woman in her sixties dressed in a western shirt and jeans approached the two.

"There you are," she said smiling at Fred, "I've been looking all over for you."

Fred introduced the woman, another volunteer. Her name was Emma Blanding, from Granby, Colorado. After acknowledging Dean, she gently tugged at Fred's elbow.

"You'll have to excuse us," she said to Dean, "I have some friends I just have to introduce to Freddie."

"Freddie" rose and followed the woman after agreeing to meet Dean later in Durango. Dean smiled as the two walked away and then gingerly mounted his bike, renewing a few aches and minor pains.

The afternoon was a blur as Dean's mind alternated between the task at hand and the sobering fact that he might be within miles, or perhaps yards, of Cynthia Byrne's missing husband. One minute he'd be drinking in the beauty of the countryside and the next feeling a wave of anxiety, realizing what had begun as a mild suspicion was close to culminating in a face-to-face confrontation with Jeffrey Byrne. And Dean didn't have the foggiest idea what he would do when that meeting occurred.

With a full water bottle and a full stomach and legs warmed to the rhythm of the ride, he became molded into a near trance as he churned up the Colorado miles. He slid in behind another biker and followed the crouched figure evenly, absentmindedly matching the rider stride for stride for several miles as he pondered his course of action.

The two bikers had started down a slight but long downhill, less than a bike length apart, picking up speed as they rolled along. Suddenly a rabbit darted from the brush directly in their path. With a squeal of brakes Dean narrowly missed the rider in front, who shouted a profanity and spun sideways to a stop in the roadside gravel, miraculously maintaining balance.

"Sorry," Dean apologized. "Guess I was tailgating too close. Are you all right?"

The other rider doffed her helmet, spilling waves of blond hair. She was a gorgeous creature in her early twenties with a figure that would make a monk sigh.

"Were you drafting me or just checking out my ass?" she asked with a smile, as she looked him up and down.

"Sleeping on the job was more like it. I should know better, but I kind of fell in back there with your pace. Sorry."

"No harm done. We'll just blame it on the rabbit." She extended her hand. "Hi, I'm Betty, from Boise."

"David from Pennsylvania" didn't have the same ring as he shook her hand and introduced himself as she remounted her bike.

"It's my turn to check out *your* buns," she said, still smiling. "You take the lead for a while—I'm tired of eating all the bugs."

"Sure thing," Dean smiled as he mounted his bike. "But fair warning—I'm hitting a very fast pace."

"We'll see," she said as she replaced her helmet and began to follow him.

The two pedaled together most of the afternoon, enjoying the pine-scented air, the cool breeze that hugged the base of the mountains and the yellow sunshine of a perfect spring day. Their pace was sufficiently similar that neither seemed uncomfortable keeping up with the other. There was little conversation but at one point when they were exchanging the lead and Betty pedaled ahead, she called to him over her shoulder.

"Are you married?"

"Nope," he replied.

"That's nice," she answered as she sped ahead. A large group overtook them outside of Durango and they became separated in the pack as she became caught up in a blur of color and then was gone. All in all, riding together had made for a most pleasant afternoon.

Aside from the anticipation of locating Jeffrey Byrne and the uncertainty surrounding it, Dean felt pretty damn good. The first day was behind him, his muscles weren't overly sore, he seemed to be adjusting to the altitude and he had conquered more hills in one day than a year of Pennsylvania biking would offer. Lurking in the back of his mind, however, was the frightening knowledge that later in the week he would have to bike twice the first day's distance on terrain quite unlike the relative level course of the Cortez-to-Durango run.

Durango, Colorado, once one of the wildest cities in the old west, was now the home of 12,000 citizens and one of the country's last narrow-gage railroads. The Denver and Rio Grande Western made daily warm-weather trips up the mountain to the mining town of Silverton, 40 miles away. Nowadays the cargo was tourists and not precious minerals. But the bikers wouldn't have time for such excursions. They were far too busy stretching muscles and preparing for the more torturous miles that lay ahead.

Although Dean was anxious to locate "P. Corbin," he was cautious enough to wait for Fred to confirm the named party had actually joined the tour. It was after dinner by the time Fred caught up with him. Dean had showered and changed and was sitting under a tree licking a frozen yogurt desert and chatting with a group of riders from Texas when the old man strolled up. Dean rose to meet him and the two wandered to a quiet section of the park before Dean questioned him.

"He's here," Fred said with a tired smile. "He signed in and picked up his packet of information. After I checked out the list I spent the afternoon at a rest stop squinting at a couple of a thousand bikers' numbers trying to spot him, but no luck. He must have been at the front of the pack and I missed him."

"I'm surprised he's in good enough shape to bike with the leaders," Dean said. "Did the papers show where he's staying?"

"No luck there—the tour doesn't record that. It would be too confusing. There's a big bulletin board down by the information area where everyone's supposed to check for messages if they're looking for someone."

"If we left a note for P. Corbin we'd just spook him," Dean said.

"Yeah, that's what I figured. But I'll spot him tomorrow. I'm scheduled to man the first rest area and I'll get there before any of the bikers get started. That way I'll make sure I get to see 'em all."

The two exchanged the Coors beer and the evening's entertainment for a brief but pleasant stroll around the streets of Durango. They tried a couple of times to telephone Mrs. Porter back in Parkside but weren't able to get through.

"She's out there gallivanting, I suppose," Fred snorted. "Mrs. Lincoln's going to be lonely. Bad enough the kitty has to suffer without any good country music to listen to, now she doesn't have any company either."

Much as Dean wanted to telephone Cynthia Byrne, he knew it wasn't appropriate—suicide was a better word. Instead, he settled for a postcard to her and one to her son, each with a bland "Having a great time" message. He had no intention of calling the Parkside Police station. It wasn't a lack of curiosity—he needed this week away from murder and mayhem. Fred was the first to suggest they call it a night, in spite of the early hour. Either the old man's age was showing or Emma Blanding was waiting. Dean moseyed off to set up his tent while Fred tried to call Mrs. Porter one more time. Dean was surprised just how tired he was and happy to get a decent night's sleep before tackling the next day's 60-mile run to Pagosa Springs—leg two of the "Ride the Rockies Tour."

# CHAPTER XXV

**MONDAY, JUNE 14, 1999 7:00 A.M.**

It was warmer on Monday and Dean was pleased his body felt better than he expected. After a misty sunrise, a plateful of pancakes and the first ten miles, his legs hit a nice smooth cadence. All would have been peace with the world if his mind hadn't remained doggedly fixed on his search for Jeffrey Byrne. Time sped by and he was surprised how quickly he pulled into the first rest stop and spotted Fred O'Connor working on a cup of coffee and a blueberry muffin. Dean could tell by the look on Fred's face that the news wasn't good.

"I found our friend, number 1368," the old man said glumly, wiping his face. Dean looked at his stepfather as he unfastened his helmet, waiting for him to continue. "He's about 19 years old and built like a Greek god. It didn't take him long to hit the rest area—he was one of the first riders, a regular Greg LeMonde. I spotted the number right away and as soon as I saw him I knew danged well it wasn't Byrne. I went over and started chatting with the guy. It seems he was in Europe someplace and didn't sign up for the tour in advance so he stopped by Cortez just to see if he could pick up a last minute cancellation. He bumped into this guy who said he had a friend who couldn't make the tour and the Greek god could take the friend's place."

"P. Corbin," Dean said disgustedly and then thought out loud. "If he was here, that means there's a good chance he's still in the tour. Maybe he signed up under a second name when he found out someone had been asking about him in Scranton."

"Makes sense to me," Fred answered.

Dean set down his bike and began to pace. "Could you get a description?"

"I had to be cozy-like—didn't want to press the guy. I did find out he was an older man, whatever that means to a teenager. He didn't know a name or a number but the fellow had black hair. If it comes down to it and we need an ID later in the week, I can locate the Greek god guy and show him the picture, but I didn't want to take the chance this early. He did say the guy is camping—he was hauling a tent and stuff. The kid offered him money for the registration but the man said that was Corbin's bad luck and wouldn't take it. He was happy to help the kid out."

"Sounds like good old St. Jeffrey, always there with a helping hand," Dean muttered.

"Easy enough to be a saint with a couple of million bucks in your back pocket. But let's look at the bright side," said Fred, "We're hot on his trail. We know he's here."

In spite of the scenery, the weather, and all the other splendid elements of the tour, Dean was experiencing a serious sense of trepidation. In spite of his lingering and totally unfounded doubts that it was Jeffrey Byrne he was pursuing, there were far too many coincidences pointing to Cynthia Byrne's husband. The more he considered the devastation this would wreak on this woman he cared for, the more apprehension he felt about finding the man. And yet he knew he couldn't turn his back on the quest—there were too many cop years and too much history in the make up of David Dean. In spite of his hesitancy he wasn't about to quit. He knew he owed Cynthia Byrne the truth in spite of what it would do to their fledgling relationship. The image of her smile and his memory of the way he felt when he was with her remained fixed in his mind. It forced him to forge ahead like some naive knight doing battle with a windmill to satisfy his curiosity and meet this fool who'd toss away a life with this woman for a few measly millions.

Physically, while the day had started well, his body thought 40 to 50 miles was plenty. If the course had been the same distance and level as yesterday, the ride would have been a breeze. By midafternoon both legs were feeling tight and his breath was coming in rapid puffs each time he tackled one of the ever lengthening climbs. He managed to keep his body fluids up by frequent gulps to replenish his rapidly diminishing energy. By the time Dean pedaled the last of the 60 miles into the small town of Pagosa Springs, he knew he'd had a full day's workout.

Dean's gear was now being transported by sag wagon like everyone else's. One day of hauling it had been enough. Fred, in a particularly kind mood, had not only picked up the gear but set up Dean's tent for him. After the obligatory shower, fresh clothes and a hearty supper, the tired body was beginning to revive, as long as the mind kept mum about tomorrow's 90 miles and the 10,850-foot climb up Wolfe Creek Pass.

Later that evening, while Dean and his stepfather were filling their faces with apple pie and ice cream and feeling sorry for themselves about their lack of progress in finding Byrne, a young man strolled up to them with a smile on his face. Fred introduced him as the biker who was riding on the canceled reservation of Pat Corbin. Dean and the young man whose name was Lou Gibbons chatted about the day's ride. To Gibbons, it had been a piece of cake. He had finished the 60 miles by 1:00 and then did some sprints—just to keep in shape. He could hardly wait for tomorrow's challenge.

"By the way," Gibbons said to Fred, "I saw the guy in the shower—the one who gave me Corbin's reservation. He was going to be camping down the line from me, but he had to leave."

Dean and Fred looked at each other. "You mean, leave the tour?" Dean asked, trying to sound casual.

"Naw, just for tonight. Something came up, a friend or someone I guess. He's just not staying in his tent. He asked me to drop off his gear at the sag wagon tomorrow morning so it gets hauled to Alamosa on the truck. He packed it up."

Fred took another bite of apple pie and said very slowly, "I've still been wondering if that friend of his—the Corbin fellow—is the same one that's married to my niece's daughter. Him being from Ohio and all, really makes me wonder. Tell you what, you show me where this guy's gear is and maybe I'll leave a note for the fella asking him to ask Corbin when he sees him."

"You can't miss his campsite," Gibbons answered, "It's the only one without a tent set up on it—just a pile of gear on the ground. It's about halfway down the east side of the field in the next-to-last row. I'd show you but I've got a new friend I'm anxious to get to know better!" Then he added, "The guy was real surprised someone was looking for Corbin." He left with a smile, jogging off toward town.

Before Gibbons was out of sight, Dean slumped to the ground, with a look on his face that mirrored both of their disappointment that the man they were pursuing was now aware the two-man posse was closing in.

"Dang!" said Fred. "I was just about to pat myself on the back for weaseling out the location of Corbin's tent. Instead I should be ashamed of myself for not telling Gibbons to be mum about our looking for the guy."

"Don't blame yourself. Gibbons would have been suspicious if you told him to keep quiet about your interest in Corbin."

"Yeah," Fred answered. "Do you suppose he's really meeting someone, or is that just an excuse to beat it?"

"Probably just an excuse. The odds say he skipped now that the word's out we've followed him here."

"There's still a chance he'll think it's another Pat Corbin who sounded familiar. Why else would he leave his stuff?"

"Why not? He's a millionaire. And he's in a hurry."

Fred thought a moment. "Let's at least give his stuff a look-see."

"You took the words out of my mouth," Dean answered as he rose and walked with Fred to the camp area.

They found the gear with little trouble where Gibbons had directed. There was a large backpack, a smaller one, a bagged tent and a rolled-up sleeping bag. Fred and Dean didn't stop to examine them but continued to casually stroll by. At a glance it appeared the gear was newer than usual and Dean could read the L. L. Bean label on the backpack. There were numerous other tents in the area, many occupied and others with campers sitting outside enjoying the setting sun.

"How do you see this coming off?" Fred asked in almost a whisper. "We can't just sit down and pull the stuff apart. Someone may know the owner."

"I've got an idea," Dean said. "Come on back to my campsite."

When they had crossed the field to the spot where Dean's tent was pitched, he began to dismantle it. "I figure we just set up this tent right on the other site and pull his stuff inside. That way, we can poke through everything in privacy. When we're finished we take the tent down and bring it back here. People will figure they reassigned the site."

"I gotta hand it to you. That's like something they'd do in a book!" Dean wasn't sure he appreciated the compliment but the pair made fast work of folding up his tent and moving the small enclosure to the new site. The two re-pitched the shelter in minutes. As Dean had predicted, no one paid them any heed. They both crawled into the tent and pulled in the gear behind them just as the last of the day was fading.

"You know," said Fred, "I suspect this business is illegal as all get out, don't you think?"

"Of course it is—I should know, I'm a cop, aren't I? But I didn't come halfway across the United States to pass up a chance like this." He fumbled with the backpack, dumping out the contents.

"I didn't say we shouldn't do it—I was just making an observation." Fred turned over a wrinkled nametag. "J. Graham, number 888, Dallas, Texas. This guy does move around. If he's still in this here tour, at least now we got a number."

"Texas is a long way from Kansas," Dean said. "I just hope we're not busting into some innocent guy's belongings."

"I'll bet Dallas is a fake address," Fred said. "He probably booked a bunch of reservations, all in different aliases, all over the country."

Dean smiled as he continued to search. It took less than ten minutes. The knapsack contained nearly all new clothes, both dirty and clean. There were no toilet articles; presumably the owner took them with him for his alleged overnight trip. The second, smaller knapsack contained a bulky sweater, rain gear, three sweatbands and a rolled up cap. That was it. Another brick wall.

Fred began to open the bag containing the tent while Dean untied the sleeping bag. The bag was an expensive, down-filled model, and like everything else, showed little if any signs of wear. As he reached inside, his hand touched something solid. He smiled, and looked over to Dean who felt his pulse quicken. But it was only a pair of shoes, fastidiously wrapped in newspaper to prevent them from soiling the fabric. Fred unwrapped the paper, tossed it aside, and thrust his hand into the toes of the shoes, but came up empty.

"Danged," he exclaimed, "I thought I had something."

"You just might," Dean said as he took notice of the wrinkled newspaper. He pulled in a deep breath and let it out slowly. It was a double sheet from the *Parkside Sentinel*. Fred scrambled over to look. The paper was dated Sunday, June 6. It was the issue listing the graduates of Parkside High School.

They took extra time replacing the gear, trying to duplicate exactly the way they'd found it. Dean was re-rolling the cap when he noticed the emblem. It was a Philadelphia Phillies baseball cap. Dean held it aloft for Fred to see. Both recognized it as the same headgear Jeffrey Byrne was reported to have been wearing when he crossed the road to the beach in Norfolk.

"That just about locks it up, doesn't it?" Fred said. Dean didn't even bother to answer.

They dismantled the tent in silence and returned with it to Dean's campsite. After once again setting up Dean's tent, this time in the dark, Fred suggested they go someplace quiet and talk. The two men found a bench on the edge of the field, out of earshot of the hundreds of campers.

Fred prattled excitedly about the Parkside newspaper and baseball cap and how the two finds represented proof Jeffrey Byrne was alive. Dean let him talk it out, half listening, half trying to make sense of all the details. Finally, Fred summed up their feelings. "The big question—has he already skipped or will he ride tomorrow?"

"We know he didn't leave his bike here, and we know his number. We can't do anything until morning but keep our fingers crossed." They were both quiet for a few moments, breathing in the cool night air before Dean spoke. "There's one thing I can't figure. Where did he get the paper? They sure don't sell the *Parkside Sentinel* in Kansas or Durango, Colorado and he didn't have the newspaper forwarded from Scranton."

"He's got help. I said that from the beginning. He's probably with some lady friend right now, in one of the motels or in the motor home."

"If that's the case, why did he bring his tent?"

"Maybe his girlfriend just arrived," Fred answered. "Anyway, he's nice and warm while I'm sitting here getting damp and cold." He rose. "I'm calling it a night as soon as I try telephoning Mrs.

Porter back in Parkside. In spite of the time difference, she's a night owl."

Dean accompanied Fred as far as a bank of pay phones. "Say hello to Mrs. Lincoln," Dean called as he continued on to his campsite.

He took his time strolling down row after row of tents, pausing briefly to answer a young man's question about directions. Just as he reached his campsite, Fred hobbled up, out of breath, a paper in his hand.

"That guy Brunel called and left a number with Mrs. Porter!" he managed to gasp.

At first Dean didn't recognize the name but then remembered Fletcher Brunel as being the missing Norfolk employee of World Wide, one of the last people to speak with Jeffrey Byrne the day he disappeared.

The two men returned to the pay phones. Dean fished for pocket change but Fred waved him off. "I've got one of them phone cards," he said, taking the instrument and entering the requisite numbers, then handing the phone back to Dean. A man's voice answered on the second ring.

Dean introduced himself and apologized for the late hour. Brunel answered that he'd just received the message—he'd been "on the road," and only recently learned Jeffrey Byrne drowned. Brunel made the usual comments of "plucked from the prime of life" and "you never know."

"God, here I am running around the country and he's out there swimming with the fishes. Who'd have guessed?" Dean remained silent for a moment, and then asked how well he knew Jeffrey Byrne.

"Just from the job. He was an okay guy. Not like Mayer and half those whoozies."

"Looks like you were the last person to talk to him."

"No shit? That's kinda like...sobering, you know?" Again, Dean didn't interrupt and Brunel continued. "He didn't like have any final words of wisdom, if that's what you're wondering. We both had a few—especially me."

"Was there anything unusual about Byrne's demeanor the afternoon the two of you were together?"

"You mean like maybe he was despondent and killed himself?" Brunel asked.

Dean answered by insisting his questions were routine. "Just anything out of the ordinary. How much booze did he put away, for instance? Did he seem...distracted? Did he mention going for a swim?"

Brunel seemed to consider his answer. "The swim-bit is a hoot and a holler. I can't even picture Jeff doing something stupid like that. He had a couple of drinks—not as much as me—but he wasn't drunk. He was sort of on edge, now that I think about it, like something was distracting him. It kind of ticked me off—like I was an assignment he had to take care of, and our going out wasn't a social thing. I was all set to have a few more at the motel and a big dinner but he begged off—just dropped me at my place."

"You planned on having dinner with him?

"He never actually asked me but I was expecting it."

"Was that unusual?"

Brunel thought a moment. "He was like from the head shed— the home office. That made it his call. He said he had a chore to do. He hadn't mentioned anything earlier about cutting the evening short so I figured it was an excuse. I left town first thing the next morning."

"What kind of chore? Something to do with his work?"

"I guess. I don't know what else it could have been, him being in a strange town and all."

"What did you talk about when you got together?"

"Just business—I mouthed off about everybody, he just listened—and some chit-chat. He was the only guy at World Wide who wasn't a shark. I've known him since Scranton. We'd talk sports and stuff, and maybe have a beer. He had a son who was a hot shot baseball player and I played two years in the minors."

"Did he talk about biking?" Dean asked.

Brunel paused. "I guess—along with other sports. I think he used to bike and I do some myself."

"Did either of you stop and buy bike shoes?" Dean asked.

"Nope. Our only stop was for a couple of beers."

It was apparent Brunel had nothing more to offer so Dean thanked him for his help and hung up. While he was disappointed, he hadn't expected much else. He filled in Fred before the two once again parted.

Dean figured with everything happening, sleep would be slow in coming. However, no sooner had he entered the tent, stripped, and crawled into his sleeping bag than his exhausted body began to drift to another world. Unfortunately, the trip to dreamland was short in duration. He'd just nodded off when he heard a sound outside and a whispered greeting. He fumbled for the light just as the zipper on his tent opened to reveal the bright smile of Betty from Boise.

"Hi. I was pretty sure this was your tent. I recognized you earlier."

"Hi," Dean responded, bewildered as he rose up on his elbows.

"Can I come in?" she asked, opening the flap the rest of the way.

"Into the tent?"

She was in before he could answer. "I've got this problem," she said as she pulled in her open sleeping bag, and turning, re-zippered the tent flap behind her. "This gang of us came down from Boise together and some of them are getting a little rowdy—you know, into funny pills and stuff—shit like that? You look like a nice safe guy, not some whacko, so is it okay if I crash here for the night?" She crawled forward on her hands and knees. "This creep Hal is hot for me and this is the last place anybody would look."

"You want to *sleep* here?" Dean asked incredulously.

"Yeah. I was going to bunk outside but I'm scared shitless of thunder and it looks like rain. Then I thought of you." Dean figured it hadn't rained in Pagosa Springs in months but she began to spread out her sleeping bag in the narrow space next to him, nudging him closer to the side with her hip. "I won't be any bother and you're not married and all and we *are* adults. I mean, you don't have to do anything—we can just sleep, if you want to. 'Course if you want to ball, I got the Trojans if you've got the time." She laughed merrily and raised her arms in one motion, pulling up her t-shirt. Dean flipped off the flashlight just as he caught sight of two very attractive breasts.

"Look," he said in the darkness, "I really don't think we should..."

"Hey, it's cool—I know you're old and all. I understand. Sometimes I come on a little too strong—half the time I don't know myself if I'm kidding or serious. But I gotta tell ya it's great for relaxing the muscles. Just give me a nudge if you change your mind—I'm a light sleeper. Good night. And, hey, thanks for being so understanding."

Dean felt her wiggle out of her bike shorts and then turn to her side, facing him. He could smell her sweetness in the night air and her breath was only inches from him.

Dean sighed deeply, "You know, guys dream about this sort of thing," he said.

"So, let's dream a little!" He felt her warm arm on his bare chest.

Why not, indeed? It had been nearly a month of empty Thursday nights since his no-show session with Ethel Rosewater and the beautiful Betty from Boise was offering an effective way to make sure that embarrassment was a temporary happening. Still, he harbored misgivings about casual sex, and god knows this was as casual as it could get. He was suddenly not sure just how strong those misgivings were.

Just as Dean turned to kiss her, they both heard the distinct sound of a footfall outside the tent. There was the yellow movement of a flashlight much too close and Dean sat bolt upright, a frantic vision of Bob from Boise, or Hal the creep, or someone ready to avenge the chastity of a wife or sister. The zipper opened in one motion to reveal the lighted face of Fred O'Connor.

"Oh, sorry," Fred said. "I figured you were alone."

"Shit!" said Dean but when Fred didn't answer, he mumbled an introduction. "This is...Betty," and then added, "from Boise. My stepfather, Fred O'Connor...."

"Pleased to meet you, ma'am," Fred said as Betty pushed upright, a little too far, and waved a greeting. Fred looked to Dean. "I gotta talk to you."

"Talk," Dean answered, "And talk quickly, will you? You know, your timing..."

"I just looked at that phone number you called—Brunel's number—when I was putting it in my notes."

"So?"

"It ain't long distance. It's the same area code as here! Fletcher Brunel is in Colorado."

Fred, with a love for the dramatic, began exiting the tent on that pronouncement.

"Wait a minute!" Dean called. "Let's think this thing through."

"It's simple. Jeffrey Byrne is dead and Brunel killed him."

Betty bounced upright making no move to cover herself. "Oh, my God! Oh, shit! I'm sorry as hell!" She wrapped an arm around Dean in comfort. "I sorry!"

"It's all right, really!" He tried to move away but she continued to console him, deep mother instincts from a hundred generations of genes.

"I know how you feel. My grandmother died and I cried for days..."

"Look," he said, trying to extricate himself. "I never even met the guy..."

"But somebody *killed* him! That's terrible!" Betty began to cry and held Dean all the closer.

"Damn," Dean muttered as he looked up at Fred. "We're jumping to conclusions. Just because he's in Colorado doesn't mean he knows anything about this business. We knew he was moving out west." Betty looked from one to the other.

"Brunel had a connection with Scranton and he skipped out of Norfolk without even filing his expense account. He knocked off Byrne and took the loot."

Betty looked as if a night with Hal-the-creep might have been a better choice.

Dean sighed, putting his hands to his head. "I don't know what I'm doing." He looked at Fred. "None of this answers who in hell is 888?"

Betty looked up, mouth agape. "Are you guys spies or something?"

"No, darling," Fred said calmly, "It's just a bit of a mix-up."

Dean plopped back down, trying to think. "Colorado is a big state. He could be 500 miles away. It doesn't change anything."

Betty still looked completely bewildered. "Do you want me to leave?" she asked in a meek, questioning voice.

"No, it's okay. I'm sorry it sounds so confusing." Dean put an arm around her bare shoulder, giving her a hug. "We all need a good night's sleep. We're not thinking clearly and there are too damn many unanswered questions."

"Yeah," grumbled Fred. "My mind is in high gear too." To Betty, he added, "Good night, Miss Boise. Sorry to have disturbed you," and he was gone.

"He's cute," Betty said as Dean snapped off the flashlight.

"Yeah," answered Dean. "Everyone thinks so."

It was a very long night, a night of whispering secrets to strangers and sharing life stories and holding and thinking aloud and even some kissing and touching stuff—lots of stuff. He told her about Cynthia and she talked about someone named Jack who was a med student whose family thought she was a jerk and they both decided life was too damned complicated and lots of the times it sucked, but not at times like this. It was a long night, but a nice night; certainly not a night with an adequate allotment of sleep—not with the naked body of beautiful Betty from Boise beside him and a world gone topsy-turvy, and wondering lord knows what lay ahead in the towering mountains that surrounded them.

# CHAPTER XXVI

Dean had arisen thousands of times in his nearly 40 years; risen to the fear of final examinations, to the anxiety of court appearances, to the dreaded knowledge there was a war going on outside. He had risen in the arms of beautiful women, after nights on the town when headaches would make you scream for mercy, and on a fifth-grade morning when Frankie Cataldo had bragged to the world he would kick the shit out of David Dean. He had woken the morning after a doctor had excised tonsils from his six-year-old throat. He had risen to fear, heartache, anxiety, bliss, pain and a hundred other feelings that made you beg to be able to bury your head beneath the covers and stay in the warm cocoon of sleep forever. But never, never, never in his entire life had David Dean felt less like crawling out of his sleeping bag and mounting his bicycle than on the misty Colorado morning of June fifteenth.

Betty had murmured something about jogging, kissed him on the nose, wiggled on her meager duds and left the tent, with the flap open just enough to admit the predawn chill and a red glow that would soon be sunrise. Dean only half remembered hastily packing his tent and gear, washing up and putting away a plate of waffles and fruit. The emerging brightness of the new day, while inviting, did nothing to sort out the tangle of thoughts crowding his brain like the line of a snarled fishing reel.

Dean was one of the earliest bikers on the road. It wasn't unbridled ambition that put him at the head of the pack—he knew if he didn't get a jump on the crowd he wouldn't see the town of Alamosa before sunset. He was hardly underway before he geared down for the long climb and gradually fell into a rhythm of sorts, muscle-pulling pain and gasps of breath as he inched his way up the first long incline.

A part of him kept asking why he was doing this—not the biking but chasing after a ghost wearing number 888 who was probably hundreds of miles away. There was no police case, nothing official about the person he was pursuing—Byrne or Brunel, or some unknown soul who was simply the culmination of a series of incredible coincidences. Who really cared who wore number 888 anyhow? Let him, whoever has the millions, keep it and leave us peons in peace.

Dean could be back on Collingswood Avenue, listening to John Coltrane or Charlie Parker and patting Mrs. Lincoln, or catching a Phillies game on the tube, or eating pizza and slugging down a cold Coors beer. Instead, he was working his backside off trying to climb an 11,000-foot mountain that never ended with the only power provided by his two aching legs. It did no good to protest. Every time Dean argued with himself, he lost.

The highway to Pagosa Springs followed the San Juan River up the pass to the top of the Rocky Mountains while side streams, arush with melting snow, ice cold to the touch, cascaded down from the roof of the sky, thousands of feet above. He was biking in the forest now, pine-scented and cool in the early morning air, watching more nimble cohorts pedal on by him as if he were standing still. The tortoise and the hare, he kept saying to himself as he checked the number of each rider as they passed. Raucous Stellar Jays squawked their encouragement while buzzards circling overhead seemed to keep out a careful eye for fallen bikers. He emptied two water bottles before 10:00 and replenished them in one of the ice-cold streams, too thirsty to heed the literature of a possible parasite from elk urine or something. What the hell, it wasn't fatal and couldn't be worse than dying of thirst. It couldn't make him hurt any more than he did, legs aching and breath heaving as he struggled higher and higher up the Rockies.

He climbed and climbed and then climbed some more. With each turn in the road he expected to see the summit but was only greeted with another long uphill climb until he lost track of the numbers. In time the trees began to thin and patches of old snow appeared in ever increasing numbers, tucked in dark crevices, left over from winter storms of months long past. The air cooled appreciably and the ever-thinning atmosphere caused Dean to labor all the more as he struggled upward. The roadside drop offs became more and more precipitous, opening on breath-stopping views of chasms so deep they made him dizzy just to look down to the bottom. There was always a river, eating away at the mountain as it had for eons, carrying with it minute particles, piece by piece in its frantic torrents.

It was after 11:00 by the time Dean struggled around the last turn and reached the summit of Wolf Creek Pass. He stood atop nearly 11,000 feet of mountain gazing in wonderment at the spectacular view below him as he strained to catch his breath. He had covered only 23 miles but each mile had given him a sense of accomplishment that astonished him. It seemed every other rider had passed him on the climb until he looked down the mountain and saw hundreds of dots of color still struggling up the incline behind him.

There was a rest area at the summit already crowded with riders. Fred O'Connor, in the company of Emma Blanding, was passing out coffee and hot chocolate to the grateful line of chilled cyclists. As soon as he spotted Dean he came over. The old man held out a cup of coffee to his stepson, who continued trying to catch his breath.

"No sign of number 888, whoever he is?"

"No, but it's so cold up here lots of the bikers are wearing jackets and sweats that cover up their numbers. But it's a long day and I'll spot him if he's here."

Dean sipped the hot coffee, thankful Fred didn't raise any questions about Betty from Boise. "More than half the riders must have passed here already," he said. "Chances are our guy skipped out yesterday when he learned we were interested in him."

Fred didn't disagree, a sure sign he too was discouraged. He changed the subject. "I called Mrs. Porter again this morning," he said, "just to check in. Got her out of bed. There was some other news. The Feds busted a gang of Colombians in Philadelphia and one of them is implicated in slitting the throat of that fellow Homer Flanders." Fred waved back to Mrs. Blanding, who was waiting anxiously for her favorite helper.

"Jonathan Winston will be getting a medal."

Fred moved his toe around in the dirt. "I don't much like getting out foxed by Byrne, whether he's alone or with someone else, but if he's gone, I can't for the life of me think of what to do next to track him down. It played out as smooth as an old harmonica the way we had it figured too. It would be a shame to lose him after all our work."

Dean reluctantly agreed. "Everything points to Byrne skipping. That's the only way it makes sense. As much as Brunel being in Colorado surprised me, I've thought about it and I think it's just a coincidence. There's still too many coincidences and things that don't add up and we'll probably never get the answers, but I agree—it looks like this is the end of the line if we can't locate him on this tour." He patted Fred on the shoulder. "Just keep your fingers crossed old man—this is our last shot." Dean put on his helmet and mounted his bike.

"By the way," Fred called after him. "Congratulations on making the climb—at your age. That's one beaut of a hill."

A bank of clouds tumbled down the slope to the left of him, bathing the summit in cold dampness. Dean stopped a few hundred yards down the road and swapped his sweat top for a nylon windbreaker. Others ahead of him were doing the same as the fog-like cloud blocked out the sun. He was re-zipping his front bag when he glanced down at a biker a switchback below him pulling off a jersey and donning a bright yellow jacket. Dean only had a brief glance at the rider, not enough to even tell if the helmeted figure was a man or a woman, much less recognize the person. But it was enough to catch the rider's number before the jacket covered it. It was 888!

Dean pushed off with a vengeance at the same time as the other cyclist below him. The lateral of the switchback was longer than it appeared and by the time he reached the spot below where the cyclist had stood, the other biker was long out of sight. Shifting to his highest gear, Dean raced in pursuit down a long incline. Although there was a scattering of other bikers, he was sure the bright yellow windbreaker would be easy to spot, unless the biker became lost in a large pack.

The bicycle built up speed and Dean was aware that only one square inch of brake pad separated him from oblivion. His digital speedometer read 54 miles an hour, faster than he had ever ridden in his life, and his eyes watered from the rush of cold air. The first curve frightened the hell out of him and he knew the brake pressure necessary to slow him from this speed could not be engaged all the way down the mountain without overheating the tiny pads to the point of ineffectiveness.

He rolled into a series of curves but he couldn't take his tear-streaked eyes from the road long enough to see if he were gaining on the other rider. When the road straightened once more, he heard a noise behind him and a dozen daredevils in the tuck position sped on by him with a wave and a rush of air. He fell in behind them, taking advantage of the quieter air in their wake and kept pace with them. At this speed he was sure he was gaining ground on the other biker.

The edge of the highway to Dean's left, absent any guardrails, was a drop of thousands of feet but the roadway suddenly leveled and then climbed sharply over a rise before continuing downward. Dean lost his convoy of younger bikers on the short uphill and he paused momentarily at the crest to wipe his eyes and scan the roadway below him for his prey.

He was still above the timberline, devoid of any trees that would impair visibility so it was clear enough to follow the road with its many switchbacks and curves traversing the mountain below him, a black line clinging to the side of the cliff like a pencil drawing. There were scores of dots of color but Dean had little trouble catching sight of a yellow blur rounding a corner, further below than he would have guessed. He pushed off once again, committed firmly to the pursuit.

In spite of the chase, the pure magnificence of the mountains overwhelmed him. Flying downhill produced an exhilaration that defied explanation. Spectacular scenery was never ending. One moment, he was a speck of nothing in this vastness that defined his insignificance; another, this whole world was his. He'd never seen so much of nature at one glance and it produced an incredible sense of euphoria. Here he was, in total control, independent of outside power—only his arms and legs and gravity. For all the misery of the uphill climb, this downhill dash was fused in his memory forever, and in one brief moment he knew this Colorado country was where he belonged.

It was a brief lapse of concentration from his purpose at hand, catching the yellow-clad figure flowing through the curves and bends below him. He could spot the rider now and again with occasional glances and by counting off the seconds between points they both passed, knew he was gaining, if ever so slowly. The cluster of 12 riders who passed him further up the mountain was now about to pass the other rider. If the rider were able to draft them, Dean would have trouble matching their pace, so he quickened his. There was another concern—once the bikers hit the lower elevation and the heat of the afternoon, they would be shedding outer gear and perhaps identifying numbers with them. The yellow jacket and telltale 888 were Dean's only clues to the biker's identity.

It was unreal rocketing down this mountain, in pursuit of an unknown someone, one minute, surely Jeffrey Byrne, the next minute someone else. Brunel? Cece Baldwin? The players sped through Dean's mind like a theater curtain call—Vinnie and his friends, Mayer from World Wide, or Arthur Atherton's nefarious clients. Or perhaps some unknown person. Or Cynthia.

Suddenly facts fell into place, previously homeless happenings began making sense, and a picture arranged itself in Dean's mind. It wasn't a flash of understanding, but a spark. As sore and tired as his body felt, all aches and pains were forgotten with what was not a complete revelation, but a scenario that suddenly seemed plausible. He felt a new breath, a new strength, as if he were just beginning his ride in a young and fit body.

Dean picked up the pace and closed the gap on the yellow-shirted rider, low on his bike to minimize the wind resistance as he raced downward at a dangerous speed. If exhaustion truly was mental as much as physical, he'd conquered its demon as he edged to the side of the road without slowing his pace, allowing an infrequent car to pass. He braked carefully as the last of a series of curves came up before the level of a long valley was spread out before him.

Dean pulled out of the curve, searching ahead for a glimpse of his quarry as he continued to hug the right side of the narrow roadway. He could see the biker clearly now, six or seven telephone poles ahead. He was shifting up for a sprint when it happened.

The sound was like a rifle shot and for a fleeting second Dean feared someone had fired. Then his front wheel twisted violently and he knew the tire had blown a second before he hit the sand at the shoulder and felt himself twisting and rolling in the grass and sharp rocks at the edge of the roadside. His head slammed against something hard and he lay there, momentarily stunned to the brink of unconsciousness before turning slowly to his side and opening his eyes. His bike lay several feet from him, its front wheel still turning lazily, its back wheel twisted at a grotesque angle.

A group of bikers stopped with a squeal of brakes and ran down the slight embankment to his side just as he gingerly moved himself to a sitting position. He could tell his left leg was bleeding through his long bike pants and his head felt rattled but in one piece. The rest of his body, although bruised, seemed unbroken. If he could only get his heart to stop racing.

"I'll live," Dean said in answer to the anxious questions of the approaching group as he tried to catch his breath. He knew the yellow shirted rider was long gone, but strangely, it didn't seem to matter anymore. Now he was sure he had some answers. At last it was all making sense.

"You better lay back down, mister," said one of the first arrivals. Someone pitched a jacket to the man who carefully placed it behind Dean's head. "You're looking kind of fuzzy."

"How about this," said another biker while still another whistled. The first arrival unfastened Dean's helmet, the object of their curiosity. When the protective headgear was removed, Dean saw why. The helmet was cracked down the entire length of the left side.

"You're one lucky son-of-a-bitch," someone said. "Looks like you got your money's worth out of that helmet." Another added, "You picked a pretty good spot to land, too. If you had dumped back up the road a couple of miles, you'd still be falling."

Dean was still trying to catch his breath when another car rolled to a stop on the road above him. He turned to look as the door opened. Standing there, in the afternoon sun, with a look of shock on her beautiful face, stood Cynthia Byrne.

# CHAPTER XXVII

The vision disappeared in a moment, after someone stepped in front of Dean and helped him steady his legs and rise to his feet. He was assisted up the slope to the vehicle of a tour monitor and placed in the back seat. There was no sign of Cynthia Byrne or another car. Dean's damaged bike was stowed in the trunk and in a matter of minutes he went from being an integral part of a wide and wonderful biking world to just another simple observer seated behind glass and peeking at life at 50 miles an hour.

Dean strained for a glimpse of the yellow jacket he had pursued so vigorously but either he had missed the rider or the biker had shed the jacket to the warmth of the valley. He was disappointed but it mattered little now he was convinced he knew how to find his quarry. They rolled past South Fork, and 20 miles later, Del Norte, where the lead cadre of bikers hummed their way toward Monte Vista, 14 miles further, and then the final 17 miles to Alamosa. The entire trip took just over an hour with the driver, a volunteer from Amarillo, Texas who never stopping his constant drawl of friendly conversation, little of which Dean heard.

The vehicle contained a roll of gauze and Dean bound his own stiffening leg after spreading a disinfectant on the oozing abrasion. While the limb was sore, the injury was minor. If this had been the Tour de France, he'd still be on the road. Of course the pros had someone shove a new bike under them before they stopped rolling. One look at his bike told him it was unridable.

Dean declined to visit the hospital. He had far more important chores to do. After thanking his benefactor and dropping off his bike for repairs, he stopped for a quick bite to eat. After locating his gear, he found a campsite, showered and changed. Surprisingly, many of the speedier bikers were already there, looking as if they'd spent the day loafing in the late spring sun.

It was only late afternoon and if Dean was right, he had plenty of time to find his prey. He located a public telephone and, with a pocketful of coins, he commenced dialing.

Alamosa was a college town of about 7,000, ringed by a number of motels. Dean spent a pocket full of coins before he found the one housing the person for whom he was searching. He considered calling for a taxicab but when he found the motel was close by he decided to exercise his tightening leg and walk.

Dean couldn't believe how calm he felt. It was six weeks today since Jeffrey Byrne's disappearance and ever since, Dean's world had revolved around that happening like a long-playing record. He'd become obsessed with finding the man. Now that he knew the story he was as cold and precise as if he were giving out a speeding ticket to an out-of-state Caddy.

The sun was warm and he walked with a slight limp but an easy stride, past the shops of the small central section to the west side of the quiet town. The majority of the bikers remained on the course and with college recessed, the streets held only a few locals, waiting for the later rush of the 2,000 riders who'd roll into town. Dean found the motel without difficulty and with the use of his police badge, he obtained access to the empty room. Thank goodness for Colorado hospitality—the friendly room clerk was more than willing to oblige a law enforcement agent.

Dean sat on the bed and waited. It seemed more of the investigation time of this case had taken place in motel rooms than anywhere else. And they all looked the same. This one smelled of over cleaning with a telltale aroma of cigarette smoke. It was dark with the shades drawn and Dean felt a desire to nod off as he waited.

While he'd considered bringing his revolver to Colorado, he had no official reason to do so and was reluctant to lie about being on police business. Now as he sat and waited he wondered if the decision had been a prudent one. He would soon know.

The wait lasted less than an hour before Dean heard the metallic sound of a key in the lock. He felt a wave of apprehension and accelerated heart beat as the door opened. There, standing silhouetted in the brightness behind him stood the pride of the FBI, Jonathan Winston.

Winston seemed to sense someone sitting on the bed but he could not recognize Dean in the darkened room. True to form, he showed no reaction to the surprise visitor as he casually flipped on the switch, flooding the room in light. A broad smile crossed his face.

"Well, I'll be damned! David Dean! What a small world it is!" He crossed to the bed and held out his hand as casually as a conventioneer. Dean declined the offering and said nothing. "Sorry," said Winston with a slight frown. "I suppose you're pissed off and looking for an explanation."

"I'm not sure most of the answers aren't obvious," Dean said in a level voice.

Winston, still smiling, pulled up a chair and sat in it backwards facing Dean. "Why don't you just run it by me for clarification? I'll stop you if you get too far off base."

"It's pretty simple. I followed Jeffrey Byrne and you followed David Dean."

Winston laughed. "Jeffrey Byrne's dead. Haven't you read your own report? He drowned on May 4th in Norfolk, Virginia."

"So the official version goes."

"Come on! A minor insurance company flunky? He couldn't pull off a fake like that!"

"No, not without the help of his friendly government agent."

Winston's smile was a tad less casual. "That's pretty farfetched, isn't it? Why would the United States government help Jeffrey Byrne?"

"Maybe not the entire government. Maybe just Jonathan Winston—for part of a few million dollars, perhaps?"

Winston shook his head. "I'm disappointed in you, David. Do you really think I'd do a stupid thing like that?"

Dean ignored the question. "It was your bug on my phone, wasn't it?"

Jonathan Winston laughed. "I have to apologize for that. When you gave us Vinnie, we wanted to make sure he wasn't a set-up, so we bugged you. Just a precaution. Then we started hearing all this nonsense about Byrne until it got us wondering if there might be something to it, so we did a little detecting ourselves. When you found the bug, I was sure we were dead ducks, but you blamed the wrong guys. Gangsters don't bug phones—us good guys do that stuff."

"I should have known. And the two suits at Willoughby's Bar? No wonder I couldn't find them in any mug books. They were your guys."

"Yeah, Henderson nearly shit when he recognized you! They thought they were busting some con artist who was trying to rip off you and the old man and then you show up and damn near kill them! We had to haul ass back to your place and pull out our bug."

"Tell them not to order ginger ale the next time. I should have known no self-respecting hood would do that. And I spent a lot of time wondering why there weren't any fingerprints on a gun that had just been used by a guy not wearing gloves."

"Nobody's perfect."

"Fred spotted one of them at the hospital in Philly after Arthur Atherton was shot but we couldn't run him down."

"Because we hid him in a broom closet until you guys left," Winston laughed.

"Were they the same guys who broke in and tied up Fred O'Connor?"

"Whoa! That wasn't us. That *was* Nota and Flanders. They broke in Cynthia Byrne's place too. But it didn't have anything to do with Byrne. They were hunting down your buddy Vinnie. They must have followed you to Maid Marian Lane and thought Vinnie might be stashed there. We picked up their voices on our bug in your house but by the time we figured out what was going on, you were already there and we backed off."

"What happened to Nota?"

"We picked him up a few days after the Colombians did in his buddy Flanders, only we didn't let the world know about it. He was just as happy. He'll become a part of the chorus and sing a song on his friends. They're all lining up now."

"So you bought the theory that Byrne had stumbled on the dough."

"Not at the beginning but the more you guys found, the more it seemed credible. When you and the old man began getting close, we stepped in. The two of you are pretty good for a couple of kitchen table detectives. So what put you on to me?"

"It was the newspaper, the *Parkside Sentinel*. The subscription was being sent to the name Cleary on Bascomb Place in Scranton but it stopped arriving there after he 'died.' When I checked with the *Sentinel*, they told me the subscription remained open but there weren't any papers lying around unclaimed, yet you said there wasn't any forwarding notice filed with the Post Office. Something didn't wash. Then it dawned on me that you lied. The newspaper was being forwarded all along."

"Smart boy," Winston replied.

"Once I questioned what you told me, everything began making sense. A bunch of gangsters chasing after Byrne was always a hard pill to swallow. You guys were the only ones with the manpower and capabilities."

"Right you are. You're on a roll."

"What about Arthur Atherton? Were you involved with him too?"

"He needed a lot of dough in a hurry so he started putting the squeeze on everyone in sight, including Cynthia Byrne. Some of the Philadelphia family took exception to it. When we got wind of what he was doing, we picked him up. I thought we had a deal with him to cooperate. We even paid off his stolen escrow account and talked him into backing off Cynthia Byrne. Sorry I lied to you about the escrow money—there wasn't any point in my doing it but I didn't think fast enough. Ol' Arthur didn't believe us when we told him there was a contract out on him and he went back out on the street. He didn't last long."

"Where did you catch up to Jeffrey Byrne?" Dean asked in a steady voice.

Jonathan Winston looked at Dean for a long minute before continuing. "It was easier for us than you. I have a lot more resources."

"So it was you who called Mrs. Glass—not Nota and his friends."

"They never had a sniff Byrne was connected to the money. That was all us. We even scared off the fellow who sold Byrne his first motor home."

"And tried to spook my stepfather in the process, only he lost your tail."

Winston laughed. "There were a couple of embarrassed agents over that, I'll tell you. The old man is something else. Then we played tag across the country chasing Byrne. He holed up in Ohio for a couple of weeks and but then in Kansas he got spooked someone was on to him. He started changing his name as often as his shorts. I was looking over his shoulder for two weeks but then I lost him."

"But you found him again, in Colorado."

"I cannot tell a lie," he smiled. "And we had a nice little chat."

"Let me guess—you let him keep ten percent? Or did you kill him?"

"God, Dean! You must think we're real bastards. He gets to keep half of it. The balance goes in a slush fund—to fix windshields of government cars that get smashed by trashcans—stuff like that."

"You really are a bastard, Jonathan. You know that?"

"You listen. I've got 21 indictments out of this mess so far and there's no end in sight. My sainted daddy used to say there are two things in life you don't want to see, sausage being made and laws being passed. Add indictments being constructed to the list."

"It stinks."

"Sure it does. No one said it was pretty but it's a war. Sometimes the good guys actually win one—like this time."

"And all this is officially sanctioned?"

"Don't give me that! We're 'officially' given a job to do and then the brass leaves the room while we discuss how to 'unofficially' get it done. That's so the big boys can be 'officially' indignant if the shit hits the fan and we get caught."

"So playing by the rules doesn't count any more?"

"What rules? Do you think the other guys have any?" Winston asked angrily. "Since the Colombians and the family started feuding over that missing dough things have been happening. As long as each thought the other stole their lousy couple of a million the fur kept flying. I wasn't about to stop it."

"So you were just as happy to see Jeffrey Byrne get away with stealing it?"

"Why not? I'd have burned the damned money before I'd have let it get back on the street poisoning kids. Byrne was a simple skip case. They happen all the time. The only difference was the

funding. Besides, what did he do? A good lawyer would say find-
ers-keepers. He didn't *steal* the money—he found it—and aside
from some name changing, it would be hell to prove he defrauded
anyone. If he wants to leave his wife, it's a free country."

"And you could care less who gets hurt in the process."

"Who got hurt? Byrne took the dough, not me. He *might* have
found his ass in jail. How would that stick with his wife and son? All
I did was help him out. Byrne's wife? Now she can mourn him in
peace. He was a son-of-a-bitch to run out on her and his son. She's
better off without him—and not knowing him for the jerk he is."

Dean considered telling Winston he'd seen Cynthia that afternoon in Colorado but it was apparent either she remained unaware
that her husband was alive or that Winston was unaware of her
involvement. He kept mum. After all, Winston hadn't exactly been
forthcoming with him. "What about my stepfather? Nota could
have killed him."

"I didn't sic Nota on anyone—that came from Vinnie Baratto
by way of Arthur Atherton and it didn't have a damned thing to do
with the Byrne case. You can blame your own big mouth. They
were looking for Vinnie. Besides, admit it. Fred O'Connor hasn't
had this much fun in 20 years!" He paused. "I saved Vinnie
Baratto's life. He was a dead man. Even you benefited. Now you
have a clean shot at Byrne's wife. If he were just missing, you'd
always wonder if he was going to pop in." He paused. "I ought to
get a public service medal."

"Wrong."

"Grow up. You're not going to blow any whistle. Who'd bene-
fit if you did and who'd believe you? We've done a damned good
job covering our tracks—painting the Scranton Apartment, swip-
ing motel receipts with Byrne's signature on them...."

"There's no dead body..."

"You want one? Don't you think we could pull that off too?
There are plenty of stiffs around. All I'd need is a little DNA and
Byrne would certainly be cooperative. Maybe that's a good idea.
We could cremate him and spread a few ashes around so the widow
has a place to mourn."

Dean shifted his position. "You can never be sure Byrne won't
get a conscience..."

"Byrne won't do diddly." Dean looked sharply. "No, we didn't kill him. We're not a bunch of assassins. We may shmuck around the facts a little and lie when we threaten him but we're still the good guys, remember? No, Byrne's just scared to death now. He won't say a damned thing." Winston stood up and began to pace the room. "I suppose I ought to thank you. It was you who put us on to Byrne in the first place. But I've got to say, this whole gig would have gone a lot smoother if you and the old man hadn't been so nosy."

"Why did you let Byrne stay in the bike tour if you knew we were close to him?"

Jonathan sighed and shook his head. "We fought that but he's a stubborn son-of-a-bitch—a fanatic about this biking business. He insisted. And," he added, "we underestimated you—he'd changed names so much we didn't think you'd ever find him."

"I'm insisting on something too," said Dean coldly. "I want to talk to your Jeffrey Byrne."

"Out of the question," snapped Winston.

"I might not be able to prove your involvement in this little charade but I bet I can ask some embarrassing questions."

Jonathan looked at him for several moments, recognizing Dean was serious. "Let me take a pee and think about it," he answered. He crossed to the bathroom and shut the door.

In a few minutes, Dean heard the toilet flush and Winston emerged. He was behind Dean and before Dean could realize what was happening, Winston grabbed his right arm and with a quick metallic click Dean was securely fastened to the brass bedpost by a steel handcuff.

"There," he said. "Isn't that cozy?"

"What the hell are you doing?" Dean growled.

Jonathan dangled a second pair of handcuffs in front of Dean. "If you agree to let me fasten your other arm and drop this pillow case over your head so you can't see, I'll let you chat with our friend, but that's the only way."

"What's the difference if I see him?"

"Maybe no difference, but I'm setting the rules. This way you could never swear in a court of law you saw him. You'd only be guessing he's alive and a lawyer would beat you to death."

Dean knew Winston was right. Winston had made sure there was no factual proof Byrne was alive. He held out his left hand. "Do it," he said.

Jonathan secured his wrist, shook a pillow from its case and pulled the cloth over Dean's head. "It might be a while before I round him up but you look pretty comfy. Make the most of your chit-chat. This is the only shot you'll get." He patted Dean on the back. "See you back east, fella. I'm flying out in the morning." The light was extinguished and Dean heard the door close to silence.

Dean remained in his cramped position, his injured leg going numb, as daylight sank into evening. At last, when he was about to begin rapping his head on the wall for attention, he heard a click at the lock and the sound of the door opening.

"Byrne?" He called as he could feel the presence of someone in the room.

"Try Cleary," a voice answered, "It was one of my favorites." The voice sounded nervous to Dean, and perhaps disguised.

"I chased your yellow jacket down Wolfe Creek Pass today," Dean said.

"Really? But you didn't catch me, huh?"

"If you'd turn the light on, you'd see my leg. I lost a wheel and a layer or two of skin. Otherwise, I'd have caught you."

"Sorry about the leg, but Mr. Winston says to keep the light off." Dean tried to picture Byrne from his photograph but nothing came to mind. They were both silent for a long while. Finally, Dean asked if Byrne planned to finish the bike tour.

"Probably not. I'm in a hurry to split. But Wolfe Creek Pass, that was really something, wasn't it? Worth every foot of the climb." Dean didn't answer but they both knew he agreed.

"Why did you want to see me?"

"I guess I wanted to ask you the classic question."

"Why did I do it?" Byrne volunteered.

"And, 'Would you do it over again?'" Dean added.

He sighed. "Mr. Winston says you know the whole business—how the dough fell out of the sky. I didn't plan any of it, but all of a sudden, there you are, every dream you ever imagined staring you smack in the face—unbelievable options—every kid's fantasy come true."

"You were taking a hell of a chance."

"I guess I've always been a dreamer and one night when I was just taking a piss I tripped over a couple suitcases with all my dreams in 'em. Sometimes there are temptations you just can't pass up."

"What about Cynthia and your son?"

The voice became surly. "That's off limits. I don't want to talk about them. Mr. Winston said I have to speak with you but he didn't tell me what I had to talk about."

"Do you always do what Mr. Winston tells you?"

"Are you kidding? He owns me. God, I thought I was so damn smart, changing names, changing vehicles and some old guy and a small town detective find me like I've got a sign around my neck. No, Winston's my salvation. It's 'Yes, sir, no, sir' from here on out." Dean didn't comment and a short silence followed. "I'm really not a bastard, at least not as much as you think."

"Cece Baldwin doesn't think so."

There was a chuckle. "So you found Cece too! Way to go! Mr. Winston was right; you are good." Dean could hear the smile in his voice, as if he was pleased.

"Where are you going from here?" Dean asked.

"Maybe the coast. Who knows? I've got a couple of million I've hardly touched."

"Maybe drink a manhattan at sunset on he Top of the Mark?"

"Where?"

"The Mark Hopkins hotel. In San Francisco." He'd forgotten, even though Cynthia hadn't.

"Are you going alone or is your wife going with you?"

He laughed, a cynical bark. "No chance of that—that was another life."

"Maybe you should tell her," Dean said. "She's here."

"You're just saying that, right?"

"I saw her. Up on the mountain. She's here—probably right in town by now."

"God!"

Dean could hear him jump up and he felt the left handcuff being unfastened and a key being pressed into his hand. Then he heard the door close with a bang and Dean was alone with his thoughts and unanswered questions.

# CHAPTER XVIII

**TUESDAY, JUNE 15, 1999  9:00 P.M.**

Five minutes later Dean was hurrying back to his campsite. While darkness had descended the town was now a hubbub of activity. Dean paid little attention as his mind remained focused on his chore ahead as he tried to put aside the stiffness in his injured leg. As he rounded a corner, he spotted Fred O'Connor walking toward him.

"Where have you been?" Fred asked. "I've been looking all over. You'll never guess who's in town! Cynthia!"

Dean grabbed Fred's arm. "Do you know where she's staying?"

"No," Fred answered, surprised by Dean's manner. The two men continued walking past clusters of bikers. "I spotted her going into a restaurant. "I saw Winston too, ten minutes earlier. What the dickens is going on? What's he doing here?"

"It's a long story but I have to find Cynthia first—it's crucial."

"She's probably still at the café. It's right down the block. Did you find Byrne?" Dean didn't stop to answer as he broke into a jog with Fred hustling to keep up.

More bikers crowded the small luncheonette, amid happy carefree chatter, all but Cynthia Byrne who sat alone at a table near the back. She looked neither surprised nor pleased to see him.

"Why did you come here—to arrest me too?" There was anger in her voice, her eyes cast downward

"We have to talk," Dean said, taking the only other seat.

Fred caught up and stood next to them. "How did you know we were out here in Colorado?" he asked.

"I called police headquarters." She continued to look down at the table. "Then Randy told me about the bike magazine and how you'd been interested in it—how Jeff marked the information on this tour." She raised her eyes to meet Dean's. "Jeffrey's alive and he's here, isn't he? And you think I'm in this with him!"

"I know you're not involved but I think you're in danger. I want you to give me your motel room key and go stay with Fred."

"No, I won't! And you can't make me! I want to see him—look him in the eye! I should be afraid of him? That's nonsense! He should be more afraid I'll kill him than the other way around!"

"Trust me. Just give me your key. This whole business is almost over." A waitress neared them but beat a quick retreat when she heard their strained tones.

"Trust you? Like I trusted Jeffrey?" she snapped. "I want to see him! I have a right! I'm his wife!"

"Listen to David," Fred said, standing over the two. "He knows what he's doing—and he cares about you." His voice had a calming effect on Cynthia. She began to cry. The fury was replaced by an overwhelming sadness.

Dean reached past her, grabbed her purse and dumped the contents on the table. He picked out a motel room key. She looked dumbfounded but made no move to stop him. He pushed back his chair, stood and glanced down at her, but no appropriate words came to mind.

He turned instead to Fred. "Take her to your room and wait there. I don't know how long I'll be but I'll run you down later and explain everything. This is important. Trust me. If Jonathan Winston is still around, tell him where I went."

"Be careful," Fred cautioned as he slipped into the vacated chair as Dean turned and left.

The key fob was the old fashioned type with the name of the motel listed on it. The lodge was in the next block and once again mirrored the others he'd visited since this business began. He located the room, which was dark when he entered, but he didn't turn on the light. Instead, he pulled up a chair behind the door and waited. While he wasn't sure what would happen, nor when, he felt certain his wait wouldn't be long. The absence of his gun was even more significant than his last vigil.

Suddenly the room was flooded with light and Dean shaded his eyes as turned to see him standing there. Dean had guessed correctly. One hand was on the light switch while the other held a gun pointed directly at Dean.

"Where is she?" asked Chip Burgess, surprised to see Dean. Dean didn't answer.

Burgess flipped off the light switch, returning the room to darkness, and sat on the edge of the bed. Dean could no longer see the gun but he knew it remained in place, pointed at him. "We'll just wait until she shows up," Burgess said. "Then all three of us will take a little ride up the mountain."

"Where you'll kill us?"

"Naw. Just drop you off to give me enough time to get out of here."

Dean didn't believe him for a minute. "You didn't have any trouble finding where Cynthia was staying. I figured it would take you half the evening to track her down."

"Just lucky and it's a small town. I recognized her from the picture in Byrne's wallet and saw her leave the room and go to the restaurant. She should be back here before long."

"Why didn't you just hustle out of town when I told you she was here?"

"I couldn't take the chance—with either of you. There was no reason for her to be in Colorado except thinking her hubby was still alive and here. Did you tell her I'm not her husband?"

"She'll know soon enough," Dean answered. Burgess didn't press him. "Aren't you afraid Jonathan Winston might show up?"

"He's already gone. He thinks I am too."

"And he still thinks you're Jeffrey Byrne." Dean fidgeted in his seat, an arm's length from the door and half an arm length from a light switch.

"Stop moving around—I've still got the gun and I'll use it. And yeah, I'm Jeffrey Byrne to him. But you know better, smart ass, don't you?"

"I figured two people found that money—Byrne and you. I'm a bit fuzzy on some of the details but I'm sure Jeffrey Byrne is dead and you played his part so well, even Jonathan Winston never considered he was chasing someone else."

"How come you made me? Did you recognize my voice?" Burgess spoke in a low tone but showed no reluctance to talk. Dean was more than willing to accommodate him while he hoped Fred could locate Winston.

"I only heard your voice once—when you biked up to Bascomb Place. I didn't recognize it this afternoon. The clincher was your not knowing about the Byrnes' dream of sipping manhattans in Frisco."

"I didn't want to meet with you. There was too much that could go wrong, but Winston insisted."

"I had my suspicions earlier. There were other hints—lots of them. Too much took place in Scranton—the mail drop, the newspaper, buying the motor home. Jeffrey Byrne spent very little time there—far too few hours to accomplish all of that business. That's why I eliminated the World Wide guy Brunel in Norfolk from consideration in spite of the trouble I had running him down and the coincidence he's now in Colorado. Norfolk was too far from Scranton. You rented that apartment for an address to set up a false identity and a place to keep the dough. That's why you changed the lock so snoopy Mrs. Glass wouldn't stumble on it. It certainly was convenient—in the same building and across the hall from your apartment." Burgess grunted, but said nothing. Dean continued. "You messed up with the newspaper too. Byrne had no reason to subscribe to it weeks before the skip date. He was getting the paper at home. You weren't. You wanted to know what was happening back in Parkside—if there was any mention of the money or Byrne reporting it. There was the Cece Baldwin business—you were a tad too pleased I discovered your anonymous thousand-dollar present to her. That was just one more way you tried to make us believe Byrne was still alive. What did you do, use the address on the postcard he'd filled out for her before you killed him?"

"Yeah. It said 'Stick with school' so I decided it was worth a thousand to send her some money—like something Byrne would do."

"It was a mistake typing the note—Jeffrey Byrne's office said he didn't type." Dean adjusted his position slightly, leaning in the direction of the door.

"I figured if you were chasing Byrne, I'd help you out," Burgess answered, unaware of Dean's movement.

"When did you start trying to blame the missing money on Byrne?"

"After you and the old guy came snooping around Bascomb Place. God, you guys shook me up! And then you traced me to Kansas."

"My stepfather was looking for Byrne. I wasn't sure who I was looking for. When I considered it might not be Byrne who rented that apartment in Scranton, I began to wonder how come you identified him from his picture. That made me take a closer look at you—a biker."

"What makes you so smart? I fooled that FBI jerk. I figured I was safe."

"I spoke with a lot of people who knew Jeffrey Byrne—Jonathan Winston didn't. I kept feeling a skip was totally out of character for him. Then, this afternoon, you didn't act or sound like the Jeffrey Byrne everyone described."

"You're doing pretty good, but you're still just guessing."

"Maybe. Correct me if I'm wrong. You worked for the contractor who built the World Wide office building in Scranton so you were at the opening dedication party there. You're a biker, so Byrne and you struck up a conversation—and I suppose shared a few drinks."

"He saw my biking magazine. I gave it to him."

"I wondered about that. Byrne wasn't near in shape to be looking into this tour and had no reason to write for information on it. You circled the article."

"Right again."

"I don't know why, but Byrne agreed to drive you out of his way—that's why he was out on Interstate 84 where you two found the money."

"I didn't have wheels and Byrne offered to take me to Blooming Grove. My ex-wife was supposed to meet me at a friend's place, only she never showed. That's when I found out she moved back to Russia on me." Dean could read the bitterness in his voice.

"Did you find the bags the way you told me this afternoon—when you were pretending to be Byrne?"

"Not exactly. I was the one who spotted the suitcases while Byrne was around the corner doing his business so I pitched them in his trunk without opening them. I figured they were left by some tourists changing a tire or something. Byrne didn't even know they were there until he got home." Burgess rose and crossed to the window. "Where is she? She should be finished dinner by now."

"There's lot's of bikers. The place will be jammed." Burgess moved back to the bed. "Where did you go after you left the interstate rest area?" Dean continued. "To a Parkside motel?"

"Yeah. I guess I sort of passed out on him after the piss stop. Byrne didn't know what to do with me so he rented me a motel room—I didn't have any money with me 'cause I was supposed to stay with my wife. I'd forgotten all about the bags I put in his trunk."

"It was after midnight so the registration said the next day," Dean said. "Why did Byrne use a fake name?"

"I don't guess he even knew my name at that point."

"When did Byrne discover the suitcases and the money?"

"When he got home and opened his trunk to get his luggage. He figured the bags must have been mine—they were still unopened. When he came back to the motel in the morning to drop them off, I told him how I'd found them. He got upset and opened them to see if there was a name. When we saw the dough, we both damned near flipped. We weren't sure he wasn't followed or something—we whispered like a couple of kids and couldn't wait to sneak out of there. He wanted to run straight to the police. I talked him out of it."

"How?"

"I convinced him he'd get in trouble with the cops and maybe the people who really owned the money—we knew it was nothing legal. Then he wanted to dump them back at the rest stop. I told him we'd get caught or maybe shot. He'd be putting his wife and family in danger. Then I said I'd turn the bags in, back in Scranton—told him I had a lawyer friend or something. He finally agreed and took the day off to drive me and the money back to my place and we crept out of there."

"But you had no intention of turning in the money."

"Are you kidding? My wife just left me, I had a shit job.... You think I was going to give away a fortune like that?"

"What made you think Byrne would believe a cock-and-bull story like that? He'd have to have been pretty naive."

"You've got to understand the guy, he didn't want to have anything to do with the dough. He was scared half to death. Like out of sight, out of mind. When he left me, I don't think he cared what happened to the money as long as he wasn't part of the picture."

"What changed his mind?"

"I guess he started thinking he might still be connected and got scared. He looked me up when he came to Scranton and I could tell there was going to be trouble. He got pushy on the phone—wanted to come forward himself. I told him I'd already turned it in. I phonied up some stuff on a computer, official-like, from the FBI receipting the dough and showed it to him I thought he bought it but I couldn't be sure."

"Why didn't you just skip as soon as you had the dough?"

"I had to set up some names and stuff—bank accounts too. That takes time." Burgess answered quickly, impatience showing in his voice. "And I had to make sure Byrne wasn't going to be a problem," he added.

"But he was. So you followed Byrne to Norfolk and met with him. Where's Jeffrey Byrne now?"

"He drowned. We were supposed to meet up the next day. I guess he was celebrating. Too bad." Once again he moved to the window and looked out. He turned to Dean. "Get up. I can't wait all night. You and me are going for a ride."

"Not unless you have a car. I don't."

"Her keys are here somewhere." Dean could hear Burgess feeling around the nightstand.

"You killed Jeffrey Byrne. He never reached the beach. You met him—where? Out at your motor home? Then you drove your bike, in his car, back to the motel. You lost your tire repair kit in the trunk. That was you who came out of his room and waved to the busboy—wearing Byrne's baseball cap. He was already dead."

"You can't prove I killed Byrne." Dean could hear him rummaging around the television and bureau. Dean moved closer to the door.

"You made a mistake taking the Phillies baseball cap. I found it in your tent."

Dean caught a flash of Burgess's smile in the light of an arriving car. "I've always been a fan. You're smart—a lot smarter than Winston."

"But if he figures it out, he can find you any time he likes."

"Naw. I'm ancient history to him. He and his pals have half the dough and could care less about me."

"He might start thinking if Cynthia Byrne's and David Dean's bodies show up."

"They won't. Just like Jeffrey Byrne's didn't."

"Where is his body?"

"Buried in back of a god-forsaken campground in West Virginia. Got it!" he exclaimed, holding what Dean presumed were Cynthia's car keys.

"Why didn't you just dump him in the Chesapeake where he was supposed to have drowned?" Dean asked as he rose to his feet. Burgess remained several feet away.

"Someone might have wondered about his skull being caved in."

Suddenly, there was a sound at the door—a key being inserted into the lock.

"Don't make a sound," Burgess rasped. This gun is pointed right at your heart." He retreated toward the bathroom just as the door opened—and just as Dean hit the light switch and rolled to the floor, flooding the room in brightness.

Jonathan Winston burst into the room and both men fired simultaneously.

# EPILOGUE

"It's been five years—tonight—since Jeff died," Cynthia Dean said to her husband. "Do you mind if I have a manhattan?"

"This isn't San Francisco—it's Ouray, Colorado."

"No, but it's even nicer here."

"I don't even mind if you have more than one, but now that we're married, I don't intend to be as much a gentleman as the last time you drank manhattans."

Cynthia laughed. "That seems a lifetime ago." David and Cynthia Dean, now husband and wife, and owners of Bird Song, a bed and breakfast in Ouray, Colorado, were seated in the Tundra Room of the recently restored Beaumont Hotel. She smiled and then asked, "You're not jealous?"

"Of Jeffrey Byrne? No. He was your husband for half your life and the father of your son," he answered. "I'm just tickled pink to be the relief pitcher." He was going to say, "for the late innings," but thought better of it.

She nodded. "We don't talk about those years very much—my life before I met you."

"Those are your memories, not mine," he said, a tad defensively. "Besides, we always seem too busy with our todays to do much looking back to yesterdays."

"Do you think that's the way it should be?" she asked.

The waiter brought two manhattans before Dean could answer. After the drinks were placed before them, he changed the subject. "Should I toast Jeffrey Byrne, or at least his memory?"

She thought a moment. "No. He's been replaced—completely."

"You seldom mention Jeff—only in reference to something else—never talk directly about him, or his death."

"It's not that I don't think of him occasionally but that was another life." She paused. "I guess I had some issues too—blaming him for his own death. At first I blamed the way I thought he died—doing something stupid and irresponsible—swimming at night."

"We all do something on the spur of the moment once in awhile."

"But if I'd looked closely at what they said took place, I'd have seen that just wasn't something Jeff would have done. Then, to make matters worse, I doubted him. I truly thought he'd skipped out on Randy and me and taken that money. It wasn't so much a question of my not being loyal to him, I began to question how well I really knew the man."

"There were some pretty strong reasons for you to think of the possibility he might have skipped. All these police-type guys were chasing after him."

"But then out in Colorado when I learned he'd been murdered, I still blamed him, in a different way. He died because he was protecting me." She twisted the stem of her glass. "Jeff never mentioned finding the money, not even after he thought it had been returned—just because of some silly sense of not placing me in harm's way. Think what that said to me—he didn't think I was capable of handling that information."

"It's tough to blame him for that."

"No, it isn't!" Cynthia said it loud enough to turn heads at the adjoining table. "Maybe I didn't want to be protected—still don't—never did! If Jeff had confided in me that he'd found the money, I'd have walked him straight to the police and he might be alive today!"

*And I wouldn't be sitting here in this elegant room, listening to classical guitar music and sipping manhattans with the light of my life,* Dean thought.

Cynthia read his mind. "Maybe there's another reason why I don't talk about it—some warped sense of guilt because I can't imagine any life without you." He smiled, but she continued.

"Don't go getting a swelled head! You almost blew it—you were just as bad as Jeff back then! You were trying to protect me too— God, why do men think we can't handle anything! Thank heavens I've managed to straighten you out."

"Duly noted," Dean said.

"If you had admitted your suspicions early on that Jeff's death might not have been an accident, perhaps we could have worked together and gotten to the bottom of the whole business before you almost got us both killed."

"Before Jonathan-on-the-spot Winston showed up, with his gun blazing," Dean said, as much to change the subject as give the FBI credit.

"He could have been killed but when you switched the light back on, it blinded Burgess."

"But not Jonathan Winston. He hit Burgess, even if he only wounded him."

"I know it's unchristian, but I'm relieved Burgess is gone." Chip Burgess was killed in a prison knifing before standing trial. "I never wanted to listen to the details of Jeff's death."

"The FBI built a good case against Burgess. His attorney would have gone for a plea bargain."

"The FBI didn't do such a great job before that. I never could understand how Winston was so positive the person you were following was Jeff when you knew all along it was that other horrid man."

Dean gulped and crossed his fingers. "That's because I'm the smartest detective in the world—and I always keep an open mind." He smiled, remembering. "Mr. Jonathan Winston had to back up a step or two and wipe the egg off his face when he realized I saved his bacon after he nearly let a killer get away."

"My hero," she smiled.

"Don't thank me, thank Fred. It was his suggestion about the newspaper subscription that started the whole business rolling— even if it was blind luck."

"You never do give the old gentleman the credit he deserves," she smiled. "You'd better treat him right. I love Fred, almost as much as I love you."

Dean said as he raised his glass. "I'll drink to that."

Cynthia's glass remained on the table. "There's something else that makes me feel guilty." Her eyes were cast downward, and her glass still in place on the table. "After I met you, I'm not sure what I'd have done if my husband walked in the door alive." Surprise was written on Dean's face. "Oh, I guess I'd have gone back to being Mrs. Byrne—I'm too accommodating to have simply left him, and I do believe in my vows. But I'd have wondered. It wouldn't have been the same." She looked across at him. "I *really* enjoyed your company and I shouldn't have—I didn't mourn my husband near as much as he deserved. He'd given me 20 years of marriage. But you were in love with me—admit it—almost from the first, and I knew it. And I liked it—very much." Dean smiled, but he didn't deny it. "You'd have never chased after that man Burgess so obsessively except for your feelings for me."

"Then why didn't I just forget about the whole business and hustle you? That would have made more sense," he said, lightening the conversation.

"That's why I love you and agreed to marry you. You needed to find the truth. You loved me enough to risk losing me, and almost did, just because it was the right thing to do. That's something special, Mr. Dean."

"Did you ever consider that your husband might not have drowned and just left you? Before little hints came up suggesting it?"

She nodded her head affirmatively. "I shouldn't have. Jeff wouldn't have left, especially for money. I can see that now. He was far too—comfortable. Perhaps that was the problem. I know now I wanted more from life than simple comfort." Then she said, in almost a whisper, "And now I have it."

"Thank you," he answered, matching her tone. Dean had never sought a comparison between himself and Cynthia's first husband. But it was nice to hear it—the nicest words she'd ever spoken.

He raised his manhattan and touched her glass. "To us," he said and they both drank to their future.